Shadows Over Shiloh

Unrest in Arkansas

The Shiloh Saga…Volume IV

Written by

Patricia Clark Blake

SCOTCHWOOD HILL

Shadows Over Shiloh

Published by:
Scotchwood Hill
3101 Scotchwood Drive Jonesboro,
Arkansas 72405
patriciacblake.com

Cover Design: Martha Rodriguez
Photograph: Serhii Nesterchuk
              123RF Stock Photos
All Scripture quoted in the book: King James Version
©1850.
1611bible.com/KJV-king-james-versopm-1850.

Copyright: ©2019. Printed in the United States of America
Shadows Over Shiloh: Unrest in Arkansas ©2019.
ISBN*: 978-0-9998416-2-4*
LCCN*: 2019905709*

DEDICATION

All I write is a gift to me from the Holy Trinity.
Without the grace, inspiration, and support from God, my Father,
Jesus Christ, my Savior, and the Holy Spirit, my Supporter, the
Shiloh Saga would be only a dream.

All I understand about family comes from my own.
I am bountifully blessed with a supportive, loving family.

All my gratitude belongs to my excellent editors,
proofreaders, and beta-readers
who help me make the Shiloh stories an
offering to God and a tribute to Arkansas.

Mary Lee Cunningham Yevon Prater Martha Rodriquez
Brenda Thakkar Beverly Thompson

CHAPTER ONE

Humble yourselves under the mighty hand of God, that He may exalt you in due time; Casting all your care upon Him; for He careth for you. I Peter 5:6-7

*A*n Arkansas homesteader's prayer lasted a long while. Water, solitary figure knelt on the bank of Lost Creek. The dancing across the boulders in the creek on Crowley's Ridge, provided an anthem for Patrick MacLayne. Only an occasional word from his prayer broke the stillness of the scene. The man, known as Mac in these parts, turned and sat on the bank of the creek, his long legs crossed Indian-style. He stared across the valley he and his wife, Laurel, had named Eden. This sanctuary was Heaven on earth. A myriad of trees in this virgin forest--every species, size, and age-provided a beautiful, perfect haven in every circumstance of his life. He sought solitude in this place whenever he needed God's presence, comfort, wisdom, and strength.

His prayer ended, yet Mac hungered to hear from to his trusted friend and companion. He spoke aloud, "Lord, my pa always told me when one phase of life ends, You always provide a new one. I've heard Brother Matthew preach on more than one occasion that You never close a door on something good that You don't open a window to something better. I believe it, but now I need help in finding my way. I'm at a crossroad, and I don't know which way to go. What I choose to do will impact not only me, but Laurel, my pa, my kids, and even the new baby not yet born. I don't think I've ever felt so lost since you lifted me out of my mired, ugly past. Please show me some sign. Let me know I'm livin' out your will. How can I be the husband I need to be? What do my kids need from me? Lord, I want to be the man You expect, but I'm not sure right now what that is. I fear my selfishness and ambition will take the place of my family again. Show me how to put all these things in priority so my life will be lived for Your glory. You've blessed me a thousand times over, so I know you've got a plan. Why can't I see my way?"

Mac continued to sit in the serenity of Eden. He had no sense of time as he remained there, just looking, taking in the wonder of his homestead. On a branch, high up in an ancient hickory tree, two robins flitted back and forth, feeding their nestlings. One was male with his bright red breast clearly visible. He sat, serenading a smaller brown hen as she tended two hatchlings with their tiny beaks spread wide to receive food that she'd had found for them. Across the opening, a doe nursed a spindly-legged fawn, splayed with white spots across its tawny fur. Not far away stood a large stag, watching guard over his new offspring. In the creek, a small school of fish, maybe a family of crappie, floated by, feeding in the clear creek water.

His meditation continued until he sensed—in a nearly audible voice—familiar scripture. *It is not good that man should be alone...And the rib, which the Lord God had taken from man, made He woman, and brought her unto the man. "This is now bone of my bones and flesh of my flesh; She shall be called woman."* "Laurel." Mac rose...homeward bound.

φ

The red-orange glow over Crowley's Ridge provided a breathtaking close to the busy day. Laurel pushed the toe of her work shoe onto the porch floor, rocking her chair to and fro, her winsome smile and closed eyes spoke of her happiness. She rose, stretched, and stared across the porch rail, taking in the awe of the Arkansas sunset. Realizing the time, she wondered where her husband had gotten off to since mid-day. In truth, a more worrisome question plagued her since Mac returned from the state capital. What had become of the man she'd married back in Washington County? He had not returned from Little Rock. She searched for an answer, but because she refused to disrupt the peace of Mac's homecoming, she didn't ask. If only he would talk to her!

Once again at their noon meal today, his unpredictable moodiness threw a shadow across the time their family spent sharing dinner together. He didn't appear to be angry or upset. He was too quiet. He simply wasn't with them. He was overly accommodating, trying too hard to please everyone at home. Mac wasn't himself and hadn't been for the nearly six weeks he'd been back in Shiloh.

Laurel continued to rock, enfolding her barely extended belly as if to embrace her not yet born child. Humming the tune of an old lullaby, she glanced across the front of her beloved doublepen cabin. How wonderful it felt to be truly at home! How blessed she was. The last sun rays laced through the branches of the budding trees to the west as Mac rode Midnight into the yard.

"Hello, Wife. I'm glad to see you restin' some this evenin'. How are you feelin' this afternoon?"

"Blessed. You've been gone a long time. I was beginning to think I'd need to send Roy out to bring you home."

"You won't ever have to do that. You know I've got no plans to leave you alone again." Mac flashed one of the smiles that endeared him to everyone.

"That's what you've said…more than once, I recall." She teased.

"Laurel, love, do you doubt my promise?"

"I know you mean to keep your word."

"Are you upset with me about something, Wife? Have I done anything to cause you to think I am planning to leave again?"

She planted her feet against the sturdy pine floor and stopped rocking. She sought his eyes. "Patrick, are you satisfied at home since you returned from Little Rock?"

"What made you ask me that? I've not talked about leavin' or even about a return to politics. We haven't argued or been at odds about plans for the homestead. Why did you bring this up now?"

"True. You have been very agreeable. You bend over backward to keep the peace, to make everything go smoothly, but you've been almost a stranger. I was just sitting here wondering where Patrick MacLayne, the man I love and sent to the legislature without me in January, had gotten off to…I'm not sure he's come home to us, yet." Laurel turned to face him in another attempt to make eye contact with her husband.

Dragging his hands through his hair, he turned and walked to the stairs to sit down. His shoulders drooped, and he cast his eyes toward his well-worn boots. Laurel felt despondency come over them both. Pushing herself from her rocking chair, she walked over to where he sat. Placing her hand on his shoulder to steady herself, she sat next to him. She took his hand, brought it to her lips, and waited for him to share what was on his heart.

"I had to get away this afternoon, Laurel. I went to Eden. I sat there a long time. Right now, I'm pretty confused—I've got so many questions that I can't answer. I spent the entire afternoon, looking, thinking, and praying for some answers. I can't say I found even one."

Squeezing his hand, she smiled tentatively, but he didn't look at her. A blank stare was contrary to the empathetic expression she wanted to display. She wanted to understood his uneasiness. Her life was better, richer, and happier than she'd ever known. Shiloh was paradise. How could he want anything more? Fearing she'd say the wrong thing, Laurel didn't respond to his honest, humble admission.

"I don't think I can talk to Matthew about all this confusion. He's so sure of his call—his place in this world. He tries to understand when I tell him of my uncertainty of whether I'm doing what the Lord wants me to do. If I were living in His will, would I have such doubt, Laurel?" He looked into her eyes with such anguish. Laurel sensed his hurt and emptiness. "If I were supposed to be satisfied here, would I find the day-to-day routine on our homestead so tedious and boring? Surely, I wouldn't feel such a draw to do more! Laurel, I prayed all afternoon. I got no answer at all."

Quiet fell between them for a while. Laurel didn't move away or relinquish Mac's hand. Tears laced her lashes as she felt the chasm between them. Yet, she'd never felt closer to him. The moon rose over the tree-lined silhouette against the night sky. Mac picked up her other hand and brought both of them to his bearded cheek.

"How I love you, Laurel Grace MacLayne. That is the one fact the Lord clearly revealed to me again today. As I admitted how lost I'm feelin' since I've been home, I sensed Him speaking to me. When I cried out 'Show me the way!' You were the one image that came to my mind. Without any sense of doubt, you will be beside me. Right now, I dread the future. I believe things are going to get hard for us and for Shiloh. Regardless, you will be with me, always loving me and supporting me. I know it to the depth of my soul."

"Somehow, whatever your fear is, I know you aren't questioning my love. I am your wife. Patrick. I do love you. I am grateful for the wonderful life we have together. As long as the Lord allows, I will always be beside you."

Mac pulled Laurel into an embrace. As he lowered his head to kiss her, the front door slammed behind Andy, a miniature of himself.

"Mama, Cathy says if y'all don't come and eat supper now, they ain't gonna be no soup left in them beans, and the roast will be dry enough to cut me soles for my boots."

"Yes, Andy. We're coming. Mac, let's finish this conversation at bedtime. I'm hungry now, and those young'uns must be starving."

Later, after seeing the kids to bed, Mac retired to the second pen bedroom, the private domain for his wife and himself. He sat near the cold fireplace and pushed his boots off. His face reflected the intensity of his troubled mood. He slumped and sighed so loudly that Laurel turned to stare at him as she closed the door to their sanctuary. An unusual downturned mouth and creases across his forehead marked his handsome face.

"You'll feel so much better if you'll get everything off your chest. Good or bad, I will listen to you. Patrick, our conversation ended mid-stream this afternoon. Please just pick it up and get the load you're carrying off 'our' chests. If it is bothering you, it is bothering me too…even more so if I don't know the reason."

"Wouldn't know where to start."

"I suggest you start where it started. When you went back to the legislature, you were optimistic and confident you were doing the right thing. What happened down there?"

"The only good thing I did was to help create a new county. Of course, that cost me my seat because now we live in that new county."

"Do you think that's bad? You told me you were ready to stay home. Or if not, you can travel south instead of north and campaign in Craighead County."

"Laurel, it's not that easy. The county has to start from scratch. Right now, we have two appointed officials—a sheriff and a judge."

"Sounds like plenty of opportunities to find a way to serve.

That is what you like to do—build things from the ground up."

"You don't understand how the political system works, Laurel."

"Teach me then."

"Awwwgh! Laurel Grace." Mac pulled her into his lap. Her spitfire behavior and lighthearted defiance lightened the mood of the room. He kissed her, and she snuggled into his shoulder. "You nagged me into talking, and I feel better."

"You aren't getting off that easily. You've been a horror to live with for more than six weeks. I want to know the rest of it. Talk."

"Are you feeling all right, Laurel? Is the baby…"

"We aren't talking about me. What happened at the legislature?"

"Nothing…too much…I didn't expect what happened, I guess. I went down there with a naïve view of what service in the state house would be and got it knocked right out of me."

"Knocked out of you? Did you get hurt, Patrick?"

"Not really. I had a brief scuffle with a couple of ruffians who didn't like how I voted. Split my lip, but I won that brawl."

"Mac!"

"I suppose that was what caused the final disenchantment with public service for me. Most everyone there seems bent on getting what they want, not what would most benefit the people who elected them. Men that I thought were honest made deals, took bribes, and threatened delegates who disagreed with them. Politics is too dirty a vocation for an ethical person."

"You knew that before you decided to run. You told me yourself how ugly men can be in a struggle over power. Mac, you said this afternoon you've come home filled with dread. You are afraid for our future. Surely, things aren't that bad. If they are, that is not like you. The Mac I know would be headed back to Little Rock to fight for what he thought was the best thing for our state.

Your faith is strong."

"Laurel, things are as bad as I've ever known them to be. State representatives talk openly about dividing Arkansas. Threats to life and property are not jokes. I want …" He lifted her hands to his cheeks.

"Please finish what you were saying. You're scaring me."
"Laurel, the old political machine that has run Arkansas since statehood is disintegrating. Men who see opportunities to get bigger pieces of political power are out to get their share. They use any means at their disposal to put laws into place that promote their schemes. That's why I had to defend myself two days before adjournment. I broke the arm of one man who threatened my family. I lost my temper."

"He must have been bluffing."

"I thought so, but the day I left Little Rock, one of the senators stopped me on the steps of the capitol. He said I'd been an obstacle to them during the entire session. He said I'd better watch out because the retribution wasn't over. Even when I told him I'd cause no more problems because I'd lost my seat, he said I'd be sorry I took up sides against the party in power."

"Do you think our family is in harm's way?"

"I don't know. I pray not, but I still try to keep up with the news around the area and reports of strangers around Shiloh and Greensboro."

"I suppose we can't do much more."

"I don't know of anything else. I'll watch out for our family, Laurel. I promise you that. I don't believe I can stand any more loss. Your papa, my ma, our baby…we've dealt with enough grief in our short time together."

"Yes, we've had some hard times, but we've shared a lot of joy, too. The Lord has seen us through."

"There is one more thing I need to tell you tonight, Wife. Through this session, I struggled with my faith. Parts of my old life slipped back into my routine during my work in the legislature. My temper became hard to control. I found myself cursing too often, and the urge to attack the people who plagued me was a daily event. Laurel, I haven't dealt with those old sins since the Lord showed me a better life. I found that old me too often. I hate that man. You'd hate him, too. No career's worth losing what I've found in Shiloh."

"Patrick, your faith is much too strong to die. I have never known that old person you just spoke of, nor do I expect to ever meet him."

"Laurel, I am serious. That is the main reason I spent so much time on my knees down in Eden this afternoon. If I can't control those things, I can never go back into the political arena.

Power is too great temptation for me. I've seen myself and how I act when I feel threatened with its loss. Pray for me, Laurel. I'm not sure if I can be a farmer like you want me to be, but I will be your husband and a good father to our offspring--all of them."

"You already are. Better than I ever thought I'd have. Thank you for telling me what you've been carrying alone. I love you. I want to share your life. We will be much happier when you let me be your full partner. I hope you see I'm not the frail, broken girl you married three years ago. Your love and belief in me have helped me grow into a better woman. You helped me claim God's grace. With that and a wonderful man like you beside me, I'll be your true helpmate. You have made me very happy, even with all the serious talk we've done today." Mac looked into the face of his wife. For the first time in six weeks, his face reflected a true smile, the first one she had seen since his return. He pressed slow kisses across her face.

"I love you, Wife. You know that, don't you?"

"Everyone one knows you love me. Just look at me! Now, let's go to bed. Your son's kicking me pretty hard this evening. I'm more tired than I knew."

CHAPTER TWO

I went by a field of the slothful, and by the vineyard of a man void of
understanding; and lo, it was overgrown with thorns, and nettles had
covered the face thereof, and the stonewall was broken down. Then I saw
and considered well. I looked upon it and received instruction.
Proverbs 24: 30-32

A new sense of normalcy evolved after Laurel and Mac's
long day of real talk. New life was everywhere around
Crowley's Ridge. Less than two weeks passed before they found
the first buds in the orchard, and Cathy came into the cabin the
same afternoon carrying two jonquils she found near the creek.
Laurel walked through her days singing happy melodies and
hymns of praise. Even though March proved to be a particularly
unpleasant time due to her daily bouts with morning sickness,
Laurel found joy in the work she did with her family.

Every day, Mac worried about Laurel's health. She hadn't
been as sick when she carried Campbell. Nearly every day, he
nagged her to talk with Dr. Edwards, but Laurel brushed away the
pleas. She knew the baby she carried was well and growing. She
told Mac that she'd never felt stronger in her life. She'd go from
project to project until her naptime in the mid-afternoon.

"Mac, dear. When will you finish breaking the garden
beds?"

"It's a bit early, don't ya think?"

"Nonsense. The weather has been glorious, and the soil is
warming every day. Getting an early start will let us make our
garden even larger this spring."

"We don't need a bigger garden. We still have plenty of food in our larder from the last harvest."

"Of course, we need a larger garden. We have Andrew to feed, and your pa will need things for his pantry. If we have more, we can always share our bounty."

"Laurel, you are taking on too much. You've got to rest more."

"Please don't caudle me, Mac! I'm pregnant, not feeble or mortally ill. Women have had babies since time began and still managed to feed their families. Let's walk out and check on the orchard."

Without waiting for him to reply, Laurel stepped down from the back porch and headed toward the orchard they'd planted the first week they'd arrived in Shiloh. The once tiny seedlings had grown to more than four and a half feet since the spring of '57. Small limbs were reaching out to the sunshine in all directions. Laurel had grown up in apple country so she knew that her trees would not produce really good apples for another six or seven years, but the hope was there. Before the child she carried was old enough to go to school, the trees would bring beautiful pink and white apple blossoms to herald the new spring. Only one tree had succumbed to the cold of winter. Laurel had pruned the trees the week before Mac returned, so there was little work to be done in the orchard, but just the idea of being in an orchard reminded her of home in Washington County. She sighed and smiled. Lots of water, a bit of manure, and the warm sunshine would create the new orchard to replace the one she'd left behind when Mac brought her to Shiloh as a new bride.

She looked to the grape vines and noticed the new shoots were strong and healthy looking. The runners on the vines were longer than she expected and told her it was time to build trellises to support the first fruit. Before the new MacLayne was big enough to run through the orchard, they would have grapes.

"Mac, there is something to keep you busy. These vines need to be tied up and soon. Of course, you will have to build trellises before you can tie them up. Maybe you and Roy can build some. I'm betting we'll have grapes within two years."

"You've taken fine care of these plants, Laurel. You've already pruned them this year, I see. They'll bring us a fine crop of fruit."

"Only because you took such care to bring them here for me. If they continue to thrive, we'll have lots of fruit to share with our family and friends at Shiloh. Selfishly, though, I'll have a piece of the Campbell homestead here in my own backyard. Bless you for being so thoughtful, Mac. I'd have never believed we could bring an orchard across the state."

"My pleasure. Just a small bribe to tempt you into moving across the state to make a home for me. I'll never leave it or you again."

"We'll see."

"You don't understand, Laurel. Serving in the legislature is nothing like I hoped it would be. When you were with me, and we were involved with proposing and writing legislation… that was the easy part. I loved the activities we found in Little Rock. After you came home, I was miserable. I had no one to talk to about what was happening day to day. I'd probably learn to deal with that, but the whole business turned mean and ugly. Some voted to maintain the status quo or to profit from the changes they tried to make. Others only touted the Family's policies, regardless of the harm it caused common folks. And the violence and threats…most from people outside the body but hired or manipulated by them…I became so disgusted. I was wrong. One man or even the small handful that were independently elected can't change anything."

"Patrick, it's not like you to quit something because you're discouraged."

"Laurel, darlin', it doesn't matter anymore. We don't live in Greene County, and I know only a handful of homesteaders west of Greensboro. My politicking days are behind us now."

The third week in April, Mac rode into the yard, returning from Greensboro. He made weekly trips to town to keep up with the news and to bring home any newspapers he could find along with the mail, which was rare now that his father was close by. On that day, he had brought Laurel two letters, one from Washington County, and another from Texas. He was also anxious to share some other news he'd learned in Greensboro. He jumped from Midnight, tied him at the porch rail, and rushed into the cabin. "Laurel, you'll never guess what I found out today." There was no answer. Mac pushed open the door of the second pen and called out a second time. Laurel was not in the house, and it was time she usually took her afternoon nap. He went to the back porch and called out. "Laurel, where are you?"

"I'm out here in the orchard, Mac. Come and join Cathy and me."

He called as he stepped down from the porch. "Al Stuart told me today…" He walked the short distance behind the barn. Mac scrunched his nose to the pungent smell of manure even before he saw his wife holding a shovel of the smelly stuff.

"What in tarnation are you doing?"

"I am fertilizing these trees and vines."

"How did you get that heavy tub out here?" "Well, it's not that heavy, but I dragged it from the barn. There is plenty of good manure from the stalls. This will help feed the orchard a good part of the summer."

"Laurel Grace! You are supposed to be takin' it easy. I could have done that, or Roy would have helped if you'd asked."

"Roy went over to his home place to see how things are, and besides, I am not helpless. I can take care of this homestead." "I want you to be more careful, Laurel. Your fifth month is

14

coming up. Your health and the well-being of our child is more important than those trees."

"Mac, I'm not an invalid. I can't go in that cabin and sit in a rocking chair until the end of September."

"You have easier things to keep you occupied. Cathy needs new school clothes before the end of the month. You need to make baby clothes. You have two new books I brought from the capital, neither of which you have read yet."

"Mac, stop fussing at me. You've never been such a mother hen! Last night you wouldn't even let me get water to wash the supper dishes."

"I wasn't busy. Why shouldn't I help you?"

"You do, all the time, but I want to do my own work."

"I want a healthy baby…and I need you here with me, strong and well, as long as I live. Don't do anything like this again." Mac clamped his fingers at her shoulders and turned his wife to face him. "Do you understand me?"

Laurel looked up at her husband who had just issued her an order. Anger was her first reaction, but after looking at his face…seeing the concern that had prompted the outburst, she realized for the first time how much her pregnancy had caused Mac to fear for her well-being. Of course, she'd been frightened at first too…afraid she would not be able to give him a child, but she'd felt so well except for the morning sickness and felt such a wonderful sense of wellbeing and peace, the worry had disappeared. She spent nearly all her time dreaming of the day she would lay the new child in Patrick's arms. She'd not noticed he spent nearly all his time looking after her, trying to do her work, and worrying about her health.

"Patrick, I am going to carry this baby to term. I won't jeopardize our child. I want this baby as much as you do. Please have a little faith and stop trying to put me in storage until fall."

"I'll stop fussing at you if you promise you'll think before you tackle certain chores and be more careful. I'm sorry I made you angry with me."

"I'm not angry…I'm just frustrated that you are being too protective. Let the time go by and live out our regular routine. Maybe you need to go read Romans 8:28 again. What happened in Greensboro? What were you saying about Al?"

"Changed the subject, didn't you? All right, I spoke with Al Stuart and John McCollough. Both of them seem to think that Greensboro may take on a lot more business since Jonesboro has been named the county seat. That settlement is new and certainly doesn't have the stores or businesses yet to support a new county. A man named Snoddy has built a fair-sized stable and livery there, not far from the beautiful old oak we sheltered under when we drove back from Bolivar. In the past week or so, several of the settlers from that area have come into Greensboro to do business at the mercantile or to have Al do some legal work for them. Even the saddler and the widow dressmaker have been doing more business with those folks. Greensboro is closer than Bolivar, and the road is a sight better."

"That's good news. Anything else?"

"One thing did concern me more than I want to admit. John McCollough told me that Robert Duncan was back in the mercantile last Saturday, buying supplies for Digby's ranch. What is he doing back here now?"

"I can't imagine they'd want to come back here to settle. With Digby losing the election so badly, I thought they'd leave pretty quickly."

"He's not been around here trying to see you, has he, Laurel?"

"Of course not. Just forget about him. He's the past, and I am perfectly content living in the present. Any other news from Greensboro?"

"I was able to get my hands on a newspaper from Little

Rock and one from St. Louis. We'll read those after supper. By the way, I asked Pa to come by for supper tonight."

"Well, I'm glad you decided to tell me. It's nearly three now, and it takes a while to make a company supper."

"Don't get into a fluster, Laurel. It's just Pa. He's surely family since he stayed here nearly all winter."

"Oh, Mac. Men just don't understand anything!"

"I understand that you like mail. I picked up a couple of letters for you while I was at McCollough's." Mac took the hoe and the shovel from her and handed her the letters. "Let's get back in so you can fix that company supper and maybe find time to read your letters."

Easter Sunday provided the opportunity to celebrate the beautiful Arkansas springtime along with the priceless gift of the resurrection of the Lord. Shiloh Methodist planned a special day. Being late in April, the weather was perfect, so Brother Matthew decided to convene a revival to be led by a circuit rider from the central area of the state. He scheduled the first service for the evening service of Easter Sunday. Between the morning service and the opening of the revival meeting, Shiloh church held their first dinner on the grounds of the season along with the afternoon singing. Laughter rose across the churchyard, and the Shiloh family felt the joy of being in community. Easter day was indeed a celebration.

At lunch, three plank tables were overloaded with food and beverages, much more than usual as the word of the circuit rider's revival had brought people from distant communities. Some families came in covered wagons or had brought tents, expecting to stay for more than one day. The wooden pews at Shiloh church were crowded that Easter morning, and a few men chose to stand rather than push into a tight seat. Knowing others in the area would come for the revival, he smiled to see the large crowd gathered. Matthew planned to call the evening service to order at five o'clock outside in the churchyard. He began to recruit several men to help him carry the split log pews outside. He also brought hay bales, barrels, and a few chairs. By mid-afternoon, more than a hundred people had come to participate in the camp meeting.

While the men were occupied, Laurel, her Aunt Ellie and her cousin Susan joined a circle of women who'd put their little ones to rest on pallets in the hickory grove. This spring revival offered the perfect opportunity to catch up on the community news since it was the first real celebration since winter had ended.

"Laurel Grace, how are ya feelin'?"

"I feel good after I have my morning bout, keepin' my food down. I can't believe how big I've gotten already. I couldn't wear my pink calico today because the bodice was too tight."

"Well, I seem to gain a little more with each new baby."

"Well, I won't mind as long as I can give Mac a healthy baby."

"You will, niece. We're all praying for you."

"I got a letter from my brother Daniel who lives down near Waco in Texas. He told me I'm an aunt again. He has three children now. I'd love to get to meet them, but that is such a difficult trip. I'm not sure we'll ever go down that way."

"Someday, perhaps, the roads will improve so travel isn't so hard."

"Mac says the state legislature is setting aside funds for road improvement, but some of the people bidding on the road construction don't build the roads the way they need to be built to make them last. He was furious when the flood report was made in the house. Scores of levees and roads were washed away in the winter floods the past couple of years."

"We had quite a bit of damage over near the Cache this winter." A visitor to their community said. "Course, we never had any levees to wash away. We sure need some."

"Daniel told me that he may decide to bring his family back to Arkansas. He is concerned because the secession talk in Texas has been strong. He wrote they've had more than a few brawls, and some people supporting the union have been the targets most often."

"Well, Arkansas government leaders ain't said this state will remain in the union if the south splits off," Susan replied.

"True, but a lot of Arkansans don't want to leave the union. Mac said most legislators would vote to stay in the union if they'd voted before the recess." Some of the women began to drift away from the circle, having little interest in the conversation.

One of the ladies took offense, though. "I'm not sure that's true. My family comes from Georgia, and we all believe state rights is just as important as the say-so of the government in Washington City."

"I hope we never find out," Laurel's Aunt Ellie had responded to sooth the tense words. "Surely we can talk out the problems and find some kind of solution that will work for everyone. Tell me, Laurel Grace. Is this new baby going to be a boy?"

Changing the subject defused the tense feelings. "We don't talk much about it. We just want the baby to be well."

Matthew Campbell called the groups together for afternoon singing. The revival service began as the congregation took whatever seats they could find outside. Brother Campbell and the circuit rider sat on the church porch, and at half past two, Matthew opened the singing with an old Isaac Watt hymn, *At the Cross*. So many of the wonderful hymns familiar to the Easter season resounded across the ridge. Tears marked the faces of Laurel and many other members of the congregation when Matthew closed the time of singing with another Isaac Watts hymn, *Alas, And Did My Savior Bleed.* The solo brought a hush. As he sang the words, not one whisper marred the precious serenity of the churchyard.

> *Alas, and did my Savior bleed,*
>   *And did my Sovereign die?*
> *Would He devote that sacred head*
>   *For sinners, such as I?*
> *Was it for crimes that I have done,*
>   *He groaned upon the tree?*
> *Amazing Pity! Grace unknown!*
>   *And Love beyond degree!*

Matthew said, "Let us pray." For several minutes, members of Shiloh church and visitors from around the area sat with heads bowed. Silent prayers were lifted up.

Mac clasped Laurel's hand almost too tightly for several minutes. Then he sighed and lifted his head. "Thank you, Lord." He spoke, joy and confidence reflected in his voice. He smiled down at his wife and kissed her cheek. Whispering, he mouthed the words, "*I love you.*" The afternoon singing ended with a favorite Wesleyan hymn, *O For a Thousand Tongues to Sing.* The beautiful words of gratitude and Jesus' passion rang out for more than ninety minutes. Before the circuit rider even began his strong, emotion-filled message, the crowd felt the stirring of the spirit among them. The devoted minister spoke with authority concerning God's love for fallen man, and the sacrifices made by Jesus. That evening several people found themselves on their knees in front of Matthew and Brother Mason, the circuit rider who'd come to hold the revival.

The first evening of the revival ended about dusk with the hymn, *Just as I am,* the perfect close to the perfect Easter. The next four evenings extended that blessed holiday for the community of believers. As Brother Matthew had hoped, new converts were added to his flock, and those who had made up the Shiloh church were renewed and strengthened in their faith.

℔

As spring passed into early summer, life on the homestead took on harvesting the bounty of the gardens, planting of fall crops, and preserving food for the next winter. Laurel's efforts paid off, and her earliest crops of pole beans and tomatoes were abundant.

She would go out every morning before the day's heat was at its height and pick anything that had reached the right stage of ripeness. Of course, that meant an afternoon of canning, as she had done the previous two years. Laurel worked hard to assure her family would have plenty to eat even if the winter proved to be long and hard. This year proved more difficult though. Laurel was well into the middle stage of her pregnancy, and the early summer was very hot and dry. As a matter of fact, there had been only one substantial rainfall since before Easter.

Laurel and Cathy had to spend a good deal of time every afternoon after school carrying water to the garden and the trees and grapes in the orchard. At least, Laurel did until one late afternoon when Mac rode into the yard earlier than expected.

"Laurel Grace, what are you doin' out here?"

"I'm tending the garden. That is my job."

"Carrying heavy buckets of water is not your job." "Mac, the dry weather will stunt our crops if we don't keep the plants watered. Anyway, I always rest when I get tired. I never fill the buckets more than half full. I had my nap at two."

"You will not carry those heavy buckets anymore! Cathy, do you hear me? If you see her haulin' water again, you come and get me at once."

"But, Papa…"

"No buts. I'll send Roy and John over in the late afternoon to help water."

"Mac, you need those boys to help with the herds and wood cutting for winter. You've got hay to put up. They don't have time to do my work." "We'll make time to do the heavy chores around here.

Calving is done. The twelve calves we have are old enough now. They'll do fine and be big enough to survive the winter. Laurel, promise me. No more heavy work."

"I haven't done any 'heavy' work. I am more than able to lift a single pail of water."

"We won't talk about this anymore. Let's go sit on the porch and rest a while."

I'm not tired. Just let me finish the last three grapevines."

"Have you been toting water out to the orchard, too?"

"I'm certainly not going to lose my orchard for the lack of a few buckets of water."

"I'm not going to argue in front of Cathy. We'll talk about his later." Mac took the bucket of water from Laurel and walked to the grape arbors he and the boys had finished earlier that month. He saw that every tree had already been doused with ample water. He muttered something under his breath that Laurel could only guess. He was trying to bite back angry words. She hadn't meant to upset him, but she felt she had to stand her ground. She felt well and strong, so there was no reason she could not take care of the task of every pioneer homemaker. She was capable of tending her garden.

Laurel turned to walk to the porch where she would sit down for a few minutes to appease her husband before she returned to the kitchen to finish the evening meal. Mac would stop fussing if she rested for a few minutes. Before Mac could follow her to the porch, the sound of hooves on the west road caught her attention. Her father-in-law rode into the yard.

"Afternoon, daughter. How are you this warm summer day?"

"Feeling fine, Pa. What brings you by on this Thursday afternoon?"

"Hoping to find my son at home. I want to talk to him about some land I've found."

"He's on his way in from the orchard. Come up and sit a spell. I'll go to the spring house and get some cool water. I wish I had some cold cider to offer, but we don't have any left."

"A cool drink will ease this parched mouth."

"Hey, Pa. I'll go bring the water, Laurel. You just sit there and tell my pa why you're in trouble while I'm gone."

"You're in trouble, Laurel?"

"Just your hovering son. He's driving me to distraction. You know the hardest thing about my condition isn't my growing body, needing naps every afternoon, or even the morning sickness, which thankfully is all but gone. The hardest thing is Patrick's coddling me. He's constantly underfoot, doesn't want me to take care of the garden, or even get water from the well. The other evening, he scolded me for carrying in three small pieces of firewood so I could heat up food for our dinner."

"Are you overdoing, Laurel?"

"No. I am just doing what I always do. And I rest when I get tired."

"Patrick is concerned. He doesn't want anything to happen to you."

"Anyway, I wish he'd relax and let me do what I need to do. I'm not taking any risks. I want this baby as much as he does. I promised him I would take care."

"Maybe I can give you a day or two without him underfoot. I'd like him to ride over to the east with me to look at some land not far from the St. Francis River."

"I think it would be good for him to get away. He's restless these past few weeks. As much as there is to do here getting ready for winter, I think he misses the hectic, chaotic life he lived in Little Rock. He says he's glad to be home, but I'm not sure the life we have here is as exciting or as meaningful to him as when he served as the state representative."

"I doubt that's the case, Laurel. Mac loves this homestead and you."

"I know he does, but that may not be enough. With the redrawn county lines now, Mac can't return to his position as Greene County's representative anymore. We don't live in Greene County now.

"Well, he'll just have to campaign in the new county when the time comes if he has his heart set on serving again."

"When what time comes?" Mac handed his father a pewter cup of chilled water from the springhouse. "I didn't expect to see you until Sunday."

"I've been told about a couple of parcels of land that may make me a nice farm. The land is near the St. Francis and would need levees and ditches, but with some work, the land would be dry and fertile. I'd like you to come with me, and let's ride over there to look at the property."

"All that land over there is pretty swampy, Pa."

"I know that, but so were parts of our land in Maryland. I had to reclaim a good part of our farm, but after I did, that acreage was some of my best-producing land."

"That's quite a trip. I don't think I can go off and leave the homestead just now,"

"Why not? Mac, you just told me the calving is done and the boys have time to do my chores. Why can't you go with your pa for a couple of days?"

"Laurel, you know good and well why! You'd be out in the pasture directly behind the barn building a shed for the cattle or maybe starting an addition to the cabin that we've been talking about."

"You're being ridiculous. I resent your suggestion that I'd do anything to jeopardize this little one."

"We'll talk about it later."

"I think the land may be just what I've been looking for, son. Enough acreage to make a nice-sized farm, and it's not more'n a day's ride from your place. I would like another pair of eyes before I buy."

"Pa, I was hoping you'd decide to settle here on this land. We've got almost five hundred acres. You could build any place you want, except in Eden, of course."

"This is your homestead. You've got a vision of what you want this place to be, and I like what you're planning. You'll always have good hunting if you keep a good share of it in its natural state. Great way to preserve it for your children. I want to make me a farm where I can do the same thing."

"What's wrong with this area here on the ridge?"

"Too much of it is already settled. If I have a section or two that's not already drained or cleared, I can turn it into usable land.
That's what I did in Maryland, and those were the days I was happiest."

"I understand, Pa. I'll go with you the day after tomorrow. Just give me time to go over and talk with Matthew."

"Why do you need to go speak to him?"

"I won't leave you here alone, not for two or three days."

"I won't be alone. I'm never alone. Cathy is here, and Roy and John are always about."

"Cathy is at school all day, and the boys are likely to be out in one of the far pastures."

"She doesn't go to school on Saturday."

"Cathy was out there watering trees and grapevines with you. I'm sure y'all did the same thing in the garden. She'll do whatever you ask her to do because she loves you."

"Mac, I need to…"

"You need to rest more and argue less." Mac's tone of voice was more than stern. She was surprised he spoke to her with such force, especially with his father standing there with them on the porch. He was demanding, not asking, her compliance. "Laurel,
I'd rather discuss this with you alone, but since you've pushed the issue, you will stop all heavy labor and exertion of any kind. I will find someone to stay with you anytime I have to leave the homestead for more than a couple of hours. Do you understand me?"

Her face reddened. She turned her back, stomped to the door, and slammed it as she left the porch. *Who did he think she was? She wasn't a child, a servant, or a piece of property? How dare he talk to her as he had… and in front of his own father!*
"Well, son, I'm not sure you handled that very well?" "Are you on her side? Do you know what I found her doing? She was carrying water from the creek to the orchard to water those apple trees and grapevines we brought from
Washington County."

"As dry as it's been, seems a logical thing to do, don't ya think?"

"Pa, you don't understand. She has to rest more." "Patrick, Laurel is a strong woman. The doctor says all is well with this baby. She is only doing what she sees as her part in keeping this homestead going. And you know what that orchard means to her."

"She is too headstrong. I want her to rest more. Pa…Laurel can't lose this baby, too."

"I thought that may be the reason for this spat. She'll have an easier time with you here."

"Pa, this is about the same time we lost Campbell."

"Go in and soothe her feathers, son. In her present temper, I'm not sure she'll let you share her bed, especially while you're in such a foul mood, too."

"What do you mean?"

"Go and let her know you trust her to take care of herself and this baby. She didn't lose Campbell on purpose. Accidents happen. You need to talk with her if she'll let you in the cabin. Come by the widow's when you are ready to go over to the eastern side of the region."

Mac stood on the porch alone as his father mounted Tartan and rode back across the valley toward the widow's cabin. Bright red colored his cheeks, and his eyes were stormy blue. Mac muttered under his breath. "My own father took her side against me!" He entered the cabin but didn't find Laurel in the main room. When he tried to open the door to their second pen bedroom, he found the door barred, just as his father hinted it might be.

"Laurel, I would like to talk to you."

"I'm too tired. I am lying down as you demanded. Go stand guard on the back porch. I'd have to come through there to get my bucket if I'm going to draw any more water."

"Laurel, don't be unreasonable. Let me talk to you about this, like we are two adults."

"You said your piece already. Go away and let me get that rest I am neglecting. After all, I only had one nap today."

"I didn't demand… or at least, I didn't intend it that way." She screamed back through the door, an action so unlike her. "I said go away! Leave me alone right now. I don't want to talk to you." With his shoulders slumped and a scowl on his face, he left the cabin and went to work off some of his frustration, cleaning the barn.

Laurel fell asleep, weeping into her pillow. Why had she let Mac upset her so? She'd never screamed at him before. Had he done anything so terrible? She slept poorly, tossing and turning, trying to find a comfortable position, but she knew the discomfort wasn't because of her swollen belly or her aching back. The harsh words she'd screamed at Mac were the reason. How long had it been, since they'd fought as they did that day? They'd not had such a serious breach since they'd returned from Bolivar when she'd run away from him before he'd ever made love to her.

At supper, Laurel tried to behave as she always did, but there was a strain in the room. Andy, Roy, and Cathy kept their eyes turned away from their parents, and the talk around the supper table that night was trite. Cathy told her parents she wanted to do the dishes after supper.

"Laurel, will you come outside to sit on the porch with me and the boys for a while?"

"Not me, Mr. Mac. I'm going over to Annie's for a spell if you don't need me."

"All right, Roy, but don't be out too late. Sometime tomorrow we need to ride those pasture fences. We've got a bigger herd to keep safe now. Those calves are running all over the pasture."

"I'll be home early."

"Mama, I want Andy to help me with the dishes. Can he?"
"Yes, if he wants to help."

"Well, Laurel, will you come and sit outside with me?"
"Yes, Mac."

"It's nice out here tonight. Smell that honeysuckle."

"Yes, I love the smell of honeysuckle, especially after a long hot day. It seems sweeter then."

"It was a hot one today. Had to be near ninety degrees."

"I suppose."

"I'm sorry I made…" Laurel interrupted Mac mid-sentence.

"Mac, I want to go over to see my Aunt Ellie in the morning."

"All right. I'll drive you over after chores."

"Thank you."

"We're being very formal with each other tonight, Wife."
"I hadn't noticed."

"You aren't going to talk to me about what happened this afternoon, are you?"

"I'd rather not. It's too beautiful out here tonight for angry words. Look, Mac, there's a shooting star over the ridge." The rest of the evening they talked about a score of insignificant things to pass the time. About nine, Laurel rose to prepare for bed.

"My pa told me I'd be sleeping in the barn for a few days, Laurel."

"Did he?"

"Do you want me to sleep in the barn, Laurel?"

"Don't be silly. I've never asked you to leave our bed. Why would I start now?"

"I don't know why we fought today."

"Mac, let's go to bed. I'm tired." Laurel once again made it clear that she didn't intend to engage in any serious conversation. "The baby's been kicking all evening. I hope I can find a way to rest tonight."

"Can I feel the little one kick?"

"Of course. Give me your hand." Laurel laid his outstretched hand on the right side of her growing torso. "Do you feel? This one is very active and will be a hand full when he or she gets here."

"Such a miracle." Mac drew Laurel into his arms and kissed her tenderly. "I love you."

"I know."

CHAPTER THREE

*T*he following morning, Mac drove his wife to visit at the Campbell homestead. They resumed their polite, less than serious conversation from the night before. As soon as they arrived, Matthew asked Mac to ride out to the Young's homestead with him. Reggie Young had asked for a little help roofing his smokehouse. Mac hadn't planned to be gone all day, but he felt Laurel was safe in the hands of her aunt, so he agreed. He departed with only one request.

"Oh, Ellie. Keep her away from the well. She can't seem to get enough water."

"Oh, Aunt Ellie, he's so insulting."

"Sounds like he is just looking out for his pregnant wife."

"If you could have heard him yesterday. He scolded me in front of his father, just as if I were a child. He's never spoken to me like that ever."

"What did he say?"

"Well, it wasn't what he said exactly. It was just the way he said it…that made the words so much worse. He sounded like a master, and I was supposed to be obedient to his every wish." "What did he demand of you?"

"Stop taking care of the garden and the orchards, and stop doing my chores around the homestead."

"That doesn't sound so harsh, Laurel Grace."

"No. You don't understand. He barked orders at me. He didn't ask me. He told me."

"I see."

"Then he came to apologize, and I screamed at him. Aunt Ellie, I never scream!"

"I've not heard you, but Laurel, you are forgetting something. You are expecting a baby, and all expectant mothers are moody at times. There were days I'd sit down and cry for no reason at all. When I was expecting Mary, once I told Matthew I couldn't stand the sight of him. Who knows where that came from? Be a little kinder to yourself and a bit more to Mac. Your moods will pass when this new baby comes."

"Aunt Ellie, I'm scared. What if I can't carry this baby to term either?"

"Niece, you are going to have this child. Don't let fear drive away the joy you both deserve. Don't fight with Mac. Let him pamper you during this time. It's a way he can be a part of all this. You know he loves you, so just let him show you."

"I will try, but I can't just go home and sit in a chair for four and a half months. I'll go crazy. I nearly lost my sanity the seven weeks we were in Little Rock last winter."

"But it's not winter now, Laurel. Go out on walks with Mac. Hold his hand. Let the family do the heavy chores, and you do lighter chores, like get things from the spring house and fold the laundry instead of pushing that heavy stirring pole. Let Cathy help with those chores. She'll like knowing she is helping you. No woman should ever have a child alone. It's far better to make it a family affair. You'll have more peace at home, too."

"You are so wise, Aunt Ellie."

"Well, I have had four opportunities to learn. I'd have had more if it'd been the Lord's will for us. I loved each and every time I was with child, I never felt closer to them or to Matthew, for that matter. It's the most blessed time in a marriage, Laurel Grace." "I will try harder. I'm so glad you are here to talk with me.

You know, I've cried for my mama several days in the past couple of months, more often than I did with Campbell."

"I know your mama would be a great comfort to you. She loved you so. She's here, watching over you now. Talk to her when you want to. You'll feel her presence and God's." Laurel wrapped her arms about her aunt's neck, and Ellie let her cry for a few minutes. Remembering her own experiences of trying to keep her emotions in check during the latter part of her pregnancies, she smiled. Ellie laid her hand on Laurel's head and rocked her for a few minutes. How blessed she felt! God let her step in for Laurel's mother.

On the following Monday, Mac went with his father to look at the land near St. Francis River. What Laurel didn't know is that he had given John and Roy special orders not to leave the immediate area of the cabin until he returned. He'd told the boys to take turns going out to check on the cattle and to do other chores beyond sight of the cabin at different times. They carried water in for Laurel at regular intervals so she never found an empty water pail at the dry sink. They filled the wash pot when it was needed, and Cathy stayed home from school that wash day complaining of a sore throat that disappeared just in time to help Laurel stir the wash tub. She also hung the clothes on the line. Laurel helped take down dry clothes and fold those that could be put away. The kids worked beside her in the afternoon when she weeded the vegetable patch, and she picked some ripened tomatoes and cucumbers. All chores were easily completed and demanded little of Laurel's energy.

Cathy asked if she could prepare the family supper that night, saying she wanted her ma to read her school essay about life in the Shiloh community before she had to turn it in the next day. That evening after John had started for home, the MacLayne household spent an easy time reading together and teasing Roy about his courting escapades.

Mac returned mid-afternoon the following day, pleased to find Laurel asleep in her chair on the porch. He saw both John and Roy working along the edge of the yard, turning over the earth, preparing the soil to plant the hedge Laurel had asked for along the road. She had commented she'd like to separate the front yard from the road with some plants and flowers. The boys had kept good watch over Laurel, just as their boss had asked. He was also relieved that his father had decided not to buy property so far from Shiloh. The trip had been a successful one. His fears had been set to rest, at least for the time being.

By the end of August, the late summer heat began to take its toll on all of them. Cathy was always at home since school had been dismissed for the harvest season. At times she seemed constantly underfoot. Laurel could not seem to find enough to keep her nine-year-old occupied. Her temper seemed on edge more than she'd ever known it to be. The hottest days seemed to last an eternity, and even with the sun down, the heat was oppressive. Laurel pushed herself up frequently from the four-poster bed and fanned herself in the rocking chair. Some nights she would be up for several hours at a time, sitting in her father's armchair in the front room, because it seemed the only place to find any comfort.

Many of those nights, Mac paced. Laurel had carried this new child longer than the first, and she'd not experienced the discomfort she knew now. Of course, she'd never been pregnant in the extreme heat of an Arkansas summer either. His concern led him to hover over her more than ever, and her moodiness and his mothering led to frequent spats and more than one full-blown argument. In late August, the day before Cathy's tenth birthday, Laurel's temper exploded.

"Laurel, let me carry that wash pan for you, darlin'."

"No. I'm not helpless, Mac. I'll take care of my own work."

"I know you can, but I just want…"

"I want you out from under my feet. Let me be!"

"Laurel, I…"

"Take the kids and y'all go down to the creek and swim or catch us some fish for supper or just go down there and get out of my sight for an hour or two! Give me a couple of hours of peace and quiet without y'all watchin' my every step. I'm sick to death of all of you today."

"I didn't mean for you to get upset with me."

"I'm not upset…I'm just hot." Laurel unbuttoned the top two buttons of her shirtwaist. "I want to be alone for a while, please. Please go out with the kids for a while. I promise I'll not try to fell one tree or slaughter any hogs until y'all get back."

"Calm down, Laurel. I'll take the kids out for a while." Reluctantly, Mac rounded up Cathy, Roy, and Andy, and they all went down to the creek. Maybe today would be a good day to catch fish.

As soon as the house was quiet, Laurel screamed her frustration and broke into body-racking sobs. Mac didn't deserve the angry words she'd thrown at him. She sunk into a chair on the front porch and after several minutes of sobs and sniffles, she slept. Shortly her nap was interrupted when a hand touched her forehead.

"Uncle Matthew." She startled. "I'm surprised to see you here."

"Just out visitin' some of the new people to the area and decided to drop by to see y'all. Where's your bunch?"

Somewhat embarrassed, Laurel replied, "I kicked them all out of the house a while ago. I think maybe they went to the creek, but I'm not sure."

"You kicked them out? Goodness, they must have done something terrible to make you kick them all out of their own home."

"Not really. I don't seem to be able to control my temper lately, but Mac is making me crazy. He's always underfoot."

"What did he do to upset you so?"

The minute her uncle had posed the question, Laurel realized how trivial the answer would sound. "He tried to take the dishpan away from me while I was moving it to the dry sink." "Oh, I see how that could cause a fit of anger, Niece…"

"Campbell sarcasm, uncle!   I know it all seems so trivial, but day after day…Mac watches me, he puts other people to watching me, and constantly someone is stepping in to do my work around here. I am so tired of this family treating me as an invalid."

"Laurel Grace, you're the one who is acting out. You've not got the sense God gave a goose…I know expectant mothers get moody sometimes, but to throw such a fit over a dishpan?"

"Uncle Matthew, please don't give me a lecture. I feel pretty foolish already. My temper got out of control, but I do wish Mac would stop playing mother hen with me."

"He will, when he knows that you and that little one are both well and safe. I probably shouldn't tell you this. Pastors are supposed to keep conversations with members of their flock private, but Mac has talked to me more than once about this new baby and the loss of the first one. Don't ya see, Mac feels guilty about the loss of Campbell. He told me that you'd even asked him to postpone his trip to Missouri to buy cattle, but he didn't."

"I don't blame him for going."

"More than just that. He said that you'd not have lost the baby if he'd been home. He thinks he didn't make nearly enough effort to get home when he said he would. He regrets not leaving one of the mules here to pull your wagon. He said it's his fault because he'd not worked with Sassy enough to make her a stable horse during stormy weather. He's got a dozen reasons that he blames himself for the accident."

"He's never said a word to me."

"Nor will he ever. He's sworn that he will not let anything happen to you this time. That's why he's been staying so close to home and trying to take over any chore that he thinks is too much for you."

"Oh…. Well, I told him more than once I'd be careful. I promised not to do too much."

"Was that before or after you mucked out the barn to fertilize the orchard?"

"It's not like that. I've been resting every day."

"So, I've heard. John said you were carrying water from the creek to the garden and orchard."

"I've been very cautious not to carry too much. Mac is being silly. I don't do any more than any other woman in our community. He's too overprotective."

"And in your stubborn Campbell way, you've fought him every step of the way when he's tried to keep you from hurtin' yourself. You're smart enough to know what it does to him every time he sees you doing strenuous work.

"I guess I didn't think."

"Laurel Grace…you have to let people take care of you once in a while. You have to learn to open your eyes and see how your stubbornness hurts people around you at times. Mac told me you've asked him a hundred times to forgive you for not carrying Campbell to term. Girl, don't you see that Mac's the one who thinks he needs to be forgiven? Haven't you two even talked about losing that baby?"

"Not really. No much about how we felt the loss, anyway."

"Laurel, in less than six weeks this new baby will be here. Until then, please just take it easy and give in for the sake of the people who love you."

"I will, Uncle Matt. I want to give Mac a healthy baby. I know he wants this child."

"You are so blind, Laurel Grace. Mac does want a baby, your baby, but above all else, he wants you. I pray someday you'll understand how he loves you." "I know he cares for me."

"No, I don't think you do, Laurel. When you have some time, read the fifth chapter of Ephesians. Start about verse nineteen and read the rest of that chapter. When you do read it, take time to think about those words. I've never known any man who tries to live out those words more than your husband. I'll see y'all at church Sunday."

Over the next several days, Laurel read and re-read those words from that passage. The more she read the scripture, the more she felt convicted by her behavior and stubbornness. She promised herself that Mac wouldn't be on the harsh end of her moodiness again. They would find a way and a time to talk about their loss and a time to forgive each other. Perhaps in doing so, both of them could learn to forgive themselves as well.

"Mac, darling, it's a beautiful September day. Not so hot as it's been. Will you walk with me this morning?"

"Are you up to walking?"

"Would I have…" Laurel lowered her voice and stifled the sarcastic remark she'd nearly spit back at her husband. "I would enjoy getting some morning air, and I do need to get more exercise. Dr. Gibson told me walking is good for soon-to-bemothers. I haven't done much in this heat."

"I'd be pleased to stroll a while with you." Mac picked up his hat and offered his arm to Laurel. "Cathy, we'll be back long before the afternoon heat sets in." Together, they ambled around their homestead, looking at all they'd done together. The fall crops were doing well, considering the long dry summer. The orchard had held its own, too. Mac had made sure Roy, John, and he had watered each tree and vine before any sign of wilting showed up to cause Laurel concern.

"You know, we may have grapes on these vines next year. They all look healthy, considering the dry season."

"I know you'd like to have new grapes. The vines have grown well this year. They're covering a good part of those trellises we made in the spring. They'll be running the cross bars by next summer."

"Mac, I'd like to walk out to Eden."

"It's too far to walk. Let me go get the wagon."

Laurel closed her eyes a moment and breathed deeply. In her sweetest, calm voice, she answered, "Mac, dearest, I want to walk with you to Eden. I will tell you if I get tired, and we'll stop to rest."

"I don't …." Laurel put her fingers to his lips and smiled up into his eyes.

"Please your pregnant wife, Mac." The change in his posture told Laurel he'd given up his argument, and he again took her arm and they walked off in the direction of Eden, at a pace that would tire neither of them. "I'm happy to be out, just walking and seeing our homestead. Even dry as it is, this place is so beautiful. I guess the creek keeps things from getting too parched."

"We are blessed to have water. Some of our neighbors farther up the ridge have seen the water levels in their wells drop seriously low this summer."

"It'll rain soon. It's strange, though, how quickly things change. We had all that flooding last winter, and now we've not seen ample rain for six months."

"Guess that's where faith comes in. We aren't even certain what the next day will bring, so we just have to believe the Lord will give us what we need when we need it."

"He did that for me. He plopped you on my doorstep at Papa's cabin in Washington County just when I needed you most. Look at how He has blessed us since that March morning in '57." "You'll get no argument from me on that point. Do you need to stop and rest?"

"No, Mac. I told you I'd tell you. Eden is just a short way from here."

The lowing of cattle in the fenced pasture, along with the rustling of the tall grass and soon to be harvested hay, wafted across the beautiful valley they both loved so much. "Looks like the boys, and I'll be busy in a couple of weeks. This hay will be ready any day. Looks like we'll have plenty to feed, even with all the new calves."

How easy the conversation seemed to pass between them that morning. For some reason, their walk that day brought her a sense of unity that brought a profound peace and contentment. How she loved this man and knew at the core of her being that he shared that love. The grand old oak came into view.

"I want to visit Campbell before we go back." They walked the last few yards into the grove of trees, and Mac helped Laurel down so she could sit near the granite cross that marked the tiny grave. "I love this beautiful carving. Mac, you paid a fine tribute to our son."

"No more than any parent would do to honor a child he loves."

"You do love him, don't you, Patrick?"

"Yes. That perfect little boy is part of both of us. I think of him every day, but now the hurt's not there. I just remember how happy we were when you gave me those tiny white booties, and all those times we talked about our plans for him. I look back to that beautiful fall adventure we had right here under this old tree…the joy and pleasure we had when we made love here those two days we stole from the world."

"I wish my faith was as strong as yours. You take the worst of sorrows and make good of them. I let every sad event of my life burden me from that time on."

"Faith doesn't happen overnight, Laurel. It's like our orchard. We plant it, tender its care, water it with our tears when we have to, and fertilize it with our repentance when it's needed. In the end, our faith matures, and we are able to share it or use it ourselves. I've seen you do both. I am still working on shedding the guilt I've carried since I failed you in April of '58."

"Mac, you didn't fail me. I was the one who didn't live up to my part of the promise. My carelessness caused that accident." "No more than my not getting home to take you to church that Sunday. I'd told you I'd be home before Easter. I would have been home if I'd not made that two-day side trip to buy that second bull."

"You didn't know about the storm."

"Neither did you. Some things happen that are beyond our control. Those times we have to learn to turn tragedy over to the Lord and trust He will make our lives whole again. That's what it means for us to live our faith."

"Patrick, I forgive you for not getting home before Easter. That is the only wrong you did to me."

"Thank you, Wife. I forgive you for not being a better horse handler. We've given Sassy too much of a sheltered life."

"Mac, I didn't give you the child you wanted."

"We have no control over the natural consequences of the actions we choose to do. All we can do is deal with the outcome in a way that God will approve. Laurel, we both need to forgive ourselves because we didn't make the right decisions. We did the best we could with what we knew at the time, but we are human. We made and will make mistakes. God forgave us so we can do no less. He is making things for good now."

"I know that now."

"I love you. Everyday life just gets better than the day before." Laurel's uncle had been right in his admonition to them both. When they allowed it to happen, and they shared their grief, the Lord had led them from the sorrow of the past into the anticipation of the new life ahead.

"Thank you for walking out with me today, Mac. I feel so much better, but I am tired. We need to go home." "All right, Laurel. At a slow, leisurely pace."

At noon, when they entered the cabin, Cathy greeted them and ushered them to the table where she'd set out a good lunch of fresh vegetables and newly baked bread. "What would I do without you, Cathy? You take such good care of things when I'm not here. You're going to be the best big sister ever."

CHAPTER FOUR

For thou hast possessed my reins: thou hast covered me in my mother's womb. I will praise thee; for I am fearfully and wonderfully made; Marvelous are thy works, and my soul knoweth right well.   Psalm 139:13-14

Laurel didn't know how soon her comment to Cathy would be tested. She lay down in the tall four-poster to take a nap after lunch. She slept well for half an hour, but then she was awakened by an unusual pressure in her lower back. She pushed the palm of her hand into the left side of her hip, hoping she'd slept in the wrong position. She grimaced when the pain didn't ebb. She pushed herself off the bed. With both hands against the bed, she stood, but when she did get to her feet, the ache in her back grew worse. Fear showed on her face. Her baby was not due for three weeks. She gasped for a deep breath for several minutes, attempting to gain control of the pain.

"Mac, please come here."

Cathy was the one to come to the door. "Mama, he's not in the house. He went out to the barn while you were asleep."

"Sweetheart, please go out and ask him to come in."

"Are you all right, Mama?"

"Yes, Cathy. Now hurry on." The girl ran as quickly as she was able, calling out as she hurried across the yard.

"What is it, Cathy?"

"Papa, Mama asked for you. I think you need to hurry." At a run, Mac and the children entered the back door. He went into the bedroom to find Laurel while Andy, Roy, and Cathy stood wide-eyed in the main pen, staring at the door.

In minutes, he returned to the front room. "Roy, take Midnight and ride to Greensboro. Ask Dr. Gibson to come. Ride fast, but safe. Hurry, son. Tarnation, where is John when I need him?"

"Papa, you know John don't never work on Saturday."

"You're right, Cathy. Today is Saturday. I guess I'll have to go."

"Go where, Papa? I can help."

"Cathy, it's a long ride to Brother Matthew's cabin."

"He'll probably be at the church getting ready for service tomorrow. Why do you want Brother Matthew?"

"I need Aunt Ellie. Laurel thinks it's time for the baby to come."

"I can ride there."

"I can't let you ride there alone. I'll go."

"I did it before. Mama may need you here. I can go in a flash. I know I can do it."

"All right, Cathy, but be very careful. You can ride Sassy. It's not storming today. She'll behave."

Mac picked up Andy and hugged him to erase the fear he saw on the little boy's face. "Andy, son, I need your help. Can you go out and feed and water the livestock in the barn and make sure the chickens and pigs have food and water? If you can do that for me, I can stay here to see after your mama."

"I can do it, Papa. I'm no baby. I can do those chores easy. Don't you worry."

"I know you can, Andy. Thank you." Mac breathed a sigh of relief...all the kids were occupied and out of the house. Thank the Lord, they were there to help him. He returned to the bedroom. "Laurel, what do you need me to do for you?"

"I'm fine for the moment. I think I'll sit in my mama's chair." He held her elbow and led her to the rocker. She shuffled, holding the small of her back where the increasing pressure was most noticeable. "Will you help me take off my shoes? My feet are huge."

"Are you in pain?"

"No, dear."

"Can I get you a glass of cold water?"

"No, dear."

"Are you too hot? Should I get a fan for you?"

"No, Mac, I'm all right." She saw the concern on his face. "Mac, I do need you to come over and sit with me. I need to have you here. Nothing is wrong. I feel well enough. It's just time for our little one to come."

"Laurel, the baby's not due until October…it's more than three weeks early."

"Babies come when they are ready. It's the most natural thing in the world. Please don't fret. Remember all you've taught me about trusting the Lord. Everything will be fine."

"You're right." He pulled a chair near Laurel. He raised her hand to kiss her palm. "I'll stay here by you as long as you want me here."

"I want you to stay with me. As long as you are here, things will go well."

"I won't leave your side." They sat together for some time, talking about their hopes and even some fears. Occasionally, Laurel would wince from the cramping in her back, but within a few minutes the ache would subside, and they would continue their conversation.

Before three o'clock, Cathy returned with Matthew and

Ellie Campbell. "We're back, Papa. I found them, just like I told ya I would."

"I knew I could trust you to get the job done. You've been the biggest help."

"Can I go in and see Mama?"

"Sure. All of you come on back."

"Laurel Grace, are you feeling all right?"

"Yes, Aunt Ellie. I'm thinkin' it's time."

"Tell me where you're feeling the pain and when did the hurtin' start?"

"Not really much pain at all. I started feeling this twinge in my back right after lunch."

"All right, you men, get out of here and let me help Laurel Grace get undressed and into bed."

"I promised her, I'd not leave her, Ellie."

"Patrick, you can go in the front room a little while, but don't go too far." Matthew held the door for his friend.

"Laurel, you know it's not usual for the father to be underfoot during these times. He'll just be in the way--not of much help."

"Aunt, I want him here. Mac needs to be here. He won't worry so much if he has to put on a strong front for me. Please help me change into my nightdress. It'll be so much cooler than these clothes. This room does seem very hot."

"It's been a warm day, Laurel Grace, but your labor may make it seem much warmer than it is. Try to relax. We have a long way to go. Do you want to lie down?"

"Not yet. I think I'd like to sit in the chair. My back doesn't hurt so much as when I try to lie down."

"Have you sent for Dr. Gibson?"

"I believe Mac sent Roy the same time he sent Cathy to bring you. I hope he can be here if there's a problem, but I know you can take care of me. This will be a normal birth. I just know it will."

"This baby will be healthy and strong, Laurel Grace. You just keep that thought in your mind."

Mac returned to Laurel's side. For a while, Matthew and Cathy remained with them. Andy peeked in the door, and Mac motioned him in. Except for being in the bedroom, the scene could have been a normal family visit. However, just before sundown, Laurel's pain worsened, and she felt uneasy with the audience. Mac asked everyone except Ellie to go back into the main room and to make a light supper. When the room was cleared, Mac picked Laurel up and carried her to their bed. He pulled the yellow coverlet over her and then sat behind her, holding her in his arms. When a pain began, he would rub her back and shoulders as he whispered words from the *Proverbs* and the *Song of Songs* they'd read together so often. This was a time they needed to be together regardless of what society told them was the expected behavior of parents during the birthing process. When each pain subsided, Mac wiped her face with a cool cloth and encouraged her to sleep.

About seven that night, Roy returned and Mac went to the main room to ask about the doctor. "Mr. Mac, Dr. Edwards wasn't at his office. Al Stuart said he'd tell him to come as soon as he got back. He told me to tell ya he'd be a prayin' for our family."

"That's fine, Roy. Thanks for making the trip. Al will get the doctor here. I can always depend on Al, just like I can depend on my kids." He returned to Laurel's side.

"You can relax, Mac. She'll sleep off and on until the labor pains get much sharper. The baby will not come anytime soon. Why don't you go in and eat a bite of supper with the family?"

"No, Ellie. She asked me to stay. That's what I intend to do."

"Well, there's no need for both of us to stay here and watch her sleep. Call me if you need me."

The labor went on for several hours with the spasms becoming more acute and closer together during the night. As the night passed, Mac cared for his wife, holding her as she hurt and bathing her face and arms as the pain lessened. Ellie returned often, asking Mac if he needed her to help. He refused to leave his wife.

At ten-thirty, Dr. Gibson arrived. He spoke with Matt and Ellie before going in to examine Laurel. He bullied Mac out of the room long enough to make an examination, and then the doctor returned to the main room. "Well, Mac and Ellie, you two seem to be doing a fine job. I don't know why you thought you'd need me. Laurel is doing fine. I believe the new MacLayne will be with us within three or four hours."

"That long? Ed, is there a problem?"

Dr. Edwards rubbed his forehead. "Look, Mac, as your doctor, I already said she is doing fine. Babies don't come in a flash, you know. As your friend, let me tell you to relax, go get a breath of fresh air, and quit fussin' so much. You'll be the patient before I can deliver your new baby."

"Laurel has been in pain since before one this afternoon."
"Labor lasts as long as it lasts. Ellie here was in labor with Mary for nearly eighteen hours. Mac, you and Matthew just need to go out for a long walk. Or go sit over there and play a game or two of checkers with me. We have some time to pass."

"I've got to get back to Laurel. Matthew will take you on or Andy. Andy beats me regularly."

"That's no place for you, man."

"Any place Laurel needs me is a place for me. Now, excuse me." He turned to go to Laurel's side.

"Matthew, you need to get him out of the house a while. You know these next few hours will only get harder."

"Don't think I can, Ed. You will just have to work around him. He promised Laurel he'd stay by her side until she asked him to leave. Nothing on earth or in Heaven will move him until he knows she is all right."

"I don't allow any man in a room where babies are comin'."

"Ed, come over here by the window and let's play a game or two."

What Dr. Gibson had predicted, came to pass. By midnight, Laurel's labor pains became extreme and almost constant. Each time she felt the intensifying pressure, Mac held her as close as he was able. He bent to whisper to her, her small hand enwrapped in his. Frequently, he'd lift it to his lips. His presence calmed her, and Laurel didn't cry out in the increasing pain. She was not aware, but Mac prayed continuously for her, begging for her relief and putting all his hopes and dreams in the hands of God. Finally, about two in the morning, Laurel gave birth to Mac's son. The healthy baby cried out loudly when Dr. Gibson slapped his backside. He laid the tiny infant in Laurel's arms and left the room. The new parents looked at their child in awe.

"Thank you, Lord!" Mac could barely stand still as he realized he had just witnessed the birth of his child. "He's just the finest child ever, Laurel. Thank you. Look at him. Can you believe how beautiful he is?"

"Yes. I can. He's your son. See that dark hair?"

"My Lord! I never knew what it'd be like to see my child take his first breath. He's my child. I can never thank you enough for what you've given me. God bless you, Wife."

"God blessed us all. Come over here." Mac moved to the side Laurel had indicated. "Here, hold him, Patrick. I want to see him in your arms."

Mac sat next to Laurel and gently lifted the tiny boy into his arms. He looked into the small face that he'd cupped in his hand. He gently touched the baby's perfectly formed hand and was overcome when the little one clasped his finger. Mac could no more hold back the joyous tears than he could stop the sun from rising over the ridge. He bent and kissed Laurel, he took her hand, raised it to his lips, and whispered a prayer of blessing for his new son.

"What will we call him, Laurel?"

"His name is Mark Thomas MacLayne, for my papa and yours. He is perfect, isn't he, Patrick?"

"Yes, Love. He is our perfect son." Mac returned the baby to Laurel's arms, lay beside them, and they fell asleep A short time later when Mac awoke, he saw both Laurel and the baby asleep. He knelt by the bed and poured out his joy in prayer. Then he arose, went to the walnut bureau, and took out the Campbell family Bible. On the family record page, he wrote:

Mark Thomas MacLayne was born to Laurel Campbell
MacLayne and Patrick MacLayne on September 18, 1859, in Shiloh, Craighead County, Arkansas.

CHAPTER FIVE

*The tongue is a fire, a world of iniquity, so is the tongue
among our members, that it defileth the whole body, and setteth
on fire the course of nature; and it is set on fire of hell.*
James 3:6

Life could be no better at Shiloh that fall. Mark Thomas MacLayne made a profound change considering his tiny stature. Every facet of life revolved around this newborn. From his first days, he totally won the hearts of his entire family. Cathy and Andrew vied to see who could do the most for his care. Roy found several excuses a day to make his way into the cabin to look in on the newborn and his mother. Thomas MacLayne doted on his new grandson and made several trips a week across the meadow to spend an hour or so rocking the baby in front of the fireplace. More often than not, Andy was seated nearby, basking in the attention of his grandfather. Blessings multiplied daily.

Mac changed most. He lost the restlessness he'd developed after his return from Little Rock. Laurel sensed the change before Mark was even two weeks old. One night as they lay together in the tall four-poster, she commented, "Mac, you're not the same fellow that came home from the legislature in March."

"Really? Is that good or bad?"

"I hope you think it's good. For a long while, you've been so restless, almost as if you felt a huge loss that you weren't returning to the statehouse."

"I'm not sure why you think that. Right now, I have no greater desire than to stay here being a good husband to you and a parent to our kids. If I can do that, I will serve a bigger purpose than I'd fulfill in the legislature."

"I'm happy to hear you say that. I'd be perfectly content if we never have to be separated again."

"Well, darlin', I'm home, my favorite place in this world."

"I agree. Shiloh is a wonderful place to call home."

"I'm not talking about Shiloh…I mean here…in our bed."

"Mac!"

"No, seriously. How could I find a more perfect place? You are here in my arms. Our new son is there in his cradle--in my cradle and my father's cradle. Our other kids are in the loft asleep.

Why would I ever want to be anywhere else?"

Laurel smiled up into Mac's eyes, reveling in his words, for she shared his dream of home and family. With the birth of their son, the dream was now real. Peace and wholeness filled their home after so long a wait. She knew that she too had changed in the two short weeks since the easy birth of Mark. Before he arrived, she'd been almost fearful of her role as the mother of an infant. She'd never cared for a new baby before, and Mark was very small, having been born three weeks early, but Laurel felt quite at ease after only a few days. She found caring for her new son the most natural thing she'd ever done. Even the time she had spent nursing the beautiful little boy, a role she'd never given thought to before, was a time of bliss. She'd not known such a bond with another person. The touch of his tiny fingers on her face and neck brought tears of joy in those first days, joy that brought unconscious prayers of thanksgiving.

The Saturday night before Mark was two weeks old, the family sat in the main room of their home together. Mac and Andy sat together near the window, either side of the side table with the checkerboard between them. This happened nearly every night. Laurel sat in her grandmother Wilsons's rocking chair, nursing Mark. Mac hardly took his eyes from the scene. Cathy sat on the hearth, working on the sampler Laurel was using to teach her basic embroidery stitches. Roy sat at the table, going over his profits from his egg and milk business. The fire had all but burned out on this first day of October. Mac continued to watch as Laurel fed Mark. The look on his face would tell anyone how content he was, there in the cabin he'd built for just such a night.

"Papa, ain't ya gonna pay attention to this game? You just gave me your last king."

"What? Oh, yeah, that was a careless move for me to make, wasn't it?"

"You know that is why I win almost ever game. You ain't thinkin'."

"Not quite so, Andy boy. I was thinking about how blessed one man can be. Look around you, son. I've got everything any man could ever want, right here in this room. I hope someday you will find yourself in a scene just like this one. A man can't ask for anything more."

"I guess, but I'd think you'd like to win a game ever now and again." Mac laughed at the pragmatic nature of his son. How like himself Andrew was proving to be.

"Time for bed, young'uns. Tomorrow is the Sabbath. We'll have to be up early and get ready for church."

As they made their way to their rooms, Mac took Mark into his arms and lay down with him in the four-poster. He held the little boy on his shoulder and felt a little hand curl up on his beard.

With his large, calloused hand, he stroked Mark's abundant mass of dark hair and rubbed a finger across the cheek of the sleeping infant.

"Thank you, Laurel, for my son…our son. You know how glad I've been to have Andy with us…bless your beautiful soul for accepting him, but Laurel, I had no idea how much I could love a child so quickly. And his mother. I've loved you since the day we met, but now…There is no way I can make you understand how much you mean to me. I can't imagine any more joy than I feel at this moment."

"I know. I feel that too. Two years ago, I'd have sworn the depth of love and connection between us could not exist between two people."

"Are you sure you're up to driving down to church in the morning?"

"I am. I can't wait to show our friends and family how beautiful our son is. Here let me put Mark in his cradle."

"Not just yet…you come over here and join us for a while." "He's too little to sleep with us. You'll roll over him. Besides, you'll spoil him, letting him learn he can sleep with us instead of in his own place."

"Could be you're right. No sense in letting him get used to sleeping with us. I'm too selfish to let him take my place beside you in our marriage bed. I'll put him in the cradle while you dress for bed." Mac rose from the right side of the bed and walked a few steps to the old family cradle. He carefully laid the sleeping child on the feathery down pillow that served as his bed. "Little man, you are a miracle. I love you." Mac brushed the sleeping child's face with a quick, gentle kiss and turned to embrace Laurel. The kiss he gave her was not gentle nor quick. "Laurel, I wish you could see how beautiful you are." "I'm beautiful because you love me."

The trip to Shiloh church was easy. The sun shone and the light breeze was warm. The trees along the road told of the coming winter. Some were bare, even this early in the month. The dry summer had contributed to the early fall. Even the grass and bushes were brown and shriveled. The wagon wheels threw up dust as Midnight pulled them along at a quick pace. Everyone in the family seemed in high spirits as they headed to their church, looking forward to the attention their newest family member would bring.

Brother Matthew delivered a beautiful sermon that Sunday based on the story of the prodigal son. Laurel had heard that scripture many times, but that Sunday, she saw the message from a different point of view. She wondered at the great love a father must feel to be able to forgive and instruct both his erring sons. The simple act of holding Mark in her arms as she listened to her uncle proclaim the gospel opened her mind to consider her role as a parent…not only in her care for the new baby in her arms, but also the care and nurture she owed to Andrew and Cathy. Her uncle's powerful words drew her not only to a deeper conviction toward her role as a mother, but also a strong sense of assurance that she could be a good parent to all her children. She was able to show them the love and guidance they needed and deserved. Mac leaned over and whispered, "Why are you smiling so?"

"Because I am a good mother."

At the close of the service, Matthew prayed for the needs of several people in the Shiloh community, asked for the badly needed rain and asked for a blessing on the newest member of Shiloh church. Just before dismissing his flock, he made three announcements. Some brought moans and others applause and excited chatter.

"Folks, before we go our ways this mornin', I want to say that we've found us a new teacher for this term. I'd like to introduce y'all to Mr. Tucker." A tall serious-looking middle-aged man rose and turned to face the congregation. "The school committee thinks he'll do us a fine job. After talkin' to most of the families, we decided to open school for the fall term early. The dry summer and fall have made our harvest earlier, and the hay is about ready to put up, so our kids will be free to return to school. We may be able to get in a couple more weeks this term. We will start the fall term on October 17." Of course, this announcement brought the most groans, but a few of the students clapped. "The last thing is we will start Sunday school back on the Sunday before school starts. My niece told me she will lead these classes for any who want to come."

Nearly all the ladies of Shiloh gathered around Laurel to see the new MacLayne for the first time. Cathy and Andrew stood close watch over their new brother. One of the ladies thoughtlessly spoke aloud, "You must be so happy to finally have a child."

"Of course, we're pleased to have Mark here, healthy, but we already have three fine children in our home, Nancy."

"Oh, yes…I didn't mean that as it must have sounded. Yours are all nice children. I meant…"

"That's all right. I know you didn't mean anything. Have a nice afternoon."

Mac had overheard the conversation, and he had also seen the confusion on Andrew's face. "Time to head home, family. We got a fine meal planned, and my pa is coming over to join us for Sunday dinner."

On the short ride home, Andy questioned his father about the comment he'd witnessed. "Papa, don't folks think I'm yours?" "Of course, they know, son. Mrs. Landers just didn't think before she said what she did. She just wanted to compliment your mama on our new son. We are proud to have him, but no more so than to have you, Roy, and Cathy. We're a family."

At dinner that afternoon, the talk centered on new plans for Thomas and Patrick. "Son, I found me another fifty acres just over near Big Creek. About half of it is pretty marshy and prone to flood, but I've looked over the whole acreage, and it's a fine prospect to build some levees and ditches to reclaim some really fine cropland. It's not more than four or five miles from here, and there's a nice rise where I can build me a fine house. Got fine trees and good grass for cattle. I'm going to Greensboro tomorrow to get the deed. If all goes well, I should be able to start the foundation by the end of the month."

"You seem pleased, Pa. I was worried you'd move off too far to visit often. I want my kids to know their grandfather."

"I've rejected some good land for that reason. This is the best I can find and still stay close. I need me a project anyway. I'm looking forward to building."

"I'm gonna do the same thing soon. We've gotta have some more room. Cathy needs a room of her own. The boys can share the loft, but with the three of them up there, it's just too crowded.

When we get your house up, I'll start building here."

"Cathy, how great to have your own room!"

"I know, Granddaddy. Mama and Papa have been so good to me since they took me in."

"It'll be fine not having to share our space with an ole girl, won't it, Roy?"

"It's not so bad now, but you and me will have lots more space when Cathy gets her stuff out of the loft. I guess she's not so bad as sisters go."

"Well, family, looks like we'll have a lot to keep us busy in the next few months. You only have one more week before ya have to go back to school."

"Papa, I'd druther stay here and help with the building. Mama can teach me good enough."

"Andy, I'd love to have your help, but nothing's more important than your schoolin'. You can help in the afternoons and on Saturday."

"Oh shucks. I don't like school, Papa."

"Won't be no arguments, Andy. You'll like school better this term. You've been working with your mama all summer. School'll be easier for you this year, you'll see."

"Yes, sir…but I still druther say here and work."

"We will, for one more week."

The next weeks were busy with usual fall activities, like butchering days, candling parties, school, and haying. Mac and his father worked tirelessly on the building projects. Laurel found she had things to do from sun up to sun down, tasks related to her role as a new mother—she'd not realized how time-consuming nursing, washing Mark's endless supply of clothes, and playing with a baby would be. Yet she thrived in her busyness, loving her new role. She made special time to spend with Cathy and Andy because she didn't want them ever to feel less special.

Mac continued his checker time with Andrew. After long days of building, supervising his crew, working his cattle, and finishing the hay harvest, Mac was often beyond tired. Yet, never once did he turned the boy away when he asked for attention, whether it was helping with homework, reading to him, or playing a game of checkers. Patrick and Andrew were building a bond neither had known before. Andrew was making good progress at school, too. He didn't complain about the hard work this term. He only once commented about 'mean ole man Tucker' to his parents. Cathy had corrected him, saying that Mr. Tucker was just a stricter teacher than Miss Elizabeth had been the previous term. All seemed well until one afternoon, Andy came back to the cabin in tears.

"Papa, I ain't a goin' back to that school no more."

"Tell me what happened, son. This mornin' you were happy, telling your mama and me that you'd spelled every word right on your test."

"I did spell 'em all right – ever one of 'em."

"That's no reason to cry."

"I ain't a goin' back. I tell ya, I ain't. No one is gonna laugh at me."

"They laughed at you? What happened?"

"I didn't do nothin' to them. I thought they kinda liked me, but then at recess, one of them older boys told me to give him my coat 'cos he was cold."

"I asked him where his coat was. He said never mind, just give him mine. I said no."

Laurel looked up with some concern. She knew a couple of fifth level boys who'd been with her during the third grade could be very pushy with new students, especially younger, smaller boys. "What'd ya do?"

"I just walked away, but a couple of minutes later, I heard all of 'em laughin' and pointin' at me. I asked them what they's laughin' for." Tears once again rolled down Andy's cheeks. "One of them came over and told me to go away. They wouldn't play with me no more 'cos I was born on the wrong side of the sheets."

Mac reddened. The scowl on his face spoke of a depth of anger Laurel had never seen on the face of her husband before.

"Papa, why was they laughin' just because I was poor. I know we didn't have no nice sheets like I got here at Shiloh. My ma done the best she could to keep us warm. We had two warm rag quilts she made us." Andrew thought the boys were making fun of his poverty. The small boy, not quite seven, did not understand the boys were referring to his birth status. Andrew didn't understand, but Mac knew. He also knew people in the Shiloh community were using Andrew's illegitimacy as gossip fodder.

As the night wore on, the strain and tension grew. Mac was curt with his family, and he didn't talk much at supper as was his custom. He did play checkers with Andy, but he couldn't keep his mind on the game. Andrew won easily. When the time came to retire, Laurel breathed a sigh of relief. Mac had kept his anger pretty well in check in front of the kids, but she knew that would not be so for much longer. When she entered their room carrying Mark, Mac turned and released all the pent-up anger and frustration he'd fought back since Andy had come home in tears.

"How in tarnation can people be so heartless? Those kids were only repeating what they'd heard from people at home."

"Patrick, take a moment to calm yourself. Andy didn't understand what they said to him."

"Thank the Lord, he didn't. He didn't know this time. Still, he was hurt thinking the kids were saying he was too poor. That's bad enough!"

"Yes, that's hurtful, too."

"Laurel, it's my fault. Andrew grew up those five years not even knowing what a sheet is. He had a few pieces of clothes, but I wonder if he had shoes most of the time. How much did he suffer because I was too selfish and careless to think about what I was doing?"

"You can't blame yourself for something you didn't know about. If you'd known, you'd have taken care of them both."

"I didn't think about my actions or the impact they'd have on his mother, and now my son is paying for my misspent past."

"Patrick, you told me that the Lord forgives our past mistakes. He forgave you."

"I also said he doesn't take away the consequences of those sorry behaviors, but he does charge us to take responsibility and deal with what we've done. I can deal with my past...my six-yearold son shouldn't have to." The anger on Mac's face and in his voice didn't pass. He paced across the room more than once. Finally, he slumped in his chair in front of the fire and dragged his hands through his hair. "Lord, please forgive me. Please help me know what I need to do so my son isn't hurt again by my faults."

"Dearest, you will know what to do when the time comes. Give yourself a day or two to think and pray about it. You always do what is right…. Will you hold Mark for a few minutes while I take down my hair and dress for bed?" Laurel could have laid the baby in his cradle, but she knew Mac's anger would ease when he shifted his focus to Mark. She took longer than necessary preparing for bed, giving her husband some time to return to the sense of blessing and gratitude they'd lived with since Mark had made his way to the heart of their family. When she returned to the bed, she found them both sound asleep. Mac was fully dressed, boots and all, and Mark lay sleeping on his chest, his tiny hand curled in his papa's neat beard.

"Lord, please bring Mac peace and help him know how to deal with this problem. He will not let it go without addressing it, so please show him how to deal with Andrew's hurt and his own shame. Amen."

The following morning, Laurel knew the answer to her prayer had not come yet. Mac was too quiet, and he could not sit still for more than a few minutes before he was up pacing the room.

"Don't you have some work to occupy you today?"

"What?...Yes, of course, I do. Roy, John, and I are going to help Pa with the foundation of his new house."

"Well, the kids have already gone to school, morning chores are done, and breakfast dishes are sitting at the dry sink, waiting for me to wash…you're going to pace the best part of the day away."

"Laurel, I want to hunt down every father of the kids who spoke those hurtful words to Andrew. I'd like to beat some sense into them!"

"And that would help how? Mac, it's not like you to think of revenge."

"I've never had to protect my child before. I'm madder than I've ever been in my life. Lord, help me, I'd crush bones if I knew who'd started this."

"Don't you think a hard day's work would be more productive and help ease your mind?"

"No, but I know what will. I'm riding over to talk with Matthew." He turned and picked up his hat from the peg at the door.

"Patrick, haven't you forgotten something?"

"What did I forget?"

"Me…. Don't ever leave me without saying good-bye."

"That was thoughtless." He pulled her as close as he was able as she held their sleeping son. He kissed her and rubbed his finger against Mark's cheek. "He's so fine. Have a good day, Wife. Never let me forget to show you that I love you. No problem we face should ever replace what we have. I'll be home early."

Before the hour had passed, Mac had found Matthew in the loft of his barn, storing winter feed. "Want some help?"

"Mac, what are you doin' here today. Thought you'd be laying stones for your Pa's foundation in this nice weather."

"Couldn't keep my mind on it. Matthew, I need to talk. Can we talk while we lay up this hay?"

"What's on your mind, brother?" Mac poured out the entire story while Matt listened. After a few minutes of Mac's fast angry words, Matthew stopped work and sat to hear the rest of the story. After several minutes, Mac's voice calmed and his shoulders dropped from the tense defensive position to a more normal posture. Mac's words slowed and the bitter spiteful tone ebbed.

"Matthew, what can I do?"

"You know what you have to do. Forgive yourself for your anger as you forgive them for trespassing against you."

"Could you?"

"I hope I could try."

"I can't let Andy get hurt again. It's bad enough he thinks they don't like him because he was poor, but, Matt, you know he'll understand sooner or later what it means to be born on the wrong side of the sheet. How can I protect him?"

"You probably can't. Much as you want to, you can't change what's happened. All you can do –all any of us can do-- is to help him know it doesn't matter. He'll know he is loved and valued as a child of God and as your son and Laurel's too-- if we teach him. No different than when you had to learn it, too."

"I never doubted I was loved by my parents. I had a mother and a father who were always in my life, loving me and protecting me."

"And you're feeling guilty that Andrew didn't. You can't change what's happened, Brother, but you can make a huge change for the boy's future."

"I know that, and I will, but surely there is something more I can do to protect him."

"Let's give it some thought and prayer. He'll give us an answer. Now get to work, and let's get this hay laid up."

When Mac returned home, Laurel had already prepared the noon meal, and she sat nursing and singing to Mark. "What a fine thing to come home to: a beautiful wife, a fine son, and a good meal."

"You seem in a better spirit. What did Uncle Matthew say to you?"

"Not much. Actually, he said little more than you said. He told me to put it in God's hands and wait to see what would happen."

"Sounds like good advice. Let's eat dinner. Please call the boys in." Dinner was much more pleasant than the supper the previous night. Roy and John told Mac they'd begun to pile rocks where the new foundation to the addition would go. Laurel told him that Mark had held up his head for a short while that morning as she had laid him on his stomach during his bath. Mac smiled at the good news and relaxed. Perhaps the Lord was putting some sunshine in a dark place. Maybe he was overreacting, and the talk would just go away if he didn't intervene.

His positive attitude lasted until about 4:00 when Andrew and Cathy returned from school. Cathy carried a note from Mr. Tucker, and Andrew appeared with a knee ripped from his trousers, a swollen cheek, and a large black-purple bruise around his left eye.

"What happened to you, young man?"

"I'm sorry I tore my pants, Papa, but I ain't gonna let no one take none of mine. If my grandpa was alive, he'd skin me good for not takin' up for myself."

"Tell me what happened, Andrew."

"Mr. Tucker done wrote it all down in that letter."

"I want you to tell me your story, Andrew." The stern tone of Mac's voice told his son that an answer was expected.

"Them same three boys throwed it up on me again about the sheet. I told 'em my ma did the best she could and about our rag quilts. They laughed again. One of 'em said I's as dumb as a stump. So, I tackled him…Knocked him down flat!"

"That didn't put that bruise around your eye."

"No. That's how I ripped my pants! He pushed me off him, and we started whalin' away. He hit me a good one in my eye, but I got him some good ones, too. Mr. Tucker pulled us apart. I'm thinkin' I broke his nose…Sure was bloody."

"Andrew! Breaking another boy's nose is not something to brag about."

"Ma, I didn't start it…and I ain't gonna be no whuppin' boy for no bullies!"

"Andy, please calm down. We'll talk about it later. Let's get you cleaned up right now."

"Laurel, leave the boy be. Sit down, Andrew, while I read this note from your teacher." Mac walked the boy over to the raised hearth and sat him down. He reached for the folded sheet of paper in Cathy's hand.

Mr. MacLayne,

Sadly, I must report to you the unacceptable behavior of your son, Andrew. In the schoolyard today at noon break, he attacked another boy. Andrew knocked out one of the boy's teeth when he punched him in the mouth with his fist.

When I asked what started the fight, neither boy would explain to me what had started the brawl. I have no other choice but to excuse them both from school until the school committee can advise me what I should do.

I will be glad to discuss my decision with you if you choose.

Your servant,

S.T. Tucker

"Well, Andy, Mr. Tucker says you can't come back to school until the school committee decides what to do. Why didn't you tell him what caused the fight, Son?"

"I ain't no snitch! I don't want to go to school no ways."

"Andrew, come over here to me." Mac sat in his armed chair and pulled the boy into his lap. He looked into the too blue eyes, the very image of his own. "Andy, what you did breaking out the boy's tooth is not right. I want you to know that. We should never fight unless it's a last resort. Thinking people, especially those of us who say we follow the Lord, have to settle our differences with words and forgiveness, not our fists. Do you understand me, Andrew?"

"You ain't sayin' I gotta back down, are ya?"

"No, son. I'm sayin' we can meet the challenge in another way."

"Ain't no other way."

"Yes. A better way. This is a lesson I want you to learn. We'll talk more, later. Now I want you to go to the loft and take your readin' book with you so as not to waste the time. I am not punishin' you, Andrew. I'm not angry with you. I love you, but hittin' that boy in the face was wrong, and I want you to think about it. We'll talk more after supper." Mac picked up his hat and left the cabin.

Laurel handed Mark to Cathy and told her to watch the supper. She followed her husband to the barn where he'd begun the evening chores. "Mac, are you all right?"

"No. I'm angry and pretty disappointed with my church family. First time I've ever felt like an outcast since I joined this congregation. Andy doesn't deserve to be punished, but I can't let him grow up tryin' to settle arguments by fightin'."

"He's only seven. He'll learn."

"What will he learn? I don't want him to be a doormat, nor do I want him to solve problems with violence, but the main thing I want is to prevent my son from having to deal with shame because of me. Legally, Andrew is my son, but the circumstances of his birth will mark him if I don't figure out how to settle this gossip."

"What will it take to stifle the talk? I'm sure the fight and the boys getting suspended from school will only add to the gossip."

"I don't know yet. I just don't know."

Mac didn't sleep much that night. When he finally tossed and turned to the point of waking Laurel, he rose from the bed, dressed and left the cabin. The moon and stars had not yet left the early morning sky. He saddled Midnight and rode the short distance to the widow's cabin to talk with this father. He could not remember a time in his life that Thomas MacLayne had ever done anything that wasn't honorable and wise. Mac knew his wayward seven years had been a tremendous disappointment, and he had hurt his parents badly. Yet when he returned, they welcomed him back, without condition or condemnation. Perhaps his father could give him advice that would help him protect his son, as they had sheltered him.

As the sun rose above the ridge, Mac arrived at the cabin. His father had just risen from a fine night's sleep and was stirring a fire back to life.

"Heavens be, son. You're out and about very early today. Is everything all right at home?"

"No one's sick, but I need to talk to you. Andrew was suspended from school yesterday for fightin'."

"That's not his nature. He's always been shy. Are you sure Andrew was at fault?"

"No, he's not at fault. I am."

"Now I really don't understand. Come over here and sit a while. I'll put the coffee on to brew." Thomas set the pot over the fire and returned to the table where Mac waited. "Tell me what happened, Patrick."

Mac told his father about the two days Andrew had been provoked at school. "Pa, I can't stand to see him cry. He hasn't earned this kind of treatment. I want to do what I need to keep him from having to deal with it again, but at the same time I want him to learn not to deal with problems with his fists."

"Andrew wasn't really in the wrong. I don't like the idea of him fighting, but he was attacked first."

"Pa, you know as well as I do that the gossip won't stop if the conflict between Andy and his school mates continues. I can't let him stay out of school either. Lord, I wish I was as good a father as you. I'd be able to deal with this better."

"You've only been at this for less than a year. You're doing a good job in my eyes. Andy knows you love him, and he has a family. That's the best he's ever known."

"And that is my fault, too. That's the answer I need. This is my problem – not his. As long as he is the focus, he'll be victim to the gossip. I need to take the focus off the boy. I know what I have to do."

Mac and Laurel did not attend church that Sunday. Mac read the scripture for his family at home, and he led their prayers. Mac was especially attentive to Cathy and Andy, playing games, telling them stories, and listening to them talk about the upcoming harvest party. He took them with him to carry water to the orchard. Though the growing season was past, the fall had been as dry as the summer, and Laurel feared the lack of rain would kill the trees and grapevines. The day was a good one for the family. Even Mac had enjoyed the day regardless of the situation that still faced him. "Papa, we didn't go to church today because of me, ain't that so? I am real sorry I broke out that kid's tooth. I know you don't want me a fightin'. If I tell Mr. Tucker that I'm sorry, do you think he'll maybe let me come back to school?"

"Son, I don't want you to worry about it. I'll take care of it this week. While you're home, you can help me with the herd, and your mama will teach you your lessons."

"Anyway, I feel bad I caused all this trouble. I sure never meant to cause you no problems."

"I am glad you want to apologize to me, but except for the fist in his face, you didn't do anything wrong. It's my problem. Don't you fret about it, Andy."

Mac was true to his word. The coming week he went to the school and spoke with Mr. Tucker, and he asked Matthew to convene a school committee meeting to talk about letting both boys back into school.

"Mr. MacLayne, how can you assure me that the problem will not come up between the two boys again?"

"Mr. Tucker, I will take care of that. I assure you that Andrew will not attack anyone who does not provoke him. He is a good boy, and he will obey me."

"I will take you at your word. I will allow them to return to school next Monday on the condition there will be no more fights."

Matthew and Mac left the meeting together and continued the discussion. When Mac arrived home, he was at peace again. He believed that the problem would be solved on Sunday and that Andy would not have to face an attack from the gossips again. When the day came, Mac and Laurel went to Shiloh church, taking only Mark with them. Roy had been given the job of caring for the other two children for the morning. Mac drove slowly toward Shiloh, not wanting to arrive early. Just as Matthew was about to go to the pulpit, they took their seat in Shiloh church.

Brother Campbell rose to speak to his flock that morning without his usual smile. Concern was evident in his expression. "Brothers and sisters in faith, the apostle Paul at times wrote letters filled with words meant to expose failings to the early church. He told them he had no joy in the need to point out those sins, but if his witness failed to stop the gossip, that sin would rip apart their community of faith. He admonished them--not in anger, but in love, asking the faithful to return to the covenant, to love God and to love their neighbor. That is the place I find myself this morning.

"Second Corinthians 12:20-21…'For I fear, lest, when I come, I shall not find you such as I would, and that I shall be found unto such as ye would not; lest there be debates, envyings, wraths, and strifes, backbiting, whispering, swellings, and tumults: And lest when I come again, My God will humble me among you and that I shall bewail many which have sinned already and not repented of the uncleanness, fornication, and lasciviousness, which they have committed.'

"James 3: 7-10… 'For every kind of beast and of birds and of serpent and of things in the sea is tamed and hath been tamed by mankind, But the tongue can no man tame; it is an unruly evil, full of deadly poison. Therefore, we bless God, even the Father; and therewith curse we men, which are made after the similitude of God. Out of the same mouth proceedeth blessings and cursing. My brethren, these things ought not to be.' These are the words of the

Lord."

Matthew spoke to his people for the good part of the hour about the damage gossip can inflict on a church. His words were plain and in no way softened. He told his flock careless words, perhaps spoken without malice, brought harm to the children of Shiloh, as they tended to repeat words they heard spoken by their parents. As he ended, Matt reminded his congregation of the way members of the church were to deal with conflict. "Brothers and sisters, remember, we bring reproof in love and for the uplifting of our fallen brother or sister. Remember our covenant. Because we have been given grace, we are to love our Lord and love our neighbors. Listen to these closing words from James 1: 19-20. 'If any man among you seems to be religious, and bridle not his tongue, but deceiveth his own heart, this man's religion is in vain.' Amen."

As the pastor closed his sermon, there was quiet in the room. The Shiloh congregation rarely heard a sermon as direct as this one had been. Some of the people averted their faces so as not to meet the eyes of their beloved preacher. Others fidgeted in the pews, clearly uncomfortable with what they knew was a scolding from the pulpit. Everyone in the church knew what had happened at the school the previous week. Before asking them to stand for the hymn of invitation, Matthew nodded to Mac, who rose and walked to the front of the room.

Mac stood in front of the altar, posture erect, his gaze directed toward the members of Shiloh church, the people he'd called his church family since he'd come to know the Lord. "Brothers and sisters, I am here this morning to confess to you my shortcomings, and I am asking you to forgive me. I know nearly everyone here knows me. I have been a member of this church for more than six years. The person I am now is not the person who first came to Shiloh back in '52. That man was angry, bitter, and had no relationship with any man or God. I had lived a life I'm not proud to claim now. Thanks to our Savior, though, that man isn't alive anymore. I am a new man because I have been forgiven, by God and by Brother Matthew, and now I ask you to forgive me too.

"Andrew is my son. My wife of two years is obviously not his mother since he is now seven years old. He came to live with me back in the summer. His life before was hard. He lived with his grandfather and his mother, an outcast in the town where they lived. I didn't know about Andrew then, so I had made no provision for his care. He is not to blame for his status. I am to blame. I want to be able to give him the family he deserves from this day on. My loving wife, Laurel, has opened her heart to take him as her own. Together we have begun to build a bond with him. "But we can't give him the life we want him to have without his having a loving church family, too. If you can find it in your hearts to forgive my failures, I will be most humbled, but if you can't and have an issue with my past, please come to me and tell me of your grief. My son deserves to have a happy childhood. He will not be the subject of gossip from this day on. The fault is mine, not my son's."

Mac returned to his seat beside Laurel, and Matthew asked for the hymn of invitation, *Just as I Am.* Mac and Laurel went to the altar and knelt. Shortly several other members of the congregation also knelt beside them. Mac felt a sense of relief. He believed the risk he'd taken to bear his conscience had not been in vain. He prayed the focus that had been on Andrew would now be shifted to him, and the gossip would stop.

CHAPTER SIX

And let them gather all the food of those good
years that come...   and
that food shall be store to the land
against the seven years of famine...
Genesis 41:5,6

the Shiloh
S congregation were strained. Mac had
accused everal Sundays following Matthew
Campbell's scolding to
no one of starting the gossip, but many knew
already. Over time though, the people
returned to their familiar ways of behaving, and
Shiloh again became a comfortable place to worship
and fellowship. A few men of the church had
approached Mac to apologize for their sons'
behavior toward Andrew. Others had commended
Mac on his courage to share his witness so openly.

More importantly, the conflict between the students at the
school had ended. Andrew didn't come home beaten
or tearful after that Sunday. That would have been
reason enough to please Mac. He had taken a drastic
step to protect his son, and from outward
appearances, his plan had worked. Within a couple
of weeks, Andy was talking about his new friends
and how much he liked playing with the other
fellows.

When Mac had assured himself that Andy was safe, he

again became relaxed and contented. He didn't speak of politics much anymore, and Laurel had come to believe he was ready to dedicate his time and energies to their family and the homestead. She hoped he'd had his fill of the political life that demanded they be apart. That was especially true since Mark had been born. Travel was too hard and conditions too hazardous for an infant to make long trips to the capital. Nearly every day, Laurel offered a prayer of gratitude that the twelfth legislative session had carved out the new county where they now lived. Mac's seat in the legislature no longer existed. If he could be satisfied at home, Laurel would not have to face the prospect of long periods of separation.

Laurel's relief proved to be very short-lived. Mac was pulled back into the broader world in December when a month-old copy of the Arkansas Gazette found its way to Greensboro on a freight wagon. Mac found it on a trip to McCollough's mercantile one Wednesday morning. Reading one article in that month-old paper resurrected his old fears and concern. On the front page of the paper, Editor Woodruff had reported a raid and the capture of a renegade abolitionist named John Brown. Mac had heard stories about Brown's raids and his abolition efforts in Kansas earlier in the decade. Last year, during the legislative session, many of the representatives had disagreed over the reasons for the attacks on the slaveholders in Kansas, but this new raid seemed different to Mac—more ominous somehow. He read further. Woodruff reported that Brown had planned a raid on the Harper Ferry Arsenal to obtain weapons to arm a slave army, hoping to incite an insurrection against southern plantation owners. However, the federal troops had been alerted, and Brown was captured on October 18, 1859, after a two-day standoff with the army. Two of Brown's sons were killed during the siege. The article concluded by saying that Brown would be tried for treason before the end of the year.

The same fears he'd had during the discussions on secession came back. Violent acts, like the Brown raids, incited the hotheads in the country to push for secession. He truly feared for the future of his adopted state, and the welfare of his family if the radicals were able to divide the country…or even his state. At the close of the twelfth session, some of the delegates were proposing to split Arkansas in two…dividing the delta, the cotton-growing region, into its own sovereign state.

Mac had to find a way to know what was happening outside the community. He truly hated that they had no local newspaper in the northeast part of the state. The Little Rock paper and occasionally one from the east were the only sources of news from beyond Crowley's Ridge. Even the budding community of Jonesboro seemed too far for news to travel. Mac wrote letters to Little Rock and his old home in Baltimore, ordering newspapers be mailed to him every week. Even though the papers cost the same as a new calf, Mac couldn't hide away at Shiloh and pretend the nation had no impact on his life or that of his family.

Mac didn't share his fear with Laurel or the children. Life at the MacLayne homestead was happy for the most part. Mac and Laurel shared much of their leisure, if such a thing actually existed, watching their family thrive and change. He took intense pleasure in watching his infant son learn to roll over and respond to his and
Laurel's voices. Mark was a happy baby who loved attention from his parents, siblings, and grandfather. He had learned to squeal and coo quite early, and he was often the source of entertainment for the family who competed to find ways to make him coo for them. A week or so before Christmas, Mark laugh aloud at his older brother's antics! Andy was delighted he made his little brother laugh before anyone else had been able to do so.

The MacLayne cabin had also benefitted from Mac's presence at home. The room addition for Cathy was completed before the winter weather had become too cold for outside work.

The room seemed a bit large, twelve by fourteen feet. Mac, John, and Roy had spent scores of hours working on it. Mac had insisted that only the four, his father being one, would work on the room until the floor was completed. Neighbors had offered their help, but Mac declined any help in the early stages of construction. Laurel had wondered at that, as the digging of the foundation seemed to take overly long. She also wondered why Mac had built a five by seven-foot cellar under the bedroom floor. Their current root cellar was more than adequate for their needs and also proved to be a good shelter in severe storms. When she'd asked, he just said any good room deserved a strong foundation, and he changed the subject. Regardless, two weeks before Christmas, the room had been completed and Cathy declared her new space to be perfect. She no longer considered herself a little girl, but a grown-up young lady with her own room, a space on the main floor of the cabin, her door just next to the fireplace.

Mac's herd had also grown during the summer and fall. He had decided to take the male calves to market in the spring. Of the fourteen calves, eight had been female and would help to grow the herd, but the males were not of much use at the early stage of developing a herd. Besides, selling the nearly two-year-old steers would be a good source of income.

Thomas had also made a lot of progress in building his new home. Mac's father had chosen to build a larger two-story clapboard house with lumber he was hauling in from a sawmill on Big Creek. Wiley, the miller, had struck a bargain with Thomas to mill the lumber he needed in return for other trees from Thomas MacLayne's new land that were ready for harvest. Since there were many more trees ready than he would need, he was able to keep his cost very low. By the time the site was ready to build on, Thomas had already found two men who were willing to become tenants on his land in return for the opportunity to buy property of their own from their wages. Mac found several days when he,

Roy, and John were able to go over and lend a hand with the building.

As time has a way of doing, one month led to the next, and the year of 1859 came to an end, as the new decade of 1860 began. That winter was very cold, having many days with temperatures near zero, but it had also been very dry. One of the hardest chores that winter had been watering the orchard, finding days when the stinging cold would abate long enough not to freeze the nearly three-year-old trees and vines. Laurel, Cathy, and Andy shivered many days in their efforts to make sure the orchard was adequately watered.

On the second Friday of 1860, Mac came into the cabin with mail and copies of both the Baltimore Advertiser and the Arkansas Gazette. Laurel knew from the moment he came in something was wrong. "What happened in Greensboro? I can tell by the expression on your face something is wrong."

"Dearest Lord, Laurel, we're headed for war."

"What are you saying?"

"I didn't say anything to you back in December, but now the die is cast. The South is demanding secession if Lincoln's elected, and the North is up in arms. The military hanged John Brown on second day of December. Mac handed Laurel the papers with the story of the trial and execution. There were also stories about the bitter campaigning between Lincoln, Steven Douglas, and John Breckenridge.

"Surely, you don't think Lincoln can get elected. He's hardly known in so many places in the country. You know the south won't vote for him."

"I'm not sure. I just know one thing after another keeps piling up. One more push came when Brown was executed. Listen to what he said as his last words. 'I, John Brown, am now quite certain that the crimes of this guilty land will never be purged away, but with blood.' Dearest Lord Jesus...I pray that's not so, but Laurel, I have a dark feelin' that Brown is right."

"I hope it will not come to pass, Patrick."

"I pray it too, but I also mean to prepare in case war is in our future. I won't sit here ignorant of the peril that may come."

At that moment, Mark squealed in delight. Laurel had laid him on a blanket on her mother's rag rug near the hearth. Mark had managed to pull his booties off, and he was pulling his bare toes toward his mouth. He waved his healthy round arms up and down, and after a few minutes, he pushed himself over with his hands. It was the first time his parents had witnessed him roll over from his back. Mac's mood lightened, and he gently brought Laurel into his arms. A smile broke across his face. "God always has a way of puttin' things into perspective, doesn't he?" Mac kissed Laurel quickly and moved to pick up his son. "Mark Thomas MacLayne, you are so fine! I love you, son."

For Mac, preparing his home and family for what he believed was coming took the priority in his daily work. He told Laurel he intended to double their garden plot, and he would begin work on that area as soon as the worst of the February cold passed. He had ordered seed to double their oat and wheat fields for the next growing season.

"Mac, do you think that is a wise use of our land? We grew much more than we needed this past year."

"We will increase our harvest. I will have the boys help you with the garden."

"But Mac, we won't need…"

"Yes, dear, we will."

"Whatever you think, Mac. If you have the time and energy, you can cultivate as much land as your heart desires."

"How many more cannin' jars can you fill?"

"Mac, we put up plenty for us last year. What's come over you?"

"Laurel, the space beneath Cathy's room is the stash for our family. Startin' this spring, for every can you preserve for our pantry, there will be one for our stash. When we cure a ham in the smokehouse, we'll salt the same amount of meat to put in there. When we grind a sack of corn, we'll store the exact amount…"

"Surely things aren't that bad."

"Laurel, I don't know what's to come, but I intend to make sure our family is provided for. I may sound like a lunatic, but I don't care. When I was at Annapolis, we had to study military history. What I learned is that the civilian population suffers as much or more than any army. My kids are not goin' to starve because I can't keep the war away. I'll do what I have to do to protect y'all."

"God loves you for the lunatic you are. You have always done what you had to do to take care of us. I only hope the war doesn't come. Surely, good, faithful people will sit down and talk this out before it gets to war."

"I wish I could believe that."

"You don't think there is any hope for peace, do you, Patrick?"

"Yes, there is always hope, but I still plan for the worst while I pray for peace."

March of 1860 brought blessed relief from the long dry period of the last nine months. Crowley's Ridge saw several days of welcome rainfall. Laurel and the children all but danced in delight for the rain, as it brought an end to their carrying bucket after bucket of water to the orchard, but for Mac, the wet weather meant a delay. In the heavy rain, he couldn't turn the soil for the additional garden space, nor begin to prepare fields for the extra grain. He worried that much more delay would not allow Laurel to grow the extra food he wanted from their garden. Whenever the rain would slow to a drizzle, he would go out and try to do what he could, but the wet ground and cool temperatures added to the difficulty of the work. The progress that two weeks was very slow.

Before Saturday the second week in March, Mac's frustration level had reached its limits.

"This rain is an abomination! I wish it'd stop so I can get some work done around here!"

"What's brought up your dander, dear? You know we need this rain. The last six to eight months have been so dry. Even our well is lower than usual."

"But for two weeks, it's rained every day. I need to get the sod broke on those two new fields. The garden needs to be plowed so we can get our garden planted. This time last year, we already had half our garden in the ground."

"Mac, we still have plenty of time to make our garden. We haven't gone hungry yet. This is so unlike you. I've always been the doubting Thomas in this family."

"I'm sorry, Laurel. You're right. God has always provided for us. He's not likely to stop now."

"That sounds more like the man I married a while back."
"Hang it all, Laurel. I feel so helpless. I can't even go back to the legislature so I can try to help keep Arkansas from seceding. Now this rain is stopping me from safeguarding my family."

"I am sure we'll get back to our work in a day or two. I'm worried about this change in you, though. Why are you so sure the war is coming?"

"Laurel, if I hadn't seen those debates, or should I say arguments in the statehouse last year, perhaps I'd feel more hope. Feelings are runnin' strong on both sides, but if Lincoln gets elected in November…. All the papers are carrying stories about the firebrands on both sides who will eventually divide the country—maybe even the state. And here I sit, what can I do? Nothing…not one darn thing."

"Patrick, life is always a challenge because we really have no control. You can't stop the rain. Maybe war will come, but you know we will be all right. You've got more faith than that. Remember who you are, and where we've come from."

"I know you're right, Laurel. Sorry about the mood." He walked across the room and looked out the window. "Hey…do you know what next Saturday is?"

"I do."

"Yes, those were the words you spoke that day three years ago, Saturday."

"I thought you marked our anniversary from September 1."

"Well, that was a pretty fine day as I remember. That first night we made love in our tall four-poster is an event I'll not likely forget, but that time wouldn't have happened if you'd not married me in March of '57."

"I remember well. I was so scared of what the future would hold for me. Back then I didn't think of us. Took a lot of growing to come to that. Now I can hardly think of a life outside of us."

"The years have been full. We've had plenty of blessings but also some sorrows."

"Just like everyone, we've experienced life. For me, Patrick, it's been a good one, because I have learned you love me, so now even the hard times are good."

"We've certainly made a family faster than most. Married three years and have four kids already!" Laurel and Mac laughed together thinking about the joy their family had brought to them. "How do you want to celebrate our anniversary?"

"We could have a family supper here. We could invite your Pa, Matt and Ellie, Susan and Randall, along with my cousin Mark and his new wife."

"Whoa! That would be a houseful! I was thinking of something a bit more romantic. How about us sendin' the kids off to my Pa, and let Ellie and Matt take the baby for the weekend. How long has it been since we've had any time, just the two of us?"

"Mac, we can't do that. Mark Thomas is too little to go away overnight. He still has to be fed."

"He's eating from the table pretty well now."

"He's still nursing."

"All right, I agree, but we can still let Pa take the other three for the night so we can have some time for each other. I've been thinkin' about that copper tub..."

"Patrick!"

"Don't pretend you're shocked. We may be old married people and parents to boot, but that's no reason to let the pleasure we find in each other slip by the wayside."

"Your plans for our anniversary sound wonderful, Husband. You talk to Pa, and I'll talk to Mark. He does sleep pretty well most of the night anymore."

"Come here and sit with me." Mac reached for her and pulled Laurel into his lap. He pulled the pins from her chignon and let her hair fall down her back and across her shoulders. He drew her as closely as he could manage and kissed her. Long before he was ready to release her, Roy opened the back door, wet hat in hand

"What's for supper, folks?"

"Real life is back, Wife. I'd about forgot. Thanks for helping me get out of the low mood I've been in. I know you're right. I've been tryin' to take on all life's uncertainties when I know that's God's job – not mine."

"You're welcome. I'd never have gotten to the point I could remind you if you'd not taught me about grace."

That night at supper, the mood at the MacLayne table was much more pleasant. Mac seemed relaxed and enjoyed his family more than he had since he'd found out about the execution of John Brown. He was still convinced that war was inevitable, but he would just put it out of his mind for the time being.

After a satisfying meal, Roy spoke to his family in a very serious tone of voice. "Mr. Mac, Mrs. Mac…well, I 'preciate all y'all done for me and Cathy these past two years. You gave us a fine home and fed us good and kept us warm."

"You're more than welcome, Roy. We love havin' y'all here."

"You made us feel like family – really, but ya know, pretty soon, I'm gonna be seventeen. My birthday is comin' up at the end of the month. I'm thinkin' I'll be going back to my homestead and start making my own livin'. Cathy can come too if she's a mind

to."

"Roy, I hadn't realized you'd been thinking about going' back so soon."

"Mr. Mac, I've been thinkin' on it for nigh on to a year now. I can't go on just being a boy forever. Besides, the barn is crowded with my livestock and with yours, too. I've been afraid that land grabbers may try to take over my homestead."

"Yeah, and Roy ain't sayin' it, but him and Annie Clark are thinkin' of getting' hitched!"

"Cathy, you hush up. That ain't so and you know it."

"See, look at him get red-faced!"

"Cathy, stop teasing your brother. Roy, have you made up your mind? I was hoping you'd go back to school and get your certificate for finishing eighth grade."

"Mrs. Mac, you've taught me real good. I read, write, and I'm really good at cipherin'. I keep records on my egg and milk business. I have saved me up nearly seventy dollars. I'll be able to pay my taxes and tend my farm. Mr. Mac has taught me how to keep a homestead a-goin'. It's time for me to take care of myself and Cathy, too."

"Roy, we want you to do what is best for you. If you want to return to the Dunn place, you have our blessing."

"Thank ya."

"Do I need to find me a new farmhand?"

"Well, I figure I can work here some, but I have to get my garden in and fix up the place, take care of my animals. Maybe need to find another helper, part-time. John's good, but he'll need some help at times."

"Cathy, do you want to go back to your family's land?"

"Oh, Ma! I don't know what I need to do. Roy needs me, but I'd hate to leave you and Baby Mark. Andy's about my best friend. Will you tell me what I need to do?"

"You don't have to decide right now. Roy, will you stay on here until your birthday at the end of the month? That will give Cathy time to think and also let us get used to the idea of havin' you across the way. 'Course, your livin' in a different house still won't change the fact that you're our son. We don't care if your name is Dunn, you're still a MacLayne in here." Mac laid his hand on his heart. "I'll miss you, young man. You've been a fine help to me."

"I won't never forget what y'all did for me and Cathy."

The evening was bittersweet. Both Laurel and Mac were proud that Roy had taken the initiative to start a life for himself and that he had offered a place for Cathy in the Dunn home. On the other hand, having the two of them gone would surely leave an empty place in their home. This was just one more incident in life they couldn't control. Kids grow into young adults, and separation is a natural result. Change would always be the only constant they could be sure of… that and the unfailing strength they found in each other and the Lord.

"Andy, how about setting up that checkerboard?"

The next Saturday morning dawned with a cloudless, blue sky and a warm southern breeze. All across the ridge, trees were greening and jonquils were beginning to push their shoots through the warming earth. Dogwood trees were covered with buds, and promised beautiful blossoms within the three short weeks until Easter Sunday. The house was quiet mid-March morning. Mac had taken Andrew and Cathy to spend the weekend with his father, and Roy had gone to the Dunn place so Mac and Laurel could celebrate their third wedding anniversary together…nearly alone.

"Good morning."

"Happy anniversary, Patrick." A long, tender kiss followed their morning greeting.

"What can I do to make this a special day for you?"

"You started off pretty well."

"Flattery will only get you kissed some more."

"I have no objection to that." Laurel was happy to bask in Mac's attention, but like most six-month-old babies, Mark had needs of his own to be met, and he let them be known. Mac rose and brought their son to their bed.

"Look here, young fella, you are lucky to be here today, at all. You just behave yourself and let your mother pay some attention to your papa today." Mac's teasing brought a smile to Laurel's face. He pulled the strong, healthy infant to his face and kissed his pink cheek. "God blessed me with you, Laurel. I never knew how much joy a man has in a family."

"No more than I have known, Patrick. I know God has been especially good to us both, but I don't think I'd have known if you'd not taught me to value myself. I don't know if a person can

learn her worth until someone loves her."

"The day is yours, Laurel. We'll do whatever you want."

"Let's go out and look over our homestead. I'd like to visit Eden. I will fix a picnic basket, and we'll spend a good part of the day in this beautiful spring sunshine."

"I'll hitch the wagon. It'd be nice to ride, but Mark hasn't quite learned to sit a saddle yet. I'll do the chores while I'm out too, so you can fix breakfast, feed Mark and get dressed for a day outside."

Before nine o'clock, the MacLaynes had left the yard, driving the familiar paths across their land. They talked about their three years together, laughing now at some event that had once seemed so serious. As they rode, Mac pointed out several new calves that had been born to the herd that spring. He showed Laurel many marked trees that he'd chosen to cut for his father's quickly rising two-story clapboard. He'd made the choices carefully. He told his wife he didn't want to lose all the woods so he'd always make sure new saplings were growing near an older tree that would be used for lumber. He also planned to assure that hunting would be good in the fall. Laurel loved wild game, and if times became hard, the wild meat would assure food for his family.

Near noon, Mark made it known to his parents that he was hungry again. They were near Eden so Mac flapped the harness across Midnight's rump to hurry his pace to the creek. There they stopped for a noon meal. Mac helped Laurel down and took the quilt from the wagon and spread it near one of the mature oak trees not far from the place they loved to swim in the summer. She leaned back against the old tree trunk, undid her shirtwaist and began to nurse her son. She carefully draped the light blanket across her shoulder and Mark to protect her modesty. Mac never tired of the scene, his wife nurturing their son, and even after six months, the image humbled him with gratitude and love. Yet in the midst of this joy, the nagging fear of loss slipped back into his awareness. "Please Lord, don't let anything separate me from my family. Let Shiloh continue."

When Mark had finished feeding, he fell asleep. Laurel laid the sleeping baby on the quilt, and Mac came to sit beside her. They shared the meal she'd brought from home. Mac cradled her in his arms as he reclined against the tree. "Do you remember how you'd pull away from me whenever I tried to hold you in our first days together?"

"Yes, I remember. You scared me …you were so confident. I thought you were arrogant, and you were a stranger, ya know."

"Nonsense, I was your husband."

"A husband I had only known four days! And you hadn't built me a house."

"I nearly forgot…that promise to your father."

"Partly that…but I think most of it was just your stubborn nature."

"My stubborn nature!"

"Yes. You were the one who insisted we have our own cabin before you had the right to take me to your bed."

"I took you to my bed the first night we were wed. Remember, I told you I didn't believe in separate beds."

"I remember."

"I remember too…I remember how hard it was to wait. Even before I knew I loved you…I wanted you. Then when I came home to find you gone…that was the time of my life I was most lost – more than any time during those seven years I spent drifting in Tennessee and Kentucky. When you ran away from me, I knew what I had lost."

"That was a hard time for me, too. It seems such a little thing now that we've found each other."

"That is true. That night I carried you across our threshold, and I made love to you that first time. I knew why we had waited. Since that night we are one. The Lord knows how much I love you,
Laurel. I'm sure I'll never be able to show you."

Tears streamed unabated down Laurel's cheeks. "Why are you crying, Laurel?"

"Campbells always cry when they are happy. Haven't you learned that yet?" Mac pulled his wife into a passionate embrace and kissed her with such yearning that it left them both shaken. But once again, Mark abruptly ended his parents' lovemaking with a demand for attention.

Mac rolled to his side, "Oh, Son! I wish you were another year older." He picked up the baby and pulled Laurel to her feet. "Let's walk over to visit Campbell this afternoon."

They walked several yards into the glade and knelt to pray together at the grave of their first son. Laurel brushed away some dead leaves that had fallen on the little granite marker. She then pulled up the weeds growing on the little mound and picked up a few broken sticks and twigs that had fallen across the grave. "I want to edge this grave with some fieldstones, Mac. I'm going to plant some flowers here a bit later in the spring. I don't want anyone to disturb this place by mistake."

"Whatever you want. We'll take care of it as soon as we can. Perhaps we'd better head home. It may get too chilly out here for Mark when the sun begins to set."

"He'll want to be fed again soon, anyway." As they began to walk toward their wagon, a red strip of cloth flapping in the breeze caught Mac's attention.

"What in thunder is that?" He walked a hundred feet or so across to the tree branch where he found the red strip tied. "I didn't put a marker on this tree." "What do you think it is?"

"I know some surveyors use markers like this when they plot out sections of land, but I didn't ask for a survey on our homestead."

"Probably just an error, Mac. We've got all our land recorded in the courthouse."

"Yes, in the Greene County Courthouse, but this is a new county now."

"Let's not let some surveyor spoil our day. Monday will be soon enough to deal with a problem if one even exists."

For the next couple of weeks, Mac rode out to Eden to look for more signs that someone was surveying the property. Except for the one marker he'd found on their anniversary, nothing else out of the usual appeared. He told Laurel one afternoon that he'd overreacted, and his suspicions had been foolish. He knew all the paperwork was in order and their taxes weren't delinquent. He knew his concern over the secession talk had made him leery about anything that seemed out of place at his homestead.

Easter Sunday came along with Mac's decision to leave the doubts and fears at the church. Fellowship was good and the people of Shiloh celebrated the resurrection with heartfelt singing and a celebration of gratitude led by their pastor. Following the service, Laurel and Mac, along with all their children and Mac's pa went to Easter dinner at the Campbell homestead, a huge family affair with all Matt and Ellie's children and grandchildren.

After a feast put together by the women, the family divided into groups to rest and enjoy the beautiful Easter afternoon. The cousins ran and played together with laughter and squeals of delight all afternoon. The mothers with the infants made their place in the rocking chairs on the covered front porch—the ladies talking and sharing family stories and happenings from their various homes while babies slept in their arms. Mac, Matthew, and Thomas found themselves walking through the woods between the Campbell cabin and Shiloh church.

This was the kind of afternoon that Mac had missed. As his family obligations grew along with his travels as a state representative, he had spent less and less time with his best friend. An afternoon to catch up was an added pleasure to the fine Easter day.

"You're lookin' pretty tired, my friend."

"Is that a nice way to tell me I'm lookin' my age, preacher?"

"No, it's just plain stating a fact. I've noticed it several times since Mark Thomas was born. Isn't that young'un sleeping through the night yet?"

"Oh, yes. He's a good sleeper. He seems to learn everything pretty fast. You know the other morning, we caught him tryin' to pull up to the front of my armchair, and him just past six months. He's been sitting up by himself for a few weeks now."

"Well, if Mark's not keepin' you up nights, why are the dark circles under your eyes, and you've been pretty on edge all year."

"Matthew, I'm guilty of slippin' back to my old ways, I'm afraid, trying to make everything suit my design. You know I told you about the division I saw in the statehouse and all the stuff goin' on across the county...makes a man uneasy."

"That why you started gettin' the newspaper?"

"Yes. I just couldn't stand not knowin' what was happenin' across the country."

"You know everyone thinks you must be wealthy beyond their dreams...you get two newspapers nearly every week and in less than two years, you've added another room to your cabin. Then your pa is halfway finished with his two-story just across the county line."

"People don't like me havin' a house instead of buildin' a cabin?"

"Not that, Thomas. It's just that when something is different it makes for talk. Some folks have no idea how anyone can afford such a large house."

"They know I had a farm in Maryland. Besides this house cost very little more than Patrick's cabin. Wiley bartered his labor to cut my lumber in return for trees ready to harvest from my land."

"That's no matter. People got to have something to talk about. You know how it goes."

"Suppose you're right. Did Patrick tell you about the surveyor's marker he found on his land over by the creek?"

"No…you got land grabbers up on your acreage, Mac?"

"I don't think it was anything. Laurel and I found a red marker up by Eden a couple of weeks ago. I've been back several times since, and nothing else has shown up."

"I hope you're right. As hard as you've worked to pass those land protection laws in Little Rock last year, you've shouldn't have to worry about squatters on your own land."

"I laid the worry in the church this morning. I've got so many better things to spend my time dealing with."

"I can't believe my ears. I guess you did learn something from me after all."

"He has indeed, Matthew. When he came back to us in Maryland before my Ann died, we were both amazed to have our Patrick come home. Truthfully, we feared we'd never see him back again – whole and happy."

"That wasn't anything I did. All that credit goes to grace and part of it to Laurel Grace."

"I know that's not so. We are very grateful for what you did for Patrick. You've been the best friend he needed."

"Hey, have you two finished talkin' about me as if I wasn't here to notice?"

"Was that a little thoughtless of us, son?"

"A bit, Pa. Matthew, have you heard anyone talking about who's going to represent Craighead County in the legislature during this next session? I haven't heard anyone talkin' about the election and it's less than six months from now."

"Just some community chatter. Such a small part of the new county is made up of people we know. It's hard to figure."

"I know Greensboro is bustlin' now. Although Jonesboro has been named county seat, that settlement has got a way to go to meet what we already have in Greensboro. We gotta have a courthouse and get our county records pulled together. We gotta get someone in charge of our area…we need a sheriff and some justices of the peace to keep things goin' as we're used to."

"You thinkin' of runnin' again?"

"No. I've had my fill. Laurel has made it pretty clear that we've got too much to do at home for me to be spending weeks and weeks in Little Rock."

"I know she didn't like that seven-week stretch you were gone last winter."

"We've got a baby at home now, and I need to do my part in raisin' him."

"Are you gonna be satisfied livin' the life of a farmer, brother?"

"I've got lots to do now. My herd is growin', and I've got two more sheds to build before winter sets in again. More cows mean more forage. Who's got time to go politicking anymore? Anyway, Roy is leaving us to go back to his own homestead."

"You did a nice job not answerin' that question, friend."

"What kind of fool would I be if I couldn't appreciate what I have at Shiloh."

"I guess I got my answer."

As Easter of 1860 came to an end, the family had changed. Roy did not return to the homestead with them. Instead, he took the north road back to the Dunn land. Cathy hugged his neck and cried for a while as they parted.

"Roy, I hope ya ain't gonna be mad at me. I love you. You're the best big brother ever. I want to go with you, but Ma needs me and Baby Mark needs me. I love my new room, and well, it's scary to go back to our cabin where Gran died. Is it okay with you if I stay with Mama and Papa? You ain't gonna hate me, are you Roy?"

"Course not, Cathy. I knew you'd decide to stay. A little girl like you needs her ma and pa around. Besides, I'll see ya all the time when I come to work for Mr. Mac." "Will you still wanna be my brother?" "I'll always be your brother, Cathy.

"Roy, you know where we are if you need anything. We'll always be your family." She walked over and hugged Roy. He blushed.

"Thank you, Mrs. Mac. I'll see y'all soon."

By the time April had come to an end and school had started for Cathy and Andy, the hardest work of spring had been completed. Laurel and Mac had expanded their garden plot by half, putting in extra rows of corn and beans. Mac had planted twice the acreage in wheat, oats, and barley to provide adequate feed for his herd if the winter proved to be a hard one. Both Thomas and Mac had finished sheds to shelter the calves and heifers when the snow and ice came. During the growing season, Mac had more time to spend with Laurel and Mark, enjoying the experience of parenting he'd missed with Andrew.

CHAPTER SEVEN

Therefore, the Lord God sent him forth from the garden of Eden, to till the ground whence he was taken. So He drove out the man and placed at the East of Eden...Cherubim's and a flaming sword...

to keep the way of the tree of life.

Genesis 3:23-24

The first day of school for the spring term fell on the last day of April. Andrew and Cathy came home with all kinds of news from the first school day. There were two new families in the community, each enrolling two new students in the subscription school. Since only three had finished their schooling the previous December, the school enrollment was up again with twenty-four students filling the tables.

Mr. Tucker had returned for another term. By Andy's judgment, he was just as mean as ever. Cathy poked him and said not to criticize because next to their ma, Mr. Tucker was the best teacher they'd had. She beamed when she told her parents the teacher said the older kids they would even study some Latin this term. School was so wonderful to her because learning came so easily.

Even Andy didn't complain as much as the previous term. Laurel's tutoring had helped him catch up in reading and arithmetic. The other kids had also stopped using him as their whipping boy. The fact that Andrew had grown about two inches also helped to boost his confidence, so school was not the dreaded event he'd experienced when he first came to them.

"Ya know, Pa, one new boy named Sean Flannigan told me we live real close so we can be good friends."

"Is that so? It's great to have a new friend."

"That's what I think too, but I don't know how close he can be to us. Our homestead has lots of land, and our house is practically right smack in the middle."

"Well, new people to the area don't always know where other people live."

"I know. I liked to never have learned my way around our place."

"Well, you learned pretty fast. Maybe Sean will too."

"I hope so. I miss havin' Roy to do boy stuff with. Cathy's fun enough, but she's just a girl."

"Well, when you get a bit older son, you'll learn it's pretty nice to have girls around.

"Sean said he'd have to miss school some here at first because he'd have to help his pa raise a cabin." "We could get our church together to help if they'll let us. You know they helped us build our cabin and barn, too. Do you have any idea where exactly they're homesteadin'?"

"No, but it can't be too far. Sean said he'd walk to school because it was barely a mile away."

"Which way did he walk when he left school?"

"We walked together for a spell, then he took a path over toward the creek."

Andy's last answer was not what Mac had expected. He knew of a couple of sections open beyond the church nearer Big Creek, but nothing that would bring the Flannigan children their way. His father had looked at both of them, but the acreage was pretty small, and the trees there were not as mature as he needed to cut lumber for his house. The other area was about halfway between the church and Lorado, much farther than the one-mile trip the boy had described to Andy. All the land between the churchyard and their homestead was already claimed and most of it was part of their four hundred plus acres.

Suspicion sprang up in Mac's mind. Could this new family have settled on their homestead by mistake? He knew he had to find out as soon as possible. This was not the kind of problem he wanted to focus on right now. Land arguments were never pleasant and always ended with one party or the other losing. Tomorrow Mac would ride around his property again, just to make sure his land was secure.

The next day was a beautiful, warm early spring day. A gentle breeze tempered the heat that cloudless morning. The clear blue sky provided a perfect backdrop to the newly greening trees and flowers of every hue and shape splashing their color across the hills and valleys along the ridge. Mac hitched the team of jacks to the small wagon. He would take Laurel and Mark out with him as he drove through their land. He'd told Laurel the day was too fine for her to stay cooped up. A pleasant family ride was a perfect excuse to find out if the Flannigan's were squatting on MacLayne property. Since the acquisition of the hunting grounds, he didn't get around to visiting all the property as often as he should. He would have to step up his supervision with so many new people moving to the area.

They drove through the back paths to the new hunting woods and across the valley where he'd fenced the best parcels for his new herd. He took time out to count his heifers and new calves, which were all still in the pasture. Across the field, he pointed out his two prize bulls that were strolling, basking in the warm sunshine. He pointed out new calves lying near the feet of their mothers. Mark, who was wide awake and sitting in Laurel's lap, seemed to take in everything around him. He waved his arms and squealed with delight when Mac showed him the new calves they'd found. He squirmed trying to get down, and his parents laughed at his antics.

Before they reached Eden, Mac noticed smoke rising down by the creek. At first, he was concerned there may be a fire in the woods, but within a couple of minutes, he saw a large, tarpcovered wagon scotched near the bank of the creek with a wellcontained fire nearby. He saw a man, a woman, and three mid-aged children all dressed in homespun and calico. He knew he had found the homesteaders Andy had told him about. They were clearing brush and saplings inside an area they'd marked off for a garden. They were trying to stake out a claim for a homestead in the worst possible place on their entire property. The site they'd staked out was within a few feet of Eden.

"I've gotta go talk to those people."

"Mac, you don't have a weapon."

"We're just gonna talk, Laurel. Please take the reins and wait here with Mark. Mac jumped from the wagon and walked a score of feet. "Hello, stranger."

The man stood up and answered. "Who are you, and what are doin' on my land?"

"My name's MacLayne. I don't think we've met.

"We just got here last week. My missus, our kids, and me are homesteading our fifty acres between the ridge and that stand of trees just beyond the creek. You can see our marker over there on that oak."

"Are you sure you're in the right place, Mr...."

"Name's Flannigan. You're durn right I'm sure. I got me a signed deed that describes this here fifty acres to a tee. I bought the acreage from a swampland agent working with the federal government. He met me in Gainesville at the courthouse and brought us here himself. The deed is right here."

"Didn't Mr. Stuart, the tax collector, tell you no taxes were due on this parcel?"

"I didn't see no one named Stuart. Another danged Scotsman!   I don't remember the name of the man who sold us the land."

"Look, Mr. MacLayne, me and my man, we don't want no trouble with you, but this land belongs to us. We paid near a hundred dollars for it."

"Mrs. Flannigan, we won't have any trouble, but this land belongs to me. My grandfather was given this land for his service in the War for Independence against England in 1812. We have a land grant signed by President Madison. We have paid the taxes on this section for more than forty-five years."

"MacLayne, you get off my land. I don't know who you think you are, but this is my land. My family and me are gonna work this land and build us a strong log cabin right there in that stand of trees."

"I can't let you do that. We own this land, and this place is very special to my wife and me."

"I done told ya to git in a friendly way, but if you won't...Paddy, bring me my gun. Ain't no one gonna tell I can't build on my own land."

Mac raised his hands to show he had no intention of fighting, and he had no weapon. "Wait 'til I can bring the constable and get a surveyor here. We'll work this out."

"Ain't nothin' to work out. I bought this land. I got a deed, and no one is going to steal it from me."

"Mr. Flannigan, just give me a day before you start felling those trees. My son's grave is there beneath that biggest oak tree. Surely you saw his marker."

"We did see that carved stone over there, but no one in the family can read. Don't know what it says."

"Please just promise me you won't disturb that place until we can get to the bottom of this. That would grieve my wife more than she could bear."

"Just tell me why I should strike a deal with any blame Scotsman?"

"Because it's the right thing to do. You can't disturb our son's resting place. Just give me twenty-four hours."

"I have a cabin to raise and virgin land to be plowed for planting. I got no time to wait for you and your friends to connive me out of what I know is mine – legal and proper."

"I'll be back."

"And you'll find me right here, working me own land."

Mac returned to Laurel, a scowl telling her that the meeting had not gone well.

"Things aren't good are they, Mac?"

"That stubborn hot-headed Irishman won't listen. He said he's got a signed deed and paid up all the back taxes, so he owns the land. That family must have fallen victim to some illegitimate land agent. He said he'd signed the papers over in Gainesville."

"But our deeds are recorded in Gainesville. Didn't the tax collector see no tax was due?

"He said something about a courthouse. I don't know of a courthouse in Gainesville, just some office space occupied by the circuit judge. I have to go talk to Al Stuart."

"Patrick, he called for a gun."

"I told him we'd have no violence. He's determined to claim the fifty acres he paid for. That land is surrounded on every side by our land. It straddles the creek and includes Eden. He said he's laid out his cabin where I'd thought to build ours. Campbell's grave would be at their back door."

"Not Eden! And how can we have another homestead in the middle of ours?"

"Do you want me to take you back to the cabin, or would you like to go with me to see Al?"

"Let's go together. I'll feed Mark while we travel so he'll sleep while we talk to Al. Mac, has Campbell's grave been disturbed?"

"Not yet. Don't fret. Flannigan must know something about farming. He knows he has to get crops in the ground if they're gonna have food this winter. Besides his being Irish, I'll bet he's

Catholic. Surely, they'll respect a grave and the cross we've used to mark Campbell's place."

By shortly after noon, Mac and Laurel sat with Al Stuart in the hotel dining room. Mark slept on Laurel's shoulder and Mac laid out the problem for his lawyer over their noon meal.

"No problem for you, Mac. All the paperwork is in order in Greene County, and you've got a legal and prior claim to all your homestead. The circuit judge will rule in your favor. He won't have to think about it for ten minutes."

"How can I stop Flannigan from cutting the lumber and plowing up Eden?"

"Eden?"

"That's what we call that little part of our land. We laid Campbell there under the largest oak tree in that glade."

"Sorry, Laurel. I understand why you're upset. Mac, I'll talk to the constable. He'll ride out to talk with the squatters. The judge will take care of everything. Don't worry."

"When can we meet with him? I'll go tell Flannigan to come and bring his papers."

"I think it'd be best if you let me handle this. The judge will be back in Gainesville at the end of the month."

"Al, that's more than two weeks. He can do a lot of damage in two weeks."

"Sorry, but you know the circuit is a large area. He was here the week before Easter."

"I'll post a guard. I probably can't stop him from plowin' up a garden plot, but I'll not let him near Eden."

"Be careful, Mac. Land arguments can turn ugly real fast."

"Mr. Stuart, what can we do to help this family get their money back. I'm sure they are victims as much as we are."

"That is what Mac worked so hard on when he was in the legislature. There is a law now. Maybe we can help them."

"I hope so. Everyone needs a place to call home."

The days following the visit to Al Stuart proved to be some of the most trying times Laurel and Mac had experienced together – a time more stressful than any of the attacks they'd endured during the campaign of 1858. Mac had sleepless nights and long trying days where his normal routine was constantly disrupted. He feared Flannigan would begin to dig the foundation for a cabin and disturb Campbell's grave. He did not trust the man to leave the beautiful old hardwoods standing in Eden. They would make prime material for building a family-sized cabin. Their proximity to the site where the Irish squatter wanted to build made them even more tempting.

Mac used the tenants from his father's land and his friends to help him patrol the area. He did as his attorney had directed, and he made no direct contact with the man or his family. Yet, he made sure they were aware people were watching Eden.

Mac hated the feeling he got from having to patrol his own property. He had come to this area himself some seven years earlier for the same purpose. When he came, the Shiloh community had welcomed him and helped him build a home. Now he found himself in the role of a spoiler for another man who was trying to do the same thing. His mood was low, and Laurel was more than aware of the battle he fought within himself.

On Wednesday after dealing with an entire week of sullen and curt answers from her husband, Laurel decided to open a conversation. She tucked Mark into his bed shortly after Cathy and Andy went to their rooms. She changed into her summer night dress and sat on the side of the bed, rocking the cradle with her foot as she took her hair down.

"Mac, please come here. Go ahead and turn down the lamps and bank the coals for the night."

"I've already started. I think some extra sleep will help me get rid of this pitiful state I'm feelin' right now."

"Mark's asleep already. You know, Husband, he's nearly too big for that cradle. We are going to have to think of getting him a bigger bed soon. I think he'll be walking before his birthday."

Mac took the hairbrush from the table and began to brush Laurel's curls. "It's been a while since I brushed your hair."

"I know. We're caught up in working every day and we've forgotten life's nicest moments. I like it when you brush my hair."

"I do too. I also like this." He drew her tresses aside and kissed the nape of her neck and shoulders.

"You always know how to make me forget the cares of the day. You haven't been able to forget the land problems, have you, Patrick?"

"You know me too well, Laurel. No. Ever since I found that family down at Eden, I've had a constant sense of loss that may come."

"Al said the judge will rule for us."

"It's not just the land. Of course, I don't want anyone to destroy that special place, but you know they aren't really squatters. They tried to buy a home and carve out a place for themselves, just like we did."

"You tried to talk to them. We could have helped them, but they wouldn't let us. Is that what's bothering you so badly?"

"I know I tried, but what will happen to them after the judge sees their papers are no good?"

"Maybe then they'll let you try to help them. That was the reason you pushed for those stronger laws against dishonest land agents."

"It's true we do have laws now, but a law can't always protect the people it's meant to help. Imagine what that hundred dollars must mean to the Flannigans. I'm pretty sure they're immigrants. Mr. Flannigan has a powerful brogue still. They have so little in the wagon to start out with, and no home to return to." "Darlin', you can't blame yourself for their misfortune. All we can do is offer to help. This will all be settled by the end of the month."

"Thank the Lord! I don't want to talk about the land problem anymore. I do appreciate havin' you here to listen to me and puttin' up with my foul mood." Mac walked over to look at Mark and pulled the soft cream-colored crocheted blanket over the plump little arms of the sleeping baby. As he gazed down, he thought, *How blessed I am. Look at this beautiful boy, asleep here in my own cradle. Look at that beautiful woman sitting there on my bed. Think of those two fine kids asleep under our roof, here in our sturdy cabin with plenty to eat and good clothes to wear. How can I feel so low? Can I take all the Flannigans have and live with myself?* He shook his head. He straightened his shoulders and lifted his head.

Mac walked back to where Laurel sat. He brought her into a firm embrace and kissed her with a passion akin to the intensity they'd felt those first months after he'd taught her to be his lover. "Laurel Grace. Let me make love to you. Let's pretend we are newlyweds again. Like it was before we were parents and a stodgy old married couple. Just for tonight, I want to forget about land deals, children, times apart from you…everything that has ever caused us a second of worry. I just want you – the two of us together—leaving the rest of the world outside that door."

"What rest of the world, darlin'? There is only one person in my world, and I want you to love me as much as you want me."

Mac turned the lantern down, bent to pick Laurel up and carried her to their four-poster. There they spent the rest of the night in a world where only two exist.

CHAPTER EIGHT

Cease from anger, and forsake wrath: fret not thyself in
anywise to do evil. For evildoers shall be cut off: but those
who wait upon the Lord,
    they shall inherit the earth.
               Psalms 37:8-9

M to talk with Al Stuart again. Al confirmed the meeting Mac made a trip to Greensboro the following morning with the circuit judge in Greensboro on April 30th. The judge had several issues to deal with for the new county, so he'd planned to hold court in the dining room of the Greensboro Hotel. Al assured him once again that the case would go in his favor, but Mac felt little pleasure in the news.

He went to the general store to pick up the mail before he returned home. He got several letters for his father and two or three from former constituents who still asked him for help with legal or political problems, even though he no longer had the authority to do anything. The last letter belonged to Laurel. He arrived back at Shiloh in a good frame of mind, remembering the previous night and feeling good that the hearing in front of the judge was scheduled soon.

"Laurel, I brought the mail. I think this one looks to be in Elizabeth's hand. It's been a while since she wrote."

"I'm glad to have news from Hawthorn. I'll put it in my pocket and read it after supper. The kids finished their chores and told me they were starving. We have some blackberry cobbler for dessert. I'm afraid I used my last jar of blackberries."

"We'll put up more this summer…all the extras we can find. Kids, wash up and come eat."

They chatted all through supper about the goings on at school. Cathy said Brother Matthew came to school that day to talk about moving from the Carolinas nearly twenty years earlier.

"Goodness, Andy. That is your third helping of potatoes. You'll have no room for dessert."

"Well, Pa, I'm right hungry today."

"Didn't ya eat your lunch at school today?"

"Yes, Mama, I did but I gave most of it to Sean."

"Why did you do that?"

"Well, he didn't have none. His brother Paddy didn't neither, and that little sister only had one cold biscuit."

"Did they forget to bring their dinner pail."

"I don't know. They ain't never brought no dinner to school any day they've been there."

"Pa, I don't think they got much food. They're just now starting to plant a garden."

"Cathy, how do you know that?"

"That girl…her name is Maureen…she told me they'd planted stuff yesterday after school. They planted some corn, peas, and potatoes. It's late to plant that stuff, ain't it?"

"We try to plant ours in mid-March when the ground is warm enough."

The conversation at dinner increased Mac's concern over Eden. The Flannigan children were going hungry, and he was begrudging the family's plowing the earth near Eden. No child should have to be hungry. He'd never been hungry. He doubted Laurel had, although they'd not spoken about it. He knew it was his Christian duty and blessing to feed those who had no food. He didn't know how he could offer food to the family he was being sued by. He doubted the head of the family would take a handout from him, but perhaps Matthew Campbell would be able to help. "Laurel, please gather up a food box from our pantry. I'll get Matthew to deliver it as a gift from the church. Cathy, you and Andy go down to the root cellar and get a bag of potatoes and some yams. Do we have any meal?"

"You can take what we have in the pantry. I have enough in my meal urn to keep us until I can get to the mercantile. I'm afraid we've used all we had milled last fall. Here, you can take this jar of molasses and another of honey. Everyone needs a little sweetenin'."

"I'll go see Matthew in the tomorrow. He'll know how to make this food seem like a welcome gift instead of a handout."

"Gee whiz, Pa. We must surely be rich to have so much to share."

"Andrew, don't you say anything to the Flannigan kids about this. This gift will be our secret. Do you understand, son? We don't talk about it."

"Is it bad to be nice to folks, Papa?"

"No, Andy. The great commandments tell us to love the Lord and love our neighbors, but sometimes, people's pride gets hurt if they think other folks see them as charity cases. You remember how those boys hurt your feelin's when you thought they made fun of you because you were poor?"

"Yeah, but they don't laugh at me anymore."

"Well, we won't let anyone have the chance to laugh at your new friend."

"I'll watch after him, Papa. We won't talk about it."

"Thanks, Cathy. You're a fine big sister to Andrew. He's lucky to have you." Laurel bent to kiss Cathy's cheek. "Laurel, read us your letter."

"Oh, I'd forgotten about it." She sat down and put Mark on the rag rug at her feet. She lifted the wax seal and opened the double-paged letter.

March 10, 1860

Dear Laurel,

I hope this letter finds you and your family well and content. I'm sorry it's been so long since I wrote to you. I got your letter from Christmas time and am happy to learn of your new son. How fine you named him for your dear pa. Mark Campbell would be so proud.

I am anxious to tell you the good news. Gracie has been returned to Hawthorn. The army brought the seventeen children who survived that horrible day in Utah back to Benton County in September. Seems a man named Mitchell, hired by the army, found them with different families across Utah. He gathered them up and with a lady named Mrs. Rainey, they made sure they got back to their families. They took real good care of the ones they found. The oldest one they brought home was eight.

Thank the good Lord, Gracie can't remember nothin' about the attack. Of course, she don't remember her mother or father either. None of her brothers or sister were brought back to us. She stayed with her grandfather Wilson until he died in February. We had a bad time with the grippe here in Hawthorn during the worst of the winter.

Gracie is four now. She is stayin' with me until we decide who will raise her. You are her godmother. With no other family livin', you will be the one to make that decision. She can stay with me, but I'm near sixty and don't know how good a mother I will be to a little one like her. Oh, how I wish you were here so we could talk like we did when you were growin' up. You and Rachel...what memories I have of y'all.

I'll wait for you to tell me what you want me to do...."

Elizabeth's letter went on with several stories about Hawthorn church, the hard winter they'd had and the heated debate in the area about the possibility of Arkansas seceding from the union. Ya know, we all hold the union dear in our part of the state were the words Elizabeth had used to show her disapproval of the idea.

As they lay together in the tall bed that night, both the MacLaynes had too much on their minds to sleep. Mac shifted position every few minutes seeming to fight with his feather-stuffed pillow. Laurel's thoughts took her away from the present into the bittersweet memories of her friend, Rachel. Abruptly Mac sat up, beat his pillow several times, and then pulled his hands through his hair.

"Patrick MacLayne, are you going to beat the pillow to pieces, or will you tell me what has put you in such a state?"

"Those kids are hungry, Laurel. I don't mean just missed a meal kind of hungry, but starving. Things won't be any better after next Monday. I'd offer Flannigan his money back if he'd take it, but it's getting really late in the planting season to get a crop in and expect a decent harvest."

"Mac, why are you feelin' so guilty? You didn't take the money."

"Is it wrong for us to sit on all this land? Should I let him keep the fifty acres?"

"We agreed that section of land should never be altered from the way we found it. We'll work the rest of our homestead, but not Eden. You promised me we'd keep it just the way God created it."

"I know I did."

"Whoever heard of letting someone else homestead right in the middle of your property? We may be able to give them some land, but it can't be in the middle of our land."

"We have to do something. I can't let people starve when we have so much."

"You tried to help, and you are. You've already provided enough provisions to feed them for at least two weeks. Matthew'll get it to them tomorrow."

"I'll be so glad to see this whole mess resolved. I want the peace that Shiloh promises."

"You know where that comes from, Mac. You know it better than anyone I know. Thanks to you, I'm learning too."

"You have been my rock. Who'd of thought that shy spinster I found in the Boston Mountains would turn out to be so strong and would remind me about grace?"

"Do you think you can sleep now?"

"In a while. Tell me why you've been so quiet and withdrawn tonight. I'd thought you'd be pleased about the news from Washington County."

"I guess I have mixed feelings about the news. Thank the Lord, Rachel's baby has been found and brought home, but Mac, I miss my friend more. All I've thought of since I read Elizabeth's letter is losing Rachel. How terrible for that little girl. She'll never know her mother and father. Rachel was a wonderful mother, and Gracie will never have a memory of her." Laurel began to cry softly. Mac sat up and pulled her closer. "Now that I am a mother, I know about that bond between children and their parents. How can Rachel's baby grow up not knowing that love?" Her tears continued to run down her cheeks. Mac gently wiped them away. "What would you like to do about Gracie?"

"I don't know what I should do. I guess we just need to pray about it for a day or two. I'm sure we'll know what the Lord would have us do if we ask Him."

"Mac…would you consider taking another child to raise here with us at Shiloh?"

"You know my answer."

"No, seriously. Could you …I don't want to force you to accept the charge for another child that's not yours."

"How could I do less than you did when you took Andy into your home and heart."

"Please take some time to really think about it. We've not yet shared four years together, and Gracie will make the fifth child we'll take to raise."

"Laurel, do you remember when we were planning this cabin, you asked me why I only put the loft over the kitchen and not here in our second pen?"

"Yes, I remember we talked about it."

"As long as we have our privacy so we can keep our relationship strong and our love life our own, we can fill this cabin to the hilt with kids. I am selfish enough to demand you for myself at times, but you are capable of loving me and as many other children as the Lord sees fit to place on our doorstep."

"You are a good man. You love your neighbor, and you love me. I couldn't want more. I'll pray about Gracie's situation. I want to do what will be best for that little girl."

"You just tell me what you decide. In the meantime, come over here and let me hold you until we sleep."

𝜙

Problems continued to escalate in the next weeks. One of the tenants had been confronted by Mr. Flannigan who'd demanded to know why his family was being watched every day. No punches were thrown, but a heated argument had ended when

Flannigan had yelled for his son to bring a gun. The tenant had left the area just as Thomas and Mac had told him to do.

Andy came home on Monday and told the family Sean, Paddy, and Maureen Flannigan had brought pone to school for their noon meal that day.

"But, Papa, I didn't tell 'em I knew how come." Andy smiled and waited for Mac's approval.

"It's true, Papa. He didn't even crack a smile." Cathy's words brought laughter, and Mac felt some comfort knowing the Flannigan kids had something to eat.

Matt had told him on Sunday that Mr. Flannigan had refused the gift from Shiloh church. He also said that Peggy Flannigan had a quiet way of doing what was best for her family. She let her husband bluster and fume for a few minutes and then she took the food, asking Matthew to thank the Shiloh congregation for the warm welcome.

Finally, the day came for the circuit judge to come to Greensboro. The MacLaynes looked on the day with mixed feelings. Neither Laurel nor Mac thought the judge would rule in the Flannigan's favor, but they knew at the end of the hearing, the family would find itself truly homeless again. If they had no land to build on, they could not plant food to see them through the winter to come. Land was a must. Mac had studied the laws about land purchases, homesteading, and the swampland parceled out by the federal government. He needed to be able to prove the sale was fraudulent and not just some mistake. If he could prove the Flannigan deal had been planned, knowing the property was already claimed, he could help the Flannigans prosecute the land agent and get their money back. Of course, that all assumed Mr. Flannigan would let go of his anger and listen to Mac. Nothing had yet confirmed that he was willing to do that.

The look on Mac's face told Laurel his mood did not match the glory of the April day as he drove to Greensboro to confront the Flannigans in the presence of the circuit judge. Laurel saw the dread in his face. She knew he wanted the matter settled, but she knew he was disgusted that another man would have his dreams stripped away when the paperwork showed his deed was a worthless piece of paper. At nine-thirty, the constable called for all interested people to enter the make-shift courtroom in the Greensboro hotel. Mac held Laurel's arm as they walked behind Al Stuart into the room. Mr. Flannigan with his wife came in together, dressed in their homespun work clothes, newly washed and pressed as best they were able in their make-shift camp on the edge of Eden. In his hand, Flannigan gasped the two pieces of paper on which all his hopes for the future prosperity of his family lay.

"Mr. MacLayne, can you bring me the documents showing your right to the homestead you've claimed?"

"Yes, sir. Mr. Stuart has brought them from the court records in Gainesville."

"Why is the homestead registered in Greene County?" The judge asked.

"As you probably know, our land lay in Greene County until the legislature created Craighead in the last session."

"I see. Stuart, didn't you tell me that MacLayne was part of that legislative body?" Al Stuart nodded his agreement. "Well, MacLayne, you voted yourself right out of a job, didn't ya?" The judged chortled, and a small group of people seated around the room laughed a bit. Flannigan didn't laugh.

"Judge, as you can see, Mr. MacLayne has more than ample proof of his claim. The first 160 acres--of which the disputed deed of Mr. Flannigan is a part--has belonged to the MacLayne family for three generations. Here is a statement from the Greene County tax collector showing no tax lien on any of the property owned by the MacLaynes. We also have deeds and homesteading claims that have been filed. We have all the tax statements..."

"We don't need all that stuff. Only the property in question matters to me." The judge took the original deed and the tax records from the lawyer. He spent several minutes looking at the dates on the documents, checking for signatures, and looking carefully at the paper itself. After a while, he turned to Al Stuart, "Al, why was this case even brought up to trial? It's obvious this land deed is valid. The date, signatures, and even the quill writing shows the paper to be old and legitimate."

"Mr. Flannigan has a deed to fifty acres of the larger section, all of it falling in the boundaries of this original warrant. Mr. MacLayne asks that the Flannigan deed be voided."

"Mr. Flannigan, can you produce your deed."

"Indeed I can. Here is the paper given to my wife and me the day we bought the property. See here...this is my mark."

"How and where did you purchase this land, sir?" "Twas back in January in Little Rock. A land agent of the federal government told us the land was part of a Swamp Land Act. We paid $50.00 for the homestead, and then paid $30.00 in back taxes. The agent told us the taxes had gone many years not paid. We had to give that agent who brought us to the land another
$20.00."

The judge again spent several minutes looking at the dates, signatures, and the document itself. "Tell me about his land agent you dealt with, Mr. Flannigan."

"A very serious, dignified man in the land office in Little Rock. I don't rightly recall his name. We mostly talked to his clerk. Was him, the clerk, that brought us here in late March after the weather allowed us to travel. That man's name is Duncan. I remember him—his name was the same as me own father, God rest his soul, Robert. The man's name was Robert Duncan."

Mac looked up with anger and disgust in his eyes. Robert Duncan! He looked to Laurel at his side and took her hand. Her face blanched at the mention of Duncan's name.

"Judge, the name on that land deed doesn't happen to be Digby, is it?"

The judge looked down at the deed and saw it was signed by Digby. "Yes. Ezra Digby. Is that important?"

"Not to the land title, but I know now how the Flannigans were cheated by an unscrupulous land agent, and I know why."

"No matter. Let's get back to the issue at hand. Stuart, do you have something else to say?"

Mac's attorney shook his head. "Flannigan, do you want to add anything to what you've told me?"

"Judge – I got me a signed deed. I spent every dollar me and my wife worked for more than three years to get us a home. We paid all the back taxes. That land is ours." Mac felt Laurel squeeze his hand at Flannigan's final plea. She knew he was torn about the decision the judge had to reach. She knew he felt helpless to do anything, even though the primary work he'd done in the legislature had been directed at this very kind of injustice. He turned to look at her loving face. He shook his head.

"MacLayne, do you want to say anything before I conclude?"

"Yes, your honor. I hate what's happened to the Flannigans. Being a homesteader myself, I know what it means to want to build a home on your own land. I wish I could just give him the land, but that piece of property is surrounded by the other property of my homestead. The area is part of an untouched, natural area so beautiful that Laurel and I call it Eden. We've set it aside to leave as the good Lord made it. Our first child is buried there. I wish things could have worked out, but we must keep that land."

"You can't keep what you don't own, you thievin' cheat!" Flannigan rose and stepped toward Mac.

The judge pounded his gavel on the table and demanded, "Flannigan, stop that rantin'. I'll make the decisions in this court.

This case is open and shut, Mr. Flannigan, because the fifty acres you're on belongs to the MacLaynes. It has since the time Arkansas was a territory. The original deed predates your deed by more than thirty years. The land was not forfeited as this family has paid taxes from the time Arkansas was made a state. Sir, you have been cheated by this land agent Digby. He sold land he had no right to sell, and he took taxes not due."

Al Stuart rose and spoke, "Thank you, Judge."

Flannigan turned back and kicked over the chair he'd been sitting in. "By the Lord in Heaven, I'll not be cheated."

"Flannigan, MacLayne hasn't cheated you. You will leave that land by the end of May. That will give you a month to find another place to build."

"And what can I build with? Another three years of sweat and labor? What's my kids gonna eat while I try to build with no land and no money?"

"My decision stands. MacLayne's claim is the rightful one. Y'all can leave. Call the next matter before the court."

Flannigan rushed toward Mac. Al Stuart and the constable stepped between the men. The constable took hold of Flannigan's shirt and pushed him back. The angry homesteader yelled across his shoulder, "MacLayne, you're a thief! I see how it is. You and your cronies here taking what's mine. The judge calling your friend here by his first name…you being a mighty member of the state government. It's all rigged. Duncan warned me about the likes of you. He said you got up in front of your church and said you broke every commandment in the Bible, except you never stole nothin'…Well, now you can say you've broke 'em all." The man turned, swearing under his breath as he pushed his way out of the room. His poor wife followed with tears streaming down her face, only partly hidden behind her well-worn poke bonnet.

Mac shrugged off Laurel's hand and rushed to grab Flannigan's shoulder. "Let me help you, man. I was in the legislature and we passed a law…" Before Mac could finish his plea, Flannigan smashed his fist into Mac's face. The unexpected blow knocked him to the floor. Laurel screamed, and Peggy Flannigan grasped her husband's arm and tried to pull him toward the door. The constable pulled the angry homesteader away from the mob that had gathered and held him from returning to the fray.

"Want me to arrest him, Mac?"

"No. I'm all right."

Laurel went to Mac's side and laid her handkerchief at his bleeding nose.

"Lord help me, Laurel! Why did I ever go to the legislature? It didn't help that man. My will to sit in that body made him the victim of Digby and Duncan. They knew that land belongs to us. They came up with this scheme to pay me back for taking the seat Digby thought he ought to get. Even better for them because it gave Duncan a chance to get in one more slap at you. Now there's talk Duncan's been back in the area again." Al Stuart and Laurel helped him to his feet.

"Mac, now that it's settled, maybe we can do something to help them. We can prosecute Digby…that new law y'all passed protects people from fraud like this." Laurel spoke as she helped Mac to his feet.

"Do you think Flannigan will take help from me now?"

"We won't know if we don't try. Al, do you think we can bring charges against Digby for this?"

"Yes, Laurel. I think we'd have a fair chance of getting him on land fraud. Let me talk to the judge. The sad part is how long it will take. Legal wheels grind slowly, and time waits for no man."

Mac and Al Stuart walked back toward the judge, allowing Mac a few minutes to clear his mind. After a brief conversation, he turned back toward the constable. "Armstrong, please let Mr.

Flannigan go. I'd be just as mad if the same thing had happened to me."

The constable released the red-faced man. "No more trouble out of you, Flannigan. Can't you see MacLayne is offering to help you? You stubborn Irishman! You can't have no better friend than MacLayne."

"He's been a fine help to me and mine. He's helped himself to our fifty acres and the hope we had to make a decent life. He's done helped me enough. This ain't over, Mr. Legislator. I will fend for me own now, and I will make the deal square before I leave this place. I won't be cheated, nor my family denied its right."

"Don't you be makin' no threats, Flannigan." The constable warned.

"That was no threat. It's a promise. Let's go, Peggy. We got nothin' to stay for in this town." He stooped to pick up his bedraggled hat, placed it on his head, and stalked out of the makeshift courtroom. His face awash with tears clearly indicated the defeat and hopelessness of dreams lost.

"I can't let this go, Laurel. What on earth can I do to help this man? Did you see the loss on his face? Let's go try to talk to them again. Maybe his wife will listen."

"No, Mac. You saw what happened when you tried to help. Give it a day or two and let tempers settle. Let's talk with Matthew and let him intervene for us. We can't do this by ourselves."

"Laurel, we can't…"

"I said, no. Mac, it's not the time nor place. Let's go to the hotel and get a cup of coffee and clean you up. We've got things to do at home."

Mac stopped, turned, and looked into Laurel's face. "What did you just say to me?" He could hardly believe his wife had spoken the words he'd heard.

"I said, no. A better time and place will present itself. I want to go home."

"Yes, ma'am."

℘

Across the main street of Greensboro in the doorway of the saloon stood a man, his hat pulled down over his eyes. He laughed.

CHAPTER NINE

*See that none render evil for evil unto any man; but
ever follow that which is good, both among yourselves,
and to all men.*

1 Thessalonians 5:15

A judge approached Mac and Laurel on the s with the
they left the hotel, two men who'd witnessed
the session boardwalk. "Mr. MacLayne...
ma'am. My name's Woodson. This is Mr.
Snoddy. We live over in Jonesboro, the new county
seat. The judge said you served in the last general
assembly. Is that so?"

"I did. Can I help you?"

"Well, we have a lot to do to get things settled
for our new county. I heard you live in the Shiloh
community that's now part of Craighead County."

"That's right."

"Did ya vote to break off our county?"

"Yes, it's a matter of record. In my way of
lookin' at the matter, it was best for my neighbors, closer
to us, and easier travel for us to do our business. I was
hopin' to see Greensboro be the county seat since we
have a more established town, but I can see now that
your settlement is more central to the land area of the
county."

"You seem to be a level-headed fellow who took his role as a public servant to heart."

"That was my aim for my short time of service. I live in the wrong county now to serve as the Greene County representative again."

"Would you consider representing Craighead County?" "That's a matter I haven't even considered. Right now, I've gotta see if I can take care of this mess on my own property. If you'll excuse me."

"MacLayne, would you let us come over and talk with you about this in a week or so?"

"Gentlemen…my husband is always open to a good political discussion. You're welcome to visit us at our place any time you like." Laurel took Mac's arm and they walked away.

"Laurel, I can't believe you did that?"

"Did what? Tell the truth?"

"Open the door to the idea of me running for the legislature again."

"You don't think you've fixed every problem we're facing by you goin' down there for one short term, do you?"

"Think about what you are saying."

"All I said is you are always open to a good political discussion. That is the truth, isn't it? Let's go home. I'd rather play with my baby than clean blood off my husband."

On Tuesday afternoon, Matthew Campbell went along with Mac and Laurel to the Flannigan's camp. Matt brought food from the church, enough to provide for at least two weeks, praying that cooler heads would let them work toward a solution. Mac had come with hopes he could to talk with the family. He was determined to convince Flannigan to bring charges against Digby. He felt sure the legal system would hold in the homesteader's favor because this was exactly the kind of swindle the laws they'd passed in the last session were meant to prevent.

"Mr. Flannigan, can we speak with you?"

"I'll talk with you, Brother Campbell, but what is MacLayne doin' here? We still got time to leave. The judge gave us a month."

"My friend wants to help you."

"I saw the kind of help he gives. He helps himself to what's mine—him and his cronies stole from me. Twas the same in Ireland. Those that had took what they wanted. No matter how hard we worked, those in power kept the land. We worked for a pittance and then got shoved off the land when someone else came to power. I got nothin' to say to him."

Mac clenched his fists in frustration. "It's not that way here. We got laws, Mr. Flannigan. Please just listen."

"I listened real good. I heard you say back in that judge's room that you made that law. I got no chance that it'll help the likes of me."

Matthew cut in. "Man, he can get your money back."

"And how long will that take? And in the meantime, how can I feed my wife and kids? We had one hope…gettin' shelter and a harvest before winter. It's nigh on to the first of May…do you see that happenin' in five months? I'd say he done all he can." With red blotches growing across his face, he turned to face Mac, eye to eye. "Now git from me sight. I'll have none of your…"

Laurel stepped between them and offered her hand to the man. "Mr. Flannigan, I'm Laurel MacLayne. I don't think we've met. We want to help so your family will be sheltered and cared for throughout the winter. Shiloh is a good community, and we will be blessed to help y'all get a new home started."

"We don't live on no man's charity—especially not the leavin's of one who steals from us. Now get off my land until my time's up."

She lifted her hand, pleading with him. "It's not charity. You paid for the land. We know that we can help you get some good land nearby, but we just need a little time." He turned his back and walked away from her.

Laurel then turned to plead her case with Mrs. Flannigan. "Please, ma'am. Listen to us."

"My man has told you. We've been kicked around, beaten, and called names since we came to these shores…We found no home in the east, and when we came west to join our family in the Irish settlement near Little Rock, we found no work there. We tried to do what they told us—we worked, saved our wages, and bought our own land. We did everything we were told and still, there's no place for us."

"We can help…" Laurel tried to convince Peggy Flannigan of her sincerity, but again Flannigan stepped between them.

"Woman, we don't want nothin' from the likes of you. I'm a-tellin' ya to leave one last time. We'll give up our place to you, and we'll be gone before the time's up, like that crooked judge ordered—not because he's right, but because he's got the law…. And, MacLayne, in time, you'll get your due."

"Mrs. Flannigan, I'm leaving these supplies sent by the Shiloh families. You can decide what you want to do with the food. God bless you. I'm sorry for the wrong that's been done to y'all."

The meeting ended. No one felt any better afterward. As they rode away, Matthew spoke. "Mac, that scowl on your face is out of place. You tried to set things right."

"Matt, don't preach at me now."

"You might as well tell me not to breathe. Brother, you stretched out your hand in friendship. You did all you could."

"And not one thing is any better."

"Free will, man. Not just yours, ya know…Flannigan chose too."

Mac raised his head to look into the eyes of his friend. He held the gaze for a time, and then he felt the burden lift…not totally gone, but more bearable. His friend had willingly shared his anguish.

"Mac, we will take care of this family. They will not go hungry. You can work with the law you helped pass to get justice for this man. The Lord charges us to do no more."

Before the close of the day, Mac had pushed the dilemma from the center of his mind. He returned his focus to his family. Andy asked for a game of checkers, and Mark, whose bout with teething had made him very cranky, could only be comforted in his papa's lap. Laurel and Cathy sat at the table working on the week's spelling list. Mac looked around at the family scene and smiled. The MacLaynes were safe and comfortable in the home he and Laurel had built so they could live just this life.

"Kids, your mama and I have been talking. How would you like to have a new sister?"

Cathy clapped her hands in delight. "Mama, are we havin' a new baby?"

"Oh, no, Cathy. One baby in this house at a time."

"But Papa said…"

"Just listen to your papa. Let him tell you what's happened."

"Your mama has a goddaughter named Gracie. Gracie is an orphan now. We wanted to ask you if you would mind having to share our home with her. If you think it's all right, we will bring her to live with us here at Shiloh."

"Papa…she's just like me and Cathy. Gracie is an orphan, too."

"Well, not quite, Andy. Cathy did lose her grandmother, who was her guardian, but you are my son. None of that makes any difference here. In our family, everyone gets to share in the decision."

Cathy, in all her almost-eleven-years of wisdom, spoke.

"Papa, how could we not want that little girl to have what we got? How old is my new sister? I can share my room with her. I got plenty of space.

Laurel smiled at the girl's loving response to Mac's question. "She's four. Her mother was my best friend when we were girls back in Washington County. Gracie was named for me."

"Papa, does she have to be a girl?" Mac looked into Andy's sincere face.

"Yes, son. Gracie is a girl, but that'd be fair, you know. You and Mark are two boys, and if we bring Gracie here to live with us, then Cathy could have a little sister."

"Yeah, but she'd only have to put up with one and I'd have two!" Mac and Laurel both laughed at the logic of a seven-yearold. "I guess one more won't hurt nothin'. At least she'll not share my loft."

"Wife, it seems our family has spoken. We'll make plans to bring Gracie here at the end of the harvest. I'll look into a way to bring her across the state; then we'll write to Elizabeth and see if we can grow this family some more."

On Thursday, Mac rode to Greensboro, along with Matthew Campbell. He'd promised Laurel he'd see about stage routes across the state. He'd also planned to stop in and talk with Al Stuart about the fall election. His chance encounter with the men from Jonesboro outside the judge's' makeshift court had not been far from his mind all week. Perhaps he could persuade Al to ride with him to Jonesboro to talk more with the men.

"Mornin', Al."

"Bless my hide, Mac. We'd just been talkin' about you."

"We? You seein' things, Al? I don't see anyone to talk to here." Mac circled his finger around in circles near his temple.

"I ain't losin' my mind. Less than half an hour ago, I was over at McCollough's and I ran into that fellow from court the other day. What's his name? Oh, well, anyway, he told me that they probably couldn't have a full-fledged election so soon. Ya know the whole population of the new county is barely 3,000 folks, and they're scattered over more'n 700 square miles of land." "I hate that. I was hopin' to talk with that committee they are working with to organize the county government. I want to get them to back me in askin' for help with the Flannigan problem."

"Ain't no *their*, man…We're just as much a part of this new county as the folks in Jonesboro. We got a bigger portion of the people up here than they have in that new settlement. Maybe we can convince them to send you back. At least you know how things work. You sure know about that land agent law since you and a couple of other men were responsible for gettin' it passed." "Whoa, Al. I didn't say I wanted to go back. I need some charges brought up on Digby and Duncan. They knew I owned that land. They did this to get back at me and to hurt Laurel."

"How better could you serve everyone involved than by returnin' to the legislature?"

"That'll take some serious talk with Laurel before I will even consider it.

"Well, it never hurts to talk. Let's go over to the mercantile to see if he's still here."

"I need to go there anyway." Together, they walked the short distance down the plank sidewalk to the mercantile. Woodson was leaned up against the counter, paying for the supplies he'd come to buy. He greeted Mac and Al and a long conversation ensued. A couple of other men from Greensboro, along with McCollough and Matthew Campbell, joined in and shortly the store became an arena for a full-fledged political discussion. Questions and comments about the entire political state of Arkansas came into play. One man talked about secession. Another mentioned the winter floods . One complained of no leadership in the new county…the issues seemed to snowball. Finally, the widowed dressmaker stomped her foot.

"Mr. McCollough, please! I can't make my livin' without some yard goods. Can you wait on me any time soon?"

Laughter erupted across the store. How long had the impromptu debate been going on? Obviously too long to suit the local seamstress. Mac picked up a pound of sugar Laurel had asked for and went to the front of the store.

"Got a sweet tooth, Mac?"

"No. I got a sweetheart who threatened my life if I forgot this sugar. She's bakin' a cake for my Pa's 65th birthday. We're havin' a family dinner to celebrate on Saturday evenin'."

"That'll be ten cents."

"Cost went up again?"

"Freight costs are up, ya know. And before you go, I wanted to tell you…the squatter on your land came to town yesterday afternoon. He's been in the saloon for a long time. Someone said he traded an old fiddle for some coins and he's been drinkin' pretty heavy since. Roscoe threw him out of his dram shop for disruptin' the place with his rantin'. Heard he's been shoutin' about how you robbed him of his land, and how you'll pay for it. He said you'd never live to see the good of your thieving ways."

"He's just angry…I feel for him. I'd like to help him get his money back from Digby. He was a victim. I'm sure he'll come to his senses once the whiskey's out of him."

"Just wanted you to know, Mac. Tell your pa best wishes for me."

"Hey, Al…why don't you and McCollough and Dr. Gibson come over with some of these fellows to Shiloh on Saturday. Invite some of the Jonesboro folks. We'll finish our discussion. Bring the wives. We'll have a party."

"Sounds like a plan. November is only six months away." Mid-spring, with the crops in the ground and no harvest to attend to was a perfect time for an impromptu social. Little encouragement was needed and within a very few minutes, the party was a go.

That Saturday was a busy day at Shiloh. Laurel had invited the family, including Roy and Annie to join them for the birthday celebration, but now she had no idea of how many people would show up at her house. They would celebrate more than Thomas's birthday, though. There was much to be thankful for…family ties, good weather all spring, the prospect of having Gracie in her home, two new calves, and a husband who had lost much of his gloom. Mac had returned with a plan to bring Gracie to Shiloh. He had even suggested that Elizabeth may be able to come for a visit if she felt she could make the trip. She and Gracie could take the stage to Little Rock and Mac or one of the tenant farmers would meet them there to bring them the rest of the way, either overland or by the river, depending on the early fall weather.

By noon, the crowd began to gather. Laurel had laid out many dishes of food on long plank tables near the porch. She'd wanted to make an apple cake for her father-in-law but the dried apples and the canned ones had long ago disappeared from the family's menu. She decided chocolate would have to do. Beside the tall four-layer cake, she'd added new onions and greens from her garden, fried chicken, potatoes and many dishes made from her still ample pantry.

Mac drew the group together and spoke from the porch. "Folks, today is the birthday of the finest man I know, my pa. We decided a party would be a good way to wish him many more birthdays with us. Pa, please bless the food so we can get this evening started."

"Father God, there's only one word. Thanks. Except for missin' my Ann, I could ask for no more. My family with me here celebratin' another year of a good life. Bless this feast made by my daughter and our friends, and bless my young'uns who call me Granddad. Thank you, Jesus. Amen."

Andy spoke up. "Amen, Granddaddy, I'm sure glad you're getting old. Look at that fine cake Mama done made for us." Andrew set the tone for the entire night. Laughter rang out across the yard. Until dusk, the Shiloh community, along with visitors from Jonesboro, Big Creek, and Greensboro fellowshipped together and enjoyed the day, talking politics, telling jokes, listening to music provided by a local fiddler, and building new friendships. A new community was coming together.

After dark, the MacLaynes sat down together in the main room. Laurel saved part of the birthday cake for an evening treat. The family's laughter filled the cabin. Mark played among his family and crawled from one family member to the next, trying at times to pull himself up at his grandfather's chair. Abruptly, Roy told his family that he'd asked Annie to marry him. That brought a silence to the room for a minute or so until he added they'd gotten permission from Mr. Clark to wed when Annie turned seventeen. Mac and Laurel were visibly relieved at that news because Annie had just turned fifteen at the beginning of the year so Roy would be near twenty before they would wed. The gaiety returned. Thomas returned to his role as the family storyteller, and he shared tales of life in Maryland with Patrick and Sean until Mark's fussing told them it was bedtime for the MacLaynes.

"Daughter, before I call it a night, how about another round of that fine cake you made for me?" Laurel got up and started toward the dry sink. Mac followed her, but not to serve the family cake. When she stopped, he pulled her into his arms.

"Laurel, life is so perfect. This day has seemed like a dream. All those rotten years I spent searching. This is what I wanted…needed. God bless you. Do you know how much you mean to me? I love you." Patrick kissed his wife.

"Granddad, make them stop…they're at it again!" Once more laughter filled the world where the MacLaynes lived.

By eight-thirty, the family had settled into their end of the daily routine. Andy had set up the checkers near the window as he did nearly every night. Cathy had gone to her room to prepare for bed. Thomas went out to the barn to check on his horse and to make sure the stock had water for the night. Roy and Annie were sitting at the hearth, holding hands and talking. Laurel picked up Mark, held him so Mac could kiss the sleeping boy goodnight and took him into the bedroom to nurse and put down for the night. "Well, Son, it'll be nice and quiet here for our game of checkers tonight. Was a fine party for your granddad." Mac took his chair and looked across the table at the miniature version of himself. The light flickered in the red crystal lantern on the mantle. For a minute, he thought of his mother who'd often read by that lamp. He pulled his pocket watch from his vest and saw it was nearing nine o'clock, the end of one of the finest days of his life. "Son, I like to end our days like this, just the two of us playing checkers. I think you'll have to bear a loss tonight."

Then the shots rang out…first one…then another… and another.

CHAPTER TEN

Oh, Lord, how long shall I cry, and Thou wilt not hear!
Cry out unto Thee of violence, and Thou wilt not save!
Why doest Thou show me iniquity and cause me to behold
grievance?
For spoiling and violence are before me:
Habakkuk 1:2-3

*A*ndy's footsteps as she approached the cradle in the second pen. screams brought chills that stopped Laurel in her Mark, who had been sleeping in her arms, screamed at being woken abruptly. She ran to the door and jerked it open. Flames streaked up the side of the fireplace from the floor where pieces of the red crystal lamp lay shattered. Annie's skirt blazed at the hem. Cathy ran out of her room. "Here, Cathy, take Mark and Andy. Go out the back door. Hurry. Go to the barn and tell your granddad I need him. Stay there until I call you in. Run! Andy, go!"

Only then did she turn toward the window. She saw Mac lying near the broken window. A circle of blood widened, surrounded his head and shoulders. He lay still. Was he breathing? In that moment, an eternity passed. What had happened to the perfect life she'd left only a moment earlier? Laurel stood--frozen.

Her old helplessness tried to push its way back into the situation. Her chin trembled, sobs about to erupt. Then quiet, strong words came to her. "Laurel Grace, my grace is sufficient. Pull yourself together. You are needed here." She pushed the panic away.

"Roy, jerk that skirt away. Don't let Annie get burned. Get her out of here and then take that rug and put out the fire before it gets out of control." Roy ripped the burning skirt off Annie, wadded it up, and threw it into the fireplace. He pushed her out the back door and returned to fight the flames, ever-growing toward the ceiling.

Laurel rushed across the room and sank to her knees at Mac's side. *Lord, please don't take him from me.* She saw the bloody area around him grow even larger. The sticky, thick blood made her gag. Nevertheless, she put her hand to her husband's chest, praying that he still lived. She felt his heart beating very fast. When she picked up her hand, it was covered with blood. That was when she realized the wound in Mac's chest was the source of most of the blood and not the one across the right side of his head.

She ripped away his shirt and saw the site of the bullet's entry, just a mite from his heart. Instinctively, she knew to stop the bleeding. She ripped off her apron, wadded it into a ball, and pressed the wound, hoping it would stem the flow of blood from his chest. She told herself the head wound was not as threatening so it could wait...at least the blood loss there seemed small by comparison. The bleeding at Mac's chest did not stop, so she pushed even harder. Mac groaned.

"Mac, can you hear me?" There was no response.

She knelt beside Mac, praying constantly. Roy worked as hard as two men, beating back the fire. The rag rug was dense, and therefore, very heavy. Yet, he swung it time and time against the stubborn flames. The smell of kerosene, burnt wool, and cotton filled the room as the rug scorched but blessedly did not burn. Both Roy and Laurel began to cough from the smoke-filled air in the room. After several minutes, the fire ebbed. Thankfully, the lamp, shattered after being struck by one of the gunshots, had only been half full of oil. The fire had not burned hot enough or long enough to ignite the logs around the fireplace. When he completely extinguished the fire, Roy dropped the badly burned rug and came to Laurel. "I think it's all out now, Ma."

Thomas came into the back door. "Laurel, are you all right?

Mac?"

"Please find me some more cloth. Mark's blanket on the armchair will do. This apron is soaked through." "Oh, my dear Father in Heaven! Is he still alive?"

"Yes, but I need help."

"The fire, Roy…Need help?"

"Granddaddy, the fire's out. It was mostly just the lamp oil."

Thomas noted the badly burned hands of the young man. "Rub those burns in butter, Roy. I'll help Laurel."

"Pa, Mac's hurt badly. Please go get Dr. Edwards. Ride Midnight and start calling out. They can't be too far yet. Hurry. I can't get this bleeding stopped." Thomas ran out, and Laurel again increased the pressure against Mac's chest, using the tiny baby blanket to scotch the flow of blood. "Roy, go bring me a blanket and a pillow from our room. Please hurry."

Roy ran, as quickly as his unsteady legs would carry him. He returned and covered Mac's still body and offered the pillow to Laurel. "Put it under his head and then get a clean cloth and try to remove that blood on his face so I can see how bad that wound is."

Roy returned quickly with two towels. He worked for a few minutes and removed the blood from Mac's face. "Mrs. Mac, this one ain't bleedin' at all. There is an opening here that goes up to his hair, but the blood seems stopped now."

Laurel handed Roy the small blanket, which was too bulky to do much good, and replaced it with the clean towel. She could do nothing more, so she prayed…one short prayer again and again. "Lord, spare my husband's life."

As time passed, seconds were as hours, and hours seemed to be days. Laurel continued to press the towel into the bloody wound, and she prayed. How long had it been since she'd heard those three shots ring out? How much blood can a man lose and still live? Will help come? "Lord, spare Mac. Please Lord, help me."

In the distance, Laurel heard the hoof beats of several horses. She heard her father-in-law call out to her. "I'm bringing the doctor, Laurel." The front door of the cabin was flung open and Laurel's uncle entered, followed immediately by Dr. Gibson and Al Stuart. Thomas MacLayne came in last, closing the door. His face reflected fear.

"Laurel Grace, are you shot?"

"No, Uncle…it's Mac. Dr. Gibson, please help him. Please don't let him die."

Matthew pulled Laurel to her feet and out of the doctor's way. Ed Gibson pulled the bloody towel away and ripped off the blood-soaked shirt. "Get me some hot water. Quick."

Al Stuart turned to the fireplace, looking for a kettle to push over the coals. He saw the fire-charred wall and the blackened fireplace. He took the poke iron and stirred the coals into a larger flame, added kindling to the small fire and several small split logs. As soon as he had a fire blazing, he pushed the spit with the black kettle over the flame.

"Roy, go out to the well and bring more water." Dr. Edwards ordered as he stooped to listen to Mac's heart with his long wooden stethoscope. He counted Mac's pulse. He looked up at Matthew and shook his head slightly. The wound was serious, and Mac had lost too much blood. He didn't want to say it, but he had little hope that any man could survive such injuries. "Help me carry him to the table. I've gotta get that bullet out if I'm gonna stop that bleeding." They carefully lifted Mac and laid him on the table.

"I need more light. Hurry, bring me some lanterns." Laurel rushed about the cabin and brought as many as she had. She took the remaining red crystal lamp Mac's mother had sent to him from the bureau in the bedroom although she knew its dim light would be of little help. As she set it near the table where Mac lay, she pointed to the last oil lamp on the table beside Mac's armchair. They raised the wicks, and together the four lamps provided light for Dr. Gibson to begin his exploration for the bullet.

As the doctor probed the bloody wound, Mac moaned and shifted away in pain. "Hold him still. Best I can tell, this bullet is near his heart."

"Can't you give him something for the pain, Doctor? He's suffering."

"Get that woman out of here." Matthew Campbell took Laurel in his arms and tried to lead her away.

"No. Stop. I'm not leaving him."

"We've got some scared kids out there to check on."

"Leave me be. Mac needs me more. I won't leave my husband."

"Then stand quiet and let the doctor do what has to be done."

"Mac needs some laudanum."

"He's lost too much blood for that. There it is. I think I can reach it without having to cut any more. Ed, hand me those forceps from my bag." The doctor worked for several more minutes and finally, he pulled the bullet from Mac's chest. With the extraction, Mac cried out in extreme pain, and the blood flow increased.
"Hold him down. He's not got enough blood left for all that exertion." The doctor again applied pressure to scotch the flow of blood. After what seemed hours, he removed the pads and carefully looked into the wound again. "I think I was able to extract that blasted thing without tearing the vein any further. Thank God, the bullet missed his heart by an inch or so." He continued to work for several more minutes, stitching the tissue to stop Mac from bleeding more. When he was sure that he'd done all he could for that wound, he turned his attention to the shot just above his right temple.

"There's no bullet here. Seems that a second shot must have grazed his head. Not much blood loss here." He washed the area thoroughly, shaved away an area of Mac's hair, and put three small stitches into his scalp. He finished by winding a bandage around Mac's head, much like the tight bandage he'd tied around his chest.

"Help me carry him to bed, men. I've done all I know to do. Careful. Don't jostle him around any more'n you have to." Matthew, Roy, Al Stuart, and Mac's father carried him to the tall bed. Before they could get there, Laurel had gone ahead and turned back the coverlet and arranged Mac's pillow as she did every night. "Laurel, put those pillows under his legs. Let his head lay flat on the bed." Dr. Gibson removed Mac's boots, and with Matt's help, they removed the bloody trousers.

"Doctor, will my son survive?"

"Mr. MacLayne, it's not in my hands now. We'll wait and see. Only God can provide the healing that is beyond my ability. I wish he'd not lost so much blood. If he can hold on…well, Laurel, you did the best thing that could be done."

"I'll bathe him. Y'all go make yourselves at home, and I'll be finished in a few minutes." Laurel cared for her husband, washing away all the tell-tale signs of the violent attack. She covered him with the yellow coverlet they slept under during warm weather. She bent and kissed his face. "Lord, watch over Patrick. Please, I need him."

She returned to the main room. "Thank you for saving him. Thank all of you for coming back to help."

"What happened here tonight?"

"I don't know for sure, Uncle Matthew. I went to the other room to feed Mark. When I heard the shots, I came back to chaos. We need to check on the other kids. Roy, will you go out to the barn and bring them into Cathy's room? After I see to the children,

I will need to return to Mac. He needs me there."

"Laurel, please sit down here a minute…Be aware…Mac lost considerable blood. I have no way to know how serious that head wound is. Mac may not be able to survive these wounds."

"Yes, Dr. Gibson, Mac will live. You stopped the bleeding. Thank you for saving his life."

She went to Cathy's room to comfort her children. Mark was frightened by the noise, by being taken away from his papa and mama, and the strangers in the house, but Andy was terrified. He witnessed every horror of the night. He saw his father rise at the first shot and come forward to push him to the floor out of harm's way. He cringed when the red crystal lantern on the mantle exploded from another gunshot. He witnessed his father stagger from the second shot, which had grazed his head. Andy felt the weight of his father's body when the final shot knocked Patrick MacLayne to the floor. He'd felt the sticky, warm blood from his father's chest wound and felt his own face was streaked with blood and tears that continued to fall. Laurel reached out to him and drew him into her arms. "Andy, Papa will be all right after a while. I need you to say a prayer for him. Will you do that?"

He looked up into her face and nodded. "I'll pray real hard for Papa."

"Cathy, will you let Annie and Andy stay here with you in your room tonight? I'll take Mark with me. I'm sure he'll want to be fed and his bath finished before I put him down for the night."

"Mama, ain't you scared for Papa? Ain't he hurt real bad?"

"Yes, Cathy. Your papa is hurt, but I'm not scared, and I don't want you and Andy to be scared either. Remember the Lord is taking care of your papa. In time, he'll be well again. Just remember to pray for him. We have to keep praying. If we will stay strong, our prayers will be answered."

Laurel believed all she told her children. She refused to allow any doubts that her husband would be well in time to enter her thoughts. She turned her mind to the tasks that had to be done. She remembered the softly spoken words that had come to her when she'd seen Mac lying in the pool of his blood. *Pull yourself together. You are needed here.* Then she noticed Annie sitting on the edge of Cathy's bed. Her right leg had been burned in the fire.
"Annie, come and let Dr. Gibson tend to that burn. I'll send Roy to tell your father what happened so they won't worry you're not home."

Laurel then took Mark and returned to Mac's side. She sat next to him in the tall bed. She leaned back against the headboard and nursed her sleepy son, and she sang a lullaby to him. When Mark fell asleep, she rose, gently washed his hands and face and tucked him into the cradle. She quickly returned to Mac's side and took his hand in hers. "Mac, dear, you've got to get busy and make your son a new bed. He'll not fit in that cradle in another month."

Her uncle Matthew opened the door. "Did you call someone, Laurel Grace?"

"No, Uncle Matthew, I was just talking to Mac. I'm fine and I'll call if I need something."

Laurel pushed her shoes off with her toe and moved closer, hoping Mac could feel her presence. She kissed his unresponsive hand and prayed. All night, she remained by his side, talking to him and brushing his hair back. She moved away only when Mark roused. Dr. Gibson came into the room frequently to look for renewed bleeding and to check Mac's pulse. He saw no change so he'd return to the front room. Laurel continued her vigil.

In the front room, the visitors sat and waited, talking in a low voice at times, and dozing as the night wore on. Roy returned after midnight from his trip to the Clark homestead. He brought Annie a change of clothes which he would give her the next morning.

"Is Mr. Mac all right, Doc?"

"No change that I can see, Roy. It's a miracle he's survived at all. Laurel saved his life by stopping the bleeding, but I don't know if he'll make it or not. He's not responded to anyone yet. That head wound may be more serious than it looks. If the bullet cracked the skull, there could be pressure building up. I just don't know what else I can do."

"Roy, what happened here tonight? Do you know who would shoot Mac?"

"Gee, Brother Matt, we didn't see no one. All I know …I heard three shots. There could've been more. The first one hit the lamp on the mantle. The glass just exploded and the coal oil spilled down the wall. The fire broke out. Annie's skirt caught fire. I got really scared when she screamed. I did hear a second and third shot, but I didn't know Mr. Mac got hit 'til Andy screamed."

"Did ya hear anything outside?"

"No, sir. Too much goin' on in here. Is Mrs. Mac okay? She takes things pretty hard, especially when her family is hurt."

"She's strong, Roy. I don't think I've ever seen her take charge in a crisis as she has tonight. She's tending to Mac and she's determined he will be well." Matthew Campbell responded.

"I think we need to pray for Papa. That's what he'd do for us."

"You're right, Roy. That's exactly what Mac would do."

Morning came, and no change had occurred with Mac. The doctor found no bleeding at either gunshot wound, but neither had the patient awakened from the coma. He feared that the bullet impact had caused a compression on the brain he had no way of seeing. A lack of response to voices and the excessive blood loss offered little hope for Mac's life. The doctor would wait--stay until he was called to another emergency.

Several of the women from the Shiloh community came to the homestead shortly after sunrise. Ellie Campbell and Susan were the first to arrive. They came into the kitchen and began to make a large breakfast for the congregatopm of men who sat watch through the night with the MacLayne family. Susan took charge of Mark while her mother Ellie and two other women began to clean the room where the incident had occurred. Ellie brought a pail of hot soapy water and tried to scrape away the blood from the walnut plank floor.

"Let me help, Aunt Ellie."

"Cathy, are you sure you want to do this?"

"Yes, ma'am. I want to help my mama anyway I can. She'll be busy takin' care of Papa until he is well."

"I'm sure you are right."

When the day had fully broken, Matthew Campbell and Al Stuart went out to see if any clue might remain to suggest who might have shot through the window. Al sent another man toward Jonesboro to search for the constable so they could report the shooting.

"Who would have done such a cowardly thing, Al?" "I'm not certain. I know of two men who are holding a grudge against Mac. Lemuel Flannigan threatened him more than once. I'd hate to think he'd do it, but then we know he's been drinkin' pretty heavy since Wednesday. Drunk men do stupid things."

"Who else could it be?"

"Robert Duncan. He's scoundrel enough to shoot an unarmed man through a window at night...in sight of his family! Flannigan told the judge that Duncan's been back in the area."

They continued to search the area outside the front of the cabin. They found two spent shell casings from a rifle, and some trampled grass, but nothing to tell them who had fired the gun. They went in to breakfast and to await the arrival of the constable.

W.T.E. Armstrong had held the position of Craighead County constable since the county was carved out during the twelfth legislative session in which Mac had served. He arrived at the MacLayne homestead shortly before noon. "I met MacLayne a time or two. Nice sort of fellow. Why'd anyone try to kill him?" "That's a question we'd all like answered, Armstrong. What are we goin' to do?"

"Well,, Brother Matthew, I've gotta gather up some facts so maybe I can ferret out the man who did this act. I need to talk to the family that was here."

"My niece is Mac's wife. She won't leave him, but she'll talk with you in there. Annie Clark and Roy Dunn were here and so were Mac and Laurel's children and his pa. Except for the baby, no one else was on the place."

"Brother Campbell, did anyone look about for horse tracks or anything else that could have been left behind?"

"We did, as soon as it was light enough to see. We only found two spent cartridges."

"Doctor, is the fellow gonna make it? Or are we tracking down a murderer?"

"It's in the Lord's hands now. I'd swore he'd not lasted this long. Mac's in a coma right now. He's not roused himself at all."

"Never mind. The culprit's got a head start. We need to get started. Let me talk with those two older kids first."

Constable Armstrong began questioning the family, but they were not able to tell him much. He went into the bedroom where he found Laurel sitting in a rocking chair pulled to the side of the bed. She held her sleeping son on her shoulder, and she held her husband's hand. She was talking to him as if he were awake and understanding what she said. "Mac, I'm goin' to have to sew you another shirt or two if you're going back to Little Rock this winter. I won't be there to keep your shirts washed up for you, so you'll need a couple more."

"Excuse me, Mrs. MacLayne. I need some answers. Can you take a few minutes to talk with me."

Laurel answered all the questions he asked, but she knew she'd added very little new information to help the constable of Craighead County. "Mr. Armstrong, I hope you can find the person who shot my husband. I would like to know why he would do something so senseless. I wish I could tell you something to help." "You can help. I need your permission to talk with the young'uns. Maybe they'll tell me something I haven't heard yet."

"If you bring them in here, so I can be with them, you can ask them whatever you need to know. Andy will be especially upset because he saw his father fall in front of him."

"Won't that disturb Mr. MacLayne?"

"No. I've been talking to him, and I'm gonna have the kids talk with him and read to him until he comes back to us."

Cathy wasn't able to tell the constable anything. She'd been in her room reading when she heard the shots. Andy stood next to Laurel's chair with his head low and tears in his eyes.

"Is my papa going to wake up soon, Mama?"

"I hope so, Andy. Just keep praying for him, like you said you would."

"I sure hope Jesus will listen to kids a-prayin'."

"He listens especially to the prayers of children. Remember those stories we read in the Bible?"

"Can I touch him, please?"

"Of course. See, he's breathin' fine."

"Son, did you see or hear anything last night when the shootin' happened?"

"I didn't see nothin'—Papa pushed me down before he staggered back. Then when he fell, I screamed for Mama. I didn't hear nothing after that."

"Think real hard, Andrew. Anything could help. Did you hear anything before the shootin'?"

"When I was settin' up the checkerboard, I heard something out by the rail fence. I looked out the window, but I didn't see nothin'. I just about forgot. I heard someone say somethin' like 'thievin' rogue…and about land or somethin' like that. I couldn't make it all out. I don't even know what a rogue is. I was gonna ask Mama. The talk sounded funny, talkin' different than us…I think he said 'me land.' I didn't think nothin' about it." "Andy, are you sure you heard someone with a strange accent?"

"Yes, Mama. I think I did, but maybe I didn't. The words were mushy like, and I was awful scared."

"I know you were." Laurel brushed a kiss on Andy's cheek. "Mr. Armstrong, we have a squatter family living on our property. On Monday, the judge ordered them to leave by the end of the month. I hate to think it, but Andy may have heard Lemuel Flannigan."

"No, Mama. Sean's papa wouldn't hurt my papa! Sean's one of my best friends at school."

Tears ran down Andy's face. Laurel reached out for the small boy and pulled him to her. "Shhh…Andy, don't think about this now. We'll talk about it later. Sean is still your friend."

"I'll do some checkin'. Your uncle told me about a man named Duncan who'd caused you some problems. Can you tell me about him?"

"Yes, I will in a few minutes. Cathy, you and Andy take Mark out to your Aunt Ellie. Ask her if she'll bathe him, please. I didn't get his bath for him last night." After the children were out of the room, she told the constable the whole ugly history of Robert Duncan.

By noon, the constable had left the homestead. Most of the men who'd come with Matt and the doctor had gone too, some to help the law and some to return to their own homes. Matt, Ellie, and Susan remained with Dr. Gibson, hoping Mac would awaken, but fearing they were sitting deathwatch. Dr. Gibson knew long periods of unconsciousness did not bode well for Mac. By midafternoon, he took Matthew out to the porch to talk.

"Matthew, as the time passes, I'm losin' more hope that Mac can recover. Even if he could survive the blood loss, I'm worried about the long time he's been unconscious. Could mean the head injury is bad. I don't know anything else to do to help.
Nothin' I ever learned taught me how to open a man's head, and even if I could, what would I be lookin' for? The bullet didn't go through."

"Ed, you've done the best you can."

"I think we should talk to Laurel and prepare her for the worst. She's thinkin' Mac will rise up out of that bed, good as new. I'm losin' hope he'll ever rise up again, and if he lives, will he be the same man?"

"Laurel has taken this much better than I expected."

"She's been calm all right, but she's in denial, just foolin' herself, thinkin' all this will pass?"

"I'll see if she'll let Thomas sit with his son for a while. If she'll do it, I'll bring her out here so we can talk with her. To tell ya the truth, I don't think anything we say will make the least bit of difference to her."

Laurel did consent to join her uncle and the doctor for a few minutes.

"Did you need to see me, Uncle Matthew? Is something wrong with one of the children?"

"Did you talk to Thomas, Laurel? How is he takin' all this?"

"We haven't spoken much. He was here when it happened...out in the barn. He'd stayed after the party."

"Laurel, as a doctor, I feel I have to tell you things don't look good for Mac. He's been unconscious nearly a whole day now, and he's not shown any sign of waking. I know you've been prayin' and talkin' to him, but he may not be able to survive these injuries. Of if he does, he may not be the same person he was. I'm worried about compression on the brain."

"Dr. Gibson, please don't tell me your fears and worries. I know you are just tryin' to prepare me, but I won't listen to any talk about losin' Patrick. He will be well again. He has more work to do. The Lord's not gonna to let him come home until he's finished with his work down here. Now excuse me. I need to get back to Mac. "

Before she returned to the bedroom, Laurel poured fresh water into a pitcher and picked up a clean cloth. She called Cathy and Andy who were sitting on the back porch and told them to do their evening chores. "I want you two to be ready to come read to your papa directly after supper. He always likes to hear y'all read to him.

She picked up Mark from the rug on the main room floor and returned to Mac's side. She laid the baby down next to his father, and then she sat next to her father-in-law. "Mac, I brought your son to visit for a while. Though for the looks of his sleepy little eyes, I'm thinkin' he'll be wantin' a nap, just like his papa." Laurel took the cloth and dipped it in the cool water and gently washed Mac's face, hands, and arms. She checked the bandages, which remained dry and clean. "You know, Mac, the work is piling up around here. You're gonna be mighty busy tryin' to catch up. Just saying, the longer you play the slug-a-bed, the more time it'll take you to catch up." Even though Mac didn't respond, Laurel continued to talk to him, asking questions that didn't get answers and telling stories that were not heard.

About sundown, Andy and Cathy came into the bedroom with their readers. Laurel asked Andy to read first. He picked out a fable from Aesop that told of a grasshopper and an ant. Andy picked that story because it was the first one Mac had read to him before he'd learned to read for himself.

"Ya know, Mama, that ant is a lot like Papa and you."

"You think we're like ants, Son?"

"Well, sorta. You work all spring and summer in the garden and in the fields, growin' food to put away for the winter. We ain't been hungry, not once since I been here goin' on two years." "Yeah, but Mama and Papa ain't stingy like that ant.

They're always sharin' what they got with folks that don't have."

"I know that, but that grasshopper ain't like the folks we know. He flittered his time away and wouldn't work. Our folks all work hard around Shiloh, don't they, Papa?" Andy looked up to see if his father would answer, but he got no response. "Mama,

Papa is hurt real bad, ain't he?"

"Yes, Andy."

"Is my papa gonna die?"

"No, Andy. Your papa loves us too much to leave us alone. You just keep prayin' for him. Cathy, please get your papa's Bible from the table and read scripture for us before bedtime."

"Yes, ma'am. What do you want me to read?"

"You can choose."

"Papa likes the Psalms. I'll read one." Cathy opened the well-worn book and found a yellowed crocheted lace cross. "This is pretty, but it's old. Is this yours, Mama?"

Thomas MacLayne answered Cathy. "No, darlin'. My Ann made that when Patrick was just a baby. She carried it in her Bible 'til the end of her days. She gave it to our son to bring home. He's kept it in his Bible since then. He said it reminded him to thank God for his good mother when he prayed every night."

Cathy handed the delicate cross to Thomas while she read. "The cross was by Psalm 30, so I'll read it tonight."

"Your papa will like that one. Read it aloud so we all can hear."

Cathy moved nearer the lamp and began to speak in a calm, sweet voice.

"Oh Lord, Thou hast brought up my soul from the grave! Thou hast kept me alive, that I should not go down to the pit.
Sing unto the Lord, O ye saints of His and give thanks at the remembrance of His holiness.
For His anger endureth but a moment. In His favor is life: Weeping may endureth for a night, but joy cometh in the morning.

"You read that so well, Cathy. Come over here to me, Andy...Cathy. Let's share our family prayer time like we do every night. Pa, will you pray for Patrick and our whole family?"

They all knelt around Mac's bed, and Thomas prayed for some time. When he finished, together they spoke the Lord's Prayer. Before he rose, though, Andy wanted to end the prayer.

"Jesus, I ain't always been a knowin' about you, but my papa says you're a good friend. Papa wouldn't tell me no lie, so please be my friend and get my papa well. We need him real bad, and especially me...I only had my papa a little while, and he's got a lot more for me to know. Amen."

Andy's words demolished the barricade that had kept Laurel's tears in check all day. She turned her back and, choking out her words, sent her children to bed. "Kids, say goodnight to your grandpa, and let's get ready for bed. Pa, please stay with him until I can get them down for the night." With her sleeve, she quickly wiped away the traces of the tears, picked up Mark Thomas from his grandfather's lap, and left the room.

φ

At midnight, Laurel returned to the main room to get cool water. Dr. Edwards warned her not to allow the fever to rise much. This would add another complication Mac's body would have to fight. As she neared the dry sink and her water pail, in the quiet of the night, Laurel heard muffled weeping from the loft. As much as she wanted to return to Mac, she feared one of the children had been awakened by a nightmare. She climbed the steps to the loft. Andy was sitting up against the headboard of the bed his father had made for him when he came to live with them. His dark head, covered with his arms, lay on his knees. He trembled and occasionally jerked violently in his attempt not to cry aloud and disturb his brothers, sleeping nearby.

"Andy, dear. Did you have a nightmare?"

"No, ma'am. I ain't been asleep." Another spasm jerked his small frame.

"Can you tell me why you can't go to sleep?"

"I guess I'm thinkin' about my papa. That's all." Laurel reached to the bureau and lit a single lamp. Mac's son turned his face to the wall. Laurel attempted to pull him into her arms. Her own fear had not allowed her to think about how the night's tragic events had impacted the children of their household. Her concern for Mac pushed her mothering instinct to the back of her mind.

"Andy, I'm sorry I forgot to check on you. Of course, you are worried about your papa. We will take extra good care of him. He's asleep right now, and the doctor says that is the best thing."

"He's gonna die, ain't he? Ever body I loved already did. I don't wanna be no orphan."

"Andy, your papa is alive. The doctor got the bullet out and stopped the bleeding. You saw him downstairs before you came to bed."

"He didn't talk to us. He's just a-layin' there, white as can be."

"Andrew…your papa will be well again. I believe that with all my heart. We prayed together, remember?"

"Maybe so, but I heard the doctor say Papa's heart ...."

"Please, darlin', don't give up on your papa. He needs your strength. He needs you to believe he will be well."

"I try but the ugly stuff keeps comin' in my head." Laurel pulled the small boy into her arms. He buried his face in her shawl and clasped his arms behind her back. His soft crying lasted for a few minutes, and then Laurel heard these nearly inaudible words, "Will you send me back to Tennessee when my papa dies?"

She was speechless. She pulled Andy to her so hard, he flinched at the embrace. She rocked him back and forth, and the tears that started at his prayer for his father at bedtime resumed in earnest. He raised his head and looked at her finally. The stormblue MacLayne eyes of Mac's son heightened her emotions and she cried even harder.

"Andy, my son, I'll never let you leave me. I love you. Do you not know that I love you?"

"You care about me 'cause you care about my papa. If he's gone, well...if he's gone..." Andy began to cry again.

"He's not going anywhere. God knows we need him here with us. Andy, you know we adopted you. We have written you and Cathy and Roy into our will."

"That's just legal stuff. Papa is my for real father, but not you...I know you are good to me, but I'm scared. I don't want to lose you too."

"I wish I could be your for real mother, too, but it didn't happen that way. Nothing can change how I feel about you. You are my son, Andy. As much as Mark Thomas is my son, you are that important to me. What can I do to make you know I'll never send you away?"

"If you say it, I'll try to believe it. I won't never have my birthday put down in our family Bible the way Papa's name is there and how he wrote in Mark's. I'll just have to believe you."

"Do you think that having those things in the Bible makes them more important?"

"'Course it does. Ever thing in the Bible is true. Brother Matthew told us that at church lots of times."

"Well, we can fix that right now, Andrew MacLayne. Let me go check on your papa, and I'll be right back." Laurel rushed down to her room where Mac seemed to be resting. She brushed her fingers across his forehead and detected a small fever, but not one so high that it brought fear. She picked up Mac's Bible from the bureau near his side of the bed and then opened the drawer beneath to get a pen and ink pot. She returned to Andy. She also picked up the Campbell Family Bible before she returned to the loft.

"Andy, I'm going to write your name in our Bibles. This is a serious occasion. A woman has never written in this book before." She wrote in her clear, steady hand:

Andrew Tollison MacLayne is the legally adopted son of Laurel MacLayne of Shiloh Community in Craighead County, Arkansas. He was born on April 25, 1853, in Davidson County, Tennessee. His mother was Dorinda Tollison and his father is Patrick MacLayne. He will always be the beloved son of Laurel Campbell MacLayne.

She then copied the exact notation in Mac's personal Bible. "Do you see now that you are officially adopted, Andy?"

"Yes, Mama. I'm in the Bible now, so I know it has to be true. Read it to me so I can go to sleep now. I'll dream about it and think about my papa getting well. And Mama, I didn't mean to make you cry. I love you."

Laurel read the words. Kissing his forehead, she pulled the sheet over his shoulders and extinguished the light. She continued to sit by his side until he slept. He, too, was healing from a serious wound.

CHAPTER ELEVEN

If ye shall ask anything in My name, I will do it. And I will
pray the Father shall send you another Comforter,
that He may abide with you forever.
John 14:14,16

*A*nd time continued to crawl by…one more hour…one more the days' demands. On Sunday, Matthew held Sunday worship at Shiloh church and led a prayer service for his friend. Ellie stayed to prepare meals and to relieve Laurel of the responsibility of her anxious children. Dr. Gibson was called back to Greensboro to deliver a baby. Thomas and Laurel sat, talking to Mac, spooning water and broth into his mouth when they were able, holding his hand, and continually praying for him to return to them.

day… another night. People came and went, taking care of

On Sunday night, Mac began to moan from pain. His sighs were low and long. When Laurel tried to wash his head with cool water, he moaned louder and seemed to wince.

"Pa, call my uncle Matthew in."

For a good part of an hour, Mac continued to cry out in pain, unaware of those around him but reacting to their touch. Laurel removed the bandages from his head. She saw his temple pulsing, and when she tried to clean the area around the wound, Mac brushed her hand away and groaned deeply.

"Laurel, does he know who you are?"

"I don't think so. He's in so much pain. Do you think it's a good sign?"

"I hope it is, but I should go get Dr. Gibson. I'll return as soon as I can."

"No, please stay here. I don't think the doctor can do anything we can't do."

For a time, Mac was quiet once again. He lay still and appeared to rest. Laurel lay down next to him with her hand on his arm so she'd wake if he roused up. She didn't plan to fall asleep, but her vigil and the high emotion of the past two days had left her drained. She fell asleep nearly as soon as her hand closed around Mac's.

Near sunrise, Mark Thomas awoke in his cradle and bawled for attention.

"Laurel, the baby's cryin'…" Laurel sat up instantly. The voice she'd heard, though weak and rasping was Mac's. "Wife…don't you hear Mark?"

"Yes, darlin'. Thank God, I hear him crying." She stood and walked to the right side of the bed. She looked into the storm blue eyes of her husband. The muted light of early morning was enough to allow her to see the recognition in his eyes. He had been spared and returned to her. "I knew you'd come back to us." She sank to her knees. "Thank you, Lord…"

"What happened?"

"I'll tell you…do you need anything?"

"Water…."

"I'll get some fresh water. Are you in pain?"

"Yes, my head aches…I'm so tired."

"Just rest. I'll bring you some water." Laurel hurried to the other room and called to her father-in-law and uncle. "He's awake. He heard the baby crying, and he woke up!"

"Thank the Lord. Now, I'm riding to bring the doctor back. He'll want to see this miracle."

Dr. Gibson did indeed proclaim he'd seen a miracle happen. "Mac, truthfully, I didn't think I'd ever talk to you again. Your wife and this community prayed you back to life, my friend."

"How long do you think I'll be laid up, Ed? I don't know why, but I've got a feelin' that I've got a hundred things to do around here that I've been neglectin'. Have I been down long?"

"Four days, but your friends and family have kept your chores done."

Mac struggled to keep his eyes open. His fatigue and pain were more than obvious to all in the room. "Still, I sense a burden that I've left too much undone."

Laurel smiled. She knew she'd said things like that to him often over those long days. Mac had heard her on some level.

"I don't know why, but I think someone was talking to me constantly. Do you think I could hear y'all when I was out?"

Doctor Gibson shook his head. "If not, it wasn't for the want of trying. Your wife talked to you and sang to you. She had your kids readin' to you and tellin' you about their days. She wouldn't let you go."

"He couldn't. Patrick still has work to do right here. Our baby can't sleep in a cradle forever."

Dr. Gibson still didn't know if Mac would recover completely. He knew that it would take weeks for his body to replace the blood he'd lost. He knew Mac would be lucky to regain most of his strength by harvest time. He gave Laurel a tonic made of yellowroot, a golden elixir, and cherry bark for Mac to take morning and night. The tonic seemed to help build blood for some people. He also directed her to feed Mac beef broth until he was able to keep down solid foods, and then feed him red meat, especially calf liver, several times a week. As he was about to leave, he took Laurel by the arm and directed her out to the front porch.

"Laurel, you'll see some improvement within a few days, but Mac will be weak for some time. One of our hardest chores will be keepin' him from overdoin'. If he is to return to his former strength and energy, he has to rest. No strenuous labor until I tell him. I know I seemed to be a doomsayer since this happened, but I have to warn you…when a person has lost as much blood as Mac did, the heart has to work too hard. Most people develop heart problems. I know Mac, and he'll be a hard man to keep down. Too much hard work too soon could bring on severe heart damage. If you want him to live to a ripe old age, you have to keep him an invalid for some time." Before he'd finished, the door opened.

"What are you tellin' her, Ed? Is there a problem with my son?"

"Tom, we have to make sure he doesn't work for some time. He's got to have rest and time to rebuild his lost blood and regain his vitality."

"I'll see to it. I'll bring in a couple more tenant farmers to take over the work around here."

"That'd be best, Tom."

"Good for us all. I've got my eye on another fifty acres of swampy land over near my place on Big Creek. I'll have to hire more help to build levees and ditches so we can drain the land anyway. I'll just get 'em a little early."

"Mac can help with the plannin' and accountin' when he feels up to it. That'll keep him occupied, but Laurel, no physical exertion for some time. I'll tell you when he's sound enough to be up and around."

"I'll do what I must."

"Laurel, that means no romancing, too." Red blotches rose to Laurel's cheeks as she left the porch and returned to Mac's side. ∮

The doctor was right. Mac did not take easily to life as an invalid. He was restless and anxious about things he felt he was neglecting. The first week after he awoke, he got out of bed for only a few minutes at a time. He leaned on Laurel or his father, and at times Roy for support simply to walk to a chair and back. He slept a good deal of the time, mostly from fatigue, but partly from boredom. He was not used to the inactivity. He had frequent visitors, but people were busy with late spring chores and life at their own homesteads, so those visits were brief and slacked considerably as time passed. Laurel made the children return to school the second day after he'd awakened, so even their banter and play was missing. The MacLayne cabin was too quiet.

"Hang it all, Laurel. There must be something I can do around here. I'll lose my mind in sheer boredom without something to occupy my time. It's been nearly two weeks of lying here in this bed. I'm never gonna have any strength if all I do is lie here and turn into a vegetable of some kind."

"Patrick MacLayne, you will do what the doctor tells you. I don't plan to spend my golden years toting you around because you are too stubborn to listen to sound advice."

"I know what Ed said about building back my blood, but I'm sure I can at least get out and walk on the porch. How strenuous is that?"

"When he comes back, we'll ask him."

"And I'm darn tired of sleeping alone? When did you decide that you could sleep with Cathy? I've told you since the time we met I don't believe in separate marriage beds."

"I just thought you'd rest better. We'll ask the doctor about that too."

"Did Ed tell you not to sleep with me?"

"Not in so many words. Are you hungry?"

"Don't try to change the subject. Whether I sleep with my wife is none of his business."

"I don't think it was the sleeping he's concerned with. Now quit complaining. You're getting better every day. If you weren't, you wouldn't be so cranky. Do you want something to read?" "Only if I can get up and sit in a chair for a while. Nosy doctor, telling my wife to leave my bed! Wait 'til I get a chance to give him a piece of my mind."

Within the week, two things helped to make the time pass a bit more normally. Mac's father came to him with a proposition. Thomas wanted to sponsor several more tenant farmers in the area. Mac liked the idea of being able to help hard-working people get a foothold on building a home of their own. He also knew he could work on many of the details while he was restricted to the cabin. The second matter came from frequent visits from Constable Armstrong. The Craighead county lawman had begun looking for the gunman the second day after the attack. He told Mac and Laurel he'd sent word to Gainesville to inquire about

Robert Duncan. He said the messenger should return by the week's end. He also reported that Lemuel Flannigan had not been back at the camp where his family waited. Watchmen had been posted around the area, thinking to arrest Flannigan when he returned for his family.

Mac's first question came. "Are the Flannigan children still in school? Do you know if they've food enough?"

"The kids have been at the wagon the two times I was there. Mrs. Flannigan had stew over a fire. I think they've had a few early vegetables, some onions, and a few carrots. They got a pretty nice little garden growing over there. Not big, but the plants are growing strong."

"I can't imagine he's deserted his family."

"I'm not sure the woman is tellin' us the whole truth. He ain't been there since we visited, but I think she might know more than she's sayin'. We aim to watch 'em."

By the end of the second week, Mac was able to walk to his chair in the main room without help and sit up for more than an hour. During his time in the main pen, he could spend time with his family. He was able to sit back in his armchair and enjoy holding his son.

Mark had reached his seventh month, and he was an active, lively baby. He didn't want to sit and be held for long periods of time. He wanted to pull up and crawl and roll around in the floor to play. Before twenty minutes passed, Mac found it necessary to return Mark to Laurel. Not only was his energy gone, but the fatigue brought on excruciating pain in his head.

"Laurel, please come take Mark Thomas."

"Patrick, are you all right?"

"Ahhh—the pain's...." Mac could go no further. He pressed both his hands against his temples, rocking back and forth. "Laurel, the light is too bright. Help me lie down." She put the baby on the floor and supported Mac as he stumbled his way back to the bedroom. "Please close those curtains..."

"What can I do?"

"Let me be... in the dark. Please don't make noise...don't talk to me."

Mark Thomas began to wail in the other room. " Please, get him quiet!"

She rushed to pick him up, began to rock him and whisper calm words, trying to quiet the little one. Even from the other room, Laurel could hear her husband groan.

Dr. Gibson came about dawn the next morning at Laurel's calling. Concerned about the return of the severe headache, she'd sent her father-in-law the previous evening to bring some help.

The doctor was bewildered when he saw Mac because he found no reason for the onset of the pain when his patient appeared to have overcome the head wound. "Laurel, I don't know what to tell you. I can't see anything to have caused this relapse. The surface wound has healed. Of course, I can't see what's happenin' on the inside."

"Can't you help him with the pain?"

"Only the remedies you know about. I could give you some laudanum for the worst times, but with Mac still bein' so weak, I don't like to use such a strong drug. I haven't even been thinkin' about the head wound. Frankly, I've been more concerned that Mac's heart may have been damaged by the stress caused by the blood loss."

"If he could sleep when the pain comes, he wouldn't suffer so."

"You know a cup of strong boneset tea or chamomile will help him rest. There is a kind of headache some people have, but I don't think that's Mac's problem. I believe he's just havin' healing pangs right now. You have to be patient with him. Put cool cloths on his forehead and block out the light. He'll heal in time."

That long, chaotic time didn't seem to be a path to wellness. Mac's strength was slow to return and his bouts with the headaches were frequent, usually every three days or so. Mark Thomas was teething, so naturally, he was cranky and cried easily and often. Andy and Cathy came home nearly every day needing help with schoolwork, and Laurel's workload had been increased by the supervision of John Campbell and the two tenant farmers her father-in-law had recruited to take over Mac's work at the homestead.

The garden was at a stage where almost daily, Laurel had to spend two or three hours making sure her family would have ample food for the winter ahead. Because they'd increased the vegetable plots, along with the corn, oats and wheat parcels, Laurel seemed to be outside more than she was inside most days. Frequent afternoon showers encouraged a huge harvest that year, much more than Laurel needed to can, yet she continued to fill the larder and the stash that Mac had insisted they supply. One blessing came with the rain, though. The orchard and grape vines didn't have to be watered every day. By nightfall, she was exhausted and ready to fall into bed.

She found little comfort in the nights because she missed the intimacy she'd shared with her mate in their private time. Dr. Gibson allowed her to return to the four-poster at Mac's request for her company. Of course, it came with the promise that their lovemaking would wait for several more weeks. With Mac in pain many nights, he didn't even hold her. Because the teas for the headaches made him drowsy, they found little time for private talks. The sharing between them had all but disappeared, and because of the increased demand on her time, Laurel wanted to be able to share those concerns with her life mate. Yet, at the end of the day, more often than not, she felt alone and helpless as she lay beside her unconscious husband.

In those times she prayed…asking for Mac's healing and a return to health, thanking God He'd spared Mac's life, and pleading for the strength to go on. She realized in those times that despite her fatigue and loneliness, she had not fallen into despair.

She'd never lost hope in Mac's complete recovery and their return to the life they'd known before that terrifying night had nearly taken her life mate away.

Laurel surprised herself. When she looked back on the other times of tragedy in her life, she'd always fallen to pieces and became dependent on her family and Mac. Her father had supported her and sheltered her when her mother and sister died, and he'd protected her when she'd been attacked by the boys from Hawthorn school. He'd allowed her to withdraw from the hard things life had dealt her.

Mac had stepped into that role when her pa had died and when Rachel was killed. He tried to step between her and Robert Duncan when he'd attacked her at the campaign rally, but Mac had not let her escape. He helped her to know grace.

Now she stood on her own accord. She had finally grown up to know she'd never have to deal with life's difficulties alone, not as long as she chose grace. Her strength, engendered by love undoubtedly…her family's, Mac's, but most of all, the indwelling of the Holy Spirit had sustained her in a way she'd never known before. "Thank you, Father. I like this new feeling of confidence and security. You promised never to leave me alone, and I know I have experienced your presence in this hard time. I am so grateful."

She was uplifted with a sense of peace. Mac was not well, and he may never be totally well again. If the worst happened, she'd still not have to face the problem alone. She was tired, but the fatigue could be erased with a good's night sleep. She lay her Bible on the side table and lay her head back on her pillow. She reached across and laid her open palm on the chest of her sleeping husband. The words of Romans 8:28 ran through her mind. That night she slept.

CHAPTER TWELVE

*But whoso hath this world's good and seeth his brother have need,
and shutteth up his bowels of compassion from him, how dwelleth
the love of*
*God in him? My little children, let us not love in word, neither in
tongue,*
but in deed and truth.
1 John 3: 17-18

Several days later, Laurel awoke to an angry gray sky streaked with storm clouds, ominously dark. The summit of the ridge was barely visible. Before the kids could get dressed and eat breakfast, the winds started howling and lightning slashed its way across the sky in powerful bolts, careening down toward the ground. The rain fell, not in drizzles, but in sheets of water. Laurel rushed out the back door and pulled the shutters over the windows. Cathy and Roy followed her lead with the windows sheltered by the front porch. Mark shrieked out in fear when the thunder cracked outside.

After shuttering the windows, the MacLayne's were soaked through to their skin. "Kids, go and change to dry clothes. You'll not go to school today. This storm looks to be a bad one, and I don't want you away from home on a day like this." "Laurel," Mac called from the bedroom.

"I'm comin', Mac." She stopped long enough to pick up her frightened son. He snuggled his face into her collarbone and clasped his tiny hands into her hair. "It's all right, sweet baby.
Mama and Papa are here to keep you safe. Let's go see what your papa needs."

"Laurel…the storm…"

"Rest, darlin'. We've shuttered the cabin. Morning chores were done just before the worst of the wind came up."

"Help me get up and get dressed. The wind sounds pretty strong. We may be in for more than a thunderstorm."

"Mac, there is no need for you to exert yourself."

"I said I'm getting up."

Mac pulled on his clothes and with a little help, he walked into the front room. Mac was determined to stay up that day. He wouldn't stay in bed if his family was in danger, even if it killed him. If he couldn't put up shutters, the least he could do was to encourage his children and play with his infant son to relieve Laurel of some of her responsibilities. When had she become so capable? She'd taken control of things that in the past would have devastated her, or would it? So many things about his woman, he didn't know. He would make himself of some use. Laurel still needed him around, didn't she?

"Andy, bring us a book, son." He'd ask Andy and Cathy to come read for a time, as the wind continued to bluster outside.

"Papa, what's that whistlin' noise outside?" Andy dropped the book from his lap.

"Laurel, come over here, quick." Mac hollered out to his wife. She rushed in from Cathy's room where she had been trying to bathe Mark. "Cathy, take that baby. You, Andy, and Mark get into the stash under your bed. Now."

"What is wrong, Patrick?"

"Nothin' maybe. As soon as you help the kids get into the stash, let's go out onto the porch and see what's happenin' with those storm clouds. Hurry!"

As Laurel helped the children move the bed covering the door to the hidden cellar, Mac went to the front porch. He gasped at the heat from the howling wind, almost as if he had breathed in air too close to a blazing campfire. Beyond the borders of his land, he saw the building storm clouds, shelves of them, each somewhat blacker, more hostile looking than the one above it. Near the horizon, the threat appeared to lie on the ground. Nearer, whirling eddies of black and gray swooped down for a moment and then jerked their spinning tales back into the ominous clouds above, where they would disappear momentarily only to fall down again.

As the cloud bank approached Crowley's Ridge, the entire structure took an upward turn and mocked the shape of the landscape as it pushed east and north.

Laurel joined him. "What do you think, Mac? Is this a tornado?"

"I'm not sure, we'll see one here, but that is a huge storm system. The ridge may be our saving grace. I've been watching and it seems just as the funnels are about to develop, the wind pushes them into the ridge, and they are blocked. Could be the land we bought may have its own built-in tornado protection."

"Praise the Lord! What about the rest of Shiloh?"

"I guess we'll wait and see. Let's go out to the back and see how it looks out there." About the time they opened the back door of the cabin, the rain became much stronger. "My goodness, I can't believe the difference in the temperature out here. In the front, it felt like a baking day in August. It's almost chilly out here. We must be in the middle of the storm. Pouring down rain on this side and cool and still and hot in the front. Strangest thing!"

"I think I can deal with strange if we don't have to live through a tornado. Should I let the kids come up yet?"

"No, I'm not sure this thing is over yet. Let's watch a while longer, but I do need to sit down now. Let's go back to the front room and watch through the front door to see how things play out." Within half an hour, the threats of tornadoes at the MacLayne homestead diminished. Laurel went to the door of the stash and called for the kids to come out. Cathy handed Mark up, and then she and Andy made a beeline to the front door to see if anything had happened while they were stowed away in safety below her bedroom. Except for small branches, many leaves blown from the trees, and a downed bird's nest, they found nothing out of order.

"Golly, all that sittin' was fer nothin'," Andy complained.

"And aren't we all grateful?" remarked Laurel to the boy. "I hope the same is true of the rest of the area. Tornadoes can cause a lot of serious damage and even kill people."

"I know. I wasn't thinkin' about that."

"Papa, can we play dominoes until the rain stops?" Cathy asked.

"I don't know if we can play that long, but we'll play a game or two." Mac winked at Laurel. "Maybe your mama can even join us when she finishes fixing lunch." Mac put up a valiant effort, trying to entertain Andy and Cathy while he joggled Mark on his knee. But the storm did little to help. Every loud clap of thunder or extraordinarily bright flash of lightning turned Mark into a scampering, thrashing imp, doing everything in his power to hide from the intrusion into his safe, tranquil world. Laurel was in the kitchen, and while he could see her plainly, his papa held him in his grip. The fight between Mac and his son began to take its toll. Unfortunately, Mark Thomas appeared to be winning.

By mid-afternoon, Mac had exerted the last of his energy wrestling with his son. With his fatigue came the onset of another headache. Exertion was the usual trigger, or at least that is what he told himself.

"Cathy, please come take Mark. See if you can feed him something. Laurel, I'd determined I'd stay up today, but I can't. I hate to ask you when you're so busy, but will you help me into the bedroom? I've got to lie down for a while."

"That's no bother, Mac. Kids, go ahead and have your dinner. It's ready there on the dry sink." Laurel laid her hand on Mac's forehead, hoping to find no fever. Instead, she felt her husband jerk away and heard him groan. Such a slight touch had brought pain. "Here, lean on my shoulder. A nap will do you good."

Once inside the privacy of their room, Mac turned to Laurel. He saw how tired she was. He saw also the concern in her eyes, and he knew he was the source of the worry.

"I'm useless. Laurel, I never wanted you to have to carry the weight of this family alone."

"Patrick, you are too hard on yourself."

"Look at you. You can't go on doing this by yourself."

"Hush! A few weeks ago, I believed I was going to be a widow. If you are never able to work again, as you did before…" "I'd want to die. What kind of man would I be letting you carry this family? I can't let you shoulder every task here on the homestead, even mine. I tried to take care of a toddler for a couple of hours and even that wore me out. I'm no good for you. Truth be known, I am part of the burden."

"Don't you ever say those words to me again! As long as you are here with me and as long as you love me, I have all I need. Why do you think I prayed so hard, night and day for the Lord to spare you? Mac, everyone thought you couldn't live, even Dr. Gibson and Uncle Matthew. I know God let you stay with me because I'm not strong enough yet to stand on my own."

"Laurel, if I'm to be an invalid, never regaining my strength, I'm just another mill stone for you to carry. I wanted to stay up today. I told myself that at least I could help with the kids. I couldn't even sit in a chair and hold Mark."

"You were up two hours longer today than yesterday. You gave me time to wash dishes, knead bread, mend one of Cathy's skirts, and sit down to rest for nearly fifteen minutes while the kids read to us. Your presence comforted all the children. They weren't afraid of the storm with their papa nearby."

"And you did all the mornin' chores, told the hands what they needed to do today, and laid out feed for the horses, mules, and hogs. Then you milked the cows. Those are things I'm supposed to do."

"And you will soon. You know the doctor said a person who lost half the amount of blood you lost would need four to six weeks to feel his strength return to normal. You have to give yourself time."

"I heard him. That does nothin' to change the fact that you are burdened with my work."

"Patrick, your father is helping. Matthew and Ellie are helping. The tenant farmers and John are doing a good job takin' care of the stock. We will be all right until you are well again."

"You're becoming a strong woman. My dearest life mate, where did you find the courage and energy to carry this load?" Laurel sat on the bed and embraced her husband.

"Right here, my love. You tore away my fear and destroyed the walls that held the world away from me. You led me to find my worth and my faith. You taught me to love and how to be loved. Through watching you, I learned how to rely on the Lord. You showed me grace, Patrick. If you hadn't loved me, I'd never have been able to know how the Lord loves me. Remember…Romans 8:28."

"I don't deserve you. I needed to hear the things you said to me. I'll rest. I will regain my strength because I need to be the man you fell in love with. I guess I'd forgotten to claim grace."

"You sleep now. I may need you up again to help with the kids if the storm gets worse." She drew a light coverlet over him and walked toward the door.

"Laurel Grace. I love you. I have no want to leave you ever."

"I know. Rest now."

Heavy rain and strong winds continued most of the day. Just about dark, the downpour slackened to a light drizzle. The dense cloud cover brought the dark early that night. Laurel knew this was the opportunity she needed to return to the barn to milk, gather eggs, and settle the stock for the night.

"Cathy, you and Andy watch Mark for me, and go ahead and put those bread pans in to bake. I'll help you finish supper when I get back." When Laurel got to the barn, she saw some things were not as she'd left them that morning. The door was closed, but the latch had not been set. Her milk pail was missing from the peg by the milking stall. She didn't remember carrying in both pails that morning. Her nerves sent a shiver down her back. Had the shooter returned to hurt them again? Was Robert Duncan back to bring her more nightmares? She lifted the lantern higher, hoping to see farther into the dark barn. She saw no one but did notice that straw had been moved into a heap in the corner farthest from the door.

"Is anyone here?" Silence was the only answer. "If someone is here, make yourself known or I'll scream." She heard a slight whimper. "Who's there?"

Out of the dark corner, Peggy Flannigan walked, holding the shoulder of her youngest son, Sean. "I'll be a sayin' I'm sorry for comin' here. I didn't know this is yer place."

"Mrs. Flannigan, what are you doin' here, out in such weather?"

"I had to find a shelter for my babes. The wind took the canvas off our wagon. Couldn't stay there with no cover, so we just started walkin', lookin' for any place to git in out of the storm. This barn was the first place we found. I didn't know this place belonged to y'all."

"Of course, you had to shelter."

"I took some milk, too. My young'uns ain't ate since before the storm broke. I'll try to find some way to pay fer what I took." "Don't mind that. We'd have shared it with y'all anyway. Come into the house and have supper. We will eat in a short while."

166

"No, ma'am. We can't do that. I know you think my Lem was who shot your man."

"Be that as it may, your children are hungry." "Ma'am, I don't know if he did it or not. Lem's a good man—works hard to take care of us, but when he comes to his cups, he does things that he'd not do if he'd not been a-drinkin'." "Mrs. Flannigan, let's just forget about all that right now. Tonight, you are just a neighbor who needs help in a storm. Come on, kids. Let's hurry. We need to get inside before the rain picks up again." Laurel led the family into the main room of the cabin and asked them to sit down.

"Hey, Sean. I'm sure happy to see ya! Golly, what a storm! Don't ya think?"

"Hey, Andy."

"Mrs. Flannigan, please make yourself at home. I've got to finish my chores, and then I'll be back and get supper ready. Cathy, how's the bread?"

"Not done yet, Mama, but it will be before long."

When Laurel returned, she found the Flannigan family sitting close together on the hearth. The room was silent, and the tension was strained. Mac had made his way from the bed to his chair. Seeing his poor state frightened Peggy Flannigan. She'd been told Patrick MacLayne had been wounded, but she couldn't believe the man who sat in front of her was the same strong, virile man she'd met at their camp.

"Mac, did you come in by yourself?"

"Yes, with a little help from Andy."

"We have visitors, dear."

"I see. How did they come to be out in this weather?"

"Looking for shelter. The storm took the canvas from their wagon."

Mac looked to the woman at his hearth. "It's good you came here to find shelter."

"They were in the barn. I brought them in to eat and dry their clothes. Are you ready to eat supper with us at the table tonight?"

"I think I can. Seems some of my strength came back while I napped. I'd like to stay up a while. My head has eased considerably."

"Thank the Lord."

Shortly, Laurel and Cathy laid out an abundance of food. Laurel knew the Flannigans had lived on rations too small to really sate the hunger of growing children.

Mac offered a blessing over the food, "Lord, thank You that this house knows no hunger, and You've given us a sturdy shelter from the storm. Thank You for our neighbors who share Your blessings with us this night. Bless the food before us and let it nourish us so we may serve You better."

Then the hungry children ate-- until every morsel was gone from the pewter plates. Mrs. Flannigan, however, ate sparingly, even though the table held plenty for all.

"Mrs. Flannigan, please eat your fill. There is ample food for us all."

The tired looking, bedraggled woman looked up into the storm blue eyes of the man who'd just spoken to her. She looked at the three-inch jagged scar on his forehead and lowered her head. After some time, she turned her gaze to Laurel and then back to Mac. Her face could have been carved in stone. "Why're ya doin' this?"

"Have we done something to offend you?" Mac asked. "You know what I'm sayin'. You prayed over us like we's friends. Ya take us in your house, and put a feast in front of us. Why ya doin' this?"

Mac laid his fork back on the table. He looked into the rigid, cold face across from him. "Mrs. Flannigan, we do this every night we are able. We sit together at our supper table with our family and ask the Lord to bless the food. We eat until we aren't hungry, and then we spend family time together. When we have company, we share what the Lord has given us."

"Why with us?"

"Because our Lord told us to love our neighbors as ourselves. Please eat your fill."

"You weren't so big on sharin' when you took us before that judge of yours. We only wanted what we'd paid for."

Laurel looked toward Mac. She feared he was not strong enough to deal with Peggy Flannigan's anger. He was calm.

"We wanted to help y'all. We would have worked out a settlement if your husband had let us. Just that piece of land was not something we could share. Our son is buried there. The very place you wanted to build is the place where he rests. That fifty acres is surrounded by our land, but nevertheless, God doesn't allow us to make judgments. He told us to take care of those in need. We'll be blessed if you will share our supper tonight, here around our table. We'll worry about tomorrow's trouble, tomorrow."

"You think my man shot you?"

"I'm not sure, but the constable is the one who will deal with that. It's not my place."

"I don't understand, but for the sake of my babes, I thank you for the meal. It's been a spell since we sat down to a meal as good as this one."

"Well, let's eat. My wife's a fine cook." Peggy began to eat, and after a while, she cleaned her plate. She even took a second piece of bread Cathy offered her. Paddy, Maureen, and Sean looked up sheepishly at their mother when Laurel offered seconds. Hesitantly, she nodded her approval. They ate their fill, each thanking Laurel and praising her fine cooking.

"My mama lays a nice meal. Sometimes we even get sweets, but not usually on bread bakin' day."

"My ma cooks fine too, but it's hard to cook over an open fire. She doesn't let us go without when she can help it."

"Hush up, Sean. That's not talk to share."

"Yes, ma'am."

"I"ll be washin' these dishes if you'll allow." Peggy Flannigan rose and began removing the dishes.

"I'd be glad for the help, but we can do the work together." Laurel replied.

The tempest outside the sturdy cabin walls erupted again about eight o'clock. The wind was stronger than it had been all day. The rain came intermittently, first in light drizzles, which increased to steady rainfall. For short periods, the rain would fall in torrents, and then it would ebb only to return again and again.

"We should make our leave the next time the storm eases. Thank you for supper and for the shelter. I'm a-thinkin' we intruded long enough.

"You're very welcome, and you don't need to go out tonight."

"Would you let us shelter in your barn for the night? We'll go at sunrise."

Laurel answered, "No, Mrs. Flannigan. The barn is for animals. Visitors stay in the house. We have a nice dry loft where our kids slept until we could add on another room for Cathy. I'll send all the boys up there to sleep on pallets. You and Maureen can share Cathy's room in here. Cathy, bring your nightdress, and you can sleep in our room. Come, sweetheart, and help me gather some night clothes for everyone."

"Hoo-ray!!! I've wanted Sean over to spend the night, and now it'll be just like when Roy was home. Fellas in the loft. How fun is this!" Even in the howling storm, Andy's enthusiasm at the thought of his friend spending the night bubbled over. "Come on. Let's go up, Sean."

The two boys made their way up the ladder to the loft, although Sean lagged behind Andy by several steps. "Come on, Sean."

"Is this your room?"

"Yep. Did belong to me and my big brother, Roy, but now he's moved back to his own homestead. Now it's just for me."

"Jeepers! I never knew a kid that had his own room before."

"It's just a loft. Cathy's got her own room down by the fireplace, but I don't care. I like it better up here." Andy sat crosslegged on the floor and pointed to the extra bunk for Sean. "Go ahead and set yerself down. I don't usually plop on the bunks because then I have to make'em up. Mama don't like it when I'm too sloppy."

Sean sat with his back against the cot that had belonged to Roy. "Do you think this storm is 'bout over? That wind this mornin' all but blew our wagon to pieces. Don't know where we are gonna stay now. I sure wish my papa could come home." Sean dropped his head and turned his head, so he didn't have to look into Andy's face. "I'm sorry about your papa, Andy."

"That ain't none of your fault, Sean. Why ain't ya been comin' to school this past week? Mr. Tucker said y'all are gettin' sorta far behind."

"Ma said we didn't have to go for a while."

"But why not?"

" 'Cos of what the kids been sayin' about Pa."

"What have they been sayin'?"

"You know. They called me a killer's son. My pa didn't kill no one."

"What in tarnation are ya talkin' about, Sean? I didn't hear nothin' about that."

"Sure, you had to. They all talked about my pa shootin' your pa."

"Nah...your pa didn't do that."

"All the kids said it. They told me the law is tryin' to find him so they can hang him."

"That's gotta be wrong. My papa didn't tell me that. I know someone shot him from outside our window, but we don't know who did it."

"The kids said you told the sheriff that my pa did it. That is why I was surprised you been treatin' me so nice since your ma found us in the barn."

"I never did no such thing. When the sheriff asked me about that night, I told him I heard someone who talked like your pa outside. I know your pa would never hurt my papa. He knows we're best friends." "Then why did he run away and leave us alone?" Sean laid his head on his arms.

Andy sat beside his friend. Shoulders tensed and eyes upward, he spoke. "I'm gonna ask my papa about all this. He'll tell me. Papa never lies to me about nothin'."

Andy dashed down the loft stairs and made a bee-line across the crowded room to his father's armchair. He attempted to throw his arms around his father's neck, but Mac still held the sleeping Mark Thomas in his arms. "Careful, Andy boy. Don't wake your brother."

"Papa, did Sean's pa try to kill you?" His blurted words resounded throughout the cabin. Mrs. Flannigan's countenance blanched to a ghostly gray-white.

"Andy. This is not the time or place for such a question." Laurel approached Mac. "Here, give me Mark."

Mac stood tentatively, handed the sleeping toddler to his wife, and bent to lay his hand on his older son's shoulder. He turned the boy to look him directly in the face. "Andy, you owe Mrs. Flannigan an apology for your outburst. I think you must have forgotten she's our guest."

"But Sean said…"

"Andy, I said it's not the time or place to discuss this. We'll discuss this another time. Now make your amends to our company."

"Pa…"

"Andrew. You will mind what I told you."

"Yes, sir. I didn't mean no disrespect to you, Mrs. Flannigan. I am sorry. I wouldn't want you mad at me. Sean is my best friend."

"Say your goodnights and get to bed. We'll talk tomorrow."

"Yes, Sir." Andy turned his back and slowly climbed to the loft, much more thoughtfully than he'd come down. At the third step, he turned to look at his father. His eyes downcast and sparkling with unshed tears. Disappointing his father had not been his goal.

In the loft, Sean was already in the cot Andy had pointed out to him. His blanket nearly covered his head, even in the hot steamy night. Slowly and methodically, Andy removed his clothes and slipped under his sheet. As he extinguished his lamp, he heard his best friend say, "Andy, I don't want it to be so. I don't want to know my pa tried to hurt yours. I don't want no killer for a pa." ⌀

At the close of the tense evening, the eeriness of the storm seemed the appropriate backdrop for Mac's mood. The noise of the thunder and bright flashes of lightning glaring in the windows caused Mark Thomas to whimper now and again. He would only be comforted in the arms of one of his parents. Mac held the boy as Laurel tried to close the house down for the night, but only at a great cost to himself. Once again, he sat in agony from the pain in his head. His temple throbbed, and the light from the lanterns and the noise from the crowd in his cabin ripped at the center of his brain.

"Laurel, please help me to bed." When she saw the grimace on his face, Laurel's fear arose again. For a brief moment, her control faltered—the weak helpless Laurel wanted to run away. Then she remembered the scene in that very room on that horrible night. Again, she heard those words that had allowed her to act. *Calm yourself. You are needed here.* The words were as clear as if someone had spoken them.

"I'll be there in a minute, Patrick." Before she could help him to his feet, they heard a loud rap on the front door."

"My Lord, who'd be out in this storm?"

"Rest here a minute. I'll get the door."

Allowing Mac a minute to return to his chair, she hurried to open the door. Her uncle Matthew and Constable Armstrong stood on the porch with a third man she didn't know. Water ran in streams from their hats and down the oilcloth coats they wore. She had to brace the door with her shoulder to prevent the wind from pulling it from her hand. "Come in out of this storm, Uncle Matthew."

"Brother, what are you doin' out tonight?" Mac called over the shrieking wind.

"Trying to take care of the flock, Mac. Been a sad night at Shiloh."

Mac leaned his head back against the high back of the wellworn armchair. "What's the trouble?"

"Mac, are you all right?"

"No, Matthew. I'm about as useless as a man can be. Tell me what's happened. Is our family all right?"

"Yes, we're fine, but there's been a tornado in the midst of this storm. A lot of damage near the Stephensons' farm. One of our families lost their cabin. Some barns down east of here. Some hurt, but no one in our congregation was hurt too bad. We found the wagon blown over in the glade and worried about the Flannigans." "Ya worried about us?" Peggy Flannigan walked out of the corner of the room and questioned again. "Why? We ain't none of your flock."

"You and the kids were out there alone. Just wanted to know you were safe."

Constable Armstrong took two steps toward the woman. "Mrs. Flannigan, this is Karl Perdue. He's one of my deputies. I'm afraid we got bad news for you. Tonight, while they were out checking on the folks in the storm path, Karl here ran upon a man at the bottom of Buck Snort Hill. Looked like the man fell with his horse from the top of the path. That's a steep hill when it's dry, but in this storm, well…. The horse broke a leg, and the man's neck was broke. Karl didn't know the man, so he came for me. I hate to say it, but I'm pretty sure it's your husband. Looked like he was tryin' to get back to your camp. Buck Snort would've shortened the trek, if it'd been dry. I'm sorry for bringin' hard news to ya."

"My dear Lord, NO." Mac pressed his hands to his throbbing head. "Please, Lord. No more."

Chapter Thirteen

Except the Lord build the house, they labor in vain that build it.
Psalms 127:1

*T*he intensity of the pain increased into the next day-sleep being Mac's only reprieve. That came only after a strong dose of laudanum. Matthew rode to bring Dr. Gibson back to the homestead. After an examination, the doctor could find no reason for Mac's continuing pain. The visible part of the head wound had healed completely.

"Laurel, there's nothin' more I can do. I've read about doctors in Europe opening the skull to relieve pressure after a bad head wound, but Mac had a few days without the headaches, so I doubt that is the cause. Even if it is, I've got no skill to undertake that kind of surgery."

"How can he continue when the pain is so bad?"

"Use the laudanum and let him sleep. Did anything happen to bring the headache back? Did he fall?"

"No. He was just sitting at the supper table. He said he could feel the pressure behind his eyes and wanted to lie down. Then the constable came with my uncle and that man who found Lemuel Flannigan's body. That was when the worst began."

"Did the Flannigans eat supper with y'all yesterday?"

"Of course. We couldn't turn them out in the storm. The constable told us the tornado had destroyed their wagon. Naturally, we gave them shelter."

"How did Mac act during supper?"

"He was quiet. I assumed he was beginning to tire and hurt again. The pain just worsened as the bad news came, one thing after another. He started to press on his temples when the constable told us about Mr. Flannigan. He cried out and said, 'Dear Lord, no. Please no more."

"Let him sleep as long as the medicine will allow."

When they reentered the main room, Peggy Flannigan rose from the bench where she'd been waiting. "Mrs. MacLayne, I'm a thankin' you for the vittles and a dry place to sleep last night. Me and mine will be a headin' back to see what we can salvage."

"You can't stay at the camp if your shelter is gone. You can stay with us, at least until we can help you see to your husband."

"We can't be a burden, 'specially with your man so sick." Just as Matthew Campbell was about to pack up the Flannigan family to leave, a knock came on the front door of the cabin. The constable had arrived with two deputies, bringing her husband's possessions back to Mrs. Flannigan.

"Ma'am, would you have a few minutes to answer a few more questions for me? We'd like to wrap up this investigation if we can."

"I don't know nothin' more to tell ya."

"I know you said your husband sometimes did thoughtless things when he was in his cups. I know he was upset with Mac about the decision of the judge about the property title. Has he ever shot anyone over an argument before?"

"No, sir. My husband was a good man. He wanted to build us a homestead on the land we bought and paid for. We got cheated, plain and simple. Last I talked to him, he'd said that he knew Mr. MacLayne wasn't the one who stole his land. He understood after he took some time to think about what the judge told us. We still felt cheated, mind ya, and we surely didn't know which way to turn with our money stolen and the land not belongin' to us, but we were gonna try to find a way to go on with our plans. What other choice did we have?"

"Mrs. Flannigan, I brought back all your husband's belongings, along with his body. Did your husband have a second firearm of some kind? The only gun we found was this muzzleloader. It doesn't use the kind of ammunition that the doctor took out of the wound in Mr. MacLayne's chest."

"My husband only had one gun, the old military long gun his father brought home from his service with the military in England when he was conscripted a long time ago. He used it to hunt mostly, but he would use it for defendin' our family if it came down to the need."

"Matthew, I'm thinkin' that maybe Mr. Flannigan may not be our shooter after all. We searched the area around Buck Snort pretty thorough. We didn't find another gun."

"What a blessin' for my kids. My young'un Sean's been frettin' about people callin' his pa a killer." Peggy Flannigan bent her head in silent prayer. "I need to go find my kids and talk about what happened to their pa. I'm relieved I can tell 'em their pa was comin' back to help us, and he didn't try to hurt Mr. MacLayne." Matthew Campbell spoke for his congregation. "Mrs.

Flannigan, you come with me. We'll go gather your belongin's, and then y'all come be the guests of our Shiloh community for a few days."

"Mr. Campbell, what call do you have to do for us?"

"Lots of reasons, but for a start, I'd like for you to teach my Ellie how to make that fine Irish stew I smelled cookin' on your campfire the other day. I've been cravin' it ever since I smelled it."

"Ma, we gotta go somewhere or stay here."

"Paddy, ya know Flannigans don't take no charity."

"Ma, these folks, they been good to us. I can help ya find a way to repay the good they done us. I'm old enough and strong enough to work now."

"You're just twelve and not done with your schoolin'."

"Ma. We gotta eat, and Pa'd want us to keep the family together."

Mrs. Flannigan drew her firstborn into her arms and allowed her tears to flow. "All right, Mr. Campbell. Me and mine will take your offer for today, and then we'll see." "Ma'am, all the folks at Shiloh call me Brother Matthew. Mr. Campbell makes me think about my blessed father. I lost him a score of years ago."

After the visitors had gone, the cabin was quiet and strangely empty. Both Andy and Cathy returned to school the next day. With Mac asleep and Mark her only company, Laurel was acutely aware of the solitude. She began the day's chores and tried to push her worrisome thoughts to the back of her mind. She sang familiar hymns to keep the dreary thoughts at bay. "Thou, O Christ, art all I want, more than all in Thee I find; Raise the fallen, cheer the faint, heal the sick and lead the blind; Just and holy is Thy name." Words from *A Mighty Fortress is our God* and *Rock of Ages* also filled the quiet of the cabin. Then she paused…Mark was sitting on the scorched rag rug, looking at her and smiling. What a blessing on such a hard day!

The next day, just at the noon hour, Matthew Campbell came through the back door. "Do you need help with your chores, niece?"

"No, Uncle Matthew. Mac's father has sent two of his tenant farmers to look after the cattle. Mac is up today. He is outside, sitting on the front porch if you want to visit with him."

"I want a word with you first. What has Mac said to you about Flannigan—since the meetin' with the judge?"

"Not much. Those few days before the shooting, he mentioned a time or two that the Flannigan family was as much a victim as we were. He was happy the judge gave us back Eden, but he hated the family had lost all they'd hoped for."

"Didn't ya say he'd gotten some better until the storm brought the Flannigans to your doorstep?"

"He still had some headaches, but not the kind he had on Monday night."

"Have you talked to him about what the constable told us the day of the storm? Does he know that Mr. Flannigan is probably not the man who shot him?"

"No. We've hardly talked at all. He has spent a lot of time asleep and his headaches have been unbearable. I don't know what to do. He can't live his life drinking laudanum and sleeping."

"Mac's dealin' with more than a gunshot wound. Knowin' him as I do, I believe he's blaming himself for the loss the Flannigans are facin'. Follows suit, he reacted pretty much the same way when he was in that duel with his friend back in Maryland, except he physically ran away that time."

"If you're right, what can I do about it now? He ran from that duel for more than seven years."

"He ran alone last time. I think he's got a better foundation now. I'm gonna have a talk with my brother."

Laurel returned to the kitchen as her uncle opened the front door to the porch.

Matthew found Mac sitting in his rocking chair, dozing. "How much sleep does one man need, Mac?"

"Hello, Matthew. I guess a lot. The medicine is so strong that I sleep more than I'm awake."

"Good reason to quit takin' it, I'd say."

"I'd like to, but the pain from that head wound is the worst I've ever felt, a hundred times worse than the wound in my shoulder."

"I'd like to see you well and back among us, Mac."

"No more than I would."

"Good. Then lay all that guilt and blame where it belongs."

"What the devil are you talkin' about, Matthew? I didn't do anything to cause that man to shoot me and try to burn my house to the ground."

"What man was that?"

"What are you getting' at?"

"You know who shot you? The constable found Flannigan's gun. He's pretty sure he didn't do it. He thinks Flannigan was headed home to his family during the storm. He died in an accident. As far as I know, you didn't sell him that fake land deed. I'm pretty sure you got no powers to create a tornado to rip up a wagon or a campsite."

"All right, all right! I know what you're sayin'. No, I didn't cause any of this to happen."

"Then why do you feel guilty? Mac, that blame headache's not brought on by any puny scratch on your head. You know I'm tellin' you the truth. It's just like that time with your friend in Maryland."

"Wait a minute."

"No, you wait…you can't run for seven years this time. You've got a wife and kids who depend on you. Have you looked at Laurel? She's worn to a frazzle. She's taken on your work on top of her own."

"Don't ya think I know that. I hate her doin' so much. She's just tryin' to keep me quiet and restin' like Ed told her."

"Ed can't fix what's botherin' you, my friend. Lay it at the cross and then get yourself up and well. There are problems to be solved, and you can't do it in a drugged sleep."

"Uncle Matthew! Those are harsh words. Don't talk to Mac like that. The doctor told him to rest for quite a while. He's not healed." Laurel had stepped out to the porch just as Matt had admonished Mac to get on with his life. "How can you blame him…I thought you see him as your brother…"

"Laurel, enough. Matthew is right." Mac pushed himself from his chair and walked across the porch to pull Laurel into his arms. "When I think about what has happened to the Flannigans, the pain gets bad, but this pain, as bad as it is, hasn't done one thing to fix any of the problems. That family still got cheated, and that crime has led to the death of a man who wanted the life I have. Now there is a widow and children who are in need and will likely go on in need if we don't intervene."

"That's the Mac I know." Matthew Campbell slapped his friend on the back.

"A far cry from it, but I'll mend. Thanks, Matthew. I needed that sermon today. You're a good friend." Mac stepped near his minister and clapped him on the back. A smile passed across his face. "Laurel, can you help me inside? I think it's time for my son and me to have our afternoon nap. Mac took Laurel's arm and let her support him as he walked to the tall bed. He took Mark from her, and they nestled together to nap. Mac slept, without the laudanum.

Laurel returned to the front porch and walked into the open arms of her uncle, where she cried in relief and fatigue. "God bless you, Uncle Matthew. You did for Mac what I haven't been able to do. He went to sleep without anything for pain."

"You need a nap too."

"I'll sleep much better tonight because of you."

The day following Matt's visit, Mac mentioned the problems the Flannigans faced. "How is Mrs. Flannigan going to bury her husband?"

"I don't know, Mac. Peggy left with Matthew yesterday. I'm sure they made some kind of decision."

"Send John to find out. We can at least help with a marker or pay for a coffin."

"She may not let us. She said they're not charity cases."

"Where are they goin'? They've got no money. The wagon may have been damaged too badly to travel. Besides, they only have one horse left since the other broke its leg in the fall."

"I don't know that either, Husband. Why don't you rest and not worry about it until we know more."

"No need to worry at all. Let's sell them the Widow's place. We already said we don't want it settin' empty. Pa's been in his new place for a couple of months already."

"How can she pay for it?"

"With the money we'll get from suing Digby and Duncan." Mac's voice was animated for the first time in a long while. This was a good solution. All the MacLaynes had to do was explain the sell in such a way that Peggy Flannigan would understand they were not 'giving' the homestead to her, but selling it to her.

"Mac, that's a fine idea. Now, can you rest a while?"

"I believe I can. One problem solved and more to tackle tomorrow. Kiss me goodnight, Wife." She bent down and kissed Mac lightly before he pulled her down into his arms, but almost immediately he winced. "Lord, please heal these pains. I'm missin' my wife." Mac kissed Laurel tenderly. "Wife, I'm more than ready to be well!" Almost daily, Laurel could see Mac's strength returning. His activity was still limited by the doctor, and he had to take his afternoon naps. At times, he would become so fatigued he'd have to sit down for several minutes. Laurel continued to dose him with the tonic made of bitterroot and honey, which the doctor had provided as a blood builder.

Not one supper went by that Mac did not have a large portion of red meat, and Laurel served him calf's liver at least once a week. All of them hated the taste of that noxious dish, but Laurel insisted they all eat. "It must be good for us. The doctor said so." Laurel made sure her husband cleaned his plate. She would accept nothing less than his complete return to health, and she brooked no argument from him.

Early the following week, Matthew brought Peggy Flannigan to the homestead as Mac had asked. He was beginning to feel the return of his stamina, and he managed to stay up most of the day, sitting in his armchair, holding his son, and talking to Laurel. When they heard the knock on the door, Mac laid aside the Baltimore newspaper he'd been reading and walked to the door. "Thank you for coming, Mrs. Flannigan. Matthew, y'all come in and have a seat here at the table. Laurel, will you bring us some coffee?"

"I'm a-hopin' you're better. Brother Matthew told me those gunshots came nigh on to killin' ya."

Matthew walked over to Mac and slapped him on the back. "The Lord has work for this old outlaw to do, yet. He's got a new son to raise and a new neighbor to help get established here at Shiloh. Besides, he's my best friend, Mrs. Flannigan, and I still have need of him, too."

"Mrs. Flannigan, I'm sorry you've lost so much. I hoped the laws we passed in the last session of the legislature would bring an end to the fraud and thievery of the land agents."

"Would you like milk or sweetenin' in your coffee?" Laurel offered coffee to those at the table.

"No, ma'am. What do you want of me, sir?" "I'd like to help you get settled here at Shiloh."

"Don't be a'frettin' yourself, Mr. MacLayne. You did us no wrong. We'll be a goin' back east as soon as school's out. My young'uns missed school last year while we moved across the country. The school committee offered me room and board to clean the church and the school while I stay here. We've got enough to eat and shelter 'til spring term ends in a couple of weeks."

"But you need more than room and board. You need a place to grow a garden so you can begin to fill a larder for winter."

"The Lord will provide." "He did already." Mac replied.

Matthew looked questioningly at his friend and then back to Laurel.

"I don't know what you are sayin' to me, Mr. MacLayne." The confused expression on Peggy Flannigan's face matched the gaze on Brother Matthew's own.

"You and your husband bought land for a farm. While I can't give you the parcel that Duncan led you to, there is a good piece less than two miles from there that is available if you'll have it."

"I got no more money to buy land. Even if I did, me and Paddy couldn't get a cabin up before winter."

"No need. There's already a sturdy cabin there, not big, but tight and strong. Even has a small barn and a sweet water well. There are thirty acres, plenty of room to plant a garden and raise a few animals and forage."

"I done told ya, we got no money. We ain't takin' your charity, 'specially not from you, Mr. MacLayne. You don't owe us nothin'."

"No. I know I don't, but we know two men who do. We already had the constable put out a call to arrest them." Mac spoke, trying to make her understand.

Laying his arm across her squared shoulder, Matthew explained, "Peggy, dear lady, my friends are not offerin' charity. I think they have a plan to help you regain part of your loss if I'm not mistaken."

"When the law I told you about is used, dirty land agents can be sued to get back what they took illegally. We are gonna sue Digby and

Duncan for the return of the price you paid and for the damages caused to your family for the death of your husband."

"You can do that?"

"I can't, but a man by the name of Al Stuart can." "Mrs. Flannigan, Mac will sell you this homestead when the case is won. The cabin is lovely. We lived there before Mac built our place."

"This don't make no sense. You're not beholdin' to me."

"Yes, Peggy, we all are. Every person has the obligation to take care of the other. I don't know much about the Catholic Church, but I believe we share that belief." Matthew hugged the woman as tears streamed down her face.

"Bless my soul. No one ever showed me this kind of concern before. Thank you. I'll make the deal, only if I am able to repay the debt in one year. My kids deserve a home, and they like Shiloh school. God bless ya."

"We are happy to have you for a neighbor, Mrs. Flannigan."

"Please, I'd like it if you'd call me Peggy."

Mac was relieved he'd dealt with this first problem so quickly. In three days, the Flannigans had set up housekeeping at the Widow Parker's old homestead, and Dr. Gibson had allowed Mac to begin a few hours a week of work around his farm. He was happy to be able to ride for short periods of times, out among his cattle, supervising his help. One afternoon he convinced Laurel to leave Mark, and they rode out to Eden to visit Campbell, and then after resting by the creek for a while, they rode over to offer a house warming gift to the Flannigans.

"Please accept this small gift, Peggy." Laurel handed her a small basket holding a loaf of bread, a pound of salt, a half dozen candles, a small keg of grape juice from the mercantile, a small pot of honey, and a hand-tacked quilt. "A loaf of bread so you'll know no hunger within these walls, salt to flavor your new life here, honey for a touch of sweetness, a bottle of wine to bring you joy, candles so you'll walk in the light, and a quilt to let the warmth of friendship grow between our families. We hope you learn to love it

here in Shiloh."

Chapter Fourteen

The desire of a man is his kindness…The fear of the Lord tendeth to life: and he that hath it shall abide satisfied.
Proverbs 19: 22-23

*M*ac's knowing the Flannigans were secure and comfortable brought him peace, and with the peace came a lessening of pain and renewed energy. He felt a strong need to deal with another problem that continued to trouble his wife. As May passed into June, Mac had still found no way to bring Gracie from Washington County. The one time he'd tried to discuss making the trip himself, both Laurel and Dr. Gibson vetoed the idea before he could even finish telling them the travel plans he'd laid out. He didn't see how sitting on a stagecoach seat was much different than sitting in his armchair.

Truthfully, Mac had become extremely bored with sitting in his armchair. Although he'd been allowed to make short rides around the homestead, time lay heavily on his hands. All his life, he'd been a man who worked long hours, doing things that mattered, whether it was the physical labor of building a successful farm or the mental effort put forth in planning, negotiating, and solving problems in the legislature, in Shiloh church, and the broader community. He didn't much like the sidelines and even more, he hated feeling useless. He preferred the role of doer to the role of delegator.

One night after the kids had gone to bed, Mac took Mark from Laurel's arms and said, "Wife, let's go sit on the porch for a spell. I'm gettin' cabin fever."

"Aren't you tired, Mac?"

"Yes, frankly, I am. I'm tired of sittin' around the house when I could work. I'm tired of bein' tended to as if I were Mark's age, and I'm completely tired of feelin' less than a man—useless! What is Doc thinking? I've got nearly all my strength back. The headaches are fewer now. I want my lover back in my bed where she belongs."

Laurel knew neither of those things Mac said about his health was true. Not one day went by that Mac didn't have some kind of headache, not as severe as before, but bad enough to cause her concern. He also tired much easier than he admitted. "Mac, Dr. Gibson is tryin' to make sure the healin' is done. I suppose it's partly my fault. I made him promise you'd return to full health before he let you go back to your regular activities. I couldn't stand the idea of losin' you."

"I am losin' me, Laurel. I have to find something worthwhile to do. It's nearly two months since—well, I need a purpose."

"You have a purpose. I am your purpose. Our son there in your arms…where would he be without you? Andy and Cathy need you as much as I do."

"I don't mean y'all mean nothing to me. I didn't mean to cause a spat. It's not in my nature to let others do for me what I can do for myself. You have taken over things that I used to do. I can see how tired you are."

"Do you see how scared I am when I think I almost lost you? I will never forget the sight of you lying in the pool of blood. Even now, I can't think of it without panic."

"I will try to remain your patient for another week, but soon I have to find my routine again. Do you realize how long it's been since we made love? I miss you, our making love."

"Mac…we have a lifetime to share if you are well again."

"I'll change the subject. Since you won't hear of me goin' to bring Gracie here, how do you think we'll be able to do so?"

"I don't know, but there has to be some way."

"She can't come by herself. She's not quite five years old yet."

"If it's meant to be, the way will be provided."

"I'll be hanged if I can think of one. I've got to convince you I'm all right. The young steers need to go to market. Roy's being at his place three days a week has left us short-handed. Today John talked about leaving Shiloh to go off to school. He's convinced he needs more schoolin' if he's gonna be suited to take up Matt's callin'. I don't know why. Matthew's done pretty well without it."

"Please stop fretting. You'll bring back the headaches."

"How safe can I keep you and the kids if I can't keep this homestead together?"

"What will keep you from workin' this place after you're well?"

"Don't you mean if?"

"Now, what are you talkin' about?"

"I heard you talkin' to Ed Gibson the last time he was here. You thought I was asleep. He told you my heart may be damaged— may never be strong again."

"Mac, he didn't say it wouldn't heal. He said that sometimes a person who's lost so much blood will have a weakened heart. He didn't say you would. That's why he wants you to be so careful while you are healing."

"He told you the tiredness and poor strength I'm havin' are the signs. Laurel, I didn't marry you to become my nurse and housekeeper like you were for your father."

"I can't say anything to make you feel any better. I believe in time you'll return to health. I pray for it every day. If it's not to be, we'll deal with that when the time comes. I refuse to argue about it anymore. I love you. I know any kind of life I have with you is better than one I'd have without you."

Mac lowered his head into his hands. "Laurel, I'm sorry. This isn't the life I pictured for us."

"Well, Patrick, this is exactly the life I pictured. Here we are, the two of us – well, the three of us, sitting on our porch, talking together, and sharing our concerns. We have four fine children, food, and shelter. And you love me. I'd be awfully small if I wasn't grateful for my bounty."

"I sound petty tonight, don't I? Happens every time I put myself in the middle of my universe."

"Just be patient, my love. Things are going to work out. We'll find a way to get Gracie here, and we'll find hands to help us work our homestead. Be patient and wait on the Lord."

Mac tried to find the patience Laurel had spoken of, but the next week he was confronted with things he wanted to do and couldn't find the strength to do. A neighbor had asked several Shiloh people to help him raise another room for his cabin. Mac wanted to go, but instead, he asked one of the tenant farmers to go instead. Mrs. Flannigan had sent Paddy over to ask for help removing several large tree limbs from the roof of the barn. John and Roy went, apologizing that Mac was not able to come. The worst blow came when he'd wanted to take Andy riding one afternoon. He'd tried to lift his son up onto Midnight's back and realized he didn't have the strength to lift the boy from the ground to the saddle. Those three events, coming within a few days of each other, brought him to the lowest mood he'd experienced since he'd met Laurel.

She saw how defeated Mac seemed. He began to sit around the cabin more each day. He picked at his food at mealtime and rarely smiled. He found excuses not to play with Cathy and Andy and would hold Mark only when Laurel directly asked him for help. He became very distant to Laurel, too. Dr. Gibson had told Mac to avoid 'amorous activity' with Laurel, but as his despair deepened, he made no effort to kiss her or to show her the least affection. When she tried to talk, he would listen but not engage in conversation. This was the worst part of the tragedy.

Laurel felt hopeless to do anything that could make a difference, so she found refuge in prayer. "Lord, please restore Patrick's spirit. Help him see we need him. I need him." The answer to her prayer came one afternoon in mid-July. The MacLayne family had just finished their noon meal when four men came up to their front porch. Laurel's uncle entered the door first, and he was followed by Al Stuart and two other men Laurel didn't know. She rose to greet them, but Mac remained in his chair at the table.

"Won't y'all come sit with us? Can I get ya some coffee or cool water?"

"Yes, Laurel Grace, that'd be nice – water though. It's too blame hot for coffee." As she tried to play hostess, the men took chairs around the table. "Mac – Laurel, these are two people from the Jonesboro settlement. Joel Mosbey and Robert Watkins, this is my niece Laurel and our former state legislator, Patrick MacLayne. He served Greene County in the twelfth legislative session."

"Good to finally meet ya, MacLayne. There's been considerable talk about you of late. Stuart here told us about the good work you did in the last session."

"Thank you, sir. I tried to do what I thought was good for the folks who elected me."

"You did your job so good, you lost your seat, I heard."

"That's true, Mr. Mosby. That was what was best for Shiloh. We needed easier access to the county seat. We're hopin' that Greensboro may be the place, but even if Jonesboro is named, it's not nearly as hard a trip as it is to Gainesville." Mac's voice was cordial, but it still showed little enthusiasm.

"That is just one of the reasons I told you Mac would be our best candidate to go back to Little Rock this fall."

There was a silence in the room for a time. "Al, wait a minute…"

"Hear me out, Mac. I know you ain't quite recuperated from that shootin' yet. I've been keepin' check on you with Ed."

"Mr. Stuart, then you know my husband needs time to rest to return to health."

"Poppycock! I ain't askin' him to wrestle a steer or lift sacks of grain. Mac's smart and level-headed. We're goin' to face some mighty serious issues this year. He knows the routine of the legislature, and he knows our people. We need him to go back to the statehouse."

"No, Mr. Stuart. He's…"

Mac reached out and took Laurel's arm. "Laurel. I want to hear what they've come to say." For the first time in several weeks, light returned to Mac's eyes. He showed an interest in the conversation around him. He drew her to a chair next to him.
"Gentlemen, please speak your minds."

"I hate all this mister stuff. Is it all right if I call you Mac, too?"

"My friends do."

"Well, Mac, we've got a group over in Jonesboro who's tryin' to get our county government set up. It takes a while, especially since our folks are so spread out. Only got about 3,000 folks spread out over 700 square miles in the county. With roads like they are, we still don't know each other from one community to the next."

"Robert's right. We have tried to get organized, but we don't see an official election happening before the first of November. So, we thought we'd get a group of folks from across the county and appoint us a representative until we can get a real election organized. Hopefully, we can do that before '62."

"Mac, we want to recommend you to the committee since you've got the experience and a fair part of the county knows you already. Will you let us?"

"Al, I'm honored you want me. I'm not able to answer you tonight. You know I enjoy the politics, but I've got some family business I've not been able to deal with since I've been laid up. The doctor doesn't seem to think I'm ever gonna be back to my old self again."

"How much stamina does it take to sit in a chair in the statehouse, MacLayne?"

"Mr. Stuart, you know the sitting's not the hard part. It's the gettin' there." Laurel intervened.

"Mac, consider it. You still have a couple of months before you'd have to make the trek down to Little Rock. A man can heal a lot in a few months if he's a mind to."

"All right, Matthew. I'll talk it over with Laurel, but travel is not my main concern right now. I still have some family business that needs my attention."

"Lots of people around here might help if we knew what the problem was."

"Laurel's goddaughter, Gracie Wilson, has been orphaned. Her mother and father were part of that Methodist wagon train attacked at Mountain Meadow in Utah."

"I remember you tellin' me something about that."

"Well, her grandfather Wilson was her only living relative in Washington County. He died of influenza during the winter. We need to bring her here to live with us, but Dr. Gibson and Laurel won't let me go after her.

"She could come by stage to Little Rock and meet you there.

"She too young to come alone. She's barely five."

"I think I have a solution. My wife's uncle is a representative from Carroll County. He and his wife come to Little Rock for the legislative session by stage. They travel through Fayetteville on their way. They could bring the girl with them if you'd pay for her fare and keep."

"Of course, we'd be obliged to cover the costs."

"The old buzzard's always been a tightwad."

"Wait, I met that representative from Carroll County. He was on the appropriation committee I served on. I remember him. He never wanted to spend tax money…very frugal man."

"That's what I said. He's a tightwad."

Laughter erupted, and Mac was laughing too, for the first time in several weeks. The men continued to talk. Laurel left them to clean the kitchen. When the time came, she went to the barn to do the evening chores, all the time feeling the dilemma the men had brought to her house. She was happy to see Mac take an interest in the talk, but the idea of him taking on the role of a representative from Craighead County scared her. Perhaps he was not strong enough to make the hard trip, and even more troublesome was the idea they'd be separated again for most of the winter. Then the thought crossed her mind: *Lord, you answer prayers, but not always in the way we want them answered.*

The political discussion went on until mid-afternoon. Laurel did not join in the talk, but she was near enough to listen to every word. Mac spoke with more enthusiasm in his voice than she'd heard since the shooting. When the delegation took their leave, Mac returned to his armchair, obviously spent. "I didn't realize how tired I'd gotten. I guess we talked longer than we should have. It was good to be in the midst of political talk again."

"Let me help you to the bedroom. A short nap will do you good." She helped him remove his boots, and he lay back into his pillow. The fatigue was clear in his voice, but he wanted to talk anyway. With an alert expression on his face and his eyes so bright and alive, Laurel whispered a prayer of thanksgiving and for strength at the same time. She was relieved to see him in better spirits, but at the same time she was terrified at the level of his exhaustion. "Sleep for a while, Patrick. I think you overdid your first visit with your new political cronies."

"In a minute…come over here and let's talk about the possibility of my goin' back to Little Rock."

"We can talk about it later."

"What do you think about having Representative Montgomery and his wife bringin' Gracie to me in Little Rock?"

"Mac, this will wait until you rest a while." She walked to the door and turned, "It's so good to see the light in your eyes again." She saw the frustration on his face, but she firmly closed the door, making clear she'd not discuss anything with him until he rested.

After supper that night, Mac challenged Andy to a checker game. They'd not played together since that night in April. Andy had not even asked to play. As he sat in his place by the window, he looked around the room. The discoloration of the logs around the fireplace was still quite evident. The rag rug Laurel's mother had made for her own home lay clean but scorched in places. Mark sat at Laurel's feet. The open space where the window had been shattered was covered with heavy paper temporarily. "Son, I think I can take you tonight."

"Give it yer best try, Papa. We'll see." When the evening came to an end, Mac and Andy had each won two games. "You must be gettin' well, Papa. You ain't never played that good since you taught me how to play." When Laurel had seen the children to bed, she joined Mac in their room, thinking he'd be asleep after the full day. However, he stretched his legs the length of the bed, propped himself on both pillows, and turned to the eighth chapter of Romans.

"I thought you'd be asleep by now."

"We've got things to discuss. You promised me this afternoon, remember?"

"I'll listen." Laurel began to change into her light summer nightdress and then started pulling the combs from her chignon. She picked up her hairbrush and began to smooth the tresses back from her face.

"I'd like to do that, Laurel."

"Patrick, you're supposed to be resting."

"How hard is brushing your hair?"

"All right."

Mac pulled the brush through her tawny curls for a few minutes, remembering the days when that act had been the only touch Laurel would allow him. He laid the brush on the table, took her bare arm and pulled her down to him. He caressed her cheek and ran his hand across her back. "I love you, Laurel. I haven't shown you much lately." He brought her face down to meet his, and he kissed her. The caress was tender and unhurried. After a while, he released her. "I am going to get well. I can't believe the time I've wasted, bein' so low and feelin' sorry for myself. I am gonna be well…I want too much from life to give up." He again pulled her into his arms, kissing her over and over. "Laurel, I want to go back to Little Rock."

"That's not news to me. I've known you wanted to return since the day you came home the last time. I was walkin' on clouds thinkin' I'd have you home, but I knew you wouldn't be happy here."

"Why didn't you say something?"

"Patrick, what good would it have done? You would play the game to make me happy, pretend to be satisfied raisin' your herd because I want to stay at Shiloh. I'd rather us just be honest with each other than put on a show."

"You don't want me to go back, do you?"

"I need you to do whatever you need to do to live the life you feel called to lead. If you believe your role is to serve in the legislature, I will support your decision. Honestly, will I be thrilled to deal with all the time we'll be separated? No. I hate the time we are apart. But I've seen more of <u>you</u>, the man I love, in the last six hours than I've known in the last six weeks."

"I don't understand what you are saying. We've been together constantly since I've been laid up here at home."

"And you've shut yourself away feelin' depressed, useless, and pitying yourself. You pull away from our whole family a bit more every day." When Laurel heard her last words to Mac, she gasped. "I'm sorry, darlin'. I didn't mean it to come out that way. Forgive me."

"You didn't mean to say it, but that is how you feel, isn't it

Laurel?"

"No, no. I love you. I hate what you've gone through. I'd never want to add to your pain. I am just tired. I didn't mean to upset you."

"You didn't. I know you only act in love. You should have said something long before now. I told you that I'd lost touch with my strength, with my connection to my faith, before I left Little Rock. I felt a strong pull. Almost like an urge to go back to my old self. I'm not proud to tell you I acted on it more than once when I was gone from you. Maybe a return to the legislature is not a good thing for our family." Mac turned and walked toward his armchair near the fireplace.

"Patrick, stop makin' decisions when we are in the middle of a discussion! I didn't say that, nor anything close to it. I'm about to get truly upset with you. It's been a spell since I've been really angry with you."

"What are you mad about? I was trying to agree with you." Laurel walked over to the chair where Mac sat, her hands on her hips and a pout on her face. She turned her back to him and stared into the cold hearth, running her hands through her long, tawny tresses.

As she was about to turn to continue, Mac grabbed her arm and pulled her into his lap. "Are you mad at me, Wife?" He began to tease her with gentle kisses on her ears and cheeks.

"Stop it, Patrick. Let's get this talk over with." He continued his teasing assault.

"Let's not. I'm tired of talkin' today. Let me take you to bed instead."

Laurel pushed at his chest, trying to get back on her feet. "You know what the doctor said."

"He's an old man. What does he know about what a man needs to regain his strength and fitness? Anyway, I'm sure I don't know of any finer way to go meet my Maker than in your arms, Laurel."

"I said stop, Patrick. I can't live with the thought of your death. Have you no sense of what I've lived through these past few weeks, fearing that you wouldn't live? We will do what the doctor says." Laurel moved away from Mac's grasp and across the room. "You are doing it again. When we get into a serious discussion you deflect the decision-making by changing the subject with your charm or silly humor. I want us to make a decision."

"Yes, I learned that little trick from you. It works well most of the time."

"Patrick, I am very much in favor of your returning to the legislature if you can do so without any further damage to your health. I will miss you while you are gone, but I know you will come home when you have served the state as you feel called to do."

"Thank you, Laurel. I want to return to Little Rock. I want you to go with me, but I will not ask you to go. Mark Thomas is too young, and the kids need you here. Probably not as much as I need you with me, but I'll not be selfish. I know you can handle the homestead by yourself, with the help of our tenant farmers. Because I know you love me, I'll go serve with anticipation only slightly less than the eagerness I'll have to return to you when the term is finished."

"All right, now we have made a decision. I feel good about what we have decided. Now we can go to sleep and rest."

"Now we can go to bed. You got what you asked for, and now I want to make love to you. I am man enough to know my limits and my needs. Tonight, I need you."

Chapter Fifteen

Whoso findeth a wife, findeth a good thing, and obtaineth favor of the Lord. Proverbs 18:22

On Sunday during the dinner on the grounds, Matt and Ellie joined them under their favorite hickory tree. Mac lay resting, his head in Laurel's lap, and Mark slept on his chest.

"Mac, that young'un didn't seem to like my sermon today, or were you pinchin' him? He sure put up a squawk for a while."

"He just wanted down. He's not much for just sittin' around either."

"You're feelin' better, aren't you, Mac?"

"Yes, at least I'm not so down." Laurel brushed his hair back from his eyes. Those kinds of little intimacies were becoming very common in their day to day routine.

Laurel smiled. She'd caught herself trying to nurse Mac back to health by doing things he could do for himself. He had proved to her what he needed was his wife, not a nurse. She pulled back her hand.

"I like Ed Gibson. I respect him as a doctor. He saved my life and I'm grateful, but I think his idea of resting myself back to health is the wrong way for me. I've tried it for two months, and I'm not stronger. This week I've been doin' little chores, walkin' around the place more, ridin' some, and staying up most of the time, and I feel stronger."

"Now Mac, Ed said the stress on your heart could be too much."

"Ellie, my dear, the stress on my mind's been worse. I'm smart enough to stop whenever I feel winded or tired. I'm startin' slow, but every day I can do a little more."

"You've decided to go back to the legislature, haven't you?" Brother Matthew asked.

"I believe it's my callin'. Since I convinced Laurel to let me go, it's weighed easier on my mind. I can serve and work, even with part of my strength. She's laid down a few conditions before she'll give me her blessin' completely though."

The following day, Laurel, Mark, and Mac drove to Greensboro to talk with Dr. Gibson. Laurel's first demand was they have a frank discussion with him before she'd accept the risk. Ed was a good man and a good friend. If they asked, he would tell them the truth.

When she asked, she knew the doctor was upset that Mac had been approached by the committee from Jonesboro. He turned his back to them. Laurel went to the doctor and laid her hand on his arm. "Please, Ed. Be straight with us. How bad is the injury, still?"

He turned to look at them in a way that told Laurel he hated every word he had to speak. He said the head wound was no longer a concern. He knew the bullet had caused a mild concussion but that had healed. The lasting effect seemed to be the headaches that Mac experienced from time to time. "The bullet in his chest did not cause the worst damage. I found it and removed it without tearin' any vessels, but the blood loss caused terrible stress on Mac's heart. Even today, when I listened to his chest, the heartbeat was irregular and weaker than it should be. At times, his pulse rate is thready and faint." He pulled out his pocket watch and opened the gold case. "Mac, I thank the Lord you're alive, but for the life of me, I don't know how you are. I can only say a miracle happened." "Ed, I want to make love to my wife again. Don't you think I'm well enough for that?"

Laurel turned as red as she'd ever been in her life.

"Patrick…" She certainly didn't intend to tell the doctor about their evening after the committee from Jonesboro had visited them.

"Hang it all! I am trying to find out whether I am a man or an invalid. Well, Doc?"

"I gave you the best answer I have. You've been given a miracle. I don't know the limits of your strength or how strong your heart is. Your faith is the only thing that is keeping you alive now."

"Will it kill me to travel to the capital, Ed?"

"Only God knows that."

"Laurel, I know that's not what you wanted to hear. You decide." Mac turned to look at his wife.

"You were dyin' in front of me before those men from Jonesboro brought some life back to you during their talk last week. I'll not deny your heart's desire."

"You are my heart's desire, Mrs. MacLayne, but I need to have a purpose. I have to be useful."

"Let's go see Al Stuart."

"Wait a minute. I'm still waitin' for doc. What about the other question I asked you, Ed?"

"I gave you my answer, Mac. Hang it all! My advice is to play it on the safe side, but you have to do what you think you're ready to do."

φ

The next several weeks saw a non-stop parade of people at their homestead. Mac was holding a campaign from his porch. The people came to see him instead of his making the campaign rounds. Of course, there would be no full-blown election, but Mac would be selected by a group of citizens from different settlements around the county. Already he'd met with homesteaders from the Maumelle settlement in the south-east corner of the county, the Grinder community just southwest of Jonesboro, and the owner of a large plantation called Lester Landing near the St. Francis River. For the most part, the meetings had been amicable and productive. Only the Lester Landing plantation owner had outwardly opposed Mac's going back to the statehouse. The planter was, of course, supporting the growing movement for secession.

When Mac honestly stated he would not vote for secession, the planter rose, offered his hand, and spoke his farewell. "Mr. MacLayne, while I admire your honesty to my question, I cannot offer you my support. I believe it's my God-given right to maintain all I own, including my slaves. I thank you for your time and hope your health continues to improve."

Mac was exhausted after that meeting. He knew he'd face opposition from some of the people who live in the sunken lands of the county. That region was very much a part of the delta, and the Kingdom of Cotton so prevalent in the deep south. For the most part, he was encouraged because most of his meetings had been with pro-union people, who feared what would happen if Arkansas broke bonds with the federal government. Yet, he knew he would face more opposition in days to come, and he must have the energy to confront that opposition with confidence and moral courage. Laurel found it impossible to keep Mac's activities limited. He continued to increase the number of chores he did. He began to repair the damage the fire and shooting had done to their cabin. Over a period of several days, he built Mark a new bed to replace the outgrown cradle. To her pleasant surprise, Mac seemed to be regaining his strength little by little. Although he was exhausted by the end of the day, he would not forego reading scripture with his family. Evening talks with Laurel became even more rare, though, as he expended most of his energy meeting his constituents and caring for things he saw as crucial before he left for the capital.

Laurel missed the time they'd talked before bed, but she didn't complain. She knew it was a foretaste of what she would deal with when he went back to Little Rock. When he'd gone to the '58-59 session, he'd served nearly three months, and only six weeks of that time had she been with him in Little Rock. The time she'd spent alone had been some of the most difficult. What would it be like to be separated for the entire session? She pushed the dread from her awareness. Mac's determination to return to the legislature had brought him back to life. He'd lost his melancholy. She was grateful for that, and he slept soundly each night having reached some peace about what had happened to him.

As summer drew to a close, Laurel had less and less time to fret about losing her best friend. The harvest was large that year because Mac had insisted that they add to their garden acreage. Laurel harvested baskets of tomatoes, string beans, black-eyed peas, squash, and cucumbers. Of course, following the harvest, things had to be canned and stored. Laurel made pickles, creamed corn her papa had loved so, jar upon jar of stewed tomatoes, and peas of all sorts. When she had remnants of vegetables too small to fill a canning jar, she'd pour them together with some fatback from the smokehouse and make soups and stews for the winter. Nothing was wasted. By the time the larder and Mac's stash was filled, the grains were ready to harvest. Oats, wheat, and corn were stored for winter, and wheat and corn were carried to the grist meal to be ground into meal and flour. Time simply evaporated with the activities that had to be done.

By the time the hay was ready to cut, Dr. Gibson declared Mac able to supervise the mowing but not the lifting or storing of the forage. Thankfully, Mac's father and the tenant farmers joined him in the huge project. His not-quite-doubled herd would require a great deal of feed, especially if the winter proved harsh. The added help freed Roy and John to cut and stack firewood under the lean-to.

The first Monday in October brought the unofficial election with one man from each settlement in Craighead County coming to Snoddy's livery to select a representative for the thirteenth legislative session. The livery had become a frequent gathering place in Jonesboro. Even the Methodist congregation had taken to holding worship services there. Al Stuart, representing Greensboro, placed Mac's name before the group as their candidate. He was easily chosen with only two dissenting votes from the nine settlements, both coming from the eastern part of the county. Al Stuart brought the news to Shiloh the next day.

"Congratulations, Mr. Representative. I don't know that I'd want to be in your shoes, but I am happy to send you in my stead."

"I know this session will be a hard one. So much anger and deception about the slave issue. So much work still to be done on the land fraud problem."

"Is Laurel goin' with you this time?"

"No. She has put her foot down about that. Our baby's too little for such a trek. Our nephew John Campbell will travel with me and stay while the session lasts. He wants to look into college there. He's worked for us since we built our homestead. He'll be good company for me."

"God's speed, Mac. And, my friend, please take care of yourself. Here are your election credentials. They've been signed by the county judge, Sam Trice, and the county clerk, L.H. Sutfin. You're as official as our foundling county can make you this year. Next term it'll be more formal."

In the last two weeks before Mac's departure, things blurred with activity. Laurel made every effort to bring her family together to share special time each evening. Mac's father was invited to supper three or four times. Laurel cooked special suppers nearly every night, making dessert with berries and pecans found around the homestead, even in the middle of the week. The checkerboard was ready for Andy and Mac's nightly game. Both Mac and Laurel delighted in Mark's early attempts at walking.

Most nights, Cathy and Andy begged their papa for a story. In their nightly prayer time, they all prayed to ask for Mac to serve well and return quickly. Under her breath, Laurel asked for courage to let him go. Even with John going to watch over Mac, Laurel felt a terrible sense of fear.

Even in her dread, Laurel could not help being grateful for the change she saw in her husband. Mac was excited, eager to be up every morning, and talking about what he wanted to accomplish in Little Rock. He seemed more like himself than he had since April. Except for the noticeable fatigue after any exertion, Mac appeared well. The week before his planned departure, Mac built the first fire of the season in their bedroom's fireplace. The nights had just now begun to bring a chill when the sun passed the horizon.

"I do like a nice fire when the chill comes."

"I do too. Thanks for building us one, Husband."

"You're welcome. Come over here and let me brush your hair tonight, Laurel."

"Just a minute. Mark's kicked off his blanket. He's got more room to fidget in the new bed."

"I'm thinkin' it's time we moved that young man to Andy's room. He's got a 'big boy bed' now." Laurel didn't answer. "You're puttin' up a pretty good front, Wife."

"What are you talkin' about?"

"You're pretending pretty hard, but you're not happy I'm headed back to Little Rock, are you?"

"I'm glad for you because you want to serve."

"But?"

"Nothing else. You need to do this. I will miss havin' you here with us. You know that."

"I do know that. You've sacrificed a lot to let me go. You've worked all summer and fall, givin' me time to get well. You've done most of my work so I'd have time to meet the new folks I need to get to know. I appreciate you more than I'll ever be able to tell ya."

"I'm grateful you are well. I pray you'll stay well."

"Do you know how precious you are?"

"Yes. You've taught me well."

"Thank you for givin' me this excellent family. Life here at

Shiloh is good because you've made us a home here at the foot of Crowley's Ridge. I've been blessed since the day we met." Laurel lowered her eyes to keep him from seeing her concern. *Why couldn't Mac be happy staying home with her and their children? Why did he have to leave them to play a role as a politician?* "I hope you are able to do some good while you're away. Please take care of yourself and come back to us as soon as you can. Please come home well."

"My poor, selfless wife, you're so good to me." Patrick walked over to the small bed where Laurel stood, staring down at her son. He turned her around and pulled her to him. He lowered his mouth to hers and drank deeply of the sweetness he found. "I'll miss you. I'll miss our lovemaking. Please let me make love to you tonight."

"Are you sure you aren't too tired?"

"Shhh...no fretting...I'm well. I need to be with you. I hope you need me as much."

Laurel wrapped her arms around his neck. Her response to his kiss was the answer he'd sought. He slipped her cloud white lawn nightdress from her shoulders and picked her up to carry her to their tall four poster. There they spent the early part of the night satisfying the needs both felt.

Chapter Sixteen

The spirit of a man will sustain his infirmity, but a wounded
> *spirit who can bare?*
> > *Psalm 18:14*

O

John were go   ing to ride to Hopefield and
catch the n October 22nd, Mac left Shiloh
on Midnight. He and
steamboat to Little Rock because it was one of Laurel's
conditions. She said it would be less strenuous than riding
the questionable roads all the way down the state. Before
they'd gotten to the bend in the road, Laurel felt Mac's
absence. She'd thrived under his attention and their nightly
lovemaking the past week, but in the space of only a few
seconds that intimacy with her lover was gone. Not only
would she miss her lover, Laurel knew she'd have to
endure the painful separation from her best friend. She
brushed a tear from her cheek as she lifted her hand in
farewell.

"Mama, is Papa coming home soon?"

"Not for a while, Andy. Maybe he'll be able to get
home for Christmas."

"Gee, he'd better. Papa loves Christmas."

"Yes, he does. Now go get dressed, sweetheart. You
don't want to be late for the first day of school."

By the end of October, the weather turned decidedly
colder. The days were cold, but the nights were frigid. Several
mornings,
Laurel had to break the ice in the animals' watering trough. On the
first Wednesday in November, the temperature seemed dangerously
low, and Laurel worried about the kids walking to school. She bundled
Mark in the buckskin coverlet Mac made for him, and she drove the
children to school. The second day she made the trip, Laurel arrived to
find the school teacher had not come early to warm the church before
the students arrived.

"Cathy, sweetheart, come here and hold Mark so I can get a fire
started." Laurel knew exactly what to do and where to get the wood
and kindling. Making the school warm and a welcoming place to learn
was a top priority for teachers. When she was the Shiloh teacher, she'd

go to school many days by 6:30 to do just that. As she pampered the fledgling flame in the stove, the Flannigan children arrived, shortly followed by Susan's two school-aged children. Before the room began to warm, the other seventeen students had arrived. The teacher had yet to make an appearance, and the time was fifteen minutes to eight. Laurel gathered the group around the stove as close as she dared and continued to stoke the flames. With each thrust of the poker, she felt her anger rise.

At ten minutes to eight, Mr. Tucker opened the door. He snarled at the students gathered around the stove. "Why are you not in your places?"

Then he saw Laurel. "Mrs. MacLayne…" He stood, hat in his hand, at a loss for words.

"Good mornin', Mr. Tucker. I hope you're not ailin'."

"No, ma'am. I'm afraid I overslept this mornin'."

"The children were gathered because I told them to come closer to the heat. I trust there is no problem."

"Of course, I understand. Thank you for startin' a fire for us."

"I'll take my leave. Andy, work hard today, and Cathy, stay warm. You know you're getting the sniffles. Here let me take Mark. We'll be back at four o'clock to bring you home if the weather doesn't warm considerably."

On the ride home from school that afternoon, Laurel learned that the school was frequently cold. Mr. Tucker did not appear to be an early riser, and he often built the fire after the time for school to begin. Laurel knew that her uncle and the school committee had not been told of the teacher's lapse of responsibility. She would talk with Matthew Campbell the next time they met.

The cold continued and worsened. Laurel became more apprehensive each day. She feared the winter would be severe on the ridge after the two relatively mild winters since their first at Shiloh. Even the winter of '57- '58 had not begun as early as this year. Each day she overfilled the wood boxes on the porches. She also had the tenant farmers move the herd into the pastures nearest the shelters they'd built. She didn't know if there would be enough shelter, though, as Mac's stock had nearly doubled since he'd brought them to their homestead, even though Laurel had demanded they slaughter two head so Mac would have fresh red meat nearly every day. Regardless, it was all she could do. Perhaps the winter would not become the fierce season she feared.

Midday toward the end of the week, Matthew Campbell knocked on the back door of the cabin. "Hello, Laurel Grace and young Mac." Her uncle had taken to calling Mark, 'young Mac' because he said the baby would grow to be the very image of his father, bearing the same strong features, dark chestnut hair, and stormy blue eyes.

"Uncle Matthew, I'm so glad to see you. With Mac away, I miss having adult company."

"You'll be really glad when I give you this letter from the capital, then."

"Bless your heart!" Laurel had received a letter the previous week that Mac had posted in Napoleon, but he'd written only briefly about the mostly uneventful ride across the sunken lands and the first leg of the riverboat trip down the Mississippi. He had said that John was proving to be a good help and fine company, although he was a bit of a mother hen, just like his cousin.

"Are things goin' well since Mac's been gone, Laurel?"

"Yes, for the most part. I've been worried about this early cold spell."

"The whole community is talkin' about the cold. Those that follow the old signs say we're in for the worst winter in memory. Ransom Stevenson said he'd run across the biggest beaver dam he'd ever seen over on Lost Creek. Granny Olson brought a wooly worm to church last week…nearly solid black and so thick with hair. She said we'd better cut more wood. The persimmon seeds even had spoons in them this year. I've seen more than one."

"I don't know if I believe in those old signs, but I know it's too cold. I've broken the ice for the animals since Tuesday." "You need help gettin' in supplies?"

"No, Mac made sure we'd be fine. The tenant helpers already moved the animals nearer to shelter. But Uncle Matt, I am concerned about the students at the subscription school. Mr. Tucker not gettin' a fire built so the school is warm when the children arrive."

"Mary told me you had built a fire on Wednesday, and she said you stopped the teacher from yellin' his head off. I think that's how she put it. I'll talk to the committee, and we'll see to our kids' welfare." Matthew sat at the table while Laurel brought coffee and warm bread to him. She also put a pot of honey butter nearby.

"You look a bit puny this mornin', Laurel Grace. You feelin' all right?"

"Fine. I've not slept as well since Mac's been gone."

"I've heard talk about influenza over around Gainesville. Dr. Gibson says he's been over to the Walnut Grove community twice in the last week to care for young'uns with the grippe. I'm goin' to make my rounds today and tomorrow to check on our flock. If it seems bad here, we'll probably close the school. Seems grippe spreads like wildfire once it gets started. I'll make some kind of announcement at church on Sunday."

"Gracious. Cathy's got a runny nose. I hope she's not gettin' the flu."

"No frettin'. Kids get colds. We don't know yet if there's a problem. Don't be a borrowin' trouble…today's is enough for today."

When Matthew Campbell left, Laurel put Mark down on a pallet near the fireplace for his nap. She took the letter from her pocket and broke the seal.

Dearest Laurel,

We arrived in Little Rock yesterday. John and I will board with the Scotts again. We didn't get our big corner room, a place I have scores of memories of us, but perhaps it's just as well. Sharing the space with John just wouldn't be the same. Laurel smiled, knowing her husband probably laughed when he'd written those words. I heard the first session will convene on November 5, so I still have a couple of days to get settled. John and I are going over to the Statehouse tomorrow to see what's going on there.

The weather here is mild and sunny. The trip up the Arkansas was pleasant. We enjoyed walks on the deck all three days on the Arkansas Star. The boat was somewhat larger than the one we came on.

I met L.L. Mack on board. He is the Greene County representative. Nice fellow…I think I'll enjoy getting to know him.

I hope you and the kids are all well and happy. I miss my family already. I don't know if I can survive alone here until Christmas. Write soon and often.

Your blessed husband,

Mac

Several days later, Thomas MacLayne paid a visit to Laurel. "Pa, it seems forever since you've been here."

"Just got home, Laurel dear. I've been north to Missouri. I found two new tenant farmers. I talked to Patrick, and he'd asked me to share out a part of that woodland he bought last year."

"I didn't know. He'd talked about lettin' that area lay for several years."

"Daughter, he told me…I hope I'm not saying more than I should…he said the place is gettin' too big for him. I know he was thinkin' about his stamina. He told me the wounds are healed, but his strength has been slow in returnin'."

"I know, Pa. Dr. Gibson didn't want Patrick to go to the capital."

"He'd asked me to find a couple more men to help with the place. Up in Douglas County, I found two brothers who wanted someplace to get a start. Both of 'em are Patrick's age or better. They got some education, one of them was a school teacher at one point. Neither got a family. I think they'll make good neighbors. James and J.F. Clarke are the names. They're gonna work your homestead this winter, then in the spring we'll help build their cabin over in the woodlands."

"Where will I put them, Pa? The widow's place is occupied now with the Flannigan family."

"Didn't know that. Well, we could set up a place in the barn, I guess."

"In this cold?"

"Suppose you're right. That would be a little heartless, I guess."

"I've got room in the cabin, but I'm not sure I would be comfortable havin' two strange men livin' under my roof with Mac gone."

"What about two strange men and a father-in-law?" "What about your place, Pa?"

"I can check on it every couple of days. I've got good help on the place already. We turned a good profit last year between the lumber and the pelts we harvested. They'll do fine if I'm there or not."

"We'll make the space. All week I've been thinkin' of bringin' the kids into my room anyway so I can keep a better check on them during this cold. The fireplace in there does a good job of heatin' that room."

"It's settled then. We'll come tomorrow. We'll hibernate together for the winter, or at least until Patrick gets home from Little Rock."

At the end of November, Laurel got a third letter from Mac. It was dated the tenth of November. He told of the opening days of the thirteenth legislative session. He spoke of the new speaker, Bradley Bunch of Carroll County. Laurel remembered meeting him when she was in Little Rock the previous session. Mac said he liked this man, and they agreed on their pro-union stand. He said many of the legislators felt as he did that secession would be the wrong choice for Arkansas. The tone of his letter sounded hopeful.

Nevertheless, sweet Laurel, nearly every day some firebrand from the lowlands puts that issue back in to play on the house floor. I wish the governor would take a stand, but he didn't when he addressed both chambers the other day. He did say we need a railroad. He supports a line to connect Memphis and Springfield, Missouri, but talk is cheap. Railroads cost lots of money…We'll see. You know our biggest argument so far? Are we gonna hire a chaplain? Same thing happened last term.

Strangest thing, Laurel. For three nights this week, I dreamed about you. You and the kids are standing on the porch…the wind is blowing your hair, and you have Mark on your shoulder. Andy's waving to me. At first, it was pleasant, seeing y'all there waiting for me.
Darndest thing…the faster Midnight galloped, the further away y'all got. I couldn't seem to get all the way home. I guess I'm just missing y'all too much.

I'll stop now, darling. How I miss holding you and playing with the kids. I pray nightly all are well. I did get one letter so far. I know I left you with a huge task, but please write when you can.

I love you, Mac

Laurel sat down that night and wrote a light, happy letter downplaying the cold and the flu scare. She wanted nothing to add to Mac's worry of her being alone. She did tell him of his father's moving in with her and the Clarke brothers who came to share the woodlands. They'd told her they were hunters and planned to keep much of the forest in their fifty-acre tract. She also told him they were doing all the outside work on the homestead during his absence. Unfortunately, the letter did not get to the Greensboro post office for some time. The first winter snow shut the family in for nearly a week.

When the snow cleared during the first week in December, Laurel made a trip to Greensboro. The day had turned out to be surprisingly warm, above freezing, so she bundled Mark in his knitted blanket and buckskin cover and held him as close as the active toddler would allow. She had two errands she wanted to fulfill that day. She posted two letters to Mac and was delighted to find another letter from him. She bought salt, flour, and some candy for Andy and Cathy. She also asked John McCollough to order fruit for Christmas. She placed an order for a silver-handled brush and mirror for Cathy's Christmas present. She bought material to make a new shirt for the Clarke boys and Roy. For her father-in-law, she sent for a book on the building of Annapolis. She still had to go to the saddler down the street and order the new saddle Mac had asked her to get for Andy. Mac planned to give his son his first horse that Christmas. Christmas was a bright hope.

She wanted the perfect gifts. She wanted Mac home.

The other errand was more personal. Laurel had felt nauseous for the past several days. She feared the stories of influenza, and she knew how quickly it could spread through a family. She would seek out help from Dr. Gibson. With her cabin so crowded now, she could not risk infecting her entire household, if she had somehow contracted the 'flu.

"Well, Laurel, what do you hear from Mac?"

"He said he's busy but restin' as much as he can. He said there is too much secession talk, but so far business is still gettin' done. He thinks most of the representatives agree with him that we need to stay part of the union."

"I'm glad he took my warnin' and is restin'. He's too dedicated to his office to give it all up and come on home."

"I haven't told him about the harsh winter, nor the 'flu. Dr. Gibson, I came because I'm afraid I've caught the grippe. The past few days, I've felt pretty bad."

"Bad? How? Fever...cough?"

"No, not yet. I'm really sick to my stomach. I have thrown up my breakfast more than once. I'm not eatin' well any time of day really."

"Um-huh. Come let me look ya over. 'Flu usually starts with a bad fever." After a brief examination, the doctor pulled his glasses off and rubbed his eyes. "Tarnation! Some patients never do what they're told. They die and then their family wants to know why!"

"Die? Did you tell me to do something I don't remember?"

"Not you, Laurel Grace. Mac! I told him to avoid exertion and romancin' until I knew his heart was stronger. He didn't listen—not one whit. I'm surprised he's still with us."

"You tellin' me I don't have the grippe?"

"Not one case reported in Craighead County yet, only in Greene and Lawrence so far. No, what you got is another MacLayne on the way. I'd say about seven months or so from now."

"Thank the Lord! Thank you, Dr. Gibson. Mac will be thrilled about the new baby." Laurel knew exactly what she'd give her husband for Christmas this year...this time she'd pray for a daughter.

On the ride home, Laurel read Mac's letter aloud to Thomas—most of it anyway. She noticed the tone was much darker...sad. Laurel sensed things were not going well in the legislature. He told her about a resolution censuring the election of Abraham Lincoln and an attempt to repeal the land agent bill they'd passed in the last session. He also decried the many petitions to offer relief to private citizens who could not deal with their own financial problems.

Laurel, sometimes I get so frustrated. We can't do things to help our state with schools, better roads, or a decent levee system because our treasury is too strapped. Yet, we can let men get off without paying their debts because they know someone in the statehouse.

The secession talk is rampant here since the news of Lincoln's election. Can you believe one senator said on the floor that it's the greatest national calamity that ever happened in this country? He doesn't know any more about Lincoln than I do. I wished Douglas had won, but we did it to ourselves when we divided the Democratic vote between him and Breckinridge.

Good things have to come to pass, too. We passed a bill to compensate for the loss of property at the Mountain Meadows attack. We can't replace the families or Gracie's parents, but there will be funds to help raise her. I'm still trying to find a way to get her home with us at Shiloh. Mr. Watkin's brother-in-law was not re-elected, it seems. We also passed a bill to set a road tax to improve the Military Road between Craighead and Poinsett Counties.

The best thing I've done so far is to confront Digby. I told him I had brought charges against him for fraud on our land. He asked if there was not some way to settle this problem. He agreed to meet with me tomorrow to 'talk' about the mistake.

Mac's frequent letters became the mainstay in Laurel's days. In the beginning, she was encouraged and strengthened just to see his bold steady script, but after a time, she noticed a change. The tone of the letters was forced, and news from the statehouse was replaced with Mac's questions of home and his longing to be back with his family. Most concerns came when Laurel noticed the unsteadiness of Mac's script, the frequent corrections in what he'd written, and the scattered ink blots on the page. Mac had always been such a meticulous penman, and his script had always been so characteristic of his nature: clean, masculine, bold and deliberate.

"Take care of Mac, Lord. Please take care of my husband." She lost the sense of time as she knelt there, alone but oddly not so. So strong was the sense of comfort that she didn't want to leave.

Only Mark's crying brought her back to the awareness of her world. She rose and went to pick up her son. She nuzzled the chubby cheek of young Mac. He was growing to look more like his father every day.

"My dear little son, I love you, and your papa will be home with us soon. God keep you both safe." She resigned herself to lay Mac's health into God's hands, and as she did, the words from Romans 8:28 came to mind.

Chapter Seventeen

Strengthen ye the weak hands, and confirm the feeble knees. Say to them of fearful heart, be strong, fear not: behold your God will come with vengeance, God will recompense; He will come and save you. Isaiah 35:3-4

nthony Hotel's elegant dining room gleamed with crystal and silver at noon as Mac waited to be seated for his meeting with Digby. Fresh evergreen mixed with red and green holly provided scents reminding him of the coming holiday. The aroma added to the homesickness that he already felt, knowing he'd not be able to go home this year.

"Will you be dining alone, sir?"

"No. I have a meeting set with Mr. Digby. If he isn't here yet, I'd like to be seated to wait for him."

"Yes, sir. This way please." The impeccably dressed waiter led Mac to a table near a tall window away from the center of the room. "Would you like a something to drink while you wait?"

"Just a cup of coffee right now."

"Yes, sir." Mac scanned the room, remembering the night he and Laurel danced at the Governor's reception nearly three years ago. How beautiful she had been in her silver-gray sateen ballgown that night and how small her waist felt in his hands as they waltzed. He recalled the green flashes in her eyes as they talked and romanced each other. He moved his hand to the chair next to him as if to capture her hand...

"MacLayne, I'm sorry to be late. I appreciate you for takin' time to talk to me about our misunderstanding."

"Please have a seat, Mr. Digby. I have a couple of hours before I have to return to the statehouse for the next session. Perhaps we find some kind of solution to the problem I am now facing back home."

"Is there something more than the problem about the land? I am prepared to solve that problem immediately. I've brought the cash...."

The waiter intervened and took their order for a noon meal. He refilled Mac's coffee cup and set a second cup in front of Digby. He removed the extra place settings at the table. All this time, the two men sat without speaking and stared at each other. When they were alone again, Digby broke eye contact with Mac and used his elegant crisp napkin to wipe his forehead.

"As I was saying, I am prepared to return the price of the land today."

Mac reached over to the floor by his feet and took his buckskin satchel that he'd made to carry documents back and forth from the capitol building back to the boarding house to read during the evenings. He removed a stack of papers about four inches tall and laid them on the table very deliberately. "Mr. Digby, I've been looking into your 'work' while I've been here in Little Rock."

Digby looked over at the stack of paper Mac had his elbow on. He gulped and his eyes took on the shape of the full moon. The sweat from his forehead returned. "Now see here, MacLayne. I understood we were to work out some kind of arrangement that would solve this difficulty for both of us. What need do you have for all those documents?"

"I am always prepared when I face a worthy opponent. Remember, we already faced each other once in an election. I'll not underestimate your ability." Mac sat back in his chair and relaxed a bit. He knew Digby had fallen for his ploy.

"What exactly do you want from me?"

"First, I'd like the truth. When I know the whole story then I'll decide how much compensation will be due. As much as I hate the inconvenience of going to court, Mrs. Flannigan and I will sue you if we are forced to do so."

Red-faced and stuttering, Digby began to rise.

"If you leave before our discussion is complete, I'll have a warrant sworn out for your arrest before I return to the capital today."

Digby sank back into his chair.

The waiter brought their meal and retreated. "Let's eat, Digby. We have a great deal to talk about before I must leave."

Neither spoke while they ate. Mac relished his excellent steak, but Digby hardly tasted the fine piece of meat on his plate. Finally, Mac pushed his plate to the center of the table, motioned for another cup of coffee, and pulled the stack of papers in front of him on the table.

"I never seem to get enough coffee. My wife doesn't like coffee, but she always has a fresh pot ready for me at home. I miss that when I'm away."

"When you're finished reminiscing about your life in the northeast, I'd like to get down to business. Tell me what kind of dirt you think you've found on me. What's in that stack of documents you pulled out of that bag?"

"Very well, Digby. This first one is important to me. It's a statement from the judge in Craighead County that told me the land you sold to the Flannigan family belonged to me. Of course, I already knew that. Unfortunately, they didn't. This fifty-acres is in the middle of two hundred, forty-acre tract, handed down to me from my grandfather as part of his payment from the War of 1812. I also have a statement from the clerk in Greene County stating the taxes on that land had never been in default." Mac showed him the two documents that were on the top of the large pile of other similar looking papers. "Do these satisfy you that I own that land?"

"Well, yes, obviously someone made a mistake when they gave us that parcel to sell."

"Please remember the first thing I told you I must have for our solving this dilemma is your telling me the truth."

"I'll have to look into this. I don't know how it got into our list of parcels to be sold, but I will find out. What else do you have?"

"I have the deed you gave the Flannigan family when they bought the land from you here in Little Rock at your office." Mac showed him the third document.

"I admit that is one of my deeds. I tell you it was a mistake."

"Mrs. Flannigan identified Robert Duncan as the man who took them to that plot of land and staked off their acreage. Why Robert

Duncan? You knew he had a history with my wife from back in Washington County. All that came out at the election in '58"

"Duncan is my agent in Northeast Arkansas. He works that whole region for me. He knows the area pretty well. He told me he was raised there."

"That is a lie. He was raised in Washington County, the same community where my wife Laurel lived until we were married. He knows about as much about the northeast as you do. I don't think we can come to an agreement, Digby, because you can't seem to tell the truth about anything. Good day to you." Mac picked up his documents and stood.

Digby grabbed his arm and spoke through his teeth. "Please wait. I'll tell you what you want to know. I don't want any more trouble."

Mac returned to his chair. "If I suspect you are lying to me again, I'm going to turn these documents over to the sheriff and let him deal with your dishonesty."

"How much do you want to let this matter go away? I have the hundred dollars here and the thirty-seven dollars you told me they paid in back taxes. Will that clear the problem?"

"Digby, Mr. Flannigan is dead now."

"I didn't kill the man. I've not been back to northeast Arkansas since the election of '57."

"I know you didn't kill the man. He died when he was thrown from a horse as he ran from the law. They thought he had tried to kill me when the circuit judge ruled his land deed was a fraudulent document. His horse threw him on Buck Snort Hill in the middle of a tornado when he was trying to get back to save his family from the storm."

"He shot you? I didn't know he'd shot you. Then why are you trying to help that man?"

"He didn't shoot me. I think you know more about that than

Flannigan did."

"I … I…" Digby stopped in the middle of his statement knowing Mac would prosecute him as he'd said he would. His slumped shoulders and downcast eyes told Mac he was prepared to tell him what he wanted to know about the entire episode.

"I'm giving you this one last chance to come clean, Digby. The night I was shot, my entire family was in harm's way. A ricocheted shot struck a lamp and set my cabin on fire. My son was inches from me and when I rose to push him to the floor, a bullet grazed my skull. A second shot barely missed my heart. Had it not been for the quick actions of my wife, I'd have died that night, and Flannigan would have taken the blame for the shooting. We found later that he didn't own a weapon capable of delivering those shots."

"I tell you I was more than a hundred miles away."

"Why did you sell Flannigan a piece of my property? You know it was no mistake."

"Duncan wanted me to do it."

"Duncan is not the leader of this shady business."

"He was being paid off by a couple of planters from the Delta to get even with you, and he told me he had a score to settle with your wife. He said this would take care of both of y'all."

"What did you get out of all this? There was no money to be made on a sale this small in our part of the state. You don't like Duncan that much."

"I don't like him at all. He threatened me if I didn't cooperate with the scheme. I got paid five hundred dollars to draw up the documents and sign them as the registered land agent.
That's all I did."

"You put my family's lives in jeopardy for five hundred dollars! I ought to shoot you right here in the Anthony House. No one would blame me in the least."

"MacLayne, I promise, I did nothing to put your family in danger. When Duncan told me that he was going back to finish what he'd started, I told him I'd have nothin' more to do with his schemin'. I didn't know he was going to try to kill you. When he came back and told me what he'd done, I told him to leave the county. I said I was done with him, and he should never come back again. He said you were dead. When I saw you on the capitol steps on opening day, I thought I was seeing a ghost."

"You spineless cheat. If I thought putting you in prison would make life better for the Flannigan family back in Shiloh, I'd turn these papers over to the law right now." Mac pounded his fist on the stack of papers in front of him. "Peggy Flannigan is a widow now with three school-aged children to raise by herself.
You rotting in the hoosegow wouldn't give her kids an education or put food on their plates until they're old enough to fend for themselves. What do you think you can do to help out that poor widow with her orphaned children?"

"MacLayne, I'll do whatever you say I have to do. Please, I don't want to spend the rest of my days in prison. Please, just tell me what I have to do."

"I'll take the cost of the land and the taxes today. That goes to Mrs. Flannigan because you stole it from her and her family. I am leaving for home at the end of the session, which I hope will be in two weeks. Before I go back to Shiloh, I want a gift of one thousand dollars for each member of that family to live on. I'll take your gift of four thousand dollars back to Mrs. Flannigan to replace the husband your foul deal took from her family."

"Four thousand dollars! I'm not sure I can raise that much money in two weeks."

"I'll bet you can. That only amounts to about ten dollars a page of each sheet of paper I have on the table in front of you. Those first three sheets are enough evidence to put you away for several years…wonder what the rest would lead a jury to sentence a thief like you to serve?"

"I'll get the money. I'll bring it to you before you leave for home." Digby scampered out of the dining room without looking back even once.

Mac leaned back in his chair and laughed. He could not replace the father to the Flannigan family, but he had made it possible for them to live comfortably. His trick had worked so well. The three pieces of evidence against the land agent had been enough. The rest of the stack of paper, copies of bills and committee reports he'd brought to read in the recess, had added the "preponderance" of evidence to convince Digby he had no hope of escaping punishment. Even better, the man had given him the name of the man who had attacked his home and family. He returned to the statehouse to finish the day's work. Between the debates on the floor and three committee meetings, Mac was not able to return to the Stones' until well after nine o'clock. He had skipped supper for the third time that week, and he was exhausted. Despite his successful meeting with Digby that day, the stress took its toll. He could feel the onset of pounding in the back of his head. He slipped into bed without waking John. *db*

About three o'clock in the morning, Mac sat before the embers of the dying fire, holding the sides of his head, tears wetting his cheeks and beard. His moans, muffled by the washcloth clamped in his teeth, broke the silence of the hour. Shivering, he pulled at the quilt from his bed and drew it around his shoulders and rocked himself as a mother might try to comfort an ailing child. *Laurel. Dearest. I need you.* Again, he moaned… his agony beyond describing. *Laurel Grace, I want to come home.* Knowing he could not sleep with pain so severe, Mac reached for the bottle of laudanum he'd not used since his return to the capital.

As the sun rays pierced the darkness at the uppermost edges of the windows, Mac woke. Careful not to awaken John across the room, he pushed himself up from the place at the hearth where he had fallen asleep in the wee hours of the morning. While the pain no longer felt like a hammer striking an anvil, the vice-like tension at the back of his neck and upper spine, which typically followed a night of headaches, placed a grimace on his face. No matter, Mac rose to dress for the day. The sooner the House could finish its business, the sooner he could go home to his family. He'd not be a reason for any delay.

He made his way downstairs to the dining room and found Mrs. Scott preparing her typical country breakfast. "Good-mornin' Mac. Want a cup of hot coffee?"

"I do, Rosalee. Hot and strong. Maybe it'll kill what's left of this headache."

"Have a seat and I'll fix ya a big breakfast before you go off to the Statehouse."

"No, thanks. I've got no stomach for much. Coffee will do me just fine."

"I ain't sendin' ya off for the day without food. Laurel would have my hide if I let you go out of here without somethin' to eat. You ain't come home for the past three days at lunch."

"All right. I'll try to eat a biscuit and a couple of slices of bacon. You're as fussy as my wife."

"I'll give you one now and fix one to go. You gotta keep your strength up. I got a letter from Laurel a few days back, and she told me you're still healin' from gunshot wounds. I can't send ya home in worse shape than you came to me."

"J.W., help me. Come in here and kiss your wife and get her off my back. I need to get headed on to the statehouse." The Scotts laughed at Mac's silly attempt to change the subject.

"Rosie told me about that attack, Mac. What was all that about? Political dispute?"

"I'm not rightly sure what caused it. At first, we thought it was a dispute over a shady land deal that was carried out by a man who ran against me during the last term. We about ruled that out because the man we thought did the shootin' didn't own the kind of gun I was shot with. Still kind of a mystery."

"You all right now?" Rosalee placed a small plate with a biscuit filled with bacon before Mac.

"More or less." Mac moved back his hair and displayed the crease left when the bullet grazed his skull. "This little souvenir gives me a whopper of a headache from time to time. Well, I'm off. Want to see how much work we can get done today. Only a couple of weeks 'til Christmas and I'd sure love to go home."

Mac slowly walked the three blocks to the statehouse. As he approached the tall, stucco-covered brick columns on the porch of the building, he was stopped by Representative Griggs, the man who had been his most aggressive opponent during the last legislative session. "Thought we'd be shed of you. Did ya move
back to Greene County, MacLayne?"

"No, still in my homestead at Shiloh."

"How in the devil did you get back in the legislature?"

"The Lord just needed me, so he called me back." "Don't suppose you have changed your tune yet and now got enough sense to vote with the rest of the Arkansans in this body."

"I just told ya that the Lord needed me. He sure wouldn't send me back down here to support a losing cause." Griggs moved toward Mac just as Quinton Mason, Mac's colleague from the Appropriations Committee called out, "Hey, MacLayne, can I have a word with you?"

"Excuse me, sir. It seems I am needed. Good day."

Together with Mason, Mac walked out of harm's way toward the vestibule of the striking Capitol building. "MacLayne, are you always in trouble?"

"Seems to be. Lately anyway."

A long day of work lay before the state legislators. Again, Mac found no time to return to the boardinghouse for lunch. About two o'clock, he realized he was hungry and was glad he'd brought the extra biscuit from breakfast. He devoured it in about two bites and gulped it down with a swig of water between committee meetings. When the chairman called the assembly into session at 4:00, Mac hoped the day's work would be adjourned, as his headache had never ceased all day. He was ready to return to the boarding house and his bed.

"Gentlemen of the House, we have a bill laid before us from the Appeals Committee. They ask for an immediate floor debate. The title of this bill is 'An immediate repeal of Act 138 of 1858.'" Mac shook with indignation. This bill was the same piece of law that he'd worked so hard to pass into law just the previous session. If passed, all punitive measures for dishonest land agents would be withdrawn and the shady sale of government lands and false deeds would continue.

"Mr. Speaker?"

"The floor is granted to the representative from Craighead County."

"Why is this act just now being introduced to the body? I was part of the committee that worked to pass this law just last session. It's the first I've heard of its presentation during this session."

"Will the chairman of the committee address this question?" The speaker asked.

"The chairman is not in attendance this afternoon, Mr. Speaker."

Mac rose. "Mr. Speaker, I move this matter be tabled until the chairman can be present to address our concerns."

A large number of representatives from the southern and eastern parts of the state cried out, "Nay. Let's debate the bill."

The speaker was not pleased with the turmoil. He called for a voice vote and the debate was allowed. Mac and several other men who supported the bill began their defense of this stand against corruption and greed. Delegates from the opposing side spoke with as much passion and vehemence. The furious debate continued for more than five hours.

"Fellow delegates, the clock reads nine o'clock. It is much too late, and the room has grown much too cold for this discussion to continue tonight. I adjourn this debate until tomorrow morning at 11:00 when I would like to be able to call a vote before lunch. Appoint two speakers to rebut the arguments. This session is adjourned until tomorrow at 8:00 a.m."

The chairman from the Appropriations Committee approached the representatives who wanted to protect the bill they'd passed the previous session. "MacLayne, you need to speak for our side. You have been our strongest proponent since we passed it last year. You have dealt with it personally. Will you do it?"

"I'm not sure I am able. What else can I say that I haven't already said?"

"Tell them your story. Keep your head and lay it out straight. We need to keep this law."

Mac agreed to speak for the opposition, but at that moment, he had to rest. He'd do no good if he were unable to get out of his bed the next day. At that moment, he hoped he had the energy to walk the three blocks.

As he plodded back to the Scotts' boardinghouse, Mac stopped every block to garner enough energy to walk the next leg of his trip. The drizzling rain turned to sleet and tiny crystalline snowflakes that stung his bare skin. His fatigue added to his sense of helplessness over the turn of events in the statehouse that day. *Why am I here, Lord? I sacrifice time with my family and friends for nothing.* Mac shuffled on in the cold, wet night. As he stepped up to the Scotts' porch, he was sapped. He pushed open the door and stumbled across the threshold. Only by grasping the back of an armchair did he stop a fall.

Rosalee Scott came from the kitchen. "Mac…here, let me help you sit down. What's happened to ya, man?"

"Just ran out of strength to go." Mac slumped into the chair.

"Jay, please come help me."

In a matter of minutes, the Scotts had Mac in his bed and John on his way to bring the doctor. The doctor, who was not familiar with Mac's recent history, listened to his heart and shook his head. He examined the scars from the recent gunshot wounds and again shook his head. "Man, are you a lunatic?"

"Yes, probably. I am an elected member of the legislature."

"Now I understand your condition. I've often thought I'd like to shoot me a politician or two."

"Tonight, I am in complete agreement. Can you give me something to get me through the rest of this session so I can get back home to Craighead County?"

"I'm not sure I've ever heard a weaker heart. You've gotta stay in that bed at least a week. If you don't rest, you'll not live the week out."

"Nonsense. I'm just tired. I just need some laudanum for these blasted headaches that won't let me sleep and a good tonic to give me some strength."

"And what medical school did you attend, Mr. MacLayne?"

"Sorry, doc. I didn't mean to do your job for you. I've just got a little more work to do here in Little Rock and then I can go home for good. Can't you help me?"

"I can give you some relief from the headaches, but that heart…" Again, he shook his head. "I know only one cure for that, rest and lots of it."

"I've been resting, seems like forever. I've done nothin' but get weaker. I need to be up workin' and buildin' my strength."

"Sittin' in a chair in the statehouse isn't building back that heart muscle. Slow exercise and good food might help. We'll try that. If you don't slow down, I'll be sendin' a corpse back to Craighead County, wherever in tarnation that is. And cut back on the laudanum. Use only enough to let you sleep."

Listening from the foot of Mac's bed, John's eyes were the shape of full moons and the scowl on his face indicated his anxiety. He could hardly stand still. The doctor handed him a small vial containing the laudanum Mac had requested. "Doctor, should I write home and tell his wife, he's sick?"

Mac snapped back. "No. Laurel has enough on her hands."

"Let's see what tomorrow brings, son. Maybe Mr. MacLayne will be better after a good night's sleep and some good food in his stomach."

Laurel had lived with a sense of foreboding for the past couple of weeks. Things at home progressed well, the weather had been temperate, and the work on the homestead eased as winter continued. Her family was well, the tenant farmers were proving to be excellent helpers, and her friends and family around Shiloh had worked to keep her involved so she didn't have time to miss Mac too much. Yet, at the end of the day, there was a gnawing feeling that something was not right.

Two weeks before Christmas, a brief letter from John Campbell told her what she feared was so.

Dear Cousin Laurel Grace,

Mac would be mad as a hornet if he knew I was sending you this letter, but I had to do it. He's workin' way too much. That speaker fellow is tryin' to get this term over fast. The legislature meets from early, usually eight or earlier, and goes on until sometimes eight at night. Many days, Mac don't come back to the Scotts' house 'til near midnight.

When he gets here, he's so tired he falls into bed and goes right to sleep. A couple of nights last week he didn't eat one bite. I hate to add to your worries, but I know I'd have to face you if I let anything happen to Mac when you sent me down here to watch over him. I tell him every day...eat and rest...but he just says 'I will', and he goes right on working. Last night we went to get a doctor. He told Mac to rest more and eat better. But this morning, Mac got up and went to the statehouse to make a speech to save the bill about land agents they passed last year.

He did good, too, because they voted to keep the bill.

I went to the college here the other day. They let me sit in some classes. I am learning all kinds of things just sitting there. I wrote to my ma and pa. If I can get in, I want to enroll next term. 'Til then, I've got me a job workin' to save what I can to pay for my schooling.

Please write to Mac and make him take care of himself. I don't seem to be doing a very good job.

Your cousin

John

John's letter confirmed to her what Mac's had not. Due to the workload at the statehouse, Mac wasn't eating well nor resting enough. Fear was her first response. Laurel felt panic trying to push away her reason. She wanted to scream. Yet, before the panic won, she felt a calm peace. She sank to her knees "No, I won't let you destroy me, Satan! I am stronger than that." And then a single phrase ran through her mind…*My grace is sufficient for you. She* tried to pray, but that single phrase blocked all other thought. For the moment, that was all she needed.

Chapter Eighteen

And the Lord, He that doth go before thee; He will be with thee, He will not fail, neither forsake thee: fear not, neither be dismayed.

Deuteronomy 31:8

W hen Christmas Eve came, Mac had not made it back to Shiloh, Laurel knew the speaker had not allowed a holiday recess. Mac had been hinting in his letters that the workload was extremely heavy and that he might be delayed in returning. In his last letter, he'd written they'd taken nine rounds of votes trying to elect a new judge for the supreme court of the state, yet no decision produced a new person to sit in that important seat. The problem had not been with the candidate but in the widening split between the pro-union supporters and the abolitionists. In the same letter, Mac told again of his reoccurring dream and how it had awakened him several times in the past weeks. Seeing a ghostly figure of his most loved one made him edgy and anxious to return to her. He didn't mention his health.

Then, he wrote these words that brought tears. "Darlin', I can't wait to see Andy make that first ride on his new pony! He's gonna love that little colt." He continued talking about gifts he'd bought the other children, but the tone of his letter was not one of anticipation. Laurel could almost sense the word 'but' and a deep sigh as she read the words he'd written.

Laurel's sense of Mac's absence proved out. Christmas came and passed without her husband. Laurel managed to provide a similitude of the Christmas the kids had wanted. Presents were opened. Laurel laughed when Andy pulled the new saddle from the burlap bag.

"Golly! This ain't for me, is it Mama? Am I dreamin'?" The moment was bittersweet. Mac planned the gift. He chose the components… the reins, the blanket, and the saddle. Yet, he was not home to share the joy of the giving. When Thomas took Andy to the porch where he'd tied the black foal sired by Midnight, the boy screamed with joy!

"Golly-geeeeee! Oh, Granddad…This can't be…my own horse? Am I in Heaven?"

"Andy, son. Your papa loves you. He aimed to be here this mornin'." Thomas MacLayne stepped into his son's place and watched Andy ride the new pony for the first time.

"Geez! I gotta be the luckiest kid in the world. I'm gonna call him Sparky. I'm glad y'all wanted me." Andrew flung himself into Thomas's arms.

"We're the lucky ones, Andy boy. Let's go and see what's for Christmas breakfast."

Two days later, Matthew brought the mail. Mac's Christmas letter sat on the top of the stack. Unfortunately, the post had not arrived in Craighead County in time for the holiday. Laurel immediately sat down at the hearth to read it.

My dearest,

I pray this letter will reach you to explain my absence from our family Christmas.

The speaker allowed only one day for the holiday recess, but we are trying to complete the business of the state so we'll be finished by mid-January. I hope it is so. Home and you are my only thoughts these days.

I wish I thought my presence here was making a difference. If I thought it did, I might not feel so bad for missing Christmas. John and I shared a good meal with the Scotts, but I didn't get my new shirt this year."

Laurel smiled…how did he know she'd made him a new shirt?

I do have a surprise for you when I come back. I think you'll like this present.

We did accomplish two good things for our people in the last week. We voted a new road tax to build roads in Poinsett and Craighead counties, and Jonesboro has been incorporated as a town, which I'm pretty sure they'll name as the county seat. That village has the advantage of being in the middle of the land mass. I guess that doesn't help Greensboro much.

Stay well, my love. Kiss the kids and tell them Merry Christmas for me. I will stop now. Maybe I will have a dream of holding you in our tall-four poster.

I am always,

Your husband

She laid the letter aside. "I'm sorry, Uncle Matthew. I wanted to see if Mac was headed home. He's not. The house adjourned only one day."

"I'm sorry, Laurel Grace. I know you miss him."

"He's the one apart from us. I've got my babies and his father and you…I'm warm and eating well. Mac's sitting in that drafty chamber with only those two pretend marble fireplaces to warm that big old room. He's not eating right nor is he resting enough…maybe killing himself and for what?"

"Stop it, Laurel Grace."

Tears streamed down Laurel's face. "I've tried to stay strong, but I miss him. I need him home, healthy and permanently."

"I know...soon. Niece, he'll be home soon."

"I'm sorry, Uncle Matthew. I'll be all right. I'm just tired of the cold, tired of the lonely nights, and tired of the endless work."

"I think you're just tired...period." When is the baby due?"

"I didn't tell you about my baby..."

"I know, but I've got eyes, you know. I've seen pregnant ladies before." Her uncle's comment brought a smile to her face, but it didn't say long.

The next morning, Mark woke Laurel long before the sun rose, whimpering and fretting. The boy never woke in a foul mood. She hurried to his small bed and picked him up. As she brought him to her shoulder, she found him to be very hot. She ran her hand across his forehead and pulled it away as quickly. Mark had a fever worse than she'd ever felt.

"Pa, please come fast." She carried him to the four poster and began to remove his clothes. "Hurry, Pa." She rushed to the bath closet and took the water from the pitcher. A brief touch told her it was too cold. As Thomas approached, she handed him the bowl. "Take the chill off this water. I've got to get the fever down.
Please go get the doctor."

"Daughter, calm down. We'll take care of our boy." She knew it was the 'flu. No other ailment brought such high fever in such a short time. All she knew to do was bring the fever down. She began to wash Mark's hot body with the tepid water. As quickly as the cloth warmed with the baby's fever, Laurel returned it to the cooler water... over and over. After what seemed an eternity, Mark was not as hot as he'd been. He cried a languid sound that told his mother he was in pain. She sat in the rocking chair and began to sing to him, the old lullabies and hymns she'd learned from her own mother. When the fever rose, she'd wash him again. She did not know how many times that day she repeated the same routine.

Cathy came to help, but Laurel would not turn Mark's care over to her. She feared the spread of the illness, and she feared even more not having the sick baby in her own arms. "Cathy, can you go out and get the milk? Heat just a bit of it and let me try to feed Mark. Then make me some very watery oatmeal and put a spoon of honey in it. Maybe the sweetening will tempt him to eat it." She covered her son with the lightest blanket she had and still the heat from his tiny body crept through her clothes as she held him in the rocking chair in front of the fireplace. Mark slept fitfully in her arms.

When Cathy brought the oatmeal, Laurel told her what she would need to do to take care of the household that day. "Cathy, please keep Andy away from this room, and you don't come back either. Just bring things to the door if I ask. Will you fix a meal for everyone? I hate to ask you to take over my job, but I can't put Mark down right now."

"Sure, I can help, Mama. Mark will be all right, won't he?"

"I'm sure he will." Laurel continued to rock and sooth the boy for what seemed to be hours. Indeed, it was past the noon hour when Dr. Gibson came back with Thomas MacLayne. Ed Gibson confirmed what Laurel had known. Mark had contracted influenza, like so many other children in the area.

"Are the others sick, Laurel?"

"They haven't complained. I hope not."

The doctor shook his weary head. "Well, I hope they stay well, but it'd be a miracle. Watch 'em close. You did the right thing when you took his fever down. Keep a close watch and wash him down when it comes back. I'll leave you plenty of quinine to keep the fever in check. Give it to anyone in the family who gets the same kind of fever. I'd stay a while, but six or seven other families along the ridge are sick already. I'm headed for Susan and Randall's place now. Send for me if it gets worse. Keep him warm, try to get him to eat and make him swallow as much water as he'll allow. No milk though…don't seem to keep milk down."

The doctor left to serve others, and Laurel shook off her dread and set out to care for young Mac. Throughout the day and all night, she sat rocking the toddler, singing to calm him and praying for his healing. When the sun rose the next morning, Mark felt cooler, and he seemed in more natural sleep. Perhaps the worst was over. Laurel laid him in his bed to sleep and went out to the main room to see about the rest of her family. No one was up yet. Cathy and Andrew had moved up to the loft so that the Clarke brothers could share Cathy's room for the winter. Mac's father sat in the armchair, sleeping in front of the fire, which needed stoking. Laurel laid more wood to restore the fire, and the noise roused Thomas.

"Laurel, how's our little one this morning?"

"I think he's better. His fever is down, and he is resting better than he was last night. I wanted to check on the other kids. Are you feelin' all right?"

"Yes, darlin', don't be frettin' over me."

Laurel climbed the stairs up to the loft. When she bent to pull the quilt over Cathy, she brushed her hand across her arm. Cathy now had a fever. Before night fell that day, Andy too had fallen to the winter scourge. She had the children moved down to the second pen so she could tend to all of them. For three days, Laurel spent every minute of the time, cooling their feverish bodies, spooning broth and water into their mouths, and dosing them with quinine. She had no time to cook, see to the homestead, or tend to the animals. She didn't even think about those chores she usually did every day. While Mark seemed to have completely lost his fever by the end of the third day, she didn't seem to be able to break the fever of the older children, regardless of the number of cool sponge baths she gave them or the doses of quinine she

poured into their mouths. The night of the fourth day, Laurel used the last of the quinine the doctor had left for her. At that point, her fears returned.

She broke into tears. Her father-in-law took her into his arms and held her for a few minutes. "Pa, what am I going to do? I don't have any more fever medicine."

"You calm yourself. I'll go find Dr. Gibson. We'll get some more."

"It's too cold to go ridin' around the county when we don't even know where we will find him. That bank of clouds over the ridge is sure to bring another round of snow. No. I need you here."

"If it were summer, I could make yarrow tea, but this time of year, I wouldn't know where to find the plant."

"Dry yarrow…I think Mac put several plants to dry in the root cellar. Let's try that. We'll keep them warm and make them drink honey tea and yarrow. And we'll pray, Laurel. God will take care of our family. You've gotta get some rest, or I'm afraid you'll be down with the kids. You sit here, nap a while if you can. The kids are asleep and I'll hold Mark."

Laurel pulled the quilt over Cathy's shoulder and touched her forehead. Since her dosing with the yarrow tea, her fever ebbed a bit and the pretty foundling slept peacefully for a time. Laurel dropped two more logs into the fireplace and walked to the pallet on the other side of the fireplace and tried to cover Andy. He twisted and jerked, pushing the coverlet to the side of his pallet. As Laurel put her palm against his cheek to check his fever, he thrashed at her and moaned deeply.

"Papa, stop it. Papa." Andy's cough racked his entire body. When he stopped, he seemed to gasp for air. Frantic, Laurel pulled the boy into her arms and carried him to the rocking chair near the fire. *Think, Laurel, think! You know something that can help him. Falling apart won't make him better.* She began to sing the old hymns her mother had sung to her as a child, full of praise and hope and the love of Jesus. Shortly, Andy relaxed and seemed to rest in a more natural sleep than he had in two days. The cough did not stop, but the boy breathed easier and slept on.

While Laurel slept, James and J.F. came to ask if they could help. Thomas sent James down to the root cellar to find more yarrow, and J.F. went to the barn to start the morning chores. By mid-morning, snow began to fall in earnest. By then the tenant farmers had replenished the wood boxes and checked the cattle in the pastures. J.F. took over kitchen duties and started a beef stew for lunch. Laurel continued to sleep, exhausted for her four days of nursing her family with little to no sleep. She finally awoke about noon. She went to the main room and looked out the windows to see the transformed landscape of her land. The powdery snow blanketed Shiloh. The beauty of the view from the windows almost made her forget the fear, tension, and loneliness she'd lived with since Mac had gone back to the capital. "My Lord, how beautiful my home is. Thank you for reminding me of my bounty."

"Mama...I want some water. It's hot in here..." Andy called her from the bedroom. She ran to check on him, hoping his thirst was a good sign, but she touched his brow and found it dry and hot. Cathy too continued to run a high temperature.

Laurel cried out in frustration... "Lord, no...my kids need a doctor. Please, Father...we need your help."

Thomas came in and brought another round of honey and yarrow tea for them and a bowl of steaming hot stew. He took Laurel's place by the bed and began spooning the tea for Andy. "No, Andy...don't fight me. Drink it up. It's good for ya." He then gave the same dose to Cathy who was more compliant with his attempts at nursing her. "Laurel, see if you can get these two to eat a few bites of this stew. It's very good. I made it from dried beef.
It'd do you good to put down a couple of bowls."

"More, Pawpaw." Mark had rolled over to his grandfather to ask for another spoon of stew.

"Look at him. I was feeding him in the kitchen before we came back in here and now, he's asking for more. And he called me Pawpaw..."

238

It was a blessing. Mark Thomas had no fever at all, and he wanted to eat. "Thank God! I think he's well."

Mark's improvement was a relief. Thomas was able to take over his care, and Laurel could then turn her attention only to Cathy and Andrew. Was this a sign the worst was over?

Through the night the snow continued to fall. Six inches of snow now lay on the ridge. The storm had brought with it a sense of isolation for Laurel, although she was never alone. She struggled to push the gloom away. She again went to her knees, asking for help. She was all too aware that she was needed. Cathy and Andrew were still very ill, and she would not let them slip from her family. Andy seemed to be having more trouble breathing than he did earlier.

Laurel remembered the way Elizabeth had eased her father's struggle to breathe so many months ago. "Pa, please come here. Heat a kettle of boiling water and bring me a wash pan and a heavy cloth. Put the yarrow in the boiling water and we'll use the steam and the plant to help clear their airways. I remember that is what my mother did for us when we had the croup. It's got to help."

She took coverlets and made a 'tent' around the four-poster bed and brought hot boiling water into the enclosure and poured the steaming liquid onto the last of the yarrow roots, hoping the steam would help the young lad to breathe easier. She didn't know that it would work, but even an attempt to help was better than doing nothing at all. Both Cathy and Andy seemed to sleep easier after the steam remedy was used.

She sat down next to the fire in her room while they slept. She dozed off for a few minutes, and then she felt a tug at her skirt. Mark had tottered over to her and put his arms around her legs. He was attempting to climb into her lap.

"Mama, hold." She did just that. She pulled him into a hug so tight that he pushed her away. "No, Mama." He threw his chubby toddler arms around her neck, and then he cuddled into her lap and fell asleep almost at once. Laurel found her sense of calm and security. She had continued the steam process until she'd used all the yarrow Mac had preserved in the cellar, but she knew her family would be well now. Both Cathy and Andy breathed easily and their fever was nearly back to normal. Sleep came easily.

Three days later, a strong rap brought Laurel to the front door. As she opened the door, she found her uncle, stomping the snow from his boots. His face was somber and drawn.

"Uncle, why are you out in this weather?"

"Makin' the circuit, checkin' on our people. Are you all well here, Laurel Grace?"

"We're on the mend. The kids have all had the grippe, but the worst seems to be over now. Mark is pretty nearly back to himself. Cathy and Andy are still in bed, weak, but at least they're fever free now. Is your family all right?"

A shadow fell across Matt's face. "This sickness has dealt a hard blow to the whole community, Laurel Grace. We lost five members of Shiloh church, and three of them were children. Susan's daughter, Martha, was among them."

"Oh, dear Lord, no. I've been so busy here with my own, I haven't even thought about your family. I am so sorry for your loss, Uncle Matthew."

"Been hard for us all, but we're blessed it didn't spread worse. We've not had a new case since the last snowfall. Perhaps the troubles at Shiloh are over for now."

"Is Susan all right?"

"As good as the rest of us, I suppose. Hard to praise in the midst of the grief, but we're tryin'. I need you to pray for your Aunt Ellie, though. She's takin' it hard. She was a nursin' little Martha because Susan was pretty sick too. We'll be all right in time. The Lord will provide."

"I want Mac. I need him home."

"So do I. This is a time I could use my best friend around. Maybe a blessin' he's not here. His health may not have been good enough to survive this sickness. This 'flu took stronger people."

"All things work..." Laurel stopped. She didn't need to quote scripture for her uncle. "Uncle Matthew, tell Susan I'm so sorry about Martha. She reminded me so much of Grandma Campbell." "Bless ya, niece. Thank the Lord, your kids are healin'." ❀

That evening after she'd put the children down for bed, Laurel sat down at the writing table near the fireplace to write a letter to Mac. The somber news from her uncle that morning had been the last straw. She planned to demand that her husband come home immediately. She wrote two lines on the first page and wadded the paper up and threw it in the fire. She started again, and with the same result. With a shaking hand, she dipped her pen into the ink bottle and tipped it over onto the crocheted doily on the table. In frustration, she broke into body-wracking sobs.

"Laurel Grace, what has happened, daughter? Are you in pain?"

"Yes, I am. I've had all I can take."

Thomas MacLayne approached his daughter-in-law and drew her into his arms. "Go ahead and cry it out, darlin'. The past month has been a hard one for you...for all of Shiloh. I know you are tired."

"I'm not tired. I'm mad. I'm sick and tired of carrying the load alone, just so Mac can go play politics down in Little Rock. What good does it do anyone anyway?" Thomas nodded and let her talk. "He is ruining his own health. They are trying to dismantle all the work he did last year. Even that land agent bill that he got shot over came up for a vote, and they tried to rescind it." Laurel rose from her chair and moved toward the fireplace, waving her arms in the futility of her rant. "Mac could at least be here to comfort his friends and family when we are hurting so badly!"

"Go ahead. Get it all out. I'm here to listen to you, Laurel."

"Pa, it's too much. I wanted Patrick to feel useful and that his need to serve was important to me, but he asks too much. Why does he feel so driven to be there? Since we've been married, I think we've spent more time apart than we've spent together. We barely begin to establish a family life here, and he finds some excuse to leave home again. He's been gone in every crisis I've faced since we've been married. He wasn't here when Campbell was born and died. We could have lost all three of our children to this influenza, and he was in Little Rock, maybe killing himself with useless work. He's missed two Christmases with our kids in the three years we've had."

"His being gone has been hard on you, Daughter."

"And our kids…He's not satisfied at home. I can't seem to build the kind of home he wants to stay in. I guess I'm not really surprised. Mac is searching for something he lost. I wish I could be enough for him. I hate that he isn't happy here at Shiloh. I can't imagine any place on earth I'd rather be than here with him. I ask God all the time why I'm not enough to keep him here."

"That is more than enough of that, young woman." Laurel looked up, eyes wide and mouth agape. Her father-in-law had never "scolded" her before. "I've tried to listen to you because I know how tired you are and how worried. I won't listen to another word of your blaming yourself for Mac's absence."

"I'm not blaming myself. I don't understand what more I can do, but if I were more like …"

"No one. Mac loves you more than he has ever loved anyone in his entire life. He believes he has been doubly blessed that God allowed him to find you across the state and that you were willing to make a life with him when y'all were strangers. He said those words to me and his mother. He knows you are the best thing in his life." "Then why won't he stay at home with me and our family? We have our own son now. Andy idolizes Mac and misses him so much. I love him, Pa. I do, but I know it's not enough to keep him at Shiloh."

"Laurel, you don't understand. Mac is trying to pay off his debt for killing his friend Louis. We talked about this more than once when he was home before his mother died. He was a different man when he came home. He'd lost that restlessness he'd had when he left for Arkansas. He told me his redemption story. He explained how your uncle Matthew and the circuit rider helped him lay down his guilt over his lost years."

"I know about that part of Mac's life. He told me about the duel with his friend Louis. He told me that he'd made his peace about that, too."

"He did to a degree, but he knew Louis was being groomed for the governor's seat in Maryland. Louis's family has always been part of the political machine in our state. When his uncle decided to give up the governor's seat in Maryland, Louis would have been next in line to take that role. He would have played a serious role in the history of the region for several years."

"Then I'm afraid I don't understand Marsha's pushing Mac and her husband into that silly duel, at all."

"Marsha always preferred Mac over Louis. She thought if Mac would agree, she could have both things she wanted--the social position of being the governor's wife and hostess of state affairs in public and her own special sweetheart in private. Marsha didn't know Mac very well. She didn't know the new Mac who came home from Arkansas at all. She truly hates him now."

"What does all this have to do with the Arkansas state legislature? Patrick has never mentioned he plans to return to Maryland."

"His service here helps him feel that he is making a difference in this state. I believe he is. Look at the good he did the last term. If he hadn't been there this time, they may have abandoned the good work that has been done by the fraudulent land sales bill. He makes a difference. He's good at what he does. He just needs to find a way to serve closer to home, so he doesn't have to leave you here alone to carry the workload of family and the homestead."

"I see. I'm sorry, Pa. I never meant to criticize Patrick. I just miss him so much. I'm more than tired. Forgive my despair and the outburst. I love my husband."

"I know you do, Laurel. He loves you, too, more than he is capable of showing you. Don't give up on him. He'll be home soon."

Chapter Nineteen

And when he cometh home he calleth together friends
and neighbors, saying unto them, "Rejoice with me,
for I have found my sheep which was lost."
Luke 15:6

With the melting of the snow at the end of the first month of 1861, the cold also abated. The fall and early winter had been unusually harsh and wet, but February brought hope for a short winter. The MacLayne children were gradually returning to their boisterous natures as their strength returned with the warmth of the sun—not summer, but mild days and nights when the water didn't freeze solid.

Routine began to return to the homestead, with the men returning to their work outdoors. Laurel started the children's school lessons as a way to keep them occupied. Mark learned to run. He scampered through the cabin constantly, playing as any toddler has want to do. From time to time he fell and demanded to be held. Laurel treasured those moments. If Mac were home, Laurel would be content. She'd made it through the trials of illness and harsh winter. She felt as if she'd overcome a tremendous test.

Now she faced only one more barrier, that of her extreme loneliness due to Mac's absence and that obstacle grew greater every day.

"One day at a time, Laurel. Just make it through one more day." Each morning, she told herself that before she put her feet on the walnut plank floor. She told herself the same thing each night as she tucked Cathy and Andy into bed and placed Mark in his little bed in the corner. And every night she knelt by the fourposter and prayed long and hard as she yearned for Mac. "Please Lord, bring my family back together…all of it."

On February 2nd, about noon, a driver with a small girl drove into the MacLayne yard. Another rider rode beside a new buggy. Mac jumped down from the buggy and climbed the three steps to the front porch. "Laurel, I'm home. Thank the Lord, I'm home!"

Laurel met him before he could open the door. He enfolded her and held her, murmuring over and over. "Never again, Laurel. I'll not leave you alone again. Never again. Laurel, I'm home." Mac truly meant the words he'd spoken to his wife. Holding her had taken every other want from him. He knew how tired he was, and the frustration he felt over the legislative session ebbed away as he kissed her. He was home now, and he intended to stay. "Laurel, come with me and let me give you your Christmas present." He took her hand and returned to the new buggy he'd driven home. "How do you like your new rig, Wife?"

Laurel hadn't even glanced at the buggy. She'd hardly seen it, as a tiny black-haired girl with the saddest brown eyes had totally captivated her attention. "Rachel?" In the seat, swaddled under a heavy lap robe sat the miniature of her friend Rachel Wilson. By some miracle, Mac managed to bring Gracie home to Shiloh. The little girl looked up through her dark lashes, trying to see the woman standing next to her. Avoiding direct eye contact, Gracie shook uncontrollably. Undoubtedly, her four-year-old courage was overcome by the fear of too many strangers in this unfamiliar place.

"Gracie, my dearest angel. Thank God, you've come to us." Laurel reached to pick her up, but the girl crouched back into the corner of the seat. How could this little one have any memory of the person who called her by her name? She didn't remember her own mother or father.

"I'll bring her in Laurel. We've gotten to know each a bit over the last month since Speaker Bunch's wife brought her from Washington County at Christmas time. We're good friends, but I think she likes John better than me."

"Thank you, Mac. I knew you'd find a way to bring her here so we could take care of her, just as Rachel and Joshua would want. You are so good!"

"Well, get me in out of this chill then. I'm tired and cold."

When they entered the cabin, Laurel introduced James and J.F. Clarke to Mac and then asked them to take care of the horses and buggy. Mac saw his father standing near the hearth. He took several steps and greeted him with a strong hug and clap on his back. "Pa, how good it is to see you. Thank you for takin' care of my family this winter. Seems that you've had a much worse time of it here than we did in Little Rock."

"Come sit by the fire, son. Let me take your hat and coat." When Mac removed his coat, his family was shocked at the emaciated frame of the man who stood before them.

"Mac! You've wasted away in these three months. Have you been ill?"

"No, sweetheart. I am tired but not sick. We put in long, difficult hours workin' through the legislative agenda. Since the first of December, we met nearly every day except Sundays, usually convening by 8:00 and not ending to after 8:30 or 9:00 at night. Speaker Bunch did cut almost a month from the calendar, but the gruelin' sessions seemed to take a toll on most of us."

"How thin you are."

"You'll feed me back to normal in no time. Mrs. Scott's a good cook, but she can't hold a candle to you."

"As if you'd know, Mac...You missed more meals than you ate while we were in the capital."

"Enough of that, John. They don't want a report of my eatin' habits." Mac sank into his familiar armchair, and Andy ran to him. "Papa, you missed Christmas. We was a lookin' for ya."

"Yes, son. I hated to be away. Tell me, did you get stones in your stockin' this year?"

"You know I didn't. I love my pony. Granddad let me name him and learned me to ride all by myself – I mean taught me. Thank ya, Papa. I never thought to get me a horse of my own."

"You'll have him as long as you take care of him."

"I do it ever day...I even let Cathy ride a couple of times." Mac reached out to embrace his son.

"I've missed you, boy. Do ya think we can have us a checker game soon?" "You betcha, we can."

Mac continued to get reacquainted with his family, as John held Gracie. The sad-eyed little girl would not be separated from the two people in the room she knew. Mark, too, acted very shyly when Laurel brought him in from his nap. He turned away when Mac reached out to take him from Laurel's arms. "It looks like you're not the only one who has to rebuild connections. Mark seems to think I'm as much a stranger as you are to Gracie.   "A little time will take care of that, Mac. I'm counting on us having plenty of that. I am so glad you are home."

"Mama, you gotta give Papa his Christmas presents. It don't matter if they're late."

"We'll do it after supper, Andy. I think your papa is very tired right now. Let's just let him rest in his chair."

"Can you read us a story, Papa?"

"Yes, Cathy, tonight before bedtime, I'll read to y'all."

"Can I...I hear it too?" Laurel heard Gracie's small quiet voice for the first time."

"Yes, darlin'. The story is for all our family. Papa tells us a story every night before bed. Cathy, you and Andy, go tend to your lessons. Let your papa have some time to talk with Granddad."

"If it's all the same to you, I want to go lie down for a while. We'll talk at supper. I have a lot to tell y'all about the end of the session but not just now."

Laurel handed Mark to his grandfather and went to Mac's side. "Come along, Mac. I'll stoke up the fire in the other room so you'll be warm." He walked—very slowly and seemingly with great effort to the door of their bedroom. The concern on Laurel's face was obvious to all in the room. The man who'd come home was but a shell of the man who'd gone to the capital. Mac had been well on his way to recovery when he left in November, but the work of the thirteenth general assembly had undone nearly all the progress he'd made toward health. "Lie down, and let me cover you. The room will be warm soon."

"When you're done with that fire, Laurel, please come lie beside me. Right now, I want nothing except to hold you and know that I am home."

Supper was a time for catching up. After nearly three months of separation, every member of the family had scores of things to share. Andy couldn't seem to get enough attention from his papa. Mac was able to calm his eagerness with the promise of a ride the next day if the weather would allow.

"All right, Papa, but I want a checker match, too. Can we do it tonight please?"

"No, Andy, tomorrow night would be much better. I need to spend some time with my papa, too." The look on Andrew's face showed him that he was none too happy that his father picked up the sad-eyed girl to sit in his lap. "Now, Pa, as I was tellin' you... I am glad I went to the capital, but I doubt it did my health any good. I think we got a few good things passed that our state's been needin'. A committee is workin' on establishin' a stage route between the four corners of the state. A share of tax money has been set aside to start buildin' the Memphis to Little Rock railroad, and maybe on into Fort Smith. I doubt it's enough, but maybe it'll get one started."

"Those projects would go so much faster if the workers didn't have to float, son,"

"Funny, pa…but you're right. If we can get the beds laid to dry land the construction will go faster. The best thing we did, though, was to table the secession question. Nearly every day someone tried to push the argument on the chamber floor tryin' to get a vote to secede. Thankfully, most of the legislators have level heads. We finally put the issue to rest. One of the representatives from the northwest part of the state stood to speak against a firebrand from the delta who said Lincoln's election was a great national calamity. He said that Arkansas was not justified in following North Carolina out of the union. We could defend our rights if we had too, but for the time, surely intelligent people were capable of sittin' down together and resolvin' differences peacefully."

"I hope you're right, son. I read in the Baltimore paper that Maryland was headin' for secession, but some of the state officials got arrested on some charge or other. A lot of tobacco farmers use slave labor."

"Well, we passed a bill to take the decision to the people this summer. I think when the people vote, we'll stay in the union." Mac started to push his supper away, as he intended to continue with the political conversation with his father.

"Eat your supper, Mac. You can't get up until you eat every bite of the stew in front of you."

"Laurel, I've had too much already…"

"Don't Laurel me…eat."

Reluctantly, he pulled the bowl back and took another bite of the stew but continued his talk across the table.

"What did y'all do about the widow's request to let her maintain ownership of her husband's property?"

"That was the worst black mark on the entire session. She was denied. Those men who control the money in the state kill that bill every time it comes up. Women with money and influence scare men, I guess. That and the bill to arm the capital guard for security and the amendment to the state's militia laws were about the last topics we debated before we adjourned."   Mac laid his head back in his chair and closed his eyes.

"I'm proud of your service, son. You've represented the county well."

Mac smiled. "Those are dear words to me, Pa. I need no other praise."

"Mama, can we have our late Christmas now?"

"Yes, Cathy. I think it's about time that y'all give Papa and Gracie their Christmas presents."

"I brought home presents, too. Andy, will you and Cathy go bring my trunk from the back porch?" Mac added.

"Hooray! More presents." Gracie startled at the tremendous scream that Andy let loose. Her big brown eyes filled with unshed tears.

"Gracie, won't you come over here and let me introduce you to Mark? He's getting big enough to play now." Laurel had yet to embrace the beautiful little girl who was her best friend remade. Gracie looked toward Mac, and when he nodded to her, she took a few very slow, tentative steps toward Laurel, but she didn't get close enough to be touched. She looked at the toddler on Laurel's lap, and she smiled a minute.

Laurel tried again, speaking in a quiet, encouraging tone. "Mark, this is your new sister, Gracie. She's gonna stay here and be part of our family." Mark reached out one of his hands toward the slight girl and caught his tiny fingers in her hair, as toddlers are like to do.

"Ouch, Baby." Laurel quickly untangled Mark's hand from Gracie's curls.

"Are you all right?" An almost indiscernible nod followed, and Gracie ran her finger down Mark's cheek.

"He's a pretty baby."

"Thank you. You are a beautiful little girl, Gracie." The waif turned and walked away, seeking her safe place with Mac again.

"Here it is, Papa. Gosh, it's heavy."

"Who's first?"

"We had our presents at Christmas. Maybe you should go first. Andy, give him the present from you."

Andy handed Mac a round bundle covered in a scrap of red cloth. Mac handled it, shook it and tried to guess what it was. "Come on, Papa. Just uncover it…you ain't never gonna guess what it is."

Mac unwrapped a small log which had been flattened on one side. The six-inch piece of hickory had been carved to look like a frame, and on the flattened part of the wood, Andy had etched out the words, Rep. Patrick MacLayne, Craighead County, 1860-1861. The carving and the etchings were crude, but Mac beamed and pulled his son into a strong hug.

"What a spectacular gift. Andy, I've never had me a nameplate before. Thank you for this wonderful present."

"Granddad gave me the idea, but I done it by myself—well mostly."

"No one's ever had a finer gift, Andrew. I'm gonna put it on the mantle so I can see it every day. You now, Cathy."

Cathy handed Mac a framed sampler she had embroidered for him. She'd spent nearly two months stitching the words of Psalms 23 inside a border of vines and flowers. "You sweet darlin'…how long did you have to work on this? How fine your work is! I think you may be outdoing your mama. Cathy, I'll cherish this all my days." Mac kissed the eleven-year-old, and she blushed with pride that she'd made Mac so happy. "Mama, it's your turn now."

"Wait, I think your papa wants to give you his presents now."

"I can't wait...should I start with the youngest or the oldest?" All the children shouted, all but Gracie, "Youngest!" Mark squealed with delight when his papa gave him a red ball just the size to fit his toddler's hands. The sounds of surprise and laughter filled the room as Mac passed out paper-wrapped packages to his entire family. Andy got new boots. A pair of mittens and a scarf in pink wool made Cathy clap in joy. Finally, a pretty china doll with brown eyes went to Gracie. When Mac presented her with the doll, the shy little girl walked to him and threw her arms around his neck. She wouldn't leave him for some time, and she wouldn't let go of the doll that looked so much like she did.

"Gracie, you're gonna like bein' here with us. Our mama and papa are so good to us. And golly gee...we're rich!" Everyone in the cabin laughed at Andy's proclamation.

"Well, what about me? Do I get any more presents?"

"Darlin', I'm afraid we ate one of your presents. I'd made your mother's oatmeal cookies for you, but I knew they'd get stale so we had them for Christmas dinner."

"Drat...I love those cookies!"

"I do have a couple more small presents for you." Mac opened the soft package Laurel handed him, and he found a new blue shirt. The color was his favorite—storm blue, Laurel called it – to match his eyes.

"Thank you, Wife. I was hopin' I'd get me a new shirt this year."

"You're welcome. This little one is the last gift I have, but I will bake you some cookies later."

"Here, let me have my littlest present. They're usually the best." Laurel took the small bundle from her apron pocket. When Mac ripped the paper away, he found the tiny booties Laurel had crocheted. As he held the booties in his hand, he felt some of his fatigue and frustration begin to fade. For the first time in several weeks, Mac felt his hopes and dreams come back into focus.

"God bless you, Laurel. You make me a richer man every day of my life. A new baby... I've learned my lesson. I never want to leave you and home again. I promise—within my power to stay, I'll not go away from Shiloh again."

That night as they lay together in the tall bed for the first time in many weeks, Mac was at peace. He wrapped his arms around Laurel as they spooned together. He felt the subtle rounding of her torso, caressing the new life not yet moving in Laurel's womb.

"This is exactly what I wanted for Christmas. Another child...our baby. It's the right time for me to give you my present." "Mac, you already brought me the buggy and Gracie. Those gifts are more than anything I could ever want."

"This one isn't really new, or really from me." He reached over to the side table and moved his Bible. He picked up the beautiful emerald ring his mother had called her family ring. Thomas MacLayne had replaced her wedding ring with the emerald band when Sean, the first child, was born. "Because you are continuing to build our family heritage, I want you to wear our family ring."

"It's beautiful. I'll be proud to wear it if I can wear it along with my wedding band. I am more than pleased to be adding to our family, but Patrick, my first pledge is to you. I never want to take off your wedding band. In the past four years, I've come to understand so much. God has to come first, but you, my love, will always come next, and together we'll love our children, as many as the Lord sees fit to give us..."

Mac's answer was a kiss. "Yes, dear. We will love each other, only second to the Lord, and then we'll cherish our kids, all of them. Do you see how easily you've provided me with the family I wanted?"

Laurel coughed to the point of strangulation. "Easy? I thought you were present when Mark Thomas was born. I don't remember that being easy."

"That is not what I meant, of course." He tried to smooth that misunderstood comment with a quick kiss. "We've known each other a month shy of four years, and you've given me five wonderful kids…and soon to be another. We have an eighteenyear-old, an eleven-year-old, one almost eight, another just past five, and our beautiful son…Woman, you are a miracle worker."

"You sir, are ridiculous!"

"You're beautiful!" Mac stopped the banter with a long passionate kiss. "Wife, I'm exhausted. Turn down that lamp and come hold me. I want to sleep in your arms. And tomorrow, when I am rested, I want to make love to you as the sun rises over the ridge. I've dreamed of it for three weeks, nearly every night."

Blessedly, Mac did sleep, well into the following morning. When he awoke, he found Laurel sitting on the rag rug before the fire, playing with Gracie and Mark. Mark toddled around the room, taking a fall once in a while as he chased the red ball across the walnut plank floor. The little girl who still didn't want to be touched would hustle over to pick him up.

"Gracie, you're as pretty as your mama always was. Your brown eyes remind me of her."

"I don't got no Mama."

"You did, sweetheart. Her name was Rachel, and she was my best friend. She loved you."

"I like your little boy, ma'am."

"I hope you grow to like all of us. We're hopin' you'll want to be a part of our family.

With eyes so brown they were nearly black, the small girl looked up into Laurel's face. In the most grown-up voice, she asked. "Am I gonna stay here for very long?"

"Yes, dear. As long as you want."

"I ain't had no home yet. Where they leave me, I stay, but then someone takes me away."

Mac intervened from the tall four-poster. "Gracie, it won't happen again. So many people love you. They've been lookin' for the best place for you to grow up with a family. We're that family.

We have been searchin' for you for more'n a year. We all love you."

"Gracie, Mr. Mac is telling you the truth. You never have to go again until you want to go. Cathy, Andy, and Mark will be your brothers and sister. My husband has brought you here, and I want you to be our little girl."

"You knowed me when I was born?"

"I did. You were named after me, Gracie. My name is Laurel Grace. My family here at Shiloh call me that name most of the time. Your mother and I loved each other as sisters. We were best of friends. You are my goddaughter now, but soon we will adopt you, as we did Cathy. I even adopted Andy. Would you like that?"

Gracie stared up with a blank expression on her face. No smile touched the corners of her mouth.

"Gracie, do you know what I mean when I tell you that you are my goddaughter?"

The little girl lowered her eyes and shook her head. "Your mama and papa asked me to take care of you if they couldn't. She wanted someone to love you and keep you safe always." Laurel answered.

"And Gracie, little one, Laurel and I will." Gracie's fear continued to show on her sweet face. She didn't speak for a time. She looked over at Mark scrambling around the room. She glanced hesitantly up at Mac, and then at the lady sitting with her on the floor.

"I wanna stay."

Mark's loud delighted squeal broke the solemn scene. He had finally caught the Christmas ball he'd been chasing all over the cabin.

"Where are our other two?"

"At church with your Pa. I wouldn't let them wake you, but I did ask them to invite Matthew and his family back for Sunday dinner. I knew you'd want to see him."

Shortly before 1:00, the Campbells arrived followed by Thomas with the kids, driving in Laurel's new rig. Right behind them came Roy and Annie Clark, riding together on Roy's horse. The

MacLayne cabin would be filled that afternoon with friends and family. Conversations didn't stop from the moment they crossed the threshold until the time for Matthew and Ellie to return to church.

Matthew told his friend about the harsh winter on Crowley's Ridge and about the deaths in the community from the influenza outbreak. "Took a toll on us, brother. Susan and Randall were hit pretty hard when we lost Martha. Truthfully, we were almost as bad…. She was a beautiful little girl…she'd been old enough to start school in the spring."

"Lord bless ya, Matthew. I know how hard it is to lose a little one."

"We lost three here in the community, but Laurel worked night and day to nurse yours."

"Laurel, our kids had the grippe? You didn't tell me."

"Darlin', you just got home at noon yesterday. We've hardly had time to talk."

"You didn't write."

"They were sick since Christmas. I was too busy to write long letters. I did tell you about the things I thought you needed to know. You couldn't have done anything while you were away."

"Were all of them sick?"

"Yes, Mark first, but he was well quicker than the older kids. Anyway, they're all fine now."

"What about you?"

"Strong as a horse…didn't even get a sniffle."

Mac's father added part of the story Laurel had omitted. "Andy was the sickest of all the kids. I believe Laurel saved his life. For about three days, she refused to leave his side. Thank God, you had the foresight to dry that yarrow last fall. We ran out of quinine too early, but Laurel used the yarrow to pull them through." When he heard this story, Mac turned to look at his wife.

"Thank God and thank you, Laurel Grace, for saving my children. I want to talk more about this tonight. Matthew, Ellie, we're havin' another baby!"

"Yes, we know."

"Did Uncle Matthew tell you, Aunt Ellie?" Laurel asked.

"No, dear. Who do you think told him? You know there are signs...and when I suspected, I told him to keep an eye on you."

"You've got to be a happy man, Mac. You came home late for Christmas, but the Lord saw you got a mighty fine present."

"The best present is bein' home. I'm here to stay this time."

"Well, we're hopin' you'll be here in June. I'd like you to be my best man when my Annie and me get married." Roy stood before his family with the reddest cheeks they'd ever seen on the young man. "Her papa said we could when she turns eighteen, and that'll be on our weddin' day."

"Roy, congratulations, son. I can't think of a greater honor than to stand up with you. Lord willing, I'll be there."

\

Chapter Twenty

Behold, I have taught you statutes and judgments, even as the Lord my God commanded me, that you should do so in the land whither ye go to possess it. Keep therefore and do them for this is wisdom and your understanding in the sight of nations, which shall hear them and say, this great nation is a wise and understanding people.
Deuteronomy 4:5-6

M that first full week in February. He didn't care that Mother Nature had ac spent a blissful week chosen to deliver the biggest snowfall of the year that Tuesday night. The storm and the moderately warm thirty-degree temperature simply provided the perfect opportunity to play with his ever-growing family. He even took Mark outside to play in the snow with the other three children. Naturally, it took only one head-first fall into a snow drift to send his crying offspring back into the arms of his mother, who chose to sit inside before the blazing fire. Before they'd finished that day, Mac, Andy, Cathy, and Gracie had built a snowman taller than Mac and had pelted each other with scores of perfect snowballs. When they came in from their play, their enthusiasm carried over into laughter, stories, and teasing.

Mac bent down and kissed Mark and then his wife. "Laurel, my dear, I plan to spend the next two months doin' what I did today, playin' with my kids and kissin' my wife. He didn't know that before the end of another week, he'd be called back to Little Rock. On February 8, 1861, the southern states which had already seceded finalized work to form the Confederate States of America. In four short days, delegates from South Carolina, Mississippi, Florida, Alabama, Georgia, Louisiana, and Texas had drafted and adopted a provisional constitution. Three days later, they signed the permanent compact to create a government that would serve the southern states. Strangely, the document they framed read almost identically to the one they were abandoning.

The news spread quickly; newspapers all over the country – both countries, the USA and CSA—reported every detail they could discover. The news pushed the bordering states to choose where their loyalties would lie. Arkansas would be pulled into a frenzy sooner than anyone had suspected. When the legislature decided to table the secession vote at the end of the thirteenth session, the hopes were that calm heads and the providence of the Lord would resolve the dispute. Those hopes seemed to vanish, though, when in the middle of

February, the leaders of the state called for a secession convention to convene on March 4, 1861.

Lincoln was inaugurated in Washington D.C. on that same day, but the event meant little to Mac or the delegates who found themselves back in Little Rock. The convention would be called to order that very morning to decide the fate of Arkansas. The differences that had existed at the close of the thirteenth session were a mere crack compared to the broadening gulf between the unionists and the pro-slavery factions that met that early March morning. The papers reported the hastily-called elections to choose delegates to a secession conference reflected a split among the voters in the state, too. The final tally of the votes showed the people were torn, but nearly 6,000 more votes supported maintaining the union ties, even with Lincoln as the president. Mac was surprised so many people had even voted in such a hastily called election.

Regardless, that Monday morning in March, Mac found himself away from home, embroiled in a heated debate over secession. He stood amid a group of unionists who had been sent to choose the path Arkansas would follow. He could hardly believe he sat there back in the chambers of statehouse with only one tie to Shiloh and family seated in the visitors' loft above. Matthew Campbell watched from the gallery, as the rancor and hostility grew among the men gathered below, even before the session had been called to order.

Matthew was there to watch over his friend. Laurel had balked when the messenger came telling Mac he was the elected representative of Craighead County until the next legislature in 1862. She'd stood her ground more steadfastly that she'd ever done in their marriage. NO! Mac was not well enough to make the trip back. She declared he'd met his obligation to his office already. She would not allow duty to kill her husband. Mac's argument fell on deaf ears.

Laurel wanted her family intact. "Hang the unity of the country. Mac, your health won't stand another trip to Little Rock so soon." She would not relent until her uncle stepped up to say that he would go with Mac. Only then, and not without a sense of dread and unchecked tears did Laurel back away from her objections. She knew the man she loved could not turn from anything he considered his responsibility. He would not abandon Arkansas at a time when his home and state faced a crisis. Laurel agreed only when she had demanded several promises from

Mac…and her uncle Matthew.

Of course, Mac knew he would be hard-pressed to keep most of them. Yet, he was more than relieved his friend would help to anchor him in the storm about to arise. Matthew Campbell would serve as his one small piece of Shiloh close enough for his refuge. Mac walked away from the noise and confusion surrounding his desk and approached the roaring fire in the fireplace. He had often stood in that place during the legislative sessions when he needed to clear his head and focus on a difficult task. He reached his hands down to warm them by the fire and to whisper a word of prayer, but the words did not come. He didn't know what words to whisper. So, he stood for some time, head bowed, allowing the spirit to speak for him when he couldn't. He noticed the painted "marble" mantle and stiles were somewhat charred toward the floor. Would real stone have done the same thing? Mac chuckled at the trivial thought that had just crossed his mind in the midst of the life-altering decisions that faced them.

The speaker rose to call the session to order, and at that moment, Mac sensed the answer to his unspoken prayer. He had only one more role to fill. He would vote for the good of those who'd sent him there, and then he would go home for good to protect his family. He knew his task. He straightened his shoulders and lifted his head toward the visitors' gallery. He lifted his hand to Matt, a sign he was ready to work and able to do what had been asked of him. He walked to his place and answered the roll call.

"Present."

For seventeen long trying days, the question was laid before the assembly for discussion. The line was quickly drawn between the factions of the body; strangely, the staunchly unionist group and the firebrands of the Delta did not comprise the bulk of the delegates.

More than half of the body was made up of members of the clergy, a teacher or two, many yeoman farmers, several plantation owners, and a good number of skilled craftsmen and merchants. Arkansas had elected a body of typical citizens to sit at this crucial juncture in the state's history. Among the group, not one past governor, United States senator, nor congressman had been seated. Mac recognized a few recent delegates to the statehouse, like himself, but even those delegates were few. More than half had come with open minds, waiting to be convinced as to the right choice for their state, and because there was no clear division, the debate took on a serious, deliberate tone from the

start. If only the convention could remain in that same manner until they reached a decision.

But rancor grew as each day passed. Emotions grew higher as the speakers used every argument to support the stance they spoke for. Thankfully, the president of the convention, David Walker, was an able leader, and he refused to let things fall into chaos. He also demanded strict adherence to the convention rules of order. The session ended each day at 4:00 p.m.

At that time, Matthew took charge of the Craighead County delegation—Mac and himself—and he demanded Mac return to their boarding house where they would share a community supper with the Scotts and other delegates who were staying at the Cherry Street address. Matthew was worse than Laurel had ever been, insisting Mac eat well. When he witnessed Mac taking small portions of the excellent food Mrs. Scott set on the table, he wasn't shy to add additional spoonsful of vegetables or stew to Mac's plate. He refused to leave the table until Mac's plate was empty. He also served as moderator around the supper table, changing the topic of conversation whenever it drifted to the political arena.

Except for three or four visits to St. John's College to visit with his son John, Matt rarely left Mac's side. Because of his diligence, his promises to his niece were never in jeopardy. Mac was in bed every night by nine.

While time was ample, some nights, sleep was not. Mac was too frequently awakened by the same recurring dream he'd had before he'd returned to Shiloh earlier in the year. The images of Laurel and the kids had brought some ease to him then, but now the dream was smothered in gloom and dark shadows. A torrential rainstorm hampered Midnight's every stride. Flashes of lightning and continuous rounds of thunder echoed across the ridge. When Mac was able to see the front porch as he approached the cabin, the people he saw there were vaporous, undefined shapes, devoid of any face. As his horse ran faster to bring him home, the cabin seemed to recede in the distance. He would call out and then the picture of home and family was gone, leaving only a void. Losing sight of his family jarred Mac awake any night the dream reached that point. Some nights, he was never able to return to sleep. ⌀

As the cold gave way to warmer weather in those early days of March, Laurel found herself busier than usual. He fatherin-law was away most of the time with demands of spring planting and early calving at his farm and sometimes at theirs. The Clarke brothers took on the bulk of the outside work with the herd and spring repairs. However, Roy worked on his own farm most days, and John was away at school. Many of the everyday chores they'd done the year before fell to Laurel. With the help of Andy and Cathy, she worked taking over the day to day tasks required to keep a homestead going. She fed the stock, milked the cows, gathered eggs and began to prepare the ground for their garden. Caring for Mark was easier, at least, as he enjoyed the outdoors, and Gracie proved to be a good playmate and watchful eye for the toddler. Yet, while her days were full, Laurel missed her husband tremendously that spring.

Laurel felt good, even as she entered into the sixth month of her pregnancy. She'd work long hours, always mindful she carried a child. When she felt spent, she'd rest, either sitting in her rocking chair on the front porch or in the

tall bed, if she felt the need for a nap. Susan and her Aunt
Ellie came every few days   to visit, but Laurel
knew they'd come to keep her from overdoing. Their
concern was welcomed but hardly necessary. Laurel knew
the pain of losing a child. She would deliver Mac a healthy
baby. Perhaps this time, she'd have a little girl. That was her
prayer, anyway. She would have a healthy daughter. ⌀

By the third week of the secession convention,
emotions had reached a fever pitch. Most of those present had
decided on their positions, with perhaps eight to ten holdouts.
President Walker announced that on Thursday, March 21,
1861, a vote on secession was scheduled. He would allow two
more days of debate. Each faction was to seek out their best
spokesman to make the final argument. The unionists would
speak on Wednesday morning, and the pro-slavery faction
would speak in the afternoon. Each side would have four
hours to make its case, and they could have as many speakers
as the time would allow. The morning of the vote, the pro-
slavery group would have two hours to rebut the unionists'
argument. The last two hours before the vote, the unionists
would counter the remarks of the pro-slavery speaker from ten
o'clock to noon. After lunch on Thursday, the assembly would
vote. The unionists asked Mac to provide their summation.
The weight of the world seemed to sit on his shoulders those
two long days.

In the afternoon, the unionists had several short speeches made
by men, mostly from the northwest portion of the state. While their
oratory did not inflame the assembly as the words from the other side
had done, they made good sense. James Turner from Van Buren
County spoke before lunch to end the unionist argument. He made five
strong points each supported with details and examples that appealed
to the undecided delegates. He explained Arkansas economic growth
during the past three decades had been brought by the immigrants
flocking to the state as yeomen farmers and skilled craftsmen who

neither had nor wanted slave labor. He spoke eloquently of division being forced into all areas of daily life for Arkansans. Being a Methodist, he knew first hand of the hurt brought into the church.

He also cited a growing number of pacifist denominations that were taking root in Arkansas, and he declared they would certainly not support a war if it came to that. He spoke to the waste of resources badly needed to improve roads, levees, and education, all sorely lacking due to inadequate funding in the state treasury. His closing statement may have hurt more than it helped, but it was sorely true. "Friends, Arkansas is a fledgling state, like a toddler tryin' to get on its feet and walk alone. We have depended on support from Washington to build every major road in this state. The useable waterways are kept up by the federal money or by local citizens as the state has no revenue to support our levees, dams, and ferries. Even law enforcement, where it is not done by local constables is provided by federal marshals. Please think. Don't get carried away with misguided passions. We are illprepared to follow South Carolina into secession."

The pro-slavery delegates had chosen three men to carry the bulk of their argument. James Yell was the leader, and he was well-supported by James Totten and Thomas B. Hanley. Together they made a strong case for secession. They avoided the motive of slavery whenever they could. The men frequently spoke of Southern honor and sectional differences in the population. Many times, property rights were touted as a sacred trust, never once suggesting that the only property being jeopardized was slaves. Mac listened intently to each argument, making an occasional note that he planned to counter. One of the men insisted that Southern gentlemen were descendants of English cavaliers and could not possibly co-exist with the puritanical culture in the North. Mac knew he could speak to that issue.

Another key point arose in a letter from a former state legislator who'd moved to Texas in 1860. He'd written that Arkansas could not stand outside the Confederacy because the economic impact on the state and the cotton producers would be disastrous. The Confederate

States would boycott Arkansas cotton if the state refused to join them. Mac wrote down two strong points to counter that stand.

The last blow came when Governor Rector finally made his pro-slavery stance public. He'd abstained from calling Arkansas to secede since he'd been in office, and he'd not directly asked for a vote, but when pushed into a corner, he had openly stated his view. He said the people of the north believed slavery to be a sin, but Arkansans did not. He went on to say, "We can remain a union without slavery or we could maintain our slaves without a union. We are southerners who won't be coerced into anything." That evening, as they walked the peaceful streets of Little Rock's growing residential area, Matthew asked, "What are you gonna say tomorrow, brother?"

"Truthfully, Matthew, I'm not sure. I've got several key points I need to address, but until I hear what Yell has to say in closin', I won't know. I will pray God will put the right words in my mind. This matter is too important for me to speak alone."

"Bless ya, my friend. I'm glad I'm not in your boots, but I know the Lord has chosen the right person for this job." Mac knew that feeling, as he believed he was doing the work God had brought him to the capital to do. He did not doubt his call, but he wished he was just homesteader MacLayne that day, home with his wife and his family. That night, he awoke to his recurring dream. He sat bolt upright in the bed and trembled. The much-loved faces of Laurel and his children came to him in wisps of gray. No discernible features...not Andy's storm-blue eyes, Cathy's bowed pigtails, nor Laurel's tawny curls were identifiable... only ghostly suggestions of the last image he had seen of them brought him terror. His cabin moved farther and farther from his reach.

"You okay, Mac?"

"Yes. Sorry that I woke you."

The next morning, Mac was exhausted from his troubled sleep. He'd awakened three times during the night, thinking of Laurel, and feeling the dread that something was not right at home.

He was driven on only by the knowledge, he'd be homeward bound by 4:30 that afternoon. If they could ride no farther than the ferry landing on the other side of the Arkansas River, at least they'd be that much closer to Shiloh.

∮

The remarks made by the lead speaker brought a general summary of the major arguments presented by the other proslavery advocates. For the first half-hour, he had said nothing Mac felt he had not already planned to counter in his rebuttal. However, as he moved to a close, his strategy took another course.

"Those of you MEN out there who have the honor and courage to reject this submissionist attitude of the unionists will find no difficulty votin' for secession this afternoon. You are all MAN enough to stand up to the bullyin' North. We aren't women who have to submit to the coercion of those who don't understand the southern way of life. I know no Arkansan will go down on his knees to submit to northern aggression toward our rights and property. Think of your southern manhood. Arkansas will not be labeled as a submissionist state. I'd rather live in a state divided than allow Lincoln to believe we aren't men enough to stand up for our rights."

The new attack took Mac and many other unionists by surprise. Not at any time in this convention had attacks become so personal and viciously demeaning. This speaker had moved from discussing political ideals to suggesting that anyone who opposed him was somehow less of a man because of his opinion. This statement could not go unchallenged, yet Mac had not given any thought to such a personal attack. Regardless, he had no time to prepare for a rebuttal of the emotionally charged words, which attacked the courage and masculinity of the unionists.

"Closing statement from the delegate of Craighead County, Patrick MacLayne of Greensboro. Mr. MacLayne, please come to the podium. You have until 11:45 to make your closing argument." Mac rose from his desk, the same place he'd occupied in the last two legislative sessions. He walked deliberately toward the faux-marble mantle at the front of the house chambers. Each step brought a plea for God to give him the right words to speak. He stood for a moment before the gathered delegates, but he looked instead into the gallery. He saw the bowed head of his friend, his pastor, and his mentor. He knew he did not stand alone. "Colleagues. A man is one who stands for his convictions. Because many among this assembly take loyalty to God and country as unshakeable, that does not make us weak or effeminate in any way. My grandfather, like most of yours, fought to carve out a nation where freedom demands that every man follows his conscience and works toward the good of our citizens. I am not speaking of slavery. It is true that I own no slaves, nor has my family since they made America home nearly a hundred years ago. I ask each man to deal with that issue as his conscience demands, but every man has the right to pursue the dreams promised in our constitution. No man has the right to attack the integrity of another because they hold a difference of opinion. In days not long ago in my home state of Maryland, and even here in this very statehouse, men have been called out to the field of honor for much less." Mac paused. His eyes bore into the previous speaker, and he did not waver in his gaze.

Across the room, mumbling erupted for several moments. Some looked with questions in their eyes, fearing Mac was about to call out the representative for the insult. Mac looked up and saw Matthew had risen to his feet. He continued, "I came here in the hopes that calm and intelligent minds would look to the facts before us. We have no call to secede. If Lincoln is unfit, we will unseat him in the next election. If we want to bring prosperity to Arkansas, we have to work with the government to build roads, levee systems, and schools for our children. If we are to represent those who sent us here, we have to vote to maintain the union as did the majority of Arkansans who cared enough to vote. I will not use more of your time. Look to those who elected you, and vote your conscience. I pray to Almighty God that we all have the courage to submit to the will of our Lord and to vote the will of the people who sent us here."

Mac wadded up the prepared notes and threw them into the cold fireplace. He stalked back to his chair and sat. He didn't know how he'd influenced the body, but at that moment he had no regrets. He'd spoken as he'd been led. He was at peace, and he was exhausted. He ached to sink his face into Laurel's curls. He wanted his wife. He wanted Shiloh.

The president called for an immediate vote, even though the clock showed more than an hour before lunch recess was scheduled. The first round of votes brought no majority as a few delegates remained undecided. Mr. Walker believed the convention may be deadlocked if he failed to intervene with a plan that more than half of the delegates would support.

"Assemblymen, I propose that we allow the citizens of Arkansas to make this decision. No actual attack has been forthcoming. Mr. Lincoln has only been in office not quite three weeks. Perhaps the accounts we've heard of an imminent assault are exaggerated. We have time to make this crucial decision. Let's vote to hold an election on secession in August. That will give us five months to assess events and inform our citizens. Go to lunch and think about the proposal, and let's come back at one o'clock to vote on this proposal. Under the rules of order, a delegate from Searcy County moved for the election, and a delegate from Chicot County provided a second. With the lunch break providing time for emotions to cool, the delegates had an opportunity to allow providence to prevail and to vote with their logic instead of their rancor.

To Mac, the lunch recess seemed to last days. Matthew and he returned to the Scotts' to gather their belongings and prepare for the trip home.

"Mac, you look all in. Do you think we should rest tonight and leave at sun up?"

"No. We're leavin' this town the first minute the convention adjourns. Laurel needs me at home. I can feel something is wrong."

"There's no riverboat in port. We'll have to ride. "

"That's the fastest way to go. With a bit of luck, we'll be home by the 26th."

"Can you make that fast a trip? Laurel will never forgive me if I bring you home in worse shape than when you left."

"We're headed out! If we can leave by two, we'll have a good four hours or so to head northeast."

Chapter Twenty-One

I am for peace: but when I speak, they are for war.
Psalm 120:7

*A*and Mac were on the ferry crossing the Arkansas River. nd so, it came to be as Mac had hoped. At 2:00, Matthew Mac didn't have a route planned, but he had a compass, and he knew home was northeast. They'd head up the military road toward Batesville, and for today that would be enough. Mac was relieved that the vote to hold the August election had passed easily. He felt if the people of the state had a chance to voice their opinion, Arkansas would stay in the union.

Thank the good Lord, that fractured, contentious group had voted to allow the vote to happen. The quick thinking of Mr. Walker, the convention's president, provided time to let tempers cool and to allow careful examination of the real issues at hand. Through God's providence, surely Lincoln would find some way to reunite the two factions and heal the nation. At least Arkansas had the good sense not to rush into the fray. With that lifted from his shoulders, Mac rode toward home feeling hopeful.

The military road between Little Rock and Searcy was easy traveling. Although they could find no place to stay the first night, they did manage to get through the swampy area north of the river. The first night was chilly but dry. Mac set up a camp on a rise where the ground was drier. He built a fire and put coffee on to brew. With the food Mrs. Scott had given them, they would eat. "I hope we don't have to sleep on the ground every night." "Don't be a wimp, brother. Laurel didn't complain when we crossed the state, and the conditions were much worse. We even had to deal with snow for a few days. Did I tell you the story of when Laurel fell face front into a freezin' creek?" Mac and Matthew passed the night talking about how Laurel had come to Shiloh. Matt knew his friend had found some peace...happy the state had not left the union and happy he was going home. In those few short hours, Mac's demeanor was much lighter than it had been since he'd come to the capital nearly three weeks earlier.

"You know, Matthew, I used to envy you and your family. I thought what you had was rare. I didn't believe I'd ever know the sense of family and belongin', the kind of life you and Ellie live. Laurel brought that to me, brother. I do love her."

"I know. Let's get some rest, that is if a man can rest on this hard ground."

The third day out, they reached Jackson Port and headed across country. Going on toward Batesville would have been easier riding, but it would also take them away from home. After a talk with some freighters they'd met in the mercantile in Jackson Port, they found out about a road to Bolivar. Mac knew he could find his way home easily from there. Besides, they could find shelter for the night and a good meal at Lizzie's boarding house. Bolivar was only a day and a half ride from Shiloh. At sun up, they left the sleeping loft above a tavern in Jackson Port and headed east. After a long hard ride, they'd covered the thirty-two miles and a while after dark, Mac knocked on the door of the boarding house. Lizzie Lee ambled to the door.

"Got a room for an old customer, lady?"

"Golly me, it's Mr. Mac. Where is your pretty lady you snatched away from here?"

"She's home with our young'uns, Lizzie. I brought her uncle with me this time. We'd like a place at your table and a bed if you got an empty one."

"Got plenty of food, but the only room I have is in the sleepin' loft in the attic. Been mighty busy since those states seceded. We got travelers here nearly every day, headed back east or further west. Everyone's got itchy feet these days. Where ya headed, Mr. Mac?"

"Headed home – to stay this time."

"Take a seat and tell me about your family. By now you got at least two babies, I expect."

"Got five and one on the way." Lizzie's mouth dropped and Matthew laughed aloud.

"Tell that lady your story. She's gonna think Laurel's gave you a litter." They spent an hour or so around the table, catching up with Lizzie and her husband when he came from closing his store down the street.

"Been nice catching up with y'all, but we're leavin' early for the last day of our trip home. Lizzie, if you'll fix us a few biscuits with some ham or bacon, we'll have a decent lunch."

"You know I'll do'er. See you fellas at breakfast about five."

Lizzie was good to her word. Before 6:00, the two men were on the northbound road to Craighead County. As the sun fell, they passed through Jonesboro settlement and stopped briefly by Snoddy's livery to share the news of the convention. Some of the leaders of that settlement were always nearby. Max was surprised by the mixed reaction he got when he told the men about the upcoming election to be held in August.

One man grumbled, "Why the dickens didn't y'all just vote to git it over with? Ever one knows we'll have to secede. No one will do business with us if we don't." Mac sensed something had happened to turn the opinions of some people. He'd stop in and talk to Al Stuart later in the week. Today he didn't care. The only opinion he cared about today was Laurel's.

"Matt, it's only 7:30. Do you think these mounts can go another couple of hours?"

He mounted Midnight and turned him toward the Greensboro road. He gave the stallion free rein, and the horse broke into a quick trot...almost as if he sensed how near home was. Before two hours had passed, Mac had said goodbye to Matthew, and he went around the last bend in the road. Before he could even see his house, he heard children playing, laughter and squeals broke the quiet of the night. What were they doing up so late? Nine o'clock was always bedtime for them.

"Hey, kids, I'm home." Before he had time to dismount, Andy had already grabbed his leg and Cathy was reaching for his hand. Even Gracie crept a few steps closer. Laurel opened the door. This scene was nothing like the unsettling dreams he'd had so many times since he'd been gone. "Why y'all up so late?"

"Just a funny feelin' you'd be here tonight. They begged to stay up, and I let them."

Mac dismounted and threw the reins to Andy. He climbed the three steps and embraced Laurel. "My dearest Lord...I've never seen a more welcoming sight." He pulled her as close as he could. "How beautiful you are. I've missed you...."

"You must have...to think I'm beautiful...I've never gotten so big before. I can hardly walk anymore." Mac laid his hand on her swollen torso.

"Yes indeed, so beautiful."

"Come in and let me fix you some supper. I must say, you don't look any worse for your trials. My uncle must have taken care of you."

"He was afraid not to. I'm fine, Laurel. I'm hungry...for supper and for your company." "Did things go well, Mac?"

"I hope so Laurel. We decided to table the secession talk until the people can vote. We're havin' an election in August, just like the legislature planned. I believe our people will vote to stay in the union. That's my prayer, anyway."

That evening was manna to Mac. His family poured their attention on him from the minute he'd stepped down on to Shiloh's soil. He took every opportunity to reach out and tousle Andy's hair, pat Cathy's cheek, twirl Gracie's curls, or swoop Mark into his arms. Throughout the time his family gathered around, Mac constantly sought Laurel's hand, brushed gentle kisses on her cheek, caressed her shoulders or lay his hand tenderly on his soon to be child, hoping to feel the infant move. The contact of those he loved was proof life was good. Nothing outside his cabin walls would take this from him. That night, as he spoke grace over supper, Mac's voice broke when he spoke words of gratitude for his homecoming and the safety of his family. The sense of blessing was deep, overwhelming him to the point he could barely speak. "Are you all right, Mac?"

"Not all right…so much more. I am overly blessed. I am home, and I know Shiloh has come."

"When you are here with us, that's how I feel—like our home is a sanctuary. I'm so happy you're back…I pray that it's for good."

"That is my wish too, but I'll not make that promise to you again. I've done it twice, and I've had to break the promise each time."

"I knew from the time we met that you are a man who has to serve. You've done it time and again when you've been called."

"My duty now is aimed at y'all; each of you deserves that. I pray the Lord will let me stay here to care for those I love the most in this life."

When Mac spoke those words, he meant each of them, but even as he spoke a sense of foreboding tried to push a cloud over his homecoming. He wanted to share his dream with Laurel, that vision that had seen him through the last demanding, frustrating absence. As they lay together that night, Mac told Laurel the details of his recurring dream of her and home. "Laurel, the dream is always so real. As I ride around the bend, our porch comes into view. Behind me, building thunderclouds—so dark and threatening—follow. The lightning streaks across the ridge.

Midnight's pace is so much more than a trot…almost like he's trying to outrun the storm. He streaks toward home, his mane and tail streaming up from the blustering wind and his pace. I feel the urgency, rushing to you and our kids…then I see you, standing at the rail. You hold Mark, and Gracie's beside you, your other hand holds her close. Andy and Cathy always run toward me. I fear for them running toward the storm. You are wearing your green gingham dress, the one you made on our trip across the state, standing there heavy with our child, even more than you are now. The sunlight is only on you, and it dances off your curls. I can see the green fire flashing in your eyes. The only light I see anywhere around is around you with our babies."

"That is a strange dream, Mac, but I never even wore that green gingham dress. I think you were thinkin' of gettin' home…and you're so very tired."

"You don't understand, Laurel…No matter how much I urged Midnight forward, I'm not able to cover the distance. You seemed to get farther away with each stride. I need to hold you, but somehow I can't reach you."

"It was a dream, Patrick. You're home now, and we're all well and happy to be together again. Thank God, He's brought you back where you belong."

Spooned together with his wife, Mac slept then. With his arms wrapped around Laurel, he didn't dream that night. Yet when he rose the next morning, the peace he sought at Shiloh evaded him still. He spent the day riding around his homestead, checking everything that he'd worried over, and he found everything in order. The dread he'd felt in Little Rock had proved to be needless worry; yet, he couldn't shake the sense of an impending storm.

He pushed the concern back into his mind. He quickly returned to his routine. He worked well with the Clarke brothers, who proved to be hard-working and companionable men. Mac found he'd met new friends who shared his interest in politics and homesteading. He asked the brothers to begin a census of his livestock, counting the new calves and pulling out the young steers of a size and age to be sold. He felt an urge to sell all his stock, but he knew he could not build a ranch that way. He wanted to talk with his father. Frankly, he didn't understand what had led him to think of some of the things he did of late. Yes, a good talk with this father would help him get back to his good common-sense plan.

Unfortunately, so little seemed like common sense right then.

April came and life seemed good. The garden was thriving under just enough rain and warm sunny spring days. Laurel had even found the first tiny grapes in the trellises Mac had built in the orchard. They were tiny, hard, green pellets, and they would not develop into good fruit this year, but they were a promise of what would be. Perhaps next year or surely the year after, the apple trees would begin to flower…Life should have felt so right that spring of '61.

Shortly after mid-month, some of Mac's doubts were substantiated. The news that Fort Sumpter off the coast of South Carolina had been fired upon by rebel forces and a thirty-four hour siege followed. The following day, the commander surrendered his troop of federal soldiers to the Confederate general. Even though only one soldier had died in an accidental explosion, Mac knew the first shots of the war had been heard in South Carolina. He laid aside the Baltimore newspaper, and he laid his head back in his chair. He now knew why he was being pulled to make contrary decisions. War was coming and soon. He had to secure his family and stockpile provisions to keep them safe when danger came their way. And it would. Women and children were always the victims of war. The most basic stores they had to survive were too often taken to feed hungry armies. Cattle and hogs were confiscated with little or no compensation in the name of patriotism. Money became worthless with nothing to guarantee its value, and since there would be few supplies to purchase, even gold and silver provided little security. Yes, he knew the need to provide a stash and sell off his growing herd were all things he had to do to make sure his family did not fall into need.

A week later, scores of messengers were sent from Little Rock to spread the word. All delegates of the secession convention were being recalled to the capital. Riders were directed to ride hard into the distant counties of the state to bring the body back together. The Arkansas secession convention would reconvene at 8:00 a.m. on May 6th. Mac received his notice on April 24, barely giving him time to prepare for another arduous trip across the state. Laurel was adamant that he would not go.

"Patrick, you've done what you could. You can't make another trip so soon."

"Darlin', you've pampered me back to health. I've loved our afternoon naps and the feasts you lay out for me every night at supper, but I don't have a choice."

"You do. Tell them you won't go."

"If I were another man, perhaps I could. But if I don't go and a handful of other delegates who want to remain in the union say no, we'll not be livin' in a new county, we'll be livin' in another country. We'll be traitors to the nation our parents and grandparents sacrificed to build."

"Papa, please don't go away from us again."

Mac looked at his son and into the scared faces of Cathy and Gracie. Sweet little Gracie had just begun to move away from her protective shell into the arms of their family. In so many ways, the little girl reminded him of Laurel in their early days together. He looked up and saw his sleeping son in the arms of his pregnant wife. Everything he wanted and needed stood in that room. He had no heart to leave, but he had no choice. He had to go.

Mac bent and lifted his first child into his arms. He went to sit in his armchair, and he thought of Laurel's father who made him promise to secure a good life for her. He'd tried and he could not back away from the promise now. He sat with Andrew in his lap. It mattered that his son knew why he had to go. *How do you make an eight-year-old understand, when he could hardly understand himself?*

"Andy, son…" Mac stammered. "I love ya…I don't want to go away from ya again. Leavin' your mama and y'all is the hardest thing I ever do."

"Then don't do it, Papa. We want ya home with us. Please don't leave us here without you."

"Andrew..." Mac rarely called the small image of himself that name anymore. "I hope you can understand. If a man doesn't do his duty and stand up for what he knows is right, then our country and our state will suffer. Even good people who make bad choices can bring evil and pain to lots of people if others stand back and let them do so without opposition. Do you know what I am sayin' to you?"

"You always do your duty, don't ya, Papa?"

"I try, Andy. The Lord expects me to try." Then he looked up into Laurel's tear-filled eyes. "I have to try, Laurel."

On April 30th, Patrick MacLayne left Shiloh returning to the second session of the secession convention. For the most part, he rode alone, only his thoughts and memories of the past few weeks filling the long hours in the saddle. As he rode, he was hardly aware of time passing as he crossed through Craighead County into Poinsett and then into Jackson. The spring weather made the travel easy, if not short, and the nights outdoors were comfortable enough. The fifth and sixth day he rode through White County and into the eastern part of Pulaski County, but he would have been hard-pressed to recall much of the trip. He spent little time thinking about what the session ahead would bring. Instead, he'd filled his days planning for his children's future, growing his homestead in his mind, and making love to his precious life mate. And each night, whether he slept on the ground or in a boarding house bed, he dreamed of returning to Laurel, that same foreboding dream he'd had so often during his last trip to Little Rock in which he fought to outrun the impending storm.

The afternoon of May 5th, late in the day, Mac rode up to the Anthony House Hotel near the Statehouse. He would stay there until the next day when he would seek board with the Scotts. He was tired, and he knew the doorman at the Anthony House would see that Midnight would be well-cared for. He would find a hot meal and a soft bed. Tomorrow would come soon enough.

Mac arrived at the Statehouse well before the eight o'clock session would convene. He greeted old acquaintances and talked to delegates from his area of the state. The mood was somber, and the room was remarkably quiet to have so many men gathered there. Strangely, some delegates who'd once supported the unionist camp were standing apart this morning. New delegates gathered around the pro-slavery leaders. Mac hadn't expected this change so quickly. He'd feared long drawn out debates over several days and then another vote would sustain the earlier decision to hold the secession election in August.

President Walker had been pressured into reconvening the convention. Several new facts were brought before the assembly, and old arguments were revived. Early in the afternoon, a delegate moved to enforce the decision of the first Secession Convention to hold the August election. The motion failed miserably. The vote was fifty-five to fifteen against the motion. Mac knew the unionist stand had fallen. Too many events had happened too quickly to stem the move toward secession. Lincoln had called troops to arm and to retake Fort Sumpter. He had sent a directive to Governor Rector asking for 750 Arkansas men to be sent to fortify the armory in Little Rock against Confederate attempts to take it and to enroll soldiers for the union army among citizens of the state. Rector was under attack by Arkansans for doing nothing to protect the state. Economic boycotts had been threatened from both Louisiana and Texas. All this had brought a flood of concern and fear.

Shortly after the vote to uphold the election was defeated, the leader of the pro-slavery delegation moved that Arkansas dissolve its ties with the government in Washington. The vote was called and each delegate rose to speak his vote. At a quarter past three that afternoon, the president rose to announce the motion had passed with a fifty-five to five count. Only five men from the previous majority had cast a vote to keep Arkansas in the United States.

"Gentlemen, I ask you to consider that we must present a united front in light of the hesitation our state has shown to join the

Confederacy thus far. I want to go to the governor with a united convention. At four o'clock, I will bring the issue back to the floor. At that time, I am asking for a unanimous vote. Please take a brief recess to consider my request." The president of the convention slammed his gavel on the desk. "Body dismissed until four o'clock."

Mac shook his head in disbelief. How had this happened so quickly? The body had been in session less than six hours. Now Walker had all but demanded every man present state his approval for this insanity—whether they believed it was right or not. Isaac Murphy walked to the faux granite mantle where Mac stood.

"MacLayne, looks like you and me and three other men have been called to task. Can you vote for secession?"

"No, Isaac. I will not change my vote. I've committed enough sin in my life without adding this one to the heap. Will you?"

"No. I can't do it."

"It's been an honor knowin' you, Isaac. In all our dealin's, I've always known you to be honest and forthcoming. God bless you, friend, and keep you and your family. I am goin' back to mine. There is nothin' more I can do here."

Mac walked back to his desk and sat in his chair for one last time. His time of service to this state had ended. He continued to sit and remember for a time. He pulled his Bible from the buckskin pouch he carried and laid it on his desk. Seeking some words of encouragement, he turned over a few pages.The words of Genesis 49:10 caught his attention. *The scepter shall not depart from Judah, nor a lawgiver from between his feet, until Shiloh come: and unto Him the gathering of the people be.*

God had told him to go home. He stood, picked up all that belonged to him, and left the house chamber. Shiloh was pulling him home, and he knew he had five or six long hard days ahead before he could reach home and Laurel. He wouldn't waste another minute returning to the place he longed to be. He could change nothing if he stayed.

As he took the last step from the broad Georgian styled porch of the Arkansas State House, he heard the gavel fall, bringing the assembly to the second vote on secession. Two delegates failed to answer the call from the clerk. One lone dissenting vote was heard.

Mac rode, at times meandering across rolling hillsides and at times racing down fair roads as if Satan were chasing him through the valley. He focused solely on moving--always to northeast, back to Shiloh.

On the morning of May 12th, dark ominous clouds covered the western horizon. It seemed more like early evening as the sun could not penetrate the heavy rain-laden clouds. In the distance, thunder rumbled, and at times, lightning splintered across the sky. Mac pushed on. Jonesboro was barely behind him when the rain turned from a sprinkle to a heavy drizzle. Mac gave Midnight his head, and they sped on down the Greensboro road toward Shiloh. Tree branches whipped downward, back and forth across the road.
Thunder and lightning added to the threatening atmosphere of the day, but Mac pushed on. The boundary to his property came into sight...less than one mile and he'd be home.

As Mac urged his stallion harder when he approached the last bend in the Shiloh road, the nightmare he'd had each night since he'd ridden to Little Rock reared its hateful presence once again.

Laurel's coppery curls swirled about a whispy semblance of her face as she stood on their porch, holding the empty blue blanket where their son should be sleeping. Instead of her green- gray eyes, Mac saw only black shadows. He could hear Andy and Cathy laughing, but no children waited for him on the porch. The faintest hint of smoke drifted from the chimney, and perhaps the familiar aroma of homemade bread. Although Midnight galloped as fast as he was able, he could not reach the porch. Mac called out to Laurel, but the vaporous image of his wife vanished, and only the small blue blanket remained on the porch. As he pushed the horse on toward the cabin, the homestead receded toward Crowley's ridge and then faded from his sight.

Uncounted nights, the nightmare had jarred him from his sleep. Mac pushed the image from his awareness. Only climbing those three log steps and drawing Laurel into his arms would finally banish the fear that he could never reach Shiloh again. *Lord, help me! I should feel at home...this road is on my land. I planted those oats and cornfields. Those are the fences I built, and the cattle I brought from Sikeston.*

Midnight's hooves splashed on the wet road. With each thud, Mac felt his heart pound in the same rhythm. *Go on, boy. Why can't I see the house? Are you standing still? I need to get home. Just a few more strides, boy...we'll see the porch.* Mac seemed to be reliving the nightmare, yet he knew he was awake.

The events of the last week lay heavily on his mind and heart. How could things have taken such a horrendous turn so quickly? The people were supposed to choose; the majority would do the right thing. Yet the special recalled secession convention had been decided before the delegates could even make the trip back to the capital. One vote taken...a count fifty for secession to five for the union...had severed Arkansas from the United States. Mac grieved the catastrophe he saw before them. War was inevitable.

At that moment, he didn't care what happened to the state or the country, for that matter. He wanted to know his family and his home were safe. He had to be home. Again, he became aware of the sound of hooves on the ground. He felt an increasing tightness in his shoulders. He had to be within sight of Shiloh. Behind him to the west, large flat-bottomed storm clouds followed him. In the distance, he heard the continuous rumbling of thunder, shortly followed by a sharp recoil that sounded like a rifle, ending in the death throe of an ancient hickory tree, ripped apart by a bolt of lightning. Mac pushed his palm into the ache in his shoulder.

That damn wound...why is it bothering me now?

He had to get home. He had to get back to Shiloh. His world would be sane again when he planted his feet on his own porch, touched her hair, and held Mark. At the bend, he saw his cabin. Laurel stood on the porch with Mark in her arms. Andy pulled at her skirts, pointing down the road. He heard his son yelling, "Papa...Papa!"

Mac flapped the reins against Midnight's flanks. Only a few yards from home and the distance was taking an eternity to cover. Finally, Mac stopped and dragged himself from the saddle.

He climbed the steps, feeling the sturdy planks under his feet. Laurel was in his arms, and the tiny hand of his son was warm and real.

"Papa...Papa, you're home."

Mac pulled Laurel into his arms and drank deeply from her lips. He felt the pull of his children as they threw their arms around him. Gracie even spoke in her quiet voice, "Oh, Papa."

Mac kissed Laurel a second time, drinking in her strength to help him return to Shiloh. As he did, the thunder roared across the valley and lightning split the ever-darkening sky. Mark Thomas began to cry. Mac took the toddler and kissed his warm face. He would not release Laurel. "Don't be afraid, Mark Thomas. We're all here...your mama, and your brothers and sisters, and now your

papa's home. We're all safe here at home."

Chapter Twenty-Two

Yea, the sparrow hath found a house, and the swallow a nest for herself, where she may lay her young,...Blessed are they that dwell in Thy house:
They will be still praising Thee.
Psalm 84:34

he MacLaynes spent the evening together in their

warm sturdy cabin. Even the cold furious rain

*T*outside did not place a shadow on the joy Mac

felt, surrounded

by his family. He gazed across the room at his father, dozing in the rocking chair nearest the fireplace, and he smiled. Shiloh was so much more home to him now that his father had moved from Maryland. For the briefest moment, he caught a whiff of jasmine, the scent of his mother's perfume. That night his family was truly gathered for his homecoming. Mac relished the peace and comfort he'd missed since October. Andy refused to get more than an arm's reach from his father throughout the night. Mac's newest charge, Gracie, sat nuzzled in his lap.

At nine o'clock, Laurel walked over and took Gracie from Mac's lap. "Children, Papa is very tired after his long time of service at the capital. It's well past your bedtimes so I want you to say goodnight. Tomorrow, we'll have all day to be together."

"Please, Mama, just a little longer," Andy begged. We ain't had our Bible story yet."

"Yes, Papa. I'll get your Bible." Cathy bounded to retrieve the worn book from her papa's buckskin pouch.

"Yes, it will be good to have your papa read us the Scripture tonight and have our prayer. It seems so long since he did it."

Mac chose to recite Psalms twenty-three for his family that night. After he spoke only a few words, Andy, Cathy, Laurel, and his father joined him. *"Surely goodness and mercy shall follow me all the days of my life, and I will dwell in the house of the Lord forever. Amen."*

Andy asked. "We know that one so good. Why did you say that one tonight, Papa?"

"I suppose my heart is just overwhelmed at bein' home, young'un. Now you mind your mama. She's right. I'm beat. I'm gonna be home for a long time."

"All right, Papa. Golly, I'm glad you're back. I don't never want you to go away no more."

"Those are words I like to hear, Andy. Now go hug your granddad and up to the loft with you."

Laurel began the business of putting her family to bed. "Pa, you can take Roy's bed in the loft tonight, since he's at his homestead. He's gonna be sad he wasn't home to welcome Mac back."

"Goodnight, Patrick. So happy to have ya home."

"Night, Pa." Mac retired to the second pen. He sat in his chair and waited. After several minutes he rose and crossed to the door and called her name, but he received no answer. He returned his chair. He sat and pushed his boots off, letting them fall where they would. Too restless, in his stocking feet, he returned to the main cabin and called to Laurel again. He found her in the room with the girls, sitting on their bed listening to their evening prayers.

"And God, thank you so much for bringing our papa home to us at Shiloh. We're so happy our family is back together again. God bless Papa's work at the capital, but don't take him away again for a very long time." Cathy closed with an amen. Then Gracie whispered amen, too. The girls crawled into the bed that he and Laurel had brought from Washington County only four years ago. How his life had changed in that short time!

"Goodnight, young ladies. Thank you for praying for me. Now, to sleep with you two." Mac took Mark Thomas from Laurel's arms and helped her from the bed. As they crossed the main room, Mac again took her arm and pulled her toward their room. "Thank the Lord, I finally have you alone."

"Papa, play ball."

"Not tonight, Mark Thomas. It's time for bed." Mac carried the toddler across the room to his crib and covered him with his patchwork quilt. "Now you go to sleep, little man, and let your papa spend some time with your mama." The little boy kicked off his coverlet and stood up in the crib. He reached out his arms to his father.

"Papa, play."

Laurel went to the baby and took him from her husband. "Son, bedtime now. Play tomorrow." She put him down again and covered him. She stood and patted his shoulder and sang a few words of a familiar lullaby, and shortly the boy slept.

"Thank you, Lord." Mac picked Laurel up and carried her to his armchair and sat with her. "So much for our private sanctuary, Wife."

"Count our blessings, Mac. We have so many." "I know I have you." He kissed her without restraint. "I have been aching to do that all day. I am happy to be home with you."

"No more than I am to have you here. I've been afraid for your health. Those return trips to Little Rock were so senseless. August is only a few months from now, and a vote of the people will solve this issue the right way."

He kissed Laurel once, almost in a sense of desperation. Mac pulled her close so he could whisper in her ear. "We failed, Laurel. I failed. We couldn't stop them. Arkansas has seceded from the union. War is coming."

"Mac, I don't want to talk about anything outside these four walls tonight! I don't care if Arkansas left the union. I don't care if the nation is going to war. Our family has given enough for right now. You have served well and true. Tonight is our time. Nothing exists in this room to divide us."

φ

Mac rose and carried his wife to the grand four-poster that had become their sanctuary since they'd found each other in September of 1857. As he laid her on her chosen side of their bed, he gently kissed her palm before he enfolded her hands into his. He sank to his knees beside her.

"Dearest Father in Heaven, thank You for my homecoming. Tonight, I am overcome with the love You have given me. You know these past six months, the whole time I have been gone, I've lived in fear and pain. I would not have survived if I'd not known this woman waited for me here in our home, caring for our family. Lord, I wish I had the words to truly impress upon her how much I love her. Since I knew she was the better part of me, all my life has been truly blessed. Even the hard parts are precious because she has been right here loving me. What a good and generous God You are, giving me what I needed when I had no idea of what that was and providing Laurel for me when the way seemed impossible. I cannot measure the depth of my love for her any more than I can see the limit of my love for You. I am a man most blessed."

Laurel's tears flowed. Listening to her husband's prayer had erased every doubt she'd felt in all his time of absence. She heard the words from his own lips, but not spoken to her. He'd told the Lord, his confidant and best friend, he loved her. Never again would she allow her own doubts, loneliness, fatigue, or frustration with life blight that one truth. Patrick MacLayne, her husband, loved her—she was not a wife of convenience or second choice.

She was and would always be his life mate--his beloved wife.

"Father, thank You for this new life we are expecting soon and for blessing us with all the fine children we already have. Grant us a good rest tonight, and be with us in the coming days, helping us to be good servants and witnesses to Your glory. In

Jesus's name, Amen"

When Patrick looked up, he saw Laurel's tear-streaked face. "Darlin', why are you cryin'?"

"Oh, you!"

"Please tell me, why the tears?"

"Because you make me ashamed, Patrick. About two weeks ago, I allowed myself to get depressed and upset that you were gone so much. I sat down in your armchair and began sobbing. Your father came in and saw me. I told him that I was unhappy because I knew you didn't want to be home at Shiloh with me and that your fascination with your wife of convenience had worn off." "What did he say to you? You seem happy to see me since I've been home."

"He assured me that you cared for me and that you would be home if you could. He said you felt a burdensome sense of responsibility to do good. He spoke of your need to account for the death of your friend in that duel. He told me that you feel called to serve beyond our own home. He is proud of you, just as I am."

"Laurel, don't ever doubt that I love you. I couldn't have survived in Little Rock without knowing you were here at Shiloh, keeping my home intact. On days when the headaches bore down on me, it was your beautiful face that kept me going. At times when the insanity in the house chamber made me want to scream, your gracious spirit held my temper in check. We were apart in space only, but you were ever with me."

"I know that now. I am happy that I heard your prayer. I'll not forget it ever. Never again will I think of myself as your wife of convenience. I love you, Mac. I will always love you."

"Laurel, I am not going to leave you again. I'm not going back to the capital. Hard times are coming. I don't know how or when, but difficult challenges will come to our family, but we'll work them out together."

"Patrick, please don't make me promises you can't keep. I know if you feel called to serve, you will answer that call. You can't change who you are. I wouldn't want you to."

Laurel sat up and looked up into Mac's storm-blue eyes. Her face reflected the love and pride she felt for her husband. "Patrick, let's talk about all this tomorrow. You did all that was expected of you. No man could do more. You are home now. Nothing else matters to me. We can overcome anything as long as we're together. Remember, Husband, you built this home for me— for our family--in Shiloh."

About Patricia Clark Blake

Who is this person who asks you to support her dream of becoming a known writer? Truthfully, this is a serious question I dealt with for many months since I retired. For most of my adult life, the answer rolled off my tongue with little thought. I was a teacher. Since the age of twenty-two, I have been an educator, teaching students from grade seven through masters-level students in Arkansas's public schools and universities. I loved my role. I believe I was a good teacher and used the gifts God had given me.

In 2012, I laid it down. For some time, I struggled with an

identity crisis. If I wasn't a teacher anymore, who was I? I found in a short time that having twenty-four hours a day, seven days a week can become an overwhelming amount of time when you don't have a role to fill and a purpose to work toward.

After travelling some (I loved the trip to Israel, England, Ireland, and the Yucatan), and getting my worn-out knees replaced(Yes, both of them...the doctor said forty years on a concrete floor can do that to the best of us), I knew I had to find a new "career" in which I could invest my time. Our good Lord opened a new door. I had to write the story, which has become the Shiloh Saga.

I had started "scribbling" a story in a steno pad about a year before I made up my mind that I was going to retire. I knew the steno pad would be plenty of paper because my personal history told me that I'd get tired of this project like I had so many others in my adult life. When I started writing my Shiloh story in that steno pad, I never dreamed the final manuscript would end at 685,000 plus words. If someone had told me I'd publish four novels, with one to go, from those pages, I'd have laughed. I could fill a large closet with other "projects" I'd started and never finished...piano lessons, learning to play the dulcimer, needlepoint, quilting, major embroidery projects, community choir, watercolor...well, you see my point. None ever stuck!

Shiloh was different. I believe God meant for me to write this story of Arkansas. At times, the Holy Spirit seemed to be spilling the words on the page. The story came so fast I could hardly get the words on the paper. Of course, there were times I couldn't write a single sentence for days at a time. But the finished project has been such a blessing. I can't count the number of people who have told me they love the story.

Over the next couple of years, I learned again who I am.

Patricia Clark Blake—Christian, Arkansan, Writer.

I am a self-published author who loves her new job. Writing has led me to make wonderful new friends who also write. My new career has allowed me to reconnect with students from my days as a teacher and past colleagues, who have become my readers. Former classmates from the Bono Class of '67, distant family members whom I never get to see in person, and precious brothers and sisters from First United Methodist Church, Jonesboro, have become supporters of my Shiloh stories.

In addition, I've met many fine people who have become new friends. These readers of the Shiloh Saga are blessings in my life. Isn't the Lord good to us?

Blessings,

Pat

Getting to Know me by Fives

What are my favorite books?

- The Holy Bible

- Gone with the Wind—Mitchell

- Redeeming Love—Rivers

- America's First Daughter—Kamoie & Dray

- The Kent Family Chronicles—John Jakes **What are my**

favorite foods?

- Fried Rabbit (Back Legs, preferred)

- Banana Pudding (Homemade)

- Chocolate/Peanut Butter

- Ribeye Steak (Medium)

- Bread

Places I love

- Arkansas and the Ozarks

- Valley of the Wind and Doves in Israel

- Irish Country Side

- Chapel at FUMC Jonesboro
- Porch on Scotchwood Drive **Songs that Move Me**
- Amazing Grace
- Unchained Melody
- The National Anthem
- Sinner Saved by Grace
- Then Came the Morning

Unfulfilled Bucket List Items

- Float the Grand Canyon
- Spend a week in Sedona, Arizona
- Travel to Scotland
- Finish my Genealogy to beyond the USA
- Write a Best Seller

Other Books by Patricia Clark Blake

In Search of Shiloh:
A Journey Home through Arkansas

The Dream of Shiloh:
An Arkansas Love Story

Beyond Shiloh:
The Story of an Arkansas Family